River of Fire

Qurratulain Hyder

River of Fire

*transcreated from the original Urdu
by the author*

A NEW DIRECTIONS PAPERBOOK

1. The Time of the Peacocks

It was the first beerbahuti of the season that Gautam had seen. The prettiest of rain-insects, clothed in god's own red velvet, the beerbahuti was called the Bride of Indra, Lord of the Clouds. This one was crawling upon a blade of grass. A gust of easterly wind brought it rolling down onto the sodden earth. Gautam scooped it up tenderly with the help of a twig and placed it on his palm. Come the rains and the beerbahutis appeared all over the green. From where do they emerge, so perfect in shape and colour, and where do they go? What a brief span of existence they have, but for them it's a lifetime. This was a solitary beerbahuti and it looked so alone in the expanse and depth of the forest. Right now it sat cosily in its own silence on Gautam's palm. It could soon be crushed by an animal or a passer-by.

Gautam put it down and made a boat out of a bargad leaf. A brook of rainwater was rippling past the gnarled roots of the banyan where Gautam had been sitting. He let the beerbahuti slide into her barge and put it out to sea. For this minute creature the rivulet must seem like an ocean. "Farewell, Indra's bride," Gautam said as the waves carried the leaf-boat away.

He looked up at the sky, collected his staff and cloth bag and resumed his journey. He noticed another red beerbahuti on the lush green grass, slowly making its progress from somewhere to nowhere. He could unwittingly trample these lovely, helpless little beings. He walked carefully across the patch of green and reached the mud track.

Now he was tired. Gautam Nilambar, final year student of the Forest University of Shravasti, had walked all the way from Shravasti to Saket in pursuit of more knowledge. He had been attending a centenarian sage's lectures on cosmology till he felt that his head was overflowing with stars. The new term was about to begin in his own gurukul and he was trudging back to Shravasti, his hometown. It rained frequently and he had to stop now and then under the trees.

The journey was arduous. As a student he was not allowed to use boats or vehicles or umbrellas. Nor was he supposed to carry any money. He had to beg his food from respectful villagers and sleep under the trees. Such a life of extreme hardship could match that of any Jain ascetic, except that Gautam was neither a Jain sadhu nor a Buddhist bhikshu. His head was not shaved and he let his long Brahmanical top-knot mingle with his glossy ringlets. He was rather proud of his good looks. Gautam, in fact, was quite vain and had certainly not conquered his ego—he saw no reason why he should.

Once his friend, Aklesh, a townsman, had said that he was like the proverbial peacock that danced in the jungle, but there was nobody to admire him. Surrounded by hoary gurus, erudite shastris and pedantic students, poor Gautam had become a loner. He liked to dance and paint and make terracotta figurines. Once he had travelled on foot all the way to Kashi to learn Shiva's nritya. He had had no intention of becoming a priest like his father. He wanted to gain some insight into Saraswati's bhed as a creative artist. He wanted to partake in the mysteries of the universe as the beerbahutis did in their own tiny, weary manner—surely they must have their own perception of the cosmos! As he was the only son of the High Priest of Shravasti, he had been sent to the gurukul as a young boy. He had lived there all these years, devoting himself exclusively to the goddess of learning.

The month of Bhadon had arrived and it rained frequently. He reached the outskirts of Saket and sat down on the grassy bank of the Saryu river.

While he was piously reciting his shlokas and cleaning his muddy feet in the water, something soft touched his toes. He heard the jingle of anklets and glass bangles. A woman laughed. Giggly females jingling their bangles, he thought loftily. Then he noticed thick jasmine garlands floating past his toes. Magnolia blossoms followed. Are they sending me floral messages, he thought vainly, and stole a glance in the direction the flowers had come from. It was a bathing ghat, hidden behind a bamboo screen. Gautam peeped through the lattice and held his breath. Two fair damsels and their dark dasi were getting ready for their early morning dip. One of them was doe-eyed and was in the process of taking off her gold tiara. These were no wanton females tempting a stranger with floral greetings, they were high-born ladies who had merely discarded their stale flowers before bathing.

One of them had a golden complexion and oblong eyes. A poet would have called her Meenakshi, fish-eyed. She was removing magnolia blossoms from her braided hair and throwing them in the water. The low-caste woman carried a fancy parasol and a basketful of fresh flowers. She had bovine eyes and could be called Ellakshi—the cow-eyed one. She was earthy, like a roughly-moulded terra cotta figurine.

The fair women wore beerbahuti-red sash bodices and knee-length sarongs. Brides of Indra, surrounded by heavy, rain-laden clouds! Their bare arms and legs were loaded with gold bangles and anklets. Gautam realised that he had trespassed into the bathing enclosure of the royal family. The Raja's palace must be in the vicinity.

He felt greatly attracted to the Fish-Eyed One. She was voluptuous and magnetic, yet there was something ethereal about her. He even went into a momentary trance, just looking at her. He came to with a jolt when he remembered that he was a brahmachari and was not supposed to look at women till he graduated. Afterwards, he would be at liberty to choose his way of life. He could become a hermit or a householder. I am not cut out for permanent bachelorhood, he told himself grimly. Still, right now, lingering behind this reed screen was dangerous. He could be caught ogling royal ladies and bring disgrace to his gurukul.

Kadamba flowers glimmered like little red lamps set amidst the heart-shaped kadamba leaves. Krishna Banmali, god of the woods, used to play his flute under the kadamba trees. The easterly wind seemed to waft the notes of his flute across the eons, shaking the branches so that drops of rain fell like a shower of tiny diamonds.

A peacock danced under a flaming dhak. Magnolias were in full bloom. A lone ferryman sang somewhere in the watery expanse. The two fair women glowed like pale moons in the river-mist. The scene was like something out of the sylvan idyll of the 'Golden Age' that Gautam had heard about. Reluctantly he came out of hiding and dived into the swiftly flowing water. The cool restful waves of the Saryu filled him with a deep contentment. He began swimming across to the other bank. The three young women heard the splash and watched a gorgeous young man appear out of the water like a silver figure emerging from the waves of a dream. He disappeared again in the mist. "Some poor miserable student roughing it out," fish-eyed Kumari Champak observed sympathetically.

"How did you guess?" asked the doe-eyed one.

"He did not hire the ferry."

"Why aren't they allowed to use boats even in bad weather?" asked Jamuna, the maid.

"To make them hardy, so that they can sit tirelessly under the bargad trees and propound more philosophy," Champak replied sourly, stepping down into the river.

The doe-eyed one noted the bitterness in her companion's voice and sighed. The sight of the white-robed scholar had upset her, too. Her own brother, the crown prince, was also a student. He had not come back from Taxila. Eight long years and he had still not returned home. They waited for him patiently, praying hard for his safe return. Meanwhile poor Champak, the chief minister's daughter, had no choice but to discuss matters of intellect with visiting Chinese scholars. She had promised the Rajkumar she would wait for him. She had rejected many a fine suitor and was fast turning into a grumpy old maid. Soon, she may also have no option but to become a sanyasin or even a Buddhist nun. The princess shuddered.

Men who go away on long journeys are awaited anxiously in the rainy season by the women they leave behind. That's what all the rain songs say. But he had not come back, even in this year's Sawan and Bhadon, to end Champak's long vigil. How much more was her brother going to study, the princess wondered. Whether you acquire the wisdom of the three worlds or remain ignorant like this dasi, Jamuna, you die all the same. So why waste your precious youth squatting under the trees, cramming? I must not feel depressed so early in the morning. She said aloud: "Today I would like to try out a new hair-style when I get home."

"The other day I saw some snooty women from Pataliputra. They wore fan-like turbans jauntily fixed to one side, big-city women. They think we are dowdy and provincial." Champak, too, changed the subject. "My father says there is political trouble brewing in Pataliputra, so they have come here."

It began to drizzle.

Both of them gazed wistfully at the further side of the river. The unknown scholar had vanished behind a moving curtain of rain.

Gautam reached midstream. He turned his head once to catch a last glimpse of the girl with the champak blossoms. Then he began swimming with all his strength and reached the other bank where cranes stood about sorrowfully, drenched in rain. He spread his wet mantle on a shrub to dry. The sun was coming up. He went to the riverside village, a peacock-rearers' hamlet where they made fans from peacock feathers. Gautam stopped at the first house in the lane and knocked on the door. A jovial-looking householder peered out and seemed relieved to see a white-robed mendicant.

"Ram Daiya, a Brahmin scholar is here, not one of those saffron-robed ones. . .," he shouted. He was a talkative trader, and continued in the same breath as he came out. "I am an exporter of peacock fans, sir. The market is down these days, ever since this new movement of shunning luxuries and taking to the woods began. Do pray for me. My fans used to go to foreign countries. When I heard the knock I thought, here comes another ochre-robed character. All these newfangled notions of equality, no caste, no nothing. And this 'Renounce the World' business is catching on. Even the girls are shaving their silly heads and taking to the woods. This is what happens when you educate the women—they begin to seek nirvana."

The old householder's child-wife came out with a cane tray full of rice and lentils, ground barley and a piece of jaggery.

The scholar received the offering in his cloth bags. The girl touched his feet. He repeated the formal benediction . . .

"May the gods bless you with cattle and progeny and bountiful harvest . . . and peacock fans," he added. Since he was not supposed to indulge in unnecessary conversation with villagers or townsmen, he started walking towards the Kumhar basti. A potter gave him a new clay pot and some fire. He dug an oven in the ground and boiled his rice and lentils in the clay pot. Then he ate, slept a little and started walking again.

He spent several days moving carefully through the tiger-infested jungles of the Gond tribes. He lived on wild fruit and slept under the trees. He had ample time to memorise the lectures on the stars he had heard in Saket, and his head was full of discourses on all manner of subjects. Fortunately this was his last year at the gurukul.

The shadows of the sal trees had lengthened when he reached another bend of the Saryu. He had to cross this river once again. Shravasti lay on the other side. He dived in and crossed over to the shore of his home territory. As he picked up a few ripe wood-apples lying on the grass he noticed a rock-shrine by the river—perhaps he could spend the night there.

It was an abandoned temple of some tribal mother-goddess. He went in and spread his mantle on the floor. Being a lonely person he had got used to speaking silently to himself—I am physically tired and I am also knowledge-weary. I am suffering from wisdom-fatigue. I must have a good night's rest here before the ashram routine starts all over again. He leaned against the wall of the cave-like shrine, frightened of the quiet within the tiny enclosure. The Rig Veda says that, in the beginning, there was the Self which appeared in the form of Purush. The Purush looked around and found nobody but himself. He said: This is I. So he began thinking in terms of I-ness. He was afraid because he was alone. Therefore one is afraid when no one else exists besides oneself. So saying, he stopped being afraid. But he was not happy, because loneliness contains sadness. And sadness is fearsome, too.

When Formless, Faceless Brahma appears in the form of another human being, one becomes careful. Why doesn't one trust others? They are also Brahma.

I must not be scared of the loneliness of my soul. He remembered the Upanishads. Within the City of Brahma which was the human body, there was the heart, and within the heart there was a little house. This was in the form of a lotus and within it dwelt that which was to be sought after, inquired about and realised. What was in the macrocosm was in this microcosm. Though seated, he travels far. Though at rest, he moves all things, who is joy and is beyond joy. In the midst of the fleeting, he abides forever. Brahma, who is beyond knowledge . . .

He heard a footfall. There was silence again. Somebody peeped over the wall. A horse neighed in the distance. Gautam became alert.

"I say, who are you up there?" a faceless voice asked cautiously and in a cultured accent. Another wandering scholar, perhaps.

"It's merely I—What name can you give to the human soul?" Gautam shouted back in a manner academic.

"Names are necessary to differentiate. If you are human, not a fiery ghost, you must have a name!" The fellow seemed to be equally argumentative.

"Speak for yourself. You may be a ghost come to haunt this spooky little hole. Why, this place is so scary even the Bher adivasis have deserted it. As for this body, if you must know its eminently forgettable name, it is Gautam Nilambar," he answered, endeavouring to be modest.

"Good. Now come down to earth, Brother Gautam of the Blue Skies, I am tired of hanging on to this ledge."

"Climb up. The cliff is not slippery."

"Heights can be slippery," came the reply.

"Are you one of the ochre-robed chaps?"

"No. A mere sympathiser of the Movement. Anyway, there can be no definite answer to any question, Brother Gautam."

"There are six equally valid answers to every question. Are you a Jain Wrangler, by any chance? Jump in, sir, and we shall discuss all this over a cold drink. I am a poor student and can only offer you a wood-apple for dinner. I'll make two cups out of bargad leaves and give you cool barley water to quench your thirst. I can make very neat cups out of leaves, you know."

Who is he? Gautam wondered. One came across sophists and logisticians and atheists, former kings and princes, roving by the light of the moon as wandering philosophers. The Prince of Kapilavastu had also followed this tradition by giving up the world. He had added yet another philosophy to this vast kingdom of thought, where sixty-two systems already flourished.

Sixty-two systems of thought. And man is all by himself, alone. Gautam felt scared again.

2. The Greek Traveller

A resplendent young man finally jumped in. He was tall and fair and wore rather funny garments—a white knee-length tunic with a leather belt, and leather sandals with straps wound round his sturdy legs. He had a fringe, and his clean-shaven face seemed strangely familiar. He stood there in the rays of the setting sun, glowing like some celestial being who had come down from Indralok, the abode of gods.

"Are you real?" Gautam Nilambar gasped.

The stranger smiled impishly. "Yes, I am. Harius Sancarius at your service." He bowed from the waist in an outlandish manner. Gautam was mystified. Then he said, "Oh, a Yavana!" He had never seen a mlechha[1] before.

"I hail from Ionia and I am in shipping," the Greek informed him breezily. Gautam looked blank, feeling like a country bumpkin.

"Well, I'm not one of those Greek shipping magnates you may have heard about," Harius Sancarius tried to reassure the obviously baffled student from the backwoods. Gautam had never heard of Greek shipping magnates, either.

"I have a little cargo boat I brought from the Gulf to the

---

[1]Dirty foreigner.

River Indus. There I left it in charge of my Phoenician crew and decided to explore the land mass to the east. So I bought a horse from a Scythian and . . . may I sit down ? First went up to Taxila. . ."

"Oh! You've been to Taxila! I very much want to go to Taxila, too," uttered Gautam, mesmerised.

"Have some of this." The Greek took out dry fruit from his leather bag. "I am a mlechha all right, but you won't lose caste. It is uncooked, straight from the orchards of Gandhara!" A diamond ring flashed on his right hand which he quickly hid in the folds of his tunic, and laughed nervously. "People are so honest in this country. I have been travelling over hill and dale fearlessly. No highwaymen, no robbers."

Gautam kept quiet. Now he was gazing more intently at the Greek's weather-beaten handsome face. It was uncanny. He resembled the doe-eyed girl with the gold coronet he had spotted the other day on the royal ghat near Saket. "You speak the local lingo fluently," he observed doubtfully.

"Well, I've been around, can speak many languages," the Yavana said nonchalantly. Although he was much older, he almost looked like the tiara-girl's twin brother. Gautam was confused. He noticed the Ionian's growing discomfort and blurted out, "Look here, sir, Harius Whatever—I happened to see a buxom female wearing a crown, who looked like you— odd isn't it? That's why I can't forget her face. She can be no relation of yours, you being Greek, she a Rajput princess. Anyway, a desirable wench, if truth be told."

The Greek's face reddened. "You mean Her Royal Highness, Princess Nirmala . . .," he spoke haughtily and in icy tones. The next moment he glanced around. He had given himself away so stupidly.

Gautam smiled, still trying to fathom the mystery. All of a sudden it dawned on him. Truimphantly he said, "Sire, permit me to say that you are no Ionian. You are good old Rajkumar Hari Shankar, better known as the Missing Prince of Kaushal Desh."

The phoney Greek looked scared. "Please don't tell a soul about me, I beg of you . . .," he pleaded. Gone were his regal arrogance and international airs of a few moments earlier.

Gautam Nilambar of the backwaters of Shravasti relished this new power which he had acquired over the crown prince.

"All right," he said magnanimously, "but only if you tell me why you have become a fugitive. Why are you masquerading as a Greek traveller? Tell me, or . . .'

"Or ?"

"I'll go out right now and inform the village drummer. He'll tom-tom the news that the prince has come back and is hiding in. . ."

The threat worked. "No, don't. I beg of you." The fugitive clasped his hands in all humility.

Now Gautam assumed the role of a cross-examiner. Authority changes a person in a moment. "The King had sent you to Taxila for higher studies, right?"

"Yes."

"There you—I mean Your Royal Highness—got into bad company, right? Started frequenting dens of iniquity?"

"No. I got into the splendid company of the Buddha's missionaries. They were on their way to the steppes of the horse-people—the Turukshas. They showed me the Highway to Salvation. Still, I was not in a hurry to take the oath of monkhood. See, I had left this fish-eyed magnolia girl behind . . ."

"A girl! That always seems to be at the root of all problems," Gautam agreed.

". . . so I could not make up my mind. Eventually the world made me renounce it." The prince continued in his sad, attractive voice, "I used to live in a tiny cave-like brick cell in the quadrangle of Taxila. We had our food in a dining hall where Acharya Vishnu Sharma often lectured on political theory. He propounded the Law of the Fish—big fish eat smaller ones. What we needed, he maintained, was an empire—the days of small kingdoms are over.

"There were some Iranians in Taxila. They said their monarchs had developed a mystique of kingship which was truly awesome. I faced a dilemma. If I remained in this world of power-hungry kings and warlords and politicians I'd have to kill human beings, whereas now I didn't even want to kill animals. I left the university and set out on my long journey. I sailed on the Indus river and rode out to the mountains of the blue-eyed Pakhtas, and beyond. The Brahmins of the north-west boast that they can trace their lineage to the rishis who composed the Vedic hymns when they lived in the mountains of Aryana,[1] before the mailed warriors of Indra conquered the dark people of Hariyupia. It all seemed quite recent—the time of the gods and the heroes—and one felt very close somehow to the Source, while one lived in Khashtram . . ."

"What is that?" asked Gautam, peeved.

"North, in the Iranian language—Aryaniam Khashtram. And those Rig Vedic chants, when they were sung out there, you could almost hear the tearing north wind and the thunder of red-faced Rudra. I sat around the bonfires of fur-clad nomads and heard the caravan-leaders recount the epics of Turanian heroes, Sohrab and Rustam. I heard of the centuries-long Greco-Persian wars and the conquests of Iran's emperors. Darius I, King of Kings, had declared: 'I am Daryush, Emperor of Emperors, Lord of this Earth. Iranian, son of an Iranian, Arya, son of an Arya . . .' The Persian Kings call their language Aryani."

"Say, this Arya business is good business. We are Aryans too, aren't we, very superior people, eh?" Gautam sat up. "Which goes to show. There are people of noble birth like us and the Iranians, and there are the lesser breeds—it's all the Law of Karma."

"I am not too sure of that. Anyway, Guru Vishnu Sharma used to talk about the Wheel of Sovereignty. Persia's Wheel of Sovereignty rolled everywhere. The Achemenians had also conquered the northeastern regions of Sapta Sindhu. Emperor Xerxes, King of Kings, declared: These lands where devas were worshipped, with the help of Ahur Mazda I have shaken the very foundations of their temples. He had this carved on stone slabs."

Hari Shankar continued, "The Greeks had at last defeated the Persians, burned down Shahenshah Dara's magnificent

---

[1] Modern Afghanistan.

palace of Persepolis. And Alexander attacked Sapta Sindhu. It's a strange paradox. Men are destructive and they are seekers of knowledge at the same time. I have wondered about the mystery of languages. Look, our Sanskrit and their Persian have a common origin. Our Ramesh is their Ramish. Our 'go' is there 'gao', and so on. And some languages are totally different. How did it happen?

"During my wanderings I came across people from Soghdia, Cappodocio and Thessaly. I have met folks who have invented all manner of scripts. And they write on anything they can lay their restless hands on—they make papyrus and they write on parchment, camel-skin and even on sheep's bones. They paint word pictures on granite walls, they carve words on stone and they inscribe on clay tablets and then bake their words. They write letters on pieces of baked clay and put them in clay envelopes.

"Why, this long-haired Hebrew merchant told me that even their god had sent down his orders on stone tablets!

"I learnt some Aramaic script at Taxila, and some Kharoshti—the words sound harsh like the braying of a *khar*—donkey in Persian."

"You don't say!" Gautam was overwhelmed by the truant prince's adventures and academic achievements.

"Then I also realised that words created much confusion, they led to misunderstandings and bloodshed and wars. So I stopped believing in them."

Gautam reflected for a few moments. "You are still using words. They connect. How can you reach pure thought unless you employ words? Meaning is the thing," he countered vehemently. Now he had again become the college debater. "Therefore, word and non-word are two different Brahmas. By concentrating on the word you can reach the non-word . . ."

"I am that non-word," responded Shankar smugly.

"Word is eternal!" Gautam persisted. "M will always have the sound of M and not of F. Sound is everlasting and we remember it long after having heard it. It exists simultaneously and cannot be annihilated."

"So you would not reject the Vedas—because they are words and therefore eternal," said the prince.

"Quite right. Matter is Brahma, the Vedas are Brahma in words."

The Rajkumar sat up again and said, "Listen, young man, there is no relationship of anything with anything, except its transitory existence. All is momentary, all is pain. *Sarvam dukham*. Body and soul both are mortal. Man is like a candle, blows out. Only the continuum of events and sensations remains. She used to sing Sri Raga and Bhairav to me in the palace arbour. The notes of her ragas followed me wherever I went—in wind and rain and flowing water. . . And those notes brought me back."

Gautam listened carefully, then said, "You may put an end to words but melody remains. Notes are eternal. And also, I think you are being very foolish. If I were you, Prince, I would go right back to the Raj Bhavan. Why must you punish yourself forever, and for no reason at all? The world is so lovely and enjoyable." Gautam looked up. There was a flutter of wings. Some peacocks had flown over to sleep on the branches of the breadfruit tree overhanging the shrine.

Hari Shankar was lost in thought.

"Your Royal Highness," Gautam reminded him courteously, "You were telling me about this young lady who wore champak blossoms and sang. . ." If I can put two and two together, I think I have seen her, too, on the bathing ghat in Saket. The voluptuous Meenakshi. He resisted the temptation to say so. He had already incurred the prince's wrath when he mentioned the tiara girl. This was indeed a strange game of chance. . .

"Ah, yes." Prince Hari paused and gazed pensively at his diamond ring. "I was supposed to marry her and she gave me this ring as a pledge. I thought I must return it to her and release her from her promise, just as the Buddha freed me of all human bondage. So I decided to come home incognito and give it back to her. I bought a Greek outfit from an Ionian merchant and came here—I went halfway into town, then I got cold feet. My parents would trap me. I'll have to marry her, continue the dynasty, wage wars—No. I won't do all that. Therefore, I am going straight to Jetvan Vihar, beyond Shravasti. There I'll don the saffron robe and be done with it." He took a deep breath after making this long confession.

"Will you be able to forget her?"

"Hopefully."

The peacocks had gone to sleep. Hari Shankar made himself a pillow of leaves. Gautam pulled his white wrap up to his face and turned towards the wall. They remained awake for a while and then they, too, fell asleep.

Gautam had a nightmare. He saw the tribal goddess of the shrine turn into the girl with champak flowers, then an ugly old woman with a toothless grin. She said, "I am Vaishali's . . ." A breadfruit fell with a thud on the stone floor. Gautam awoke, shivering. Hari Shankar was peacefully asleep. Some Chandals were carrying a dead body towards the cremation ground. Gautam was too afraid to go to sleep again. He didn't want to be haunted by that hideous crone. He huddled in a corner and waited for the morning. Then it occurred to him . . . If you could somehow foresee your beloved in her old age you would never want to fall in love. Perhaps that's what the Buddhists' teaching was all about.

Rajkumar Hari Shankar awoke at daybreak. Some Brahmins had started gargling noisily on the riverbank down below. Parrots twittered in guava trees. Peacocks had flown down from their branches. Gautam sat cross-legged on the floor, facing the rising sun.

He jumped to his feet and asked Hari, urgently: "Sire, there was this famous dancer, Amrapali, who lived in Vaishali. . ."

"Stop thinking about women."

"Have you?" asked Gautam cheekily, and returned to his sun-worship. Too upset to continue his communion with nature, he got up again. "They say the courtesan called Amrapali tried to seduce the Buddha's chief disciple, Ananda. Took it upon herself as a sort of challenge."

"Whatever happened or didn't happen in the past does not concern us. Let's start on our separate journeys."

They clambered down to the edge of the river.

"The Saryu is so translucent, if you throw a coin you can see it in the riverbed," the prince remarked.

"I carry no money, Sire," Gautam replied.

Hari Shankar took out a Persian coin from his purse and flung it into the river. It lay sparkling on the grey sand. "Ah! And there is my fine Arabian horse!" the prince said and untied his black steed from the trunk of a neem tree. The next instant he rode past Gautam, shouting joyfully, "Here I go towards my new life, shall see you some other time, dear friend. May all be well with you. . ."

Gautam remained standing on the bank, surprised by the prince's abrupt departure. He looked up at the overcast sky and turned towards the road to Shravasti.

3. The Sages' Grove

Shravasti lay on the southern bank of the Rapti, guarded in the north by the pink and blue Himavat range. It was a large city divided into separate localities, where people of different castes lived and followed their ancestral occupations. Thieves, thugs and harlots had their own guilds and canons. The populace enjoyed life. Jugglers and harlequins performed in the marketplace and colourful festivals were celebrated with much merriment. Courtesans played ornate lutes at their windows. Flower girls sold jasmine garlands from door to door. Gambling was everybody's favourite pastime.

Low-born cartwrights, potters and basket-weavers lived in shanties outside the suburbs. The Chandals were the lowest of the low, inferior even to the Shudras. They were the fifth caste, destined to be pallbearers. They could only wear clothes taken off dead bodies because their karma had not decreed otherwise.

The Buddha had arrived in Shravasti nearly a hundred and

fifty years earlier from Magadh, and set up his vihara in nearby Jetvan. A lot of untouchables followed him and became touchable. It was as easy as that. He was greatly resented by the powerful Brahmin priests of Shravasti.

Gautam had inherited the prejudices against Buddhist philosophy and had argued with Prince Hari Shankar as an orthodox Brahmin. He had heard many discourses on Buddhism and was well-versed in it, mainly for the sake of disputation with ochre-robed monks. After Prince Hari vanished from sight, Gautam picked up his staff and cloth bag and resumed his journey.

The roofline of Shravasti came into view. He entered the gate and reached the town square. His father's brick-and-timber mansion confronted him—it was known as Elephant House, for carved elephant heads flanked its portals. Gautam had a great urge to go in and see his parents but he was not supposed to meet his family till he graduated. With a heavy heart he walked on. Dusk was falling. Toddy shops and gambling houses resounded with bawdy songs. A juggler was eating live coals and idle spectators cheered him on. Fops strutted about in the Street of Courtesans. He hastened out of the neighbourhood and proceeded towards the gurukul. The prince had disappeared, yet he seemed to be in hot pursuit. Both the Rajkumar and the woman, Champak, had ganged up and were hounding poor Gautam. He felt mentally exhausted and his legs ached.

At last he arrived at his kutir, hidden behind flowering creepers. This was his sanctuary, his kingdom. A few pots and pans, and a chulha. Some unstitched clothes hung from the rafters. His painting paraphernalia and unfinished figurines were stacked neatly in a corner. He took his bath in the brook which ran under his window and stepped in, feeling light and refreshed. But when he lay down on his piece of sacking and fell asleep, he dreamt of the Lady Champak.

He got up in the morning feeling angry with himself. A female and a fugitive prince have enticed me. I ought to be strong like an oak, not shaken by every wind. He resolved to get back to his studies in earnest and prepare for his final examination.

Every year from the full moon of July to the full moon of March, he diligently attended open-air classes and followed the strict rules of Brahmacharya. He got up before sunrise, brushed his teeth with a fresh twig of the neem tree, bathed in the river and prayed in the ashoka grove. In the autumn months, cranes and storks came flying in from Tibet and returned to the north in the spring. At the river bank at dawn each crane or bagla was found standing on one leg, as though deep in meditation, so fake "holy" men had come to be called "bagla bhagat".

He had followed the ashram routine day after day for ten long years. Soon, he would be twenty-four. On graduation day, early in the morning, he would be shut up in a room in order "to shame the sun by the humiliation of being confronted with his superior lustre. From now on, the sun must shine with the borrowed radiance of the scholar." In the evening he would come out, take off his white robes, roll up his deerskin, shed his thread, staff and begging bowl. Riding a chariot he would be taken to the assembly of learned Brahmins and presented before them as a competent pandit. At the time of the convocation the Acharya would read "The Advice to Lay Students" from the Upanishads.

> Speak the truth. Do your duty. Honour your teacher and your parents and your guest. Conduct yourself as a Brahmin. This is the rule. This is the true Upanishad of the Vedas.

Then he would go out into the world, get married and become a householder.

Many young Kshatriyas went to Indraprastha and joined the army of the warlike Kurus and Panchals. Wars were being fought everywhere. Wherever there was power, there was conflict. Kings and chieftains had their own priests who were also crafty politicians. He was not going to be a bagla bhagat if his heart was not in priestcraft. So what would he do after graduation? Loaf around as a rich man's son? He liked to carve in stone. But sculpture had yet not developed into a thriving art so he could not make it his career. His future was uncertain and he was in love with an unknown woman. It seemed like a hopeless situation.

Autumn arrived. On a mellow, golden Kartik eve as he sat brooding outside his hut, there was a rustling beside him in the grass. He looked up and saw a tall and distinguished-looking bhikshu standing in front of him.

"Hari! Hari!" the young man sprang to his feet happily.

"*Om mane padme hum*[1]—" the bhikshu chanted and gave him a beatific smile.

"Jewel in the heart of the mendicant's gourd . . .," Gautam uttered good-humouredly, for he had noticed the diamond ring shining in the bhikshu's begging bowl.

"Precisely! Can you do me a favour?" the visitor asked in a whisper.

"Yes, Your Highness, I mean Your Holiness."

"Look over there."

Gautam obediently turned round. The river-line was lit up with a procession of torches.

"The King has come for his sport of elephant-trapping. She must be part of the entourage. As a pandit you will have easy access to the royal camp. Find her at the earliest and return the ring on my behalf."

Gautam thought quickly and said, "I'll carry out your order on one condition, Sire."

"Wily Brahmin! The other day you threatened to inform the village drummer. What is it now?"

"May I, sort of, fall in love with her? I keep dreaming of her night after night."

A cloud passed over the bhikshu's face. "Permission granted," he answered, trying to be jovial. "Now, give this to her from Brother Hari Ananda with his blessings. And you can have my blessings for whatever kind of future you may have." He gave Gautam the ring. His hands trembled. Gautam tied the ring in a knot made with the corner of his mantle and tucked it into his dhoti. The monk was in a hurry to go back. Gautam accompanied him on the bridle path. They were quiet for a while.

The bhikshu broke the silence. "Heard any good discourses lately?"

---

[1]Jewel in the heart of the lotus.

"No. I've been cutting classes for some weeks. Too worried about the world situation."

Hari Ananda smiled fondly. "How big is your world, dear lad?"

"Where I live is my world, and I am concerned about it."

"What's happened?"

"I go to town every day on my begging rounds, and I hear rumours. A friend of mine, Vimleshwar, lives in Shravasti. He designs fancy ornaments. Sometimes I make the sketches for him. He had gone to Pataliputra on business and he says the capital is full of unrest. The Dhan King has become very unpopular. More taxes—salt, sugar, even firewood is being taxed. Moreover, your Guru Chanakya, Vishnu Sharma of Taxila, has turned up there."

"He was bound to," responded the bhikshu, jumping over a puddle. "If one wants to capture power one ought to be in the capital."

"So much is being spent on defence. Defence against whom? Both Saket and Madhya Desh are weak feudatories of Magadh, and Vimleshwar says our King is only a Rajan, not even a full-fledged Raja, with nobody to help him. His only son and heir has absconded. I didn't tell Vimleshwar about you."

"Good boy."

"Aren't you being an escapist? At a critical time like this you should have been at your poor old father's side. Look, Magadh has always been troublesome. They even fought against Lord Krishna in the Great War. They like violence . . . their king, Ajatshatru, killed his own pater."

"These things happen in royal families," the bhikshu remarked dispassionately.

"I think that's why the Princes Mahavira and Siddhartha both appeared in that land to preach peace," Gautam went on. "But I have always wondered—both of them were contemporaries and lived and preached in the same region, but they never met."

"One of those things," the bhikshu replied. They had reached the edge of the gurukul forest. "So, my friend, I bid farewell to you," he said lightly.

"That's good of you. Here you are, sending me off on a

perilous mission and you're not worried at all. What if I'm caught and questioned by your august father?"

"Let the future take care of itself. I think 'she' will protect you, I know her. Look at the chance you're getting of meeting the lady of your dreams!"

"One more thing, Sir. I have become a sort of believer in non-violence. What shall I do if war breaks out between Kaushal Desh and Magadh?"

"Our actions are the result of our thoughts."

"How do you and I find ourselves over here at this moment in time? Are we merely the result of our thoughts?"

"Our actions," Hari Shankar answered patiently, "are due to necessity, or accident, or are caused by our own natures. One is not free. And therefore responsibility has no meaning."

"Can't you be less enigmatic?"

"The Enlightened One prophesied that a time would come when Pataliputra would perish in fire and flood and war. For all of life and its glories are a passing dream. . ."

"In this shoreless ocean of events," said Gautam, "you and I are floating like stray autumn leaves. Am I responsible for what has happened before me?"

"Time cannot be determined. All is a dream and shall pass," Hari Ananda replied.

"Alarma had said to the future Buddha: happy friends are we that we look upon such fellow-ascetics as you. The doctrine which I know, you know too, and the doctrine which you know, I do too. Pray let us be joint wardens of the company—Tell me about non-violence," Gautam pleaded.

Far away in the village clubhouse the local bard had started reciting the folklore of the Great War.

"Time, for this bard in the chowpal, has been vaguely divided into the Golden Age and the Age of Wickedness. Man has bound himself in his own concept of time while all the time he is being hurtled into eternity as he revolves, dangling in time, tied to a wheel of fire. . .," the bhikshu remarked. "Now, let me go back to my vihara. May all be well with you." He walked away rapidly into the sunset, leaving Gautam bewildered and upset once again.

Gautam returned to his hut. On the way he could see rush lights beyond the mahua grove. They were setting up camp. The wind wafted the murmur of voices and sounds.

He entered his hut and flopped down on the mat. The prospect of meeting Champak was much too exciting and unexpected.

Why did women have such power over men? he wondered. The Buddha had solved that problem too: shun them. He had told his chief disciple Ananda:

"Don't look at them."

"But suppose one's glance falls on them, Sir?"

"Do not speak to them."

"If they start talking to us?"

"Keep wide awake."

Life was full of paradoxes. He thought of the sages' contradictory statements about women. Woman could never be pure, she was the root of all evil, she was shallow. Women of good families envied courtesans for their dresses and ornaments. Evil came into existence because of creation. Woman gave birth, so she was the origin of all sin. Woman was hungry for love, and therefore unreliable. And yet, despite her weaknesses, she could be immensely virtuous, faithful and self-sacrificing. She should be respected. She symbolised Shakti.

And there were all those wives who were burnt alive with their dead husbands, and Sakyamuni had told Ananda that women were stupid, jealous and vicious. Therefore his favourite disciple, Ananda, had given up his beloved Sundari. And now Hari Anand had forsaken his Champak. Doesn't stand to reason. What is wrong with women that they should be shunned like lepers ?

In the morning he went across to the open-air class. The guru had already begun his lecture.

"This is," the Acharya was saying, "and this is not."

The students nodded.

"The bound one, who is to be born again and again, has the path of his forefathers to traverse."

"Sakyamuni has questioned the very existence of a limited self. Perhaps it is the various conditions of consciousness, Sir," Gautam put in and slipped out of the copse.

The Ashram activities were in full swing. A sacrificial fire
was burning in a mandap. Vedic gods and ancient sages were
being honoured amid the loud chanting of mantras. The deities that presided over intelligence and memory were being
propitiated with burnt offerings.

A group of medical students passed by. Gautam came out
of the Hermitage. His heart was in great agony, his mind was
in doubt and his soul was certainly not traversing the right
path. The Upanishads said that for one who sought his self,
his atman, his father was not his father, his mother was not his
mother, the world was not the world, the thief was not the
thief, the murderer was not the murderer. He had no concern
with good or evil because he had conquered all the griefs of
his heart. . . Gautam loitered all day on lonely pathways.

A week passed. He did not have the courage to undertake
the mission. Perhaps it was a fool's errand. The monk had
cleverly passed the buck to an idiot. Responsibility has no
meaning, says he. Gautam began to have misgivings about
everything. At night, he was bothered by mosquitoes. Toads
and crickets disturbed his sleep. Noisy frogs used to be compared to Brahmins repeating their shlokas in unison. I am a
mere frog, he decided, wallowing in self-pity. One morning
he was awakened by an equally fretful Vimleshwar.

"I came last evening to the camp to show my jewellery designs and some gems to the royal ladies. The guards won't let
me in."

Gautam took his friend out into the open to have a breakfast of fresh fruit and milk. In the copse of plantains the guru's
pet baby elephant plucked some bananas for them. From the
ashram's cowpen they got their milk. The two friends spent
the morning strolling on the green, discussing politics.

4. Aryani, Goddess of the Woods

The royal barges were moored to the pier. Track-finders had brought the information that it was raining heavily in the foot-hills so the King had to wait. Camp was set up in the mahua grove, not far from Acharya Purshottam's Hermitage. The jungle came to life. Courtiers moved about in the tract which till now had been the haunt of deer and wild boar, or an occasional student who passed by, lost in thought. The merchants of Shravasti arrived with their wares. Minstrels and gypsies were trying to attract an audience for their ballads and acrobatics.

On a pleasant morning, Princess Nirmala set out with her bow and arrow to hunt deer. She was accompanied by Kumari Champak, the chief minister's daughter. It was very still in the fields. Snatches of a haunting song came floating in the wind. Champak stopped under a kadamba tree and plucked its leaves one by one.

"Lady of the Forest. . .," a student sang on his way to the Ashram—Gautam and Vimleshwar were passing by on a side track. The student sang the hymn to Aryani, the elusive Goddess of the Woods:

Lady of the Forest
Who seems to vanish from sight in the distance.
Why don't you ever come to our village?
Surely you are not afraid of men?

Gautam joined the singer.

In the evenings you hear the Lady of the Forest
Like a far-away voice crying,
Or as the crash of a felled tree.
She eats sweet berries
And rests wherever she will,
Perfumed with balm and fragrant,
The mother of all things of the wild. . .

The singer's voice receded in the distance. Gautam halted near a spreading mango tree. "Don't stand under a tree at high noon or dusk," his mother used to say, "some playful tree-fairy might kidnap you."

"Who is it?" he exclaimed. The two friends quickly hid themselves in the lush foliage. "Who is it, standing under the kadamba tree—a god, a fairy or a yakshi?"

Kumari Champak stood right in front holding a bough of the kadamba in her hand, languidly surveying the autumn landscape. With her elaborate hairdo, bright green bodice-and-sarong, seven-stringed gold necklace and golden waistband she seemed quite unreal. "Sudharshan Yakshini!" Gautam muttered in wonderment. "Tree-fairy, good to look at! Forest goddess!!"

All of a sudden the 'goddess' screamed and let go of the leafy branch. A number of red ants had crawled up her bare legs. She shook them off. Her royal companion, the doe-eyed Nirmala, came running. From his vantage point, Gautam observed her as well. Why does she always paint her eyebrows blue? Women do amazing things to their faces. Around her waist she had tied a length of silk part of which she had thrown over her left shoulder. This was called the sari.

"No deer, Champak dear. Let's go," she said a bit imperiously. They ambled away jingling their anklets. They were escorted by armed soldiers who followed them at a distance.

"She was the Rajkumari, the other one is a mere lady-in-waiting. Let's go before we are arrested. Look at all those security men! Why should they wear so much gold when they come on a hunting trip?" Vimleshwar grumbled.

"Don't worry, I'll put in a word for you—I'm going right now to the camp," Gautam told his friend airily. "Nobody can stop me, by virtue of my caste and status."

He started running towards the camp. His feet were bruised as he tore along on the scrub, taking a short-cut. He was already at the entrance of the encampment when the girls arrived.

"A little rice, my good ladies," he intoned, with feigned gravity. The sari-clad princess went straight into a tent, throwing down her bow and arrow. The magnolia girl stayed back and sat down on the edge of a red stone tank facing the royal tents. She regarded the student with interest. He was panting.

Great runners, these, as well as expert swimmers, she thought admiringly. This was the fellow she had seen diving in the Saryu some months back. His shoulder-length, wavy hair and his white cotton mantle were streaming in the strong river wind as he stood there against the bright sky. He looked like the young god of the woods.

"Rice and some lentils, too," he repeated cheekily. Surrounded by flowers and squirrels, he now seemed to be a talking rabbit of the *Panchatantra*, begging for a carrot. The simile was not apt, but it was so funny that Champak burst out laughing. For some unknown reason she was suddenly feeling light and happy.

He was jubilant. He laughed aloud, which was unbecoming for a scholar. So he checked himself and began: "And may the gods . . ."

She interrupted him pleasantly. "Were you invoking the forest goddess a little while ago . . . pandit?"

"Yes. I thought you were Aryani, till the ants upset you!" he answered frivolously, surprised by his own informality.

"So you are Gautam Nilambar of the Forest University of Shravasti! I have heard about you."

"My dakshina, please. I'm getting late for my devotions," he said hastily as a sentry passed by.

A dark-skinned housemaid brought him the grains. She smiled at him in recognition. She was the parasol-woman he had seen at the ghat.

He took the rice in his jholi, muttered the formal benediction and hastened out of the bamboo enclosure.

How on earth was he to accomplish his task—a poor brahmachari caught in the act of giving a diamond ring to the pradhan mantri's daughter—heavens would fall. I am already up to my ears in Woman Problems, he told himself gloomily, tramping back through the flame of the forest.

The next morning he turned up again. He had gathered that the King was out hunting bison all day. The Rani was fat and lazy and mostly slept in her tent. The women of the retinue went about doing their chores. Champak and Nirmala spent the day sitting by the lotus tank, teaching their parrots and mynas to repeat various phrases. That was the pastime of all ladies of rank. Champak and Nirmala teased each other through their talking birds. "Get up, lazybones," "Get lost, Nirmala," "Pipe down, Champak."

Gautam found them tutoring their new pahari myna. "Say, Champak is a fool," Nirmala told the bird. "Oh," she saw Gautam and laughed shyly. The young brahmachari smiled. "May I have some rice and. . ."

"You are just like our parrots. You repeat the same phrase day after day. Don't you know any other words?" Champak asked him playfully.

"We are not supposed to indulge in unnecessary conversation with laity, especially females."

"Are you training to be a purohit?" asked Nirmala.

"Yes, indeed."

"Can you perform some rituals quickly to bring my brother, Prince Hari, back?"

"Yes, I can. I'll have to come here daily at a certain time, if you get me all the rare ingredients required for the havan."

"I will," she said eagerly. He realised how easy it was to deceive women in these matters.

"I'll have to send for the stuff from the city," Nirmala told him.

"There is a thing called mohini which attracts people like nobody's business. First you get that," ordered Gautam with an air of authority about him.

"Mohini! That's used by tantrics—you are not a tantric, are you?" Champak asked dubiously.

"No, no, I am not." He sobered up. I'm getting into trouble, must make myself scarce. "Time for my classes, my good ladies," he said looking at the trees' shadows. "See you tomorrow."

At regular intervals he comes out of the wild flowers like an elf and vanishes again, Champak said to herself, wondering if she was finding some mohini in this attractive boy.

The next day he had to wait by the lotus tank for the ingredients of mystic potency which were being brought from a magician in Shravasti. He spent the day talking to Champak.

They laughed and chatted. She sang his favourite ragas. Nirmala remained doleful, probably because she had this overriding worry about her missing brother.

In the evening the footmen came back from Shravasti, empty-handed. They could not find the requisite ingredients. "Could you perhaps try some jyotish, Vaidya?" Nirmala asked him anxiously. He drew a few lines on the ground and said, "The Prince has come back from Taxila and is somewhere here in the vicinity. I'll do more calculations tomorrow." Champak had promised to sing Sri Raga tomorrow. No wonder Hari Shankar had confused her with music!

At night he went to the river bank to sleep on the cool sand. He was deeply in love, and she was not indifferent either. Perhaps he compensated for the absconding Rajkumar. At last, he was not lonely. He closed his eyes and felt light and airy like a cloud. . . He was not alone in Brahma's palace of light. A being of light had dropped from somewhere, a companion, a woman singing Sri Raga. All the grace of the universe emanated from her. After a long time Gautam slept soundly and had no dreams.

He rose with the sun, bathed in the Rapti and felt as usual for the ring tied to his waist. He got a rude shock—the ring was not there. He had been trying to find the right opportunity to break the sad news about the prince to the two women, and now the ring was gone. He searched for it frantically on the sand, in the shallow waters, in the shrubs. It would be impossible to find it in the dense forests he had been roaming all these days. He felt weak and sat down. So that's it. All happiness is short-lived. The monk Hari Anand appeared in his vision and said, laughing, "I told you so, stupid!"

It was possible the ring had been stolen while he was fast asleep. Lots of loafers and thieves were around. They had come from Shravasti hoping to gain from the royal hunt party. Then he caught sight of a fisherman casting his net on the other bank. A ray of hope flashed. Foolish, but hopes are usually foolish. He remembered the Shakuntala story. The ring Raja Dushyant had given her had fallen into the river and was swallowed by a fish. A fisherman caught that fish and sold it to the royal kitchen. The ring was found. Once again, poor Gautam hotfooted towards the camp. He went straight to the kitchen and asked a maid, breathlessly, "Have you fished any cook to-day. . . I mean. . . have you. . . ."

"Listen, what's going on here?" A guard lurched forward. "Who are you?"

"A Brahmin student," he croaked.

"A Brahmin demanding cooked food? Who do you think you're trying to hoodwink?" the fierce-looking man thundered. Gautam was tongue-tied. "A whole lot of crooks have turned up from the city and thugs are masquerading as students and sadhus. Things are being stolen from the tents." The burly sentry caught hold of Gautam's arm and produced him before the princess. She sat by the lotus tank colouring her toes with alta. She was horrified.

"Rajkumari ki jai ho. . .," the sentry announced. "We caught this man loitering in suspicious circumstances near the kitchen. Maybe some enemy Raja has sent him to poison the royal food."

"You have made a mistake!" the princess cried indignantly, "He is our special purohit, he comes every day to perform certain rites. Please forgive us, pandit."

Champak came out of her tent.

"I would like to speak to both of you in private," Gautam said grimly.

Nirmala ordered everybody to leave and spread a mat for Gautam to sit on. He took a deep breath and narrated the entire story, starting from his encounter with the "Greek" traveller. He was distressed to find the two girls reduced to helpless tears. Jamuna, their maid and confidante, had joined them and was sobbing hysterically. He tried to reassure them. "He may come back. . . He is still a novice monk, he can leave the Order. And I think he has not entirely got over his fascination for you, Kumari Champak."

In all eastern lore ministers' daughters are proverbially wise and sagacious. Champak was no exception. She wiped her tears and her nose and said calmly, "Has the hermit prince forgotten what Sakyamuni said to Mahamati?" She stood up and declaimed. "O Mahamati, just as one attains perfection in the arts of drama, dancing, music and the playing of the lute gradually, in the same manner one doesn't become an arhat in one day!"

There was silence.

"I lost the ring," Gautam said at last. "I'm sorry."

"I am not," Champak replied, stoically. "This was all my karma. What's done cannot be undone. Don't you think so, Myna?" she asked the bird.

"Done! Done!" the myna cried.

5. The Autumn Moon

As the wind shakes the grasses
So I shake your mind
So that you may desire me
So that you may not go away

Champak recalled a poem as she waited for Gautam. He had not come for several days. He had been sent here by Hari to convey a message, had done his duty and gone away. She stood near the tank, feeling lost and somehow betrayed once again. As though Hari's treachery was not enough.

A few nuns shuffled by. They looked so peaceful, *for they had all entered the Stream.* They were traversing the path of No Return. They had conquered the World of Desire. How and why? The Convent of Golden Mists was situated at a short distance from the camp. Champak left the myna's cage at the corner of the tank and began to follow the expressionless bhikkunis. They were trudging back from the city with their begging bowls full of rice. Some of them had been princesses. Shravasti had become the greatest centre of Buddhist nuns, and the convent was the Mother House.

River mist mingled with the dying rays of the sun. That was why it was called the Convent of Golden Mists. Champak reached the close-walled building and hid behind a door. The nuns trooped in. Somebody lighted an earthen lamp in the forecourt. A shadow appeared in the doorway. It was a sanyasin who had noticed Champak's presence.

The young woman was scared. She turned round and saw the distant lights of Shravasti. The sight of a human habitat reassured her. Somehow the nuns were not quite human, they were a breed apart. She looked at the distant lights again and now it seemed to her as though the city was on fire.

The sanyasin had apparently guessed her apprehension for she began to speak rapidly. She was repeating the terrible words of the Fire Sermon:

"All things, O priests, are on fire. The eye, O priests, is on fire; forms are on fire, eye-consciousness is on fire. . . the ear is on fire; sounds are on fire, the body is on fire; things tangible are on fire. . . the mind is on fire; ideas are on fire. . . with the fire of passion, with the fire of hatred, with the fire of infatuation, with birth, old age, death, sorrow, lamentation, misery, grief and despair, are they on fire. . . fire. . . fire. . . The body is like a house which is on fire, but we keep talking! We keep talking till the house is finally burnt down."

Then the woman broke into a song:

Thou that art come from where the fragrant trees
Stand crowned with blossoms,
Standest alone in the shade, maiden so fair
  and foolhardy
None to companion thee. . . fearest thee not
  the wiles of seducers?

"No," Champak replied briefly.

"Dost thou not know that Mara is in ambush aiming at frail human hearts?"

"I fear him not," said Champak staring back at the eerily youthful nun.

"In a former era, a girl very much like thee sat under the sal tree grove and lo, Mara appeared to her in mid-air and said, 'Thou that art come from where the fragrant trees stand crowned. . .', " the bhikkuni resumed her singing. And darkness was torn asunder by sudden lightning which lit up the night sky from horizon to horizon, and in that instant Champak saw that the old nunnery had disappeared and a strange fragrance filled the world for it was springtime in lovers' hearts and dark-eyed cowherds played their flutes on shady riverbanks, and village lanes rang with youthful laughter as young girls went forth to worship the God of the Woods, and the world was made for falling in love; for there was power in love and impotent misery in renunciation.

The lightning vanished in the horizon, darkness returned and the nun's voice continued, "But love lasts only an instant, it is merely a moment involved in eternity. Dreams, and the shadow of flowers and physical love, all have one thing in common. . . they fade with the light of the moon. At first Uppalavana also thought what thou dost think. . . dost know her story?"

"No."

"She, the lotus-hued, was born in Hansavati when Padmauttara was Buddha, and reborn in Shravasti in this Buddha-age as the daughter of the Treasurer. She joined the Order instead of marrying one of her rich and handsome suitors and . . ."

"Were there many Buddhas?" Champak interrupted, confused. The nun ignored her question and continued. "Uppalavana became especially versed in the mystic potency of transformation. I am Uppalavana! On this thirteenth night of the Autumn Moon I am a hundred and fifty years old." The ghostly speaker faded into the shadows.

Champak was terror-stricken. She clutched the twigs in her fingers. The leaves fell. Run, run, she said to herself. Curiosity overpowered her fear. She tiptoed up to the main hall. Worse was to come. A nun known as Sister Nanda, an ex-dancer, was ominously leading a chorus:

> *Behold Nanda! the foul compound, diseased,*
> *Impure! Compel thy heart to contemplate what*
> *Is not fit to view. . .! Behold Nanda. . . the*
> *Foul compound. . . the foul compound. . . the foul. . .*

Voices rose higher and became more terrible. Champak realised that she was present in the very corridor of Time—this Sisterhood of Shravasti founded by the Lady Gotami Prajapati had been blessed by Lord Buddha himself when he had walked by this river a century and a half ago. They were seeking the end of being—frail women whose only lot had once been to attract men and bear children. Proud princesses, generals' daughters, housewives, all turned into gentle Setters of the Wheel.

Am I a woman in these matters or am I a man, what am I not, then? Thus spake Sumedha, living in the Sophists' Grove. It was said that, incensed with the bloom of her beauty, she would talk to lads standing at harlots' doors like a crafty huntress devouring the virtues of many. Now she went about with a shaven head, wrapped in yellow robes, begging.

And Kundal Keshi, the one with the curly head, had toured the country with a rose bough in hand debating with sages, intoxicated with the pride of her intellect, before she went into a life of humility. Champak had heard about these women during her stay in the camp. Now they began to sing:

On fire is all the world, all is in flames
Ablaze is all the world, the heavens do quake. . .

The nuns chorused in sombre tones:

By reason of a cause it came to be.
By rupture of a cause it dies.

A high wind rose, scattered the clouds and fell. Champak came out. Even the moon looked like the placid face of a shaven-headed bhikshu.

"Champak—come back, come back. . ."

She heard her myna screaming away for all it was worth. Gautam carried the bird's cage. Nirmala stood beside him. The myna sang out—"Champak is a fool!"

"I have been in there and found Nothing," she announced in a hollow voice.

"This is a ghostly place," Nirmala was saying. "Gautam Pandit had just arrived when we saw you going behind the nuns, so we followed you. Gautam says it is a dangerous area known for its scorpions and snakes. Come along."

So, he had turned up. But now she resented this rapport between the princess and the pandit. Am I jealous? Quietly she began to walk back with them.

"How do these frail women live in such a frightening place full of whispering shadows?" Nirmala wondered aloud. "I think some of them could be victims of circumstances. I have seen some pretty young sanyasins over here."

"Young women can also hear the Call!" Gautam objected. "Anyway, most of them are bent double with age."

"Yes, it's heartbreaking. I saw one old sanyasin limping badly."

"Well, that is what Buddha's teaching is all about—to understand the extent of Sorrow."

"Why didn't you come the whole of last week?" Nirmala asked.

"I had gone to Jetvan Vihara to tell the ex-prince that I had done the needful, minus the ring. He wasn't there—gone to preach among the Chandals. Waited there for a couple of days, he did not turn up. May have gone further afield. Anyway, wherever they are, they come back to spend the rainy season in the monasteries. He'll be back much earlier. I'm sure he will visit Saket and bless you all."

Yellow leaves crackled under their feet. He escorted them back to the encampment. "Come tomorrow to inaugurate our Festival with your shlokas," Champak said a trifle dryly before going into her tent. Gautam noticed the subtle change in her tone. Women!

He had got this hint from Prince Hari. You can go through life incognito—as a Greek traveller, a hermit, a fop, a dancer, and nobody will ever know the real you.

A corner of his kutir served as his "studio". He took out the requisite material and made himself up in the mystic image of Natraj. Shiva's body was yellow like autumn leaves, covered with ash, and he wore an elephant hide. The crescent moon shone on his head. He seldom laughed. He danced the Cosmic Dance and Time turned into an ocean of light . . .

The sound of dance-bells, reed pipes and drums could be heard from a distance. They were celebrating Sharad Purnima.

Champak was singing Chhaya Raga, Melody of Shadows. Servants were going to and fro carrying jugs of wine. The King was fond of his goblet.

"Natraj" entered the mandap, rattling his damru. Everybody was taken aback. This was high drama—the people of Shravasti were noted for their theatricals. This was obviously a dancer from the city. Champak and Nirmala guessed his identity and were astounded as he burst into Sandhya Tandav.

He danced in a frenzy till dinner was served on banana leaves. Women retired to their enclosure. The Rajan also took him to be an eminent performing artiste of Shravasti and made him sit next to him on the gaddi. Gautam ate roast meat and drank cup after cup of strong madh. The King and the Court were all gloriously drunk.

A courtier shouted, "Sire, a young Brahmin seer has been frequenting the camp. He says the Prince has arrived in the vicinity."

In his state of elation Gautam hiccuped and blubbered: "I'll tell you the Truth. . . your shun, Shire, has become a—hic—a bhik—hic—hic—a bhikari—with a begging bowl—hic. . ."

The King was enraged. How dare he! "Throw him out. Out! Out!" He stood up, stamped his foot and roared. Gautam, meanwhile, had passed out. Two footmen carried him off the mandap and dumped him near the lotus tank. That was an equally dramatic anticlimax.

The sun was going down behind the foothills. "Get up! Get up, lazybones," the myna cried in her cage.

Gautam opened his eyes and pressed his temples. The bird's cage was lying on the tank steps.

A honey-maker stung him on his nose and he sat up with a jolt. He tried to think hard—then he repeated, dramatically, "Where am I?" as though he was still on the stage. He looked around once again. No stage. No rush lights. No revelries. Total desolation. He had a terrible headache. A terrible silence—had he hit the Shunya of the Buddhists?

He recollected slowly. He had danced, hobnobbed with royalty, eaten a lot of meat and got drunk, all in rapid succession. He had enjoyed himself thoroughly. Given a chance he would do it again. He had grown up overnight, become a man of the world. Damned good business, this Maya business. Except that he hadn't yet enjoyed the intimate company of a female.

Female. Ah, female! Where was she? He got another rude shock. She had gone away. Everybody had left.

"Champak, come back, Champak. . ." The myna cried. Gautam looked around. There was nobody. He scratched his head, puzzled. Then he saw an elephant-trapper coming towards him.

"What happened. Where are they?" Gautam asked him.

"They were deceived by the Chief Thug of Shravasti. Now we can say with some pride that our practitioners of this ancient art have surpassed those famous ones of Kashi!"

"I don't understand."

"See—the Chief Thug's chelas turned up here last night while the King was having his dinner. They shouted, 'A rogue has escaped the trappers' hold and is heading for the camp!' So the royal party left everything and ran for their lives. They got on to their barges and rowed downstream at full speed towards Saket. . ."

"Then?"

"The thugs set to work. They looted the tents in no time and went back."

"While I was sound asleep right here!" Gautam marvelled. "That is Maya. . .?"

"That is for you to comprehend, sir." The trapper nodded. "That is indeed Maha Thugee Maya[1]! Do you need any help, sir? You are not really a dancer, are you?"

"No. I am also an illusionist. I am all right. Get some seeds for this poor creature."

"Yes, sir."

The trapper brought a handful of millet from the debris of the royal kitchen. Then he took his leave.

Gautam turned to the myna.

---

[1] Illusion—the supreme con-woman.

"So, your royal mistresses left you to die of hunger and thirst, eh? They could have awakened me before they left. . ."

The bird stared at him with its beady eyes. It could not tell him the real story: when Champak and Nirmala were running towards the pier they had tried to wake him up.

"Poor shastri. He danced so strenuously last evening that he fainted," Nirmala had remarked sympathetically.

"Fainted! He simply got roaring drunk. Succumbed to temptation in a big way. He may even end up as a rake. Just like your brother gave in to the temptation of being called an arhat. He has ended up a mere vagabond, neither here nor there." Being the Minister's Wise Daughter Champak made her little speech, then added, "Get up, dear Gautam, before your skull full of intelligence is crushed by a mad animal."

He continued to snore.

"So, one who has been wide awake falls asleep one day, and one who is asleep wakes up. . ." Champak declared.

"Champak, this poor man is lying in the jaws of death and you are mouthing platitudes!" Nirmala screamed.

"Come along," the Chief Minister shouted her down, and dragged both girls towards the jetty.

Nirmala rushed back and left the myna's cage near Gautam. "Wake him up quickly, Myna. Keep repeating, Get up—get up, lazybones. . ." Then she ran back to join the rest of the fleeing entourage. . .

Gautam washed off his make-up in the tank, gave some water to the myna and picked up the cage. On the way back to the ashram it occurred to him that all was not lost. This was his final term. On convocation day his father would come proudly to fetch him. The Acharya would repeat the formal words of farewell—Do your duty and speak the truth. He would go home, put kohl in his eyes, wear silks and leather sandals and jauntily stick a comb made of porcupine quills in his hair. And he would drive around town in his own chariot, as behoved a young man of substance. He would visit Saket and find out if the Chief Minister would send his daughter's proposal of marriage to his rich and important father, the High Priest of Shravasti. . .

6. Sudarshan Yakshini—
Tree Sprite, Good to Behold

Myna was his new friend. He told her, "Look, Myna, Champak was angry with me for some reason the last time I met her outside the convent. I didn't know it was going to be our last meeting. What shall I do?"

Myna hopped about in the cage and kept quiet.

"All right. Let's draw her—would you like to see her again? I'll make a picture of her for you." He collected his painting material and made the usual preparations. He ground red brick into fine red powder and mixed indigo with water to make blue paint. He prepared yellow and orange from turmeric and saffron. He collected the required herbs from the forest, boiled them according to prescription in order to make green, white and other hues. He tried to remember what Champak looked like.

He spread a piece of white Chinese silk on a slab of stone and took out his paint brushes made of squirrel's tail. He began by making an outline—a pair of fish-eyes. Then he stopped and wondered: Meaning has no definite station. One meaning can be attained through various symbols and the symbols can be understood as different stations. They do not circumvent the meaning. A picture is not merely colours, it is the soul of the artist. Viewers can discern significance from a mere hint— the eye can only see colours which exist on the surface, just as poetry is merely an expression of the poet's inner voice. And sensibility has no precise definition.

The absolute has no form. It is beyond comprehension, it is not even an intellectual concept. Brahma Ishwar was a being who could be compared to a Form. And light was the source of that form. Its real form, Swarup, was the form of various other things, Viswarup.

Gautam put down his brushes uneasily. Thought can only be *thought*. A real person is life itself, not a symbol of life. One's attraction towards them is based on emotion. Then how do I present pure thought? I cannot remain dispassionate or even neutral. Dhyan is the real art of the artist and it cannot remain intact or whole. Pure form, the concept of a thing which is itself, is inherent in the thing—it is the real dhyan. How is the *personalness* of a thing to be ignored?

For the next few days he made and destroyed paintings, moulded figurines in red clay and dashed them to pieces. At last he completed the high relief of The Girl with the Kadam Bough—the plump, slender-waisted, broad-hipped girl who was bending the twig of the exotic tree, just as he had seen Champak do a few weeks ago.

Theorists judged it harshly. No one praised him for what he had done. Gautam made no comment. He had given up the path of philosophy, and couldn't tell them what pure aesthetic experience actually was, how it was gained and communicated. Who was he to resolve the conflict of Rup and Arup, Bhava and Abhava? He merely wished to somehow capture in clay and stone the mystery of the human form. Pure aesthetic experience was unconnected joy, it was like lightning, indivisible, and it appeared by itself. Just as the concept of the artist was inherent in the concept of Viswakarma who was omniscient, and whose swarup was the symbol of the whole universe, the beholder existed in the atma or the self, *Viswarup, rupam priti rup. . .*

The picture of the world was merely the Self which had been painted on the canvas of the Self. This was that pure existence, pure perception, pure life, the studio of the heart which contained all pictures, all imagination, where all images became one, where the same light kept passing through myriad-coloured glasses and all that which had been made with beauty and truth was a complete art-piece and a path, both for the creator and the beholder. And those who knew could understand.

He called The Girl with the Kadamba Bough, "Sudarshan Yakshini—Tree Sprite, Good to Behold". The figure was still somewhat archaic, not streamlined as sculpture was to become in later centuries. But in The Girl with the Kadam Bough a fusion and balance of lines and poise had been achieved. It was earthy and emanated strength. Gautam was very happy that he could make such a figurine, and decided to make some more. One afternoon he lifted the myna's cage and travelled excitedly to Shravasti to talk to his friend Aklesh about his work. Now he would like to make some free-standing statues and wanted to discuss new techniques with his artist friends.

Aklesh lived in the centre of town. When Gautam arrived there he found his friend's studio crowded with fellow craftsmen and artists. He placed the cage in the window and sensed the tension in the air. As if something terrible had happened. No one spoke to him. There was a knock on the door. A wild-looking bearded artist came in, panting. "Friends," he said hoarsely, "pick up your paintings and run for your lives." He sat down to regain his breath. "War has broken out. The up-start Chandragupta's army has occupied our country. This land shall be ruined in a few days. Your time is over, brother Gautam. Death will finally cancel all conflicts of Rup and Arup, Bhava and Abhava.

"The new imperial army from Magadh has arrived. Prime Minister Chanakya does not want any weak feudatories around, so Rajan and all his men were put to death."

"All of them?" Gautam felt too weak to finish his question.

"It's the Law of the Fish. I hear some young ladies swam across the river somehow, and escaped to the territory of the Panchalas. A contingent of the Imperial Army has been dis-patched in their pursuit." The man got up to go.

"Where are you off to?" Gautam asked him feebly.

"To the wars. You, of course, will not fight because, I am told, you have recently become a believer in this newfangled Jain-Buddhist business of non-violence."

"Shall we get ourselves killed meekly in the name of Ahimsa?" Aklesh asked Gautam, the theorist, agitatedly.

Gautam crossed the room and roared. "Tell me why some killing is good and some bad? I am not interested in King Nanda, Vishnu Sharma and Chandragupta. Why must they drag me into their conflict. . .?" Nobody heard him because they were running out through the front door. Soon the room was empty. He rushed out too.

A dreadful din rose from the bazaar down below. The city had been suddenly attacked by hordes of war-elephants and heavy chariots. The next moment the market square had turned into a battlefield. Gautam called out to his friends. His voice was drowned in the trumpeting of elephants, the swish of arrows and the clanking of swords. He stood horrified for a while on the veranda, watching the terrible scene. The corpses of his artist-friends lay sprawled on the main street.

Gautam walked down the steps slowly. He removed a sword from the clutches of a dead warrior and began to fight.

Outside the city, a cool wind sang peacefully in the rose-apple trees of Jetvan Vihara. Nature remains indifferent to human affairs.

Gautam fought in front of Aklesh's house and killed a few Magadhan foot soldiers till he was struck down by a spear and fainted. When he regained consciousness, dawn was breaking over a smouldering city. Lanes were strewn with the dead and the dying. Smoke rose from a building in front of him. He felt extreme pain in his bleeding hands and looked at them. His fingers had been mutilated.

Sujata supplied milk to many people in the city. Today she had come to give milk to the wounded. None of her customers was alive. She came to the chowk facing the burnt-down Elephant House. The high priest and his wife had been killed in the fire. Aklesh's studio was close by and Sujata heard a myna crying, "Come back, come back." It was eerie. A tiny bird had survived the massacre. The milkmaid went up and saw the ornate cage in the window. Then she found Gautam lying crumpled on the steps. He was still breathing.

"I would like to go to my ashram," he said weakly to her after she had dressed his wounds.

"The gurukul is deserted, sir. Everybody has fled. I am a lowly milkmaid, but you won't lose caste if you stay in my house till you get well. You can't go anywhere in this condition. We'll treat you with our herbs and things."

He accompanied the milkmaid to her village and stayed with her till his wounds healed. Sujata served him with the devotion of a bondswoman. The situation alarmed him. He could take her as his dasi but did not. One morning he said to her, "Let's go and see what happened to my little thatch. Palaces fall but humble dwellings survive, you know." He went to the silent hermitage and found his Sudarshan Yakshini lying upside down upon a heap of rubble. Luckily, she was intact. With the help of Sujata's brother he placed the slab on the milk-cart and carried it all the way to Shravasti. They stopped in front of the ruin of his Elephant House. He had dreamt of bringing Champak here in a wedding chariot. He lifted the statue and placed it in a corner of the entrance hall. The statue stared at him with its vacant fish-eyes. Well, dear lady, now I go forth in the world to find you. I have a feeling you are alive and I may still locate you somewhere. Till then, beware of the red ants which may crawl over your legs the way they did when you stood under the Kadamba tree! He wiped a tear from his eye.

Sujata asked him, "Is that a goddess you worship, sir?"

"Yes," he lied, for he no longer believed in gods and godesses. "Yes, she is Aryani, Goddess of the Woods. But she is afraid of human beings and likes to live in desolate places." Sujata made a dutiful namaskar before the statue of Champak. They came out of the burnt-down house.

On a moonless night he bade farewell to Sujata, picked up the myna's cage and crossed the Saryu in a ferry boat.

7. *Birdman of the Crossways*

Gautam became a tramp in his search for Champak and Nirmala. The country was in a shambles. War-weary people gladly gave him alms and sought his blessings. He showed them his stumped hands and declaimed—"Fingers reveal the mudras of the Dance of Shiva. They play the lute and the flute. They paint. They also make spears and arrows and swords. May the gods give you no harvest and no progeny if you go on making spears. . ."

Once he said this to a Mauryan general's wife who had come out of her house to give him alms. She was horrified by his curse and banged the door shut in his face.

I may soon become famous as a crank, he thought gloomily. Everybody seems to love wars. They just don't learn, don't regret or repent. So what shall I do now? That seemed to be his eternal problem.

He trekked from place to place and sat down at the crossroads, hoping to find Champak and Nirmala among the passersby. He came to be known as the Birdman of the Crossways. The myna continued to call out, "Come back, come back," till she grew old and tired. She had failed in her mission. She became very quiet and kept her beak in her feathers. One day she died. Gautam grieved for her. His last link with Champak was broken.

Chandragupta Maurya, the monarch with the insignia of the royal peacock, became the first Samrat, emperor, of the chaturant state of Bharat. He was not one of those "descended from the sun or the moon" because his mother was an Untouchable. He was brought up by shepherds and trained by Vishnu Gupta at Taxila where he had been considered the young man most likely to succeed. A self-made man, Alexander had invaded the north-west and Chandragupta had got up an army and driven out the Greeks from the land of the Five Rivers, Punjab, as the Persians were to call it in later eras. Chandragupta had also defeated old King Nanda of Pataliputra. His army had occupied smaller kingdoms and Sakyamuni, the Buddha, had said: Victory breeds hatred because the vanquished sleep in sorrow, and only that person is peaceful who is above victory and defeat and happiness.

Chandragupta Maurya's prime minister, Vishnu Sharma, alias Chanakya, had begun putting his theories into practice:

the only thing to be avoided in politics was making a mistake. He set up separate departments of minerals and irrigation and commerce and revenue, foreign affairs and defence, grazing lands and slaughter houses. Unsuccessful Brahmins and witty barbers, astrologers and courtesans gladly joined the newly established intelligence service. Spies dressed as sadhus loitered about. They visited the houses of prostitutes and gamblers and kept in touch with what the populace was saying in the bazaars. Manu had said that subjects did not feel insecure where black-faced, red-eyed Dand walked the earth.

Rapid changes were taking place around the vagabond Gautam. New fashions and hair-styles were coming into vogue. In the spoken language words were appearing in a new form. Commerce was flourishing. Gautam couldn't trade in anything except his learning but he was not supposed to charge any fee from his students. And he avoided the company of thinkers and sophists. He continued living on alms and looked for Champak in Buddhist nunneries, market-squares and new garrison towns of the victorious Mauryan army. She seemed to have vanished.

During his wanderings he came across a number of Persian horsemen. They had fled Iran after Alexander's invasion and lived in the land of the Five Rivers for many years. One of them, whom he met on the highway near the town of Ahichhatra, spoke a kind of polyglot language. Gautam could only roughly understand what the Parsi with the curly beard and tall black hat told him.

"We have come to Hind from Iranshahr to seek our livelihood."

"Where is Hind?" asked Gautam.

"This country in which you live!" the Persian answered, surprised. Then he said, "See, your literary language and ours are almost identical, except that we use H for S. Your *saptah* is our *haptah*—sometimes the words are almost the same, like your *namo* is our *namaz*.

"Yeah," Gautam was bored. He had heard all that before from Hari Shankar. "Affinity in languages does not keep people

from fighting and hating one another." Wearily he changed
the topic, as he observed the Persian's long coat, pyjamas and
leather boots. "What a lot of things you carry on your body!"
he commented.

"Yes, it's rather hot out here. We'll discard these clothes
when we get to Pataliputra. You know, a great deal of building activity is going on there. We are architects from burnt-
down Persepolis, but we're sure to get jobs in Pataliputra!"
said the displaced Parsi from Pars, and rode away.

The same evening Gautam noticed a touring theatrical company pitching its tents in an open space near Ahichhatra. He
had exhausted himself walking and begging. He realised that
he had done nothing else all his life. The country was full of
men and women crippled in the recent war. They had become
beggars. Will I end up as one of them? He went straight to a
stagehand and said, "I would like to see your manager." The
lad took him to a glamorous woman who sat on a cot, dying
her soles with red alta. She was Ambika, chief actress and owner
of the company. She looked up and eyed him with unabashed
interest. She was a woman of the world, and a connoisseur of
male flesh.

Gautam switched on his charm. "I am an unemployed actor, lost everything in the war. . .," he whined. "Can I join
your company, madam? See, I used to paint and carve. But
then"—dramatically he spread his maimed hands in front of
her—"I can act all right."

Despite being a seasoned courtesan and a hard-headed busi-
ness-woman, Ambika fell in love with him. He became the
chief actor and her paramour. He thought he was cast in the
mould of heroes. He was very conscious of his power over
women and grew vainer by the day. But he was too outspoken, and his curse on the Mauryan general's wife had probably been reported. Ambika was worried. Once or twice he
made a reference to the policies of the new Prime Minister
Vishnu Sharma, alias Chanakya, alias Kautilya, in a satire he
had put together. "Don't attack the powers that be in your
plays, you may get into trouble," she warned him. He didn't
care.

Then Ambika said to him, "I hear you are a fine dancer. Teach me, too."

"Teach *you*? Do you still require anything to be taught—the All-Knowing Woman?" he growled sarcastically. He had become a bitter, cynical person who liked to hurt her. She looked crestfallen. He felt sorry for her. Poor girl, she has given me a career. She looks after me and serves me as though I were a prince, not a vagrant, and I taunt her all the time for no reason. She is not responsible for my misfortunes. In a mellower tone he asked, "Who told you that I could dance?"

"Some actors from Kashi who dropped by the other day. One of them said he had seen you perform the Shiva Nritya in a royal festival in Shravasti, shortly before the war."

"Who was he? Where is he? Can I meet him?" Gautam asked anxiously. This actor might know Champak's whereabouts.

"I have no idea," Ambika replied evenly. "They left on their tour." She was used to the changing moods of this temperamental, restless man, her demon lover.

"Gautam," she said calmly, after a pause, "we have done enough travelling in the provinces. Let's go to Pataliputra."

"Yes, let's," he responded, indifferently.

8. *The Theatre in Pataliputra*

All roads led to the brand new auditorium with the sloping roof—a theatrical company from Ahichhatra had arrived in the Mauryan capital. There were rumours that they might even give a royal command performance. They were splendid. Stories about the company's legendary hero had already reached the city. The actor Gautam Nilambar, they said, was too good to be true. Tall, dark and handsome, an excellent singer and a fine thespian—in short, absolutely devastating. Women adored him—for women have this habit of confusing a fellow's good looks with his talents. They have a weakness for celebrities, poets, musicians, actors.

The hall was sold out for the first night. Quite a few Greeks were present among the audience, eagerly looking forward to seeing the latest Indian play. They had stayed back in India after Alexander left the country and followed Chandragupta to Pataliputra. The mandap was full of women of all ages and classes, princesses, housewives, young maidens—they had all flocked there in their palanquins or on foot to see the famous heartthrob.

Ambika was the best-known actress of her time. When she made up her face with the powder of ground yellow kasturi leaves and lined her almond eyes with kohl made of pure ghee and lampblack, she created a sensation. She belonged to the courtesan or vaishya caste; her mother and grandmother had been court dancers. The vaishyas were a class apart. Treatises were written for them on how to lure and captivate men. Some were trained as spies and were called vish-kanya or poison-maidens. They were reared on slow poison so that their kisses would be fatal for the enemy. Ambika was an enchantress without being a dangerous vish-kanya. She had also had strenuous training in the performing arts. As a high-class vaishya she was an accomplished entertainer of nagar-seths, warlords and princes.

Gossip-mongers said that Gautam treated her badly. He flirted with other women, drank expensive wines, dressed himself in the finest muslins from Vanga and silks from Kashi. He wore pearls and diamonds and lived like a lord—all at the expense of the wealthy Ambika. He exploited her unashamedly. The scandals and tales about Gautam were not unfounded. The fact was that he had become a thoroughly degenerate and wicked man. He had long given up his search for Champak and had settled into a kind of fake domesticity with Ambika. Now he was a middle-aged rake with a streak of silver in his ringlets which made him look more attractive than ever.

Tonight he was in Pataliputra with yet another abject audience at his feet. According to dramatic convention he came out of the wings and began his dialogue with the chief actress about the theme of the play. The crowd gazed at him, spellbound. He laughed silently for they could never view his inner drama. . . just as there is a backstage which spectators cannot see.

And then it happened. In a flush of unexpected excitement he threw up his disfigured hands.

Women gasped. Romantic young girls were shocked. There was a hushed stir in the hall. The celebrated, sad-faced hero had mutilated fingers. He always kept his hands, especially the left one, carefully concealed under his mantle. On this fateful evening his glance had fallen on somebody in the audience. It had upset him so much that he spun round with a flourish and his shawl slipped off. Ambika quickly picked it up and threw it back over his shoulders. . . He was still aghast by what he had seen.

Champak sat in the front row, dressed in purple silk, loaded with gold ornaments. She was accompanied by a little boy and her maid. She had come to attend the famous actor's first performance in the metropolis. She had also wanted to see Ambika, who was reputed to be his possessive mistress. . .

When she saw his crippled hands, burning tears welled up in her eyes. Through the mist she watched Gautam's face flicker like a dying candle. Speechless for a moment, he gathered his wrap and stared at Lady Magnolia again.

The woman he had been searching for all these years—there she sat on the floor, cross-legged, with a child beside her. A prosperous housewife and mother. No longer an ideal or a vision, just a smug matron with a double chin and a middle-age spread. Shiva—Shiva—

I hereby recognise Time the Gambler's hilarious interplay with Maya, Illusion, and resume my own play-acting.

Across the footlights Champak cried quietly, pretending to be moved by the hero's oratory. Prince Hari Shankar had given up the world and yet could not quite give it up. In order to forget her Gautam Nilambar had returned to the world and probably remained a hermit at heart. She could neither renounce nor enjoy the World of Desire. Could the sacred nuns of Shravasti ever understand the Unsung Psalm of Sister Champak? Hadn't she become wiser than the all-knowing Sister

Uppalvana? For she had undergone her own transformation: she had done what a mere woman was required to do—she had accepted her "fate".

After the First Act was over she whispered to her handmaiden who sat near her. Jamuna slyly looked around and slipped out of the exit.

"A dasi wishes to see you," Ambika said to Gautam in the green-room.

"Who is it?" he asked gently. All his irritation and harshness had vanished. Ambika was astonished by this very unusual, very sudden change in him for she noticed extraordinary peace on his face.

"The usual thing, perhaps. A message from one of your female admirers," she said and began her make-up for the next act.

Gautam came out and encountered a dusky servant-woman at the bottom of the stairs. She bowed low and joined her palms. Speaking coquettishly she delivered the message. "Milady has sent you her greetings and would like to meet you after the play."

With a sickening feeling he realised who had sent her. He stood very still for a moment. Descending to the second step he said, "No. Tell your lady on behalf of this body: *One who is awake falls asleep one day, and one who has been asleep suddenly awakens.* Consider those who are awake all the time. Further: I now am wide awake, and though the path be sharp as the razor's edge, nothing can hinder me now. Also: has your lady forgotten the injunction that, for a devoted wife all other men are in the likeness of a shadow? You may go now, my good woman. And may the gods . . ." he checked himself from reciting the benediction. In an instant he had regained the mannerisms of an ascetic.

Jingling her anklets the maid ran off. She returned after a few minutes and was not surprised to see that he was still there, backstage.

She said, bowing, "My lady says: you are so right, O Wise One! It is good that you have woken up. Further, the Lady Champak says: What, kind sir, do you know of a woman's devotion? However, it's all right, she says, for none can blunt the razor's edge. Now you may go too, quoth she, and bids you farewell."

Jamuna paused a little and added, "Milady had also asked me to tell you that after the war she was captured by the victors and brought over here. . ."

Gautam looked at her intently and recognised her: She was the royal maid-servant Jamuna, who had held the umbrella over Champak and Nirmala when he had seen them for the first time that long-ago rainy morning on the river bank near Ayodhya. Later he had met this woman in the royal camp near Shravasti. She smiled faintly. "Your honour, I was also made a captive when the palace was sacked. We were all brought to Pataliputra. Lady Champak was forced to join the harem of an old mantri. Look, sir, right now he is away on tour. Milady would like to meet you on the quiet. For a few moments . . ."

Now she was playing the traditional role of the stage kutni, the go-between between the nayika and the nayak—and in such tragically changed circumstances.

"For old time's sake," she pleaded.

He thought quickly. Should he go and meet this fat, married woman, cause her greater unhappiness and totally shatter his own world of dreams? "No," he spoke firmly and briefly. "My dear Jamuna, there are no old and new times. Only Eternity—which is also an instant."

The woman rushed back to the hall and returned with the answer: "Lady Magnolia says that in all your glory and self-assertion you may propound great philosophies but right now, at this moment, after receiving this reply from you, it is she who has become the Enlightened One. For she has realised the Supreme Truth—it is a profound misfortune to be reborn as a woman, especially since her beauty and youth have nothing to do with Eternity!"

Gautam kept quiet. The message squashed all argument. Suddenly he asked, "And where, pray, is Princess Nirmala?"

"If you ever happen to go to the Convent of Golden Mists near Jetvan, your honour, you may come across a wrinkled old woman with shaven head sitting under a wood-apple tree, telling her beads. That is Sister Nirmala, a Buddhist nun, and one of the famous Sisterhood of Shravasti. During the killings at Ayodhya she escaped to Indraprastha. She stayed there for a few years in somebody's harem. Some monks helped her to run away and reach Jetvan Vihara where her brother, the former Prince Hari Shankar, was in residence at the time."

"Shiva! Shiva!"

"Yes indeed, sir. One can't stop marvelling at the game of dice called Life. And the other day, a wandering bhikshu told us that the Reverend Brother Hari Ananda of Jetvan Vihar has passed on and entered the Void. And now I must take your leave, sir, for you are getting late for your next act." Jamuna stepped back deferentially and vanished into the crowd, leaving the famous actor dumbfounded.

9. The River

As soon as the performance was over Gautam hastily left the stage, without once looking at his audience. Back in the silent green-room he took off his unstitched silk robes and ornaments and removed his make-up. Ambika had not returned yet. Hurriedly he covered himself with a white cotton mantle and slipped out of the back door.

How easy it was to abandon Ambika too, a mere woman. On reaching a side lane he quickened his pace and made for the nearest city gate. Nervous, like a prisoner running away from gaol, he looked back from time to time to see if he was being followed, but apparently nobody had noticed a white-robed sanyasi picking his way through the jostling crowds of the metropolis and the river-front. The Street of Dancing Girls was brightly lit with torches. Crooks, jugglers and men-about-town were assembled in gambling dens. The wooden parapet of the distant Imperial Palace was visible in the moonlit summer night. Gautam smiled: at this very moment the Emperor would be playing chess with Prime Minister Chanakya. A city-woman watched him closely as she passed by. She probably worked in the prime minister's intelligence department which employed clever courtesans, and was merely doing her job.

The question, Gautam said to himself, which someone ought to put to the great Chankaya, is: Who will spy on whom?

Sentries walked to and fro on the ramparts. The city walls of Pataliputra have sixty-four gates—which of these leads to my destination?

I have been an ascetic and a libertine, a thinker and an idiot, a beggar and a grandee. I have seen it all. Perhaps now, in spite of myself, I have reached a stage of sanyas when one desires neither death nor life.

He proceeded on his journey, going through many towns and peacock-villages. Where is my final refuge? He felt lonely in a way he had never felt before. There was nothing to be afraid of, he reassured himself. He was with the earth, the earth was his mother and she was still with him. He smelt the soft smell of grass, the coolness of stones, the strength of the soil beneath his feet. He stretched his arms and touched the air.

Many days went by as he proceeded on his way. Exotic plants and flowering boughs bent down before him, birds accompanied him, whistling blithely. Raindrops played sonorous melodies on lotus petals. It had clouded over. The multicoloured stoles of peasant girls fluttered in the wind as they sang, sitting on swings under dark green trees.

He took a boat from a riverside town and got off at Saket. A drop of rain fell on his eyelashes. Black clouds thundered on the horizon. He was overcome by a strange ecstasy. Stormy rivers roared in his heart, melodious waterfalls made music within his brain. He found Indra standing by his side. The rain fell like a cascade on his face. He whispered his hymn to Rudra. . .

Like the charioteer lashing his horses forward by the whip
Does he announce the message of rain,
Lions' roars are heard from a distance,
Roar and thunder, sow the seed,

Come flying hither in your squelching car!
So that high lands and low be levelled —

It rained all night. Then the clouds gave way to the soft
light of dawn as he reached the Saryu. He knelt down on the
wet earth and saw that there was void all around. He was, as
ever, all by himself, the eternal man. He felt that he was in
God, was apart from God, was God himself. He stood up,
straightened himself and chanted softly:

O God, thou art fire and sun, and wind and moon.
Thou art the starry sky, Brahma, water, Prajapati;
Thou art woman and man,
Thou art the young girl, that old man art thou, who
*   walks by, leaning on his staff.*
Born with Thy face at every side
Thou art the dark blue fly, the red-eyed parrot, the storm cloud,
*   the ocean.*
Two birds, great friends, sit on a tree. One is nibbling a fruit.
The other watches him helplessly,
Man sits on this same tree, saddened, amazed at his
*   powerlessness.*

But one who looks at the other's contentment and recognises
his greatness puts an end to his own sorrow. The ones who
know the eternal person of the Rig Veda are sitting contentedly. When the light arises, neither day remains nor night,
neither existence nor non-existence. Only Shiva remains. The
eternal light is that of Savitri from which wisdom was born.
Its beauty cannot be perceived nor its splendour portrayed. It
exists within the heart.

Thou that was not born, one approaches Thee, trembling—
O Rudra, protect me. He is the lone bird in the world.
He is like the sun which has gone down in the sea.
One who will know him shall cross the ford of death.
For there is no other way of voyaging—

The water was flowing unceasingly under his sore feet. He
looked up. The Saryu had swollen with the rain. He had finally come back. He could visit the Convent of Golden Mists

and meet Sister Nirmala if she had survived the loneliness of the Whispering Shadows. Then he would return to his ashram. He had seen the world.

He had reached the water's edge when he heard someone shouting in panic, "Maharaj! Maharaj! Be careful, you might slip. The mud is treacherous."

He stepped back. A village girl sat on the lowest step of the ghat filling her pitcher of water.

"I'll be careful," he told her gently. "I would like to go across before it starts raining again."

"You won't get a ferry in this weather."

"No matter! I can swim."

"Swim in this stormy river?"

"There is no harm in trying, my good woman!" He raised his right hand to bless the peasant girl and repeated, "May the gods give you a bountiful harvest and good progeny . . ."

It had become very pleasant. Mango-birds sang in the foliage. A shower of flowers dropped from a bough and fell at Gautam's feet. He picked them up and put them in the river. The waves promptly carried them away. Then he jumped into the water and began swimming against the current.

He had reached midstream. A forceful torrent came rushing and carried him close to the other shore. He struggled hard against the waves but the current was more powerful. In the struggle he caught a glimpse of a crag jutting out over the water. It was the stone fragment of the temple of the adivasis where he had met the "Greek" traveller and spent a night. Gautam quickly caught hold of its edge. He was exhausted and panted heavily. He closed his eyes and clung to the rock. Time was pushing the torrent forward and there was a seemingly infinite expanse of water all around. Holding fast to the bit of stone he felt secure for an instant. A stone which has been in the past will remain in the future as well. But he couldn't hold on to the rock for more than a few seconds with his stumped fingers. The angry waves of the Saryu passed over Gautam Nilambar.

Syed Abul Mansur Kamaluddin arrived at the river bank at full

gallop. The Saryu flowed majestically in front of him. There
was a row of huts on the other shore where some dervishes in
patched smocks moved about, carrying out their ablutions for
the early morning namaz.

10. The Marvels and
Strange Tales of Hindustan

The fair, blue-eyed horseman glanced around loftily and dismounted. The long loose end of his turban indicated that he
was a university graduate but his clothes established that, despite being a scholar, he was not poor. He was a distinguished-
looking young man of about thirty who seemed very pleased
with himself. He led his fleet horse called Toofan to the water's
edge and threw his scimitar on the grass; he feared nobody for
he belonged to the ruling class. Moreover, he was not even a
native Muslim. He was a vilayati, for he had arrived from the
lands called 'Vilayat' in India because they lay beyond the distant Hindukush and the Pamirs. Even the horse he rode was
foreign.

While Toofan quenched his thirst the master took off his
turban and Persian half-coat, and rolled up the sleeves of his
linen shirt called 'kurta' in Turki. He tucked in his baggy Central Asian shalwar, discarded his pointed high-heeled boots
and knelt down on the jetty for his ritual ablutions. Starlight
had faded and temple bells had started ringing out in the distance. The young man washed his face, arms and feet thrice,
performed the massah by anointing his head with water, and
stood up. Then he spread his large handkerchief of Meshed
silk in a corner of the landing stage facing west, put on his
turban and like the dervishes across the river, began saying his
namaz-i-fajar.

Dawn broke. The wood was filled with birdsong. The cavalier finished his fajar prayer and put on his boots again, be-

cause it was bad manners not to be properly dressed even if one was in a lonely forest.

His horse was grazing. As for himself, he would have his breakfast in a wayside Sufi langar or a dak chowki where royal couriers changed horses. Anyway, he must wait here to bid her goodbye. She had said she came to this forest early in the morning to gather flowers for her idol worship. He had rushed down all the way from his inn in order to meet her. He looked anxiously at the Saryu and settled himself under a tree laden with ripe mangoes. His co-religionists called it the Fruit of Paradise. Like the Talmudic Jews, the followers of Islam kept thanking God for His blessings at every step. The world was a table-spread of Allah's immense bounty.

A boat passed by carrying early morning bhajan singers. They were chanting a hymn composed by Kabir Das, a weaver who lived in Banaras and had become popular as a mystic. There was no sign of Champavati yet. Resignedly, he leaned back against the tree and thought of this mystic phenomenon. Most mystics belonged to the working classes, like Mansoor Hallaj who was a carder of cotton-wool. The mystics in India were also humble folk and were busy attracting the masses. That reminded him of the book he was writing about this country. The sun was rising. May as well go through my manuscript while waiting for her. He took out his pen and ink-flask and a morocco-bound notebook. Half of it was still empty. He opened the volume and started touching it up here and there as he read. . .

I

I, Abul Mansur Kamaluddin of Nishapur, begin in the name of the Merciful God this travelogue of mine which I have called *The Marvels and Strange Tales of Hindustan*. In the preface I have mentioned how my honourable mother, that august lady of royal Sassanian lineage married my father, an Arab apothecary settled in Khorasan. Since my lady mother is fiercely proud of being a Persian (a weakness shared by all her compatriots), she wanted me to study in Merv, or Balkh or Herat, or even go to Samarkand and join the observatory of Ulugh Beg. But I am more interested in history and linguistics. A professor of Tunis who was taught by a student of the great Ibn-i-Khaldoon had come to Baghdad, so off I went to Iraq and, in due course, I received my black gown of graduation and my turban of scholastic eminence.

Now it happened that I met a bunch of dark-eyed Spaniards who had come from Granada for the pilgrimage at Mecca, and had wandered on to Baghdad in search of a livelihood. They belonged to a Sufi Brotherhood of Spain which had its own lodge on the west bank of the Tigris. They were staying in the rabat and often met me in an eating-house by the river. Among themselves they spoke in Spanish which had a lot of Arabic words in it. They wrote Spanish in Arabic script. They were full of their past glories and achievements and had very little to show for the present era. One evening they said, "For seven hundred years we were the teachers of benighted Christian Europe whose students flocked to the universities of Cordoba, Malaga and Seville. Or they went to the Muslim universities of Sicily . . ."

"Did all this stop the Christians from warring against you?" I countered. "And how did the theosophy of your Ibn-ul-Arabi help? Did it bring about peace and harmony between Christians and Muslims? The fact is, dear friends, that power politics has no use for mysticism and scholarship and so on." I was a student of Ibn-i-Khaldoon and had also been impressed by Ibn-i-Tammaya's anti-mystical, anti-Shia arguements. There are always brilliant arguments for both sides of a question. And I, as a son of a Shia mother, am also attracted by the rationalism of the Muatazzalites. The pull of contradictory or different ideologies has always bothered me.

The Andalusians looked very unhappy and fell silent. To make matters worse, an oily Levantine (they are always called oily) acquaintance of mine came along and joined us. The Greek owner of the restaurant brought him food. A number of Jews were squatting close by talking of their new warehouse in Anatolia. That gave me an idea. I said, "This being the Age of the Turks why shouldn't I go to Granada and teach Turkish there?" I enquired of the Levantine if he knew of a good ship which could carry me to the shores of the Caliphate of Hispania.

"Hispania!" the man repeated in surprise. "That country is full of political turmoil. Sooner than you expect, the Cross may replace the Crescent in Spain. Forget it." He leaned forward and whispered with a cheery wink, "If you want to know—in the West we Christians are on the ascent, in the East, the Turks—the Saljuks, the Memluks, the Ottomans. In India the Turks have been merrily setting up kingdom after kingdom for the last three hundred years. Go to the Orient, sonny boy. You have lost Spain for good."

I felt very angry but kept quiet. My Andalusian friends would have wept.

"India," the Phoenician continued, "yes, that is the land of tomorrow. Egypt has already become the biggest buyer of Indian cotton. All Europeans, the Genoese, the Venetians want to trade with India. You listen to this ancient mariner—this is the Year of Grace 1476, Anno Domini." Piously he made the sign of the cross and went on, "If you are twenty-four now, you will be rich in no time once you get there. Commerce and industry are flourishing out there like nobody's business!" He waved his pudgy hands which sparkled with rings. . . "Diamonds of Golconda! I have just sailed back from Gujarat. You take the high road to the North."

"I am not a businessman. Most Khorasani traders go to India," I replied evenly. "I only know the theories of Ibn-i-Khaldoon and the philosophy of Rhazes and other such subjects which do not bring in big money."

"No matter. I am told there are colleges in the southern Sultanates as well as in Multan, Lahore, Jaunpur, etc. You could easily get a lecturership. You could even be appointed a qazi in some Indian Sultan's administration."

City lights twinkled over the Tigris. There are eye-witness accounts of the Holocaust when the waters of this very river turned black with the ink of tens of thousands of books that the heathen Mongols threw into it when they destroyed the

libraries of this city. Athens fell once again with the Fall of
Baghdad in the year 1258 of the Christian calendar. We never
recovered after 1258.

Now, by the Grace of Allah, even the ferocious Tartars and
the Khans of all the Russias have embraced Islam. As my mother
says, Iran civilised them. Though in the far east the Mongols
have misguidedly taken to the worship of the colossal stone,
in Central Asia and the land of the Afghans the followers of
the But[1] have long accepted the True Faith.

After the Phoenician left one of the Andalusians said ruefully, "Do you know, Brother Kamal, a qazi of Toledo once
wrote that the Indians, Greeks, Romans, Arabs and Iranians
had cultivated knowledge while the people of northern Europe were uncouth barbarians. A time may soon come when
those barbarians will rule the world."

Talk about the loss of Spain was vastly depressing. The poor,
forlorn Spaniards left for their rabat. I walked back to my hostel thinking seriously about betaking myself to Al-Hind.

I had read my Al-Beruni and my Al-Idrisi but also looked
up Avicanna's encyclopaedia for his physiographic studies, and
Al-Beruni for his mathematical geography. The books by early
travellers were interesting but out of date, and so were the
world maps prepared in colour by early Arab-Persian astrono-
mer-geographers. Arab learning and the sciences have come
to a standstill. Like the Spaniards we have also started harping
on the past. I bought an astrolobe and a portable hourglass
from a shop selling travel gear. Since people are constantly
going on long journeys the souks are full of travel goods. That
is why I was surprised when I first came to India and learnt
that the Hindus do not go abroad for fear of losing caste—
whatever they mean by that. Although I have read that the
ancient Hindus and Buddhists travelled far and wide, carrying
their learning with them wherever they went.

From the souk I proceeded to the governor's secretariat. I
had been told that from the time of Mohammad bin Tughlaq

---

[1]The Buddha. Later the word 'but' (pronounced as in 'put') came to
mean any idol.

all foreigners' documents were thoroughly scrutinised at border check-posts in India. While I was talking to the Armenian official in charge a carrier pigeon flew in and perched smartly on the clerk's desk. "On His Majesty the Memluk Sultan's Service from Cairo," the Armenian Christian grinned. I wished this pigeon network extended up to Nishapur so that I could inform my parents of my imminent arrival.

II

Nishapur is teeming with poets. They are generally very angry with the world at large, and get together in taverns to criticize the government and the clergy which is always hand-in-glove with the authorities. That is one reason why the anti-government Sufis have always been popular with the poets. One evening a versifier cousin took me to his favourite haunt, a tavern run by a seedy hawk-nosed Zoroastrian. Young fire-worshippers called Moghbachas, or sons of the Magi, were serving the drinks. "Are you not fond of the Daughter of Grapes?" a winsome Moghbacha asked me archly. (Unfortunately, like the ancient Greeks, many people in Iran are also that way inclined.) I replied in the negative. A lot of Hafiz was being quoted by the patrons who sat around on the carpets. Opium was being smoked in a nearby den. A lovely Circassian slave-girl was dancing. The Quran and the Prophet say freeing slaves is an act of piety, for they are also entitled to buy their freedom. Some even become kings. . . Male slaves from the Caucasus were trained as soldiers, gained power and established political dynasties. Look at the Slave Kings of India and the Memluks of Egypt!

The ancient Zoroastrian observed the tavern with his hooded eyes. Like the Phoenician he, too, had seen the ebb and flow of Time. The Zoroastrians of Iran have always made me sad. Once they were the masters of this land, now they are reduced to wine-sellers. The rest have fled to India carrying their holy fire with them, as the Jews once wandered from country to country, carrying their Ark. And in recent times our Sufis and scholars escaped to India with their books to avoid persecution by the conquering heathen Mongols. In Persian poetry the Tavern signifies free thinking. Moghbacha is the saqi. The handsome, swashbuckling Turk has become the metaphor for the heartless beloved.

So to Dehli, where the stylish, dashing Turk has been replaced by Syeds and Afghans.

The international caravan-serai of Nishapur was bustling with a bewildering variety of races. Burly, fur-clad Russians, fur-hatted, cocky Turkmans and dagger-happy Georgians. Kowtowing Chinamen trading in jade, silk and chinaware. Camel-trains were leaving in all directions and all manner of beasts of burden were being loaded with merchandise and passenger luggage. It was like Noah's Ark and the Tower of Babel rolled into one. The moneychangers' din was nerve-racking. I booked a saddle-seat on a quaint-looking Central Asian camel. My father said to me, call your brothers and cousins over too, when you get a job in India.

III

The Iranians were great name-givers. 'Roos' was the name they gave to the landmass beyond the Oxus because the Volga was a sparkling river, and *roshan* in Persian meant bright. They called the region where I arrived from across the Khyber Pass after a long and tedious journey, the Punj-ab—Five Waters. The Iranians also referred to the inhabitants of Hind as Hindu and they called the country Hindustan. The word Hindu has come to mean black in Persian. In his famous oft-quoted couplet, Hafiz of Shiraz said, *Ba-khaal-i-hinduash bhakhsham Samarkand-o-Bokhar-ra*—I can give away Samarkand and Bukhara in exchange for the black mole on her cheek!

In these regions the infidels were not black. They were fair and even light-eyed. As we journeyed south the sun became stronger and we saw some Hindus. Many camel-stations later we reached Kaithal, a small, dusty town on the road to Dehli. In Lahore a Punjabi Mussalman joined the train and became

my friend. He was going to Dehli on business. We stayed overnight in the local caravan-serai, and in the evening I went out
for a walk accompanied by my Punjabi friend. We passed by a
tank where a lot of heathen females were bathing, wrapped
only in a length of unstitched cloth. Nobody looked at them.
A grey ruin attracted my attention. It was covered with nettles
and brambles and a strange melancholy pervaded the atmosphere. A cowherd passed by. He told us that the jeevan-lila of
Sultan Razia had come to an abrupt, untimely end at this spot.

Jeevan-lila. The mystic drama of life, my companion explained. I was struck by the phrase, used by an illiterate peasant. Isn't everybody's life a 'mystic drama'? "Even illiterate
Hindus seem to have a philosophical bent of mind because of
their belief in karma—" my India-expert said to me. He also
told me about Razia, this remarkable woman monarch who
styled herself Sultan, instead of Sultana. She was killed in tragic
circumstances as she rested under a tree with her husband, on
her way to Dehli. Murdered right here, where we stood, more
than two hundred years ago. Her cabinet of forty ministers
had disapproved of her enlightened policies. "She was very
popular with us Jats and Khokars," the cowherd said.

"It was an infamous victory for her opponents. They say
robbers murdered her, but in fact it was a politically moti-
vated assassination," my Punjabi friend remarked.

The cowherd continued, "Sultan Razia wanted to abolish
the poll-tax which we Hindus have to pay in lieu of military
service. Wait. . ." He went into his hut nearby and brought
back a silver coin. "I found it here in the fields. Take it as a
memento of Kaal—Time—"

I took the coin from him and thanked him with my Persian
courtesy. He looked surprised for he was obviously not used
to being thanked for anything. I gazed at the coin. Sultan
Razia's name was embossed on one side and the obverse carried the image of a goddess.

"This is the goddess Lakshmi," the cowherd said simply
and walked away with his buffalo.

I marvelled at this woman who knew how to rule over a
vast empire and a people who belonged to a very different

religion and were generally hostile to the Turks. She belonged to the Turko-Iranian tradition of able female monarchs, though the world knows little about them.

I pocketed the coin and returned to the serai. India had already started teaching me a lot of lessons.

Dehli or Dilli, is the seat of Bahlol Lodhi, the first Afghan king of North India. Being the capital city it is full of intrigues, political factions and rumours. Scribes, unemployed writers and poets seeking official patronage gather in taverns and bhatiar-khanas and discuss politics. Frequent attacks by the kings of Jaunpur are a constant source of irritation but life goes on, regardless.

In a crowd of devotees, I ran into an old Sufi acquaintance from Nishapur. He took me to his hostelry situated in the dargah complex. A beautiful kiosk of red sandstone. "Ibn-i-Batuta also stayed here!" the dervish chuckled. Then he told me that he was living in a big Sufi lodge in Jaunpur in the east, and was returning after a few days. It transpires that, like North Africa and the lands of the Turks, India too has an efficient and vibrant Sufi network with hospices, schools and free-kitchens maintained by land grants given to them by kings and noblemen. In the time of Sultan Firoze Tughlaq there were one hundred and forty khanqahs in Dehli alone. There must be many more now.

"Why don't you come along? That place has become the new academic capital of this country and a resplendent centre of high culture. There is a university, countless colleges and thousands of ulema and writers. Everybody is flocking to Jaunpur where even the king is a famed musician. The Sultans of Jaunpur claim descent from the Prophet. Allah knows best. They marry their daughters to Syed dervishes. Why, a promising young Syed that you are, you may even wed a princess of Jaunpur some day if you are lucky! I know the king and shall take you to meet him."

11. The University Town of Jaunpur

The carriage fare from Dehli to Jaunpur is only one tanka[1] bahloli. However, I bought a fine Arab horse and named him Toofan. My Persian dervish, being a poor man, rode his humble mule. Together we set out towards the east.

Jaunpur is called Sultanate-i-Sharq or the Eastern Kingdom. It was founded about seventy-six years ago by Malik Sarwar, also a former slave and a provincial governor, who took advantage of Timur's sack of Dehli and became independent.

"This Sultan business is good business," quoth my dervish, trotting alongside on the highway. "The modus operandi is simple and to the point. Wherever the government at the centre loses its grip over the provinces you gather enough military strength and a few allies, usually Hindu Rajput chieftains, and declare your independence. Then you obtain a firman from the nominal Caliph of Islam who resides in Cairo. According to this decree of the figurehead pontiff you become his deputy caliph and the Friday sermon in the cathedral mosque and all the mosques of your realm is read in your name, instead of the reigning monarch's at Dehli. You mint your own currency and send out your own envoys. You assume the grandiose titles of the ancient Kings of Iran till you are replaced, often violently, by another dynasty.

"Had there been kingship in Islam there would have been the law of primogeniture too, but as it is the sons get an equal share in their father's property. If it is a royal throne it stands to reason that all the brothers must fight to obtain it."

The ascetic took a deep breath. "Great bloodshed continues because of kingship." In Jaunpur, after Malik Sarwar, his adopted son Mubarak succeeded to the throne and after Mubarak, his brother Ibrahim who was a good king. He was a nephew of Khizr Khan, the founder of the fake "Syed" dynasty of Dehli. Ibrahim Shah's army consisted of crack regi-

---

[1] A tanka was the ancestor of the present-day Indian rupee, coined by Bahlol Lodhi.

ments of Rajputs and Iraqis. These Sultans of Jaunpur are addicted to attacking Dehli, which they do with monotonous regularity."

As we approached Jaunpur I was struck by its beautiful landscape. The lofty domes, minarets and golden spires of idol-houses were visible in the distance.

"When Firoze Shah Tughlaq was on his way to fight Sultan Sikander of Bengal, he stopped here and founded this city," my hermit informed me. "Ibrahim Shah had a massive regiment of war-elephants that were looked after by the Corps of Veterinary Surgeons. He was also a great builder. When he invaded Dehli the Syed king sued for peace and married his daughter, Bibi Raji, to Ibrahim Shah's son, Prince Mehmud Khan. Her father died and her no-good brother, Allauddin Alam Shah abdicated in favour of Bahlol Lodhi. When Mehmud Khan became king, Bibi Raji told him, "If you don't attack Dehli I will lead the army myself. That throne belongs to my family. My brother was a fool to quit." So Mehmud laid seige to the capital at the time when Sultan Bahlol was away at Sirhind. Bahlol's aunt, Bibi Masto, was officer-in-charge of the fort. Only a few members of the Lodhi family were present inside. Bibi Masto dressed the women up in men's uniforms and sent them up to the ramparts. From a distance they looked like soldiers. Then she ordered the few men inside the castle to keep shooting arrows from time to time at the enemy so that they would think the fort was well defended.

"Sultan Bahlol returned to Dehli and the ensuing battle ended in some confusion. Bibi Masto was still holding the fort when news was brought to her that the Sharqi soldiers were running away. She asked the messenger whether they were running towards the tent of their king or in the direction of their own camp. "Their own camp, madam," she was told. Whereupon Bibi Masto ordered the battle-drums to be played at once. The sound of the victory drums further unnerved the Sharqi troops. Mahmood Sharqi returned to Jaunpur, but he invaded Dehli unsuccessfully again before he died. Bibi Raji crowned her favourite son Bhikan, Sultan Mohammed Shah. The Prince was probably born after a great deal of prayers and was given away as a token bhiksha to some fakir. But look what he did to his own family when he became king! He had a nasty temper and turned out to be an awful ruler. Bibi Raji was well versed in statecraft. Like the mothers of the Sultans of Turkey she also wielded enormous political power. She doted on her son, Mohammed Shah, and also feared him because of his despotism. When he had his brother, Prince Hasan assassinated, he told her, 'Your remaining sons will also meet the same fate if you don't stop interfering in my affairs, Mama.'

"Bibi Raji was camping in Etawah. She held an emergency meeting of her noblemen. She fired Mohammed Shah and crowned her younger son, Hussain. Now there were two kings of Jaunpur. The brothers fought. Mohammed Shah was an excellent archer. When he wanted to shoot his foes he found his arrows were useless. His mother had had all their iron tips removed earlier. Mohammed Shah was slain.

"Hussain Shah is an excellent musician. He has inherited a vast kingdom, extending upto the borders of Bengal. He should rest content and devote his time to his music but Bibi Khonza, his wife, like his mother Bibi Raji is also a Syed princess. She is a niece of Bibi Raji and daughter of Allauddin Alam Shah. She keeps urging Hussain Shah to capture Dehli."

My head reeled as I heard this rigmarole. Nevertheless, I think I am getting the hang of Indian politics. Everybody wants to capture power at Dehli and for that purpose they make and break alliances, go to war and swap allegiances all the time.

We entered the city gate. I was struck dumb by the sheer magnificence and grandeur of Jaunpur's Egyptian-style buildings. And I have realised that the lives of the kings and queens who live inside these noble halls are full of high drama, tragedy and truimph. The overriding passion is the acquisition of power and glory, however transient it may turn out to be. I am staying in one of the numerous inns constructed by Good King Ibrahim. Each of these serais has a garden, a well, a mosque and a free-kitchen. There is a separate staff and free kitchen for Hindu travellers.

His Majesty is a warrior-king, but he is also popularly known as Sultan Hussain Nayak (performing artiste) and has composed a number of melodies. (Ragas and raginis, somewhat akin to our maqamat). He calls his melodies 'khayals', which means thought in Arabic. Jaunpur and Gwalior are two big centres of classical music today and there is much traffic of musicians between the two cities. Unlike Bahlol Lodhi of Dehli, Sultan Hussain is as proud as a peacock. He is fond of wine and women. Because of his mastery of Hindustani classical music and his creative genius, he is called the Supreme Nayak of the time. He must be the only monarch in the world who also carries the title of a performing artiste. His durbar contains a galaxy of famous musicians who live in an interesting locality called Dharitola—Dhari being the name of their caste. Everybody in India belongs to a caste, and the Dhari caste includes Hindus and Muslims.

One afternoon my Persian mentor took me to Jannat Mahal overlooking the Flower Tank. After going through a lot of protocol we were ushered into the royal presence. His Majesty sat on a masnad tuning a tamboura (our tembour). One cannot imagine how this gentle musician could have forcibly subjugated Orissa and Gwalior and several districts of the Lodhi Sultanate. Like his grandfather, Ibrahim Sharqi he, too, has become a formidable monarch. Only two years ago, I was told, he invaded Dehli with his huge army and war-elephants. Bahlol Lodhi humbly asked to be allowed to remain in Delhi as a Sharqi governor. Hussain Shah haughtily told him to get lost, so the Afghans fought back with all their might. He has broken many a pledge with the Lodhis in his relentless pursuit of imperial power.

I had never met a king before. He looked regal and arrogant, although he seemed pleased when he saw my certificates of excellence in Arabic, Persian, Turki and classical Greek. A hajib or aide-de-camp came forward and His Majesty said something to him in the local Hindvi language. Then he turned towards me and said, "Now you must learn another language, young man—Sanskrit. I have important work for you to do." I was speechless and couldn't quite believe my ears.

In short, I was appointed supervisor of calligraphists and copyists of the scriptorium and also attached to the Bureau of

Translations. I was given the customary robe of honour and silver inkstand and pen confirming my appointment, and I was ordered to proceed to the Fort Secretariat and get my papers. All of which was too good to be true. Like Feroze Shah Tughlaq who had had a lot of Sanskrit works rendered into Persian, Hussain Shah is also an antiquarian.

Therefore today I, Kamaluddin, am happy to record for the benefit of posterity, that I am living in the jurisdiction of Sultan Hussain Shah Sharqi who holds sway over Night and Day, who builds cities on the Foundation of Justice. The Ring of his Governance is like the Ring of Solomon. He is gorgeous like Darius and a speck of dust like myself has been illumined by the Rays of the Sun called the Mighty Monarch of the Sultanate of Sharq. Allah be praised.

Bazaar rates as of today: wheat, one maund for one tanka; 20 sers of pure ghee: one tanka. Rice, three maunds: one tanka. If you earn two tankas a month you can live well. The populace is happy and has enough time to indulge its one great passion—religion. Right now their Bhakti and Sufi cults are flourishing. The city and the countryside are teeming with all manner of picturesque hermits who remind me of the wandering dervishes of the land I come from. The qalandars of the Madari order hobnob with the yogis.

This elegant city of Jaunpur is also called Shiraz-i-Hind. It has a very large number of colleges and schools and more than a thousand eminent theologians who arrive at the Cathedral Mosque on Fridays, riding grandly in their palanquins. These Ulema-i-Zahir, Scholars of Exterior Knowledge, are quite conceited while the Scholars of Interior Knowledge, Ulema-i-Batin, the Sufis, are mostly humble folk and come to the mosque on foot. I have rented a house in the locality of these schoolmen. Most of these colossal buildings were built by Ibrahim Shah and his daughter-in-law, Bibi Raji.

In the course of my Sanskrit studies I came across a poem by Vidyapati Thakur. He has referred to the Muslims of Jaunpur as Turks and has said that they salaam one another, call each other Abay, drink a lot and read books. This is how he has described Ibrahim Shah's capital. "In his durbar, the poor petition the generous king and get what they are destined to get. In his palace there is a water fount for the public, hamams, much decoration and tall mirrors. And twenty-seven horses of the sun chariot go around a spire stamping their hooves. What there is inside the palace, I do not know."

Nor do I, Kamaluddin. But I am lucky to have been right inside the zenana gardens. It happened thus—all very honourable and above-board. The Rose Tank is an artificial lake built in the shape of a huge redstone flower. It is a marvel of underground hydel engineering, with automatic fountains and friezes which seem to float on the water. There are separate steps for men and women where they bathe. The tank is surrounded by royal residences called Roshan Mahal and Jannat Mahal which extend upto Bibi Raji's Red Gate Palace. The Queen Mother is not only an astute politician, she is a learned woman and has had a college and grand mosque built specially for women. The redstone complex is connected with the Red Gate Mahalsara through an underground passage so that the ladies can go back and forth freely.

I fell in love. One afternoon I was busy with my Sanskrit grammar in the library when a Georgian slave-girl stepped in smartly. She handed me a little note. It was from Ruqqaiya Bano Begum, a kinswoman of the Sultan, who lived in Roshan Mahal and went to the women's college inside the Red Gate every morning. I had glimpsed her once on the grand staircase of Roshan Mahal as she hurried down towards the subway. The note said she wanted a copy of Diwan-i-Rudaki. I sent it to her with the message that I was always at her service, her humble servant.

In her college the faculty consists of pious spinsters of royal blood who are unmarried because men of equal status or lineage could not be found. There are also old and learned war-widows of whom there is no dearth. Young widows remarry in no time. The teachers are called Mullani-ji, or Ato-ji. A few doddering old maulanas from the local colleges come there off and on to deliver their lectures, and the students are mostly daughters of noblemen. The next time when my lady scholar sent me a note requiring a certain book, I wrote back. "You know, fair lady, Laila and Majnun were classmates as children. It's a pity that in our Shariat a girl studies with boys in a mosque-school only up to the age of nine. If you and I had attended the same school. . .," etc., etc. So, we started corresponding.

Then we met. The rendezvous was arranged by the clever Georgian, Maria. We met in the evening in a quiet, secluded corner of the Roshan Mahal back garden. The slave-girl stood behind a tree to warn Bano if anybody was coming. Bano was beautiful and intelligent. She sat demurely at a distance, on the edge of a fountain.

Conversation was academic and intellectual. I told her about the lady scholars of Seville and Cordoba, she told me about her college syllabus. She was dressed in an azure gown of soft Banaras silk. I asked her what the silk was called.

"Gulbadan," she replied. "Queen Mother, Bibi Raji, had a very able and highly educated lady-in-waiting called Gulbadan Begum. She gave her name to this silk."

Suddenly the huge lamp in the gate-house lit up and I had to leave in a hurry. This lamp is another marvel of the city of Jaunpur. It contains certain ingredients which make it light up automatically at sunset, and it is because of this lamp that the royal ladies' residence is known as Roshan Mahal or Palace of Light.

I work in the scriptorium located in the Palace of Forty Pillars, inside the Fort. This area houses administrative offices and is adjacent to the army headquarters and barracks. The Palace of Forty Pillars was also built by Ibrahim Shah, and may have been the mansion described by Vidyapati in his poem. Hussain Shah lives in Jannat Mahal, overlooking the Rose Lake.

Later, during our clandestine meetings, Bano often talked about her remarkable family. They had certainly produced two outstanding individuals—Ibrahim Shah and his grandson, Hussain Shah.

"The friendships and alliances among kings are mercurial," said Bano. "When the going was good Bahlol Lodhi himself arranged the marriage of Dehli's last Syed King Allauddin Shah's daughter, Bibi Khonza, with our Hussain Shah. Now that she has become Jaunpur's Malika Jehan, Empress of the World, she has clean forgotten the good turn the large-hearted Pathan did her. She keeps goading her husband to topple her benefactor, Sultan Bahlol, so my cousin Hussain Shah spends half his time waging wars against Dehli, instead of composing his music," she concluded unhappily.

"What you are saying can be construed as treason against the Queen. This Georgian girl could report you, she comes from the world of Byzantine intrigue," I reminded her.

"Maria has become sufficiently Indianised to know whose salt she eats. She is my personal maid."

Bano lived within the Roshan Mahal complex. Her father was a close relative of the King and so her primary loyalty was to Hussain Shah, not his wife. Having spent some time in India I realised that blood ties, caste and regional affinities, and "salt" were what counted most in personal and collective relationships. But blood ties became meaningless in the quest for power.

"What I am saying is common knowledge. Everybody in this kingdom knows that His Majesty is madly in love with his beautiful Malika Khonza and does what she says."

12. Hussain Shah Nayak

We spent many a languid summer afternoon in the bower while the mango-birds cooed and everybody slept in the Palace. Sometimes one could hear the haunting notes of a noontime rhapsody wafting out of the King's chambers, whenever His Majesty was in residence in Roshan Mahal. In fact this music became a kind of time-keeper for us. As long as the King was doing his riaz we sat in our secluded nook in the arbour; when the singing stopped, Bano slipped away. Thus I came to recognise many a raga composed by this extraordinary man.

Once I wrote a Persian ghazal for Bano, then a qasida in

Arabic in the style of Arabic-Andalusian odes written five hundred years ago. I told her about the Age of Romance and Chivalry in Muslim Spain. Bano was fascinated. It is amazing that Indian Muslims know nothing about the west—they live in an Enchanted Forest of their own. India's Eternal Primeval Jungle has claimed them. I even tried to write a few dohas in Hindvi, the polyglot language which consists of Prakrit, Persian, Turki and Arabic words spoken by common people in the Indo-Gangetic plain. Sufis and bhaktas also use this language to preach their cult of love and free themselves from the stranglehold of the clergy. But the mullahs and pandits are ganging up against them. At present their target is a mystic called Kabir Das, a poor weaver of Kashi. The Muslims call him Mian Kabir.

Once Bano said rather pointedly, "We are also Syeds, like you. It's a canard spread by our enemies that our grandfather, Ibrahim Shah, was a water-carrier in the service of Khwaja Jehan Malik Sarwar who founded this Sharqi kingdom, and that he was an African. Do we look like Abyssinians to you?"

I knew what Bano was driving at. I took the hint, smiled to myself and visualised my glorious future as a son-in-law of the mighty House of the Sharqis. I'll even call my parents and the entire family from Nishapur. I have now spent nearly four years in royal service and am counted among the junior courtiers. Friends are urging me to take a wife.

One evening Bano said to me, "Look, I don't want to end up like those erudite spinster Mullani-jis of the Madrassa-i-Niswan. Please hurry up and send your proposal to my father."

On the way home I met my old friend and benefactor, the Persian hermit. He lived in his lodge in the forest and rarely came to town. He was accompanied by a good-looking young fellow who carried a travel kit and a staff. The Persian introduced us to each other. He belonged to Mithila, Bihar, and right now he was coming from Patan, Gujarat. "You are a wandering scholar sufi!" I exclaimed.

"And you a court historian!" he retorted, rather sarcastically. I was taken aback by his hostile tone.

"This Brother here belongs to the Order of the Chishtis," the Persian explained to me, peaceably.

"Well, are you one of those chroniclers who write that their Sultan killed so many crores of people in such and such expedition? At that rate this country should have been depopulated by now!" the young man remarked as we picked our way through jostling crowds in the main bazaar. We strolled down to a popular eating house run by an excellent cook-bhatiari called Lado. It was full, so we had to sit near the entrance. A girl came to take the order. The young man from Bihar looked up at her approvingly. She rattled off the evening's menu. I ordered chicken pulao, qorma and naan, the girl shouted the order back to her mother. I turned to the guest. "Yes, I am writing a chronicle, but not officially. It is my personal diary."

He was still thinking of the bhatiari's luscious daughter. "Our Vidyapati Thakur," he began, blinking his long eyelashes, "must have seen females like her, eh? In his ode to your Sultan Ibrahim Shah he waxes eloquent about the lotus-eyed women of Jaunpur—where the golden spires of the temples sparkle and shine and the Sultan sits in his balcony and is pleased to see the happy multitudes down below. His face is radiant like the full moon."

"I have read that poem," I replied airily. I am afraid I was not above showing off my newly and diligently acquired knowledge of Indian affairs. "When Malik Arsalan invaded Mithila, Raja Kirti Singh sought his overlord Sultan Ibrahim's help, and the poet describes the soldiers of the enormous Sharqi army as so many lotuses spread over a lake. That's an odd kind of simile—comparing a horde of military men to water-lilies!"

A literary argument followed. In between, the Persian dervish aired his anti-monarchist views.

"Hafiz has said the mysteries of statecraft are known only to the Chosroes of this world. Hafiz! You are a mere beggar sitting in a corner. Don't make a noise!" I reminded him.

"That's why we chose to live in the forest. We follow the tradition of Abuzar Ghafari. He had been a Companion of the Lord Prophet. He was so disgusted that he left Medina when the rulers started behaving like Sassanian kings. You know, I told Sultan Hussain to be less warlike. He ignored my advice so I have stopped going to the Palace."

The inn-keeper's wife continued to sit behind the platform of her massive oven, counting her tankas and jaitals, quarrelling with the customers. It was a normal, peaceful evening. The streets outside heaved with what Vidyapati had described as "an ocean of human beings which had entered the resplendent bazaars of Jaunpur". The Persian addressed me again. "Hey, Brother Kamal, listen. The bazaars are full of rumours that the Supreme Nayak is about to take on the Dehli Afghans once again. Is this so ?"

"As a matter of fact, I have heard nothing. I am busy with my books." I didn't add that I was too engrossed in my platonic affair with Bano to notice anything else. The bhatiara lad brought an aftaba and chilamchi for us to wash our hands in. Another placed rakabis and Chinese cups in front of us on a low table. Then he brought a huge round tray full of subtly fragrant pulao. "Ah," the Iranian dervish said, attacking a roast chicken, "last time when Hussain Shah reached the banks of the Jamuna—it was his third and the seventh Sharqi campaign against Delhi—poor Bahlol Shah went hotfoot to the tomb of Bakhtiar Kaki in Mehrauli. He stood beside the grave of the saint and prayed all night. At daybreak an unknown man came along and gave him a stick. A great many sheep have arrived at the gate of Delhi, drive them away, quoth he.

"And Bahlol was victorious. And he is such a kindly, nice man," the dervish sighed.

We ate in silence. The newcomer Sufi was hesitantly nibbling at a kofta.

"What's the matter?" I asked, peeved, "Why don't you eat?"

"See, brother," he replied a trifle sheepishly, "If you don't mind, I belong to the Order of Mukloom Jehanian Jehann Gasht. . ."

"So?"

"He has written in his *Malfoozat* that once, when he was staying in a hospice in Dehli, one of Sultan Feroze Tughlaq's ministers sent him dinner. He ate it, and he records that his prayers didn't reach On High that night because he had eaten food sent by a king's man."

"So?"

"You are a Royalist, too," he replied.

"Yeah, but I am also a Syed and so is the King."

That did it. The young fellow began to eat meekly. I think these Sufis are crazy.

It was a Wednesday evening. When I reached my lodgings I resolved to buy the customary perfumed red notepaper upon which wedding proposals are written. I'll buy it from the neighbourhood stationery place and compose an elegant epistle. According to custom I will address this letter to Bano's father, to the effect that since my pater is not in India I myself take the liberty of requesting you to accept me as your son-in-law and so honour me. This is the set language of proposals. The following morning I went to the library, sat down at my desk and began thinking of really flowery phrases for the proposal which I was going to send to Bano's pater on Friday. Right then a footman came in.

"His Majesty wishes to see you. At once."

The King was sitting in his Music Room, tuning his tamboura. I stepped in and salaamed in the usual courtly manner. He nodded and smiled. That put me at ease, but I was still nervous.

"Have you made any progress in your study of the Sanskrit language?" His Majesty asked.

"A little, Sire," I replied.

"I have just been informed that some pandits in Ayodhya are in possession of a very ancient treatise on classical music. Go there at once and find out all about those manuscripts. Seek the pandits' help in deciphering the texts. Off you go."

I bowed again and beat a hasty retreat.

13. "Champavati": A Sufi Allegory

Al-Hind is rife with myths, legends, folklore and old wives' tales. In Ayodhya the other day, I came across an inordinately long grave situated under a leafy tree. A local Muslim told me in his Oudhi dialect, and in a matter-of-fact tone, that it was the last resting place of Prophet Sheth, son of Prophet Nooh. How on earth did Sheth come to be buried in Ayodhya?

"Well," said the local Muslim, "There was this Big Flood— say yes."

"Yes. But it happened in Iraq, etc.,— those areas. . ."

"Only in Iraq? The whole world drowned in it— say yes."

"Yes."

"And Noah's Ark stopped at Mount Judi, didn't it? Well that was, in fact, Ayodhya."

"But where is the mountain here?" I argued.

"There must have been one all those thousands of years ago. Physical features of a place can change. Why, one stream has changed its course near my village. And the Hindus say they had a flood in the time of Manu. So Manu may have been Noah, for all you know."

I gave up, though I also often wonder about the nine-yard-long grave in Jeddah, supposedly of Mother Eve who gave the name Jeddah or Ancestress to that port town.

Well. Allah knows best.

I went on to meet a wise Brahmin. I live in a well-appointed Ibrahim Shahi serai, and in the mornings I go to this pandit's mango grove. He discusses Sanskrit texts with me, sitting at a safe distance for fear of pollution. I ought to find it very insulting but the Lord Prophet has enjoined upon every Muslim man and woman to go even to China to seek knowledge. India is en route, and in China the Buddhists may behave even more strangely. As Amir Khusro said—every country hath its own customs.

Now this pandit has a younger sister called Champavati. She is very attractive and intelligent and naturally I have fallen quietly in love with her. I can converse well with her in Oudhi which I have picked up with ease. I get a chance to talk to her because she is also her brother's student.

Champavati is utterly enchanting, so different from Bano. No regal airs, no jewellery, no make-up, no silks and brocades. She wraps herself in an unstitched piece of cotton cloth and goes about barefoot. When I want a glass of water she brings it in a clay cup and places it on the ground, then rushes back to her cow-dung plastered hut. I have not seen Rajput princesses, they must be different. But they live in purda.

And let's admit, a fellow wants variety. I'm afraid I have almost forgotten princess Bano. These infidel women have a charm of their own. They are faithful, shy, docile. They worship their husbands as demi-gods and touch their feet in obeisance every morning. They put the man on a pedestal and sing songs in his praise. That's how it ought to be. We developed this Cult of the Lady in Hispania and introduced the concept of romance and chivalry into the rest of Europe—gallant knights fighting in honour of their ladies and young poets singing to lutes on moonlit nights while the lady sat on a trellised balcony. Here the roles are reversed—man is the beloved, the woman pines for him and is forever waiting for him. That's very flattering indeed. . .

I am foolishly waiting for her. She may not turn up at all. It wouldn't be a bad idea to save her soul and show her the path of the True Faith but—

Kamal closed his book and looked at the sky. It was high noon, and the wind had become warm. He started writing again.— I am not a missionary. I am here on His Majesty's Service, and in a hurry. . . The other day I asked her obliquely if she would like to live in a town house by the Rose Lake in Jaunpur. She asked me as cryptically, "What would I do there—play chess and teach the parrots and mynas how to say Good Morning?"

Suddenly he heard a rustling in the tall grass and looked up. There she stood before him, like a tree sprite, laughing like the wind.

"You still around? I thought you had left for Behraich."

"I have waited for you all day to say goodbye—"

"Why? Won't you come back?"

"His Majesty is too busy waging his wars. I may have to go to the Front with my report."

"You Turks have a hard time of it, always fighting."

"I am not a Turk."

"All Muslims are Turks," she said in a tone of finality.

Kamal again recalled *Kirtilata* in which Vidyapati had described the Muslims of Jaunpur: "The Turks salaam one another, drink wine, address each other as Abay, and read the kitab—"

Champa noticed Kamal's sword lying on the grass.

"Throw it away in the river and relax, soldier," she said amiably.

He was annoyed. "I am not a soldier, you know that. What was I doing at your brother's place? Brandishing my dagger?"

"Then why do you carry this fearful thing?"

"A scimitar is the ornament of a man. Have you never seen a Rajput warrior?"

"I'm not too happy with Rajput warriors either."

"Who are you happy with, then?"

"Sant Kabir—"

"Who—?"

"Sant Kabir of Kashi—"

"I know about him. He spent some time with the eminent Sufis of Jhoosi and Jaunpur. And I have heard you sing Kabir songs with the bhaktas. Look, that's no way for a young girl to spend her time, singing hymns with all those morons wearing orange skull caps. They are a peculiar people—all these chaps, qalandars, sanyasis, the lot."

Champa flushed red, "Don't ever make fun of holy men. Some day they may rescue you from your delusions. Right now you are riding the high horse, captain—oh, sorry, scholar!"

"You've become quite a sadhavi, too!" he responded sarcastically.

"No, I'll get married, that is if Mars is not too strong in my house."

"What the hell is that? How would Mars come to your house? Do you know when you tie the knot with a man of your own society, and if he dies, they will either shave your head and you'll be shunned like a pariah the rest of your miserable life, or they'll push you alive onto his funeral pyre. Deck you up as a bride, put you on horseback and take you in a procession to the cremation ground with much beating of the drums. First they'll burn you alive, then they'll worship you as goddess Sati."

"If such is my fate, so it shall be."

"Listen, as a Muattazalite I must explain to you. . ."

"Motijala —what?"

"Never mind. Look, I am a believer in free will; Ibn-i-Rushd has said. . ."

"Who?"

"Ibn-i-Rushd of Andalusia—he says except for revealed religion everything should be examined scientifically."

"Revelations are a mystical experience too!"

Kamal looked at her in amazement. "You are too clever!"

"No. I merely listen carefully when my brother and his erudite friends have their discussions. Reason has nothing to do with mystical experience."

"Have you ever had any?"

"The Cult of Radha and Krishna is a Mystery." She picked up some flowers. "And, anyway, everything is in the hands of Destiny."

"No, you can make your choice here and now. If you agree to marry me you'll get such an interesting fellow in this life and as a Muslim, you will be safe in the Hereafter."

"If I was married to you in my previous janams, I'll marry you now, too."

"This is nonsense. There is only one birth and one death. The rest is speculation."

"If my karma and sanskaras are such, I'll become a Muslim and be your spouse."

She gathered some more flowers. He was rattled.

"Sanskaras or no sanskaras— will you wait for me?"

He thought he saw her nod but he was not very sure because a shower of magnolia blossoms fell between them like a floral curtain. He took it as a good omen and thought it best to leave instead of tempting fate by arguing with her some more. He packed his saddle-bag and asked, "Why were you so late in coming? You must go too, before the villagers come this way."

Then he recalled that somebody had told him, if you throw a coin in the translucent waters of the Saryu you can see it lying on the river bed. Promptly he took out a Hussain Shahi silver tanka, flung it in the river, and saw it sparkle on the soft blue-grey mud several feet below. He grinned like a schoolboy and turned towards Champa.

She stood there almost motionless, under the flowering magnolia tree, looking sad and pensive. The traditional picture of the woman in Indian rain-songs: the man is going away on a distant journey leaving her forlorn and unhappy. The Raga Malhar sung by Hussain Shah Nayak visualised such mournful, doe-eyed damsels. . .

"I'll come back soon, Insha Allah, and I leave you in the safe-keeping of Almighty God," he shouted against the wind and galloped away without looking back.

Life had certainly become very complicated.

14. The Cavalcade

A full moon sailed over the extensive ruins. All was eerily quiet. Moonbeams lit up the faint decorative designs on the floor of a roofless house. A trident, a lotus, a wheel, a 'pillar of fire'. . . what did those remote people mean by such symbols, Kamal wondered, yawning, and lay himself down upon an elephant-head made of stone.

A ghostly sound rose out of the silence—as though chariots were passing through the deserted lane outside. Strange men who wore gold earrings stood on ancient vehicles. The chariots stopped right in front of him and the men peered down at Kamal. Their teeth shone like phosphorus in the dark. The fish-eyed stone woman came alive and began to sing in an unknown tongue.

A phantom appeared in the broken doorway and announced hoarsely, "The Moon among Men, Emperor of Aryavart."

How could he be here? Kamal rubbed his eyes. This infidel king had left the world three hundred years before the birth of Prophet Isa. He had become a Jain ascetic and starved himself to death. But here he was, standing among the fallen pediments, grinning. Now another man craned his neck above the shoulders of Chandragupta and jumped out. He addressed Kamal gently: "My name is Ashok Priya Darshan. Emperor. I ruled over all of Bharatvarsh once. When I died I owned only this one-and-a-half amla." He opened his fist and threw bits of an Indian olive in front of Kamal. Then the invasion of the spirits began in full force. . .

They stepped out of the chariots, hung from the rafters, climbed the pillars and did somersaults in the dry tank of the forecourt. Twittering like birds, they encircled Kamal and danced around him, chirping—

'I am Bharat Muni, *Canons of Dance and Drama* fame.'

'Vishnu Sharma. In case you need any advice on polity.'

'Raja Bhoj.'

'I am merely Gangwa, the oil-presser.'

'Clouds are thundering in the dark skies. Kalidasa.'

'Bhavabhuti. . .'

'Bhartrihari! As I said, All the world is a stage and we the actors. You are an actor, I am an actor, ha— ha—"

Playwright Shudrak quietly drove past in a clay cart. A lot of pretty women trooped in, jingling their anklets. They looked like queens.

'Princess Rajeshwari. . . I outwitted the scholars of China!'

'Prabhavati!'

'Ratnavali!' This woman was heavily made up and coquettish.

Playwright-king Harsha, who had been sitting meekly in a corner with his pen behind his ears, raised his eyes when he heard the voice of his celebrated heroine. He took the cue and declaimed: 'We were called Sri Prithvi Vallabh. . . beloveds of the godesses of Wealth and Earth. . .'

The fish-eyed stone-woman remained nameless and continued to sing.

All of a sudden, swords clanked and the courtyard lit up with their terrible lustre. There was a hailstorm of chopped-off heads.

"We are the Chandela Rajputs!" they were shouting. "We are the Baghelas. We are the Rathors. We fought among ourselves and the Huns turned up— and the Turks!" They began to hop around on one leg each. "Like we did, you will go too . . . ." Most of them were headless, and they began singing the Ballad of Alha-Udal at the top of their voices.

Kamal thought his eardrums would burst. Trembling, he opened his eyes. Dawn had broken on the horizon and outside, some peasants were going towards their fields merrily singing the Ballad of Alha-Udal. Kamal looked around quickly, greatly confused. He could not remember where he was. Then he tried to gather his violently disturbed thoughts. This was Behraich. He had been sleeping fitfully in the desolation of Shravasti. He had had a dream, populated by all the shadowy figures he had been reading and hearing about. The Sufis have a lot to say about such dream-phenomena.

He rubbed his eyes again and began to ponder. Allah, Allah—he was all alone in a ghost-town and surrounded by ancient apparitions. Reason fails on such occasions.

What was it—a visionary dream? Or simply a nightmare?

Sheikh Mohyeddin Ibn-ul-Arabi. . . Yes, that clever Spaniard, may come to my rescue. That illustrious Sufi philosopher dwelt at length on creative imagination. He said whoever did not have an active imagination could not reach the Heart of the Matter. . .

Is my fascination for Champavati making me mystically inclined? Do I need an invisible mentor, the "Silent Speaker" of Ibn-ul-Arabi? Do I need a guide? A murshid? A living sheikh? Much perplexed he thought of the Prayer of Protection. After all these years he remembered the incantation his Shia mother had taught him when he was a child. After he had tied his turban he raised his right forefinger, waved his right hand seven times around his head and recited: "The Lord Prophet is before me, Fatima is above my head. Ali is to my right. The

Imams and the Companions are all around me." Then he repeated the invocation for Ali's aid: "Call Ali, the Manifester
of Wonders. Just call him for help and see. . ."

Fortified thus and feeling reassured, he came out of the
roofless hall. His faithful black horse stood outside tied to a
pillar, neighing. Perhaps he was saying, let's get out of here,
master, as fast as we can! He patted the animal and gave him
some grass for breakfast. Then thoughtfully, he walked down
to a pond for his ritual ablutions and early-morning prayer.

The sun came up. While Kamal was crossing the dhak forest
which surrounded the nearby stupas he saw a Shaivite sadhu
hovering over an old grave. The ascetic went around the grave
once and looked up. He had red eyes and matted locks. His
fearsome face displayed marks of white ash. He wore a red tiger-skin and seemed to have emerged from last night's nightmare. 'I need not be afraid of this Tantric.' Kamal quickly told
himself, 'but what on earth is he doing over here. . . it's as
though he were whispering to someone.'

"Maulana," the yogi who had noticed Kamal's pedagogue's
turban, spoke sternly, "Go back to town at once. You have bad
news waiting for you. Do not tarry."

Kamal was incensed. This fellow is trying his sorcery on
me. He knew one should never annoy powerful Tantrics so he
asked politely, "Baba, what are you doing over here, near this
grave?" (The Turko-Persian word Baba, father, was generally
used for Hindu holy men.)

"Don't ask questions."

"No, you must tell me. Are you in touch with the departed?"

"We have our own relationships and our own channels of
communication. Don't poke your nose in our affairs. Go away."

Kamal knew about the belief that Sufi saints have their own
unseen, parallel spiritual administration of the world, their
own ranks and grades, and so on. They have high-ranking
women saints too who are part of the occult government, and
the Khwaja of Ajmer is the Supreme Monarch, Sultan-ul-Hind.
Was this yogi in touch with them, too?

"So you were conversing with this gentleman who was buried here four hundred years ago? Do you know who he was?"

Kamal argued. The yogi glared at him, looking very cross. Kamal went on recklessly, his rationalist mind had taken over once again. "He was one of the soldiers of Salaar Masud's volunteer army—some adventurous youth from Afghanistan or Georgia or Azerbaijan. There had been a skirmish over here, too, against Sohal Dev. He must have fallen in battle and been buried here. I am a historian, so I know."

The yogi raised his hand solemnly. "You are an ignorant and arrogant young fool. Go away! There is a messenger awaiting you with bad news," he repeated and turned his back. Kamal's bravado vanished. He was scared once again.

"Come along, Sonny, off we go. We are not wanted here," he told his stallion and rode off quickly.

On the way to town the wind had become very pleasant. A drop of rain fell on his face. He tried to forget the encounter with the sadhu and glanced at the verdant, refreshing landscape. The monsoons had arrived. Champa must be sitting on a swing in her orchard, singing rain-songs.

The rainy season! Oh, the spell that the different seasons cast on one in this country! Each month had its own music and colours and scents. Yellow Vaisakh, when the mustard bloomed. Sizzling Jeth and Asarh, when wood-apples fell off langorous trees. Rain-filled Sawan and Bhadon. Kowar and Katak when autumn moonlight pours a cool paleness on his and dale. This was not his native land but he couldn't escape the enchantment of the seasons.

Kamal wondered again about the uncanny yogi. How was it that it was mostly Shaivite ascetics who found a certain affinity with the mystics of Islam? Was it because of their monotheism? Oh, well, he thought, I have had enough of the strange tales of Hindustan. Thank God, tomorrow I go back to the cosy retreat of the Royal Library in Jaunpur.

"Alas, alas, Maulana Kamal, we have lost the war!" Cavalier Udai Singh Rathore shouted in agitation from the balcony of the serai's gatehouse when Kamal entered the quadrangle. He was thunderstruck. This was the bad news the yogi had foretold in the morning. Cold sweat appeared upon his brow. Rathore rushed downstairs. Kamal dismounted. The courtyard was crowded, horses neighed, some women waited, cursing aloud. Lightning flashed in the sky.

"Our Sultan has Saturn in his House, I always said so. Nobody listened to me," someone complained sorrowfully. The crowd made way for the two officials as they entered the serai's long dalaan.

"How. . . how?" Kamal asked feebly.

"Like this," the Thakur took out his dagger. The scholar was taken aback. Rathore sat down upon a cot and drew a map of the battlefield on the mud floor, with the point of his weapon.

"Look," he said severely. "We are here. . . at Rapri. Highly strategic place, this. The old fox Bahlol attacks us from here. . . we retreat. And the Mother is very angry. . ."

"Whose mother? Bibi Raji?" Kamal asked foolishly.

"No, stupid, Bibi Raji must be turning in her grave. Mother Jamuna. She was furious and in flood. As we tried to cross the river, most of our army was swept away—in one go. All drowned.

"So His Majesty marched towards Gwalior to get reinforcements from his vassals. On the way, bandits got us. Famous dacoits of Chambal valley. They looted what was left of the Sharqi army. Provisions, money, everything. The Gwalior Maharaj supplied troops, so we fought another battle at Kalpi. Lost again. Rewa Maharaj escorted the Sultan up to Jaunpur and there the Afghans swooped down and laid siege to Roshan Mahal."

Kamal gasped as the Rathore knight rattled off the list of disasters.

"Queen Khonza and the ladies. . ."

"What happened to them?"

"Captured. Taken to Dehli." Kamal turned pale. Rathore was an old friend and knew about Kamal's romance with Ruqqaiya Bano Begum. He paused for a few moments, ostensibly studying his map with great concentration. He was trying to find the appropriate words to console the royal bookworm. As a man of action he could advise this dreamy young man to fight his way to Dehli and rescue the damsel in distress, but he knew poor Kamal was no daredevil. So he simply asked, "Shall I go and get her back for you?" He placed his hand on the hilt of his sword, twirled his moustache and stood up.

"No, no!" Kamal groaned. "How can you? It is not possible."

"All right." He sat down again. "But you must not worry. The Pathans are like us Rajputs—they have a deep sense of honour. And they treat women with respect, like we do. Queen Khonza accompanied His Majesty to the front in the last war and was taken prisoner. King Bahlol chivalrously sent her back. Besides, you know well how the Pathans venerate you Syeds. They do not even marry Syed women because that would mean disrespect to the House of the Prophet. Our Royal Family is supposed to be Syed too, so Princess Bano is safe. They will probably marry her off to some poor Syed maulvi and ask her to keep praying for them for the rest of her life. . ."

The crowd had moved in and was listening intently to the Rajput captain's gruff, crisp account of the hostilities. The sharp-tongued bhatiari shooed the audience away and brought hot lunch for Kamal. He had lost his appetite. She urged him to eat.

"Come on, Maulana Saheb, it's not the end of the world. Floods, robbers, the capture of his Queen—no calamity can discourage our King. He is made of steel. And listen, Dilli's throne belongs to his sasural, he is its rightful claimant. The son of a king, married to the daughter of a king. Who is this upstart horse-dealer, Billoo Khan, whose wife is the daughter of a common goldsmith? He must have borrowed money from her father for his stable-business before he eloped with her."

The crowd roared with laughter. The bhatiari was referring to Bahlol Lodhi's beautiful queen, Hemavati, who was the mother of handsome Prince Sikander. The charismatic Hussain Shah was the dearly beloved king of his subjects, and they were staunch royalists.

The Rajput scratched out a few dots from his map and shook his head sadly. "So we have retreated to the north. His Majesty

is camping right here, near Behraich. He has sent me to fetch
you. He wants to know if you have been able to decipher that
ancient treatise on music. . ."

The vanquished Sharqi army was encamped on the banks of
the overflowing Rapti. In the distance, across the sea-green,
rainy mist, lay Jetvan Vihara. It had been buried under the
shifting sands and slush of two thousand years. The Buddha
had once stayed here and preached of the impermanence of
things.

However, we are living in the present, and have enough for
the time being.

Abul Mansur Kamaluddin lifted the crimson curtain of the
traditionally crimson royal tent. As a Syed, protocol did not
require him to bow low before a king. "Assalam aleikum, Your
Majesty," he said calmly, standing ramrod straight.

Hussain Shah put down his tamboura. He looked very
pleased with himself, as if he had just composed an excellent
bandish. "Waleikum assalam, Maulana. How are we this morning?" he said cheerfully. "Could you decipher that Ayodhya
text?"

15. A Poet and a Musician

From Behraich, Hussain Shah and his knights marched down
to Qanauj. Queen Khonza managed to escape from Dehli and
rejoined her husband on the battlefield. The war zone was like
a bustling township. Bazaars. Entertainers. Caterers. Mobile
kitchens. Hakims and surgeons. Hordes of pack animals. Kamal
had joined the King's army on the move and was bewildered by
the tenacity and resilence of human beings. In the ensuing battle
fought near the confluence of the Ganga and the Kalinadi, the
Afghans overwhelmed poor Hussain Shah again. In 1484 Bahlol
captured Jaunpur and placed his son Barbak on the Sharqi
throne. Hussain Shah was forced to flee to nearby Bihar.

In a characteristic gesture of generosity, Bahlol Lodhi allowed him to retain his own crown lands in Mirzapur district. Hussain Shah regrouped his forces, attacked the Lodhis and lost once again.

Hussain Shah's daughter was married to a prince of Bengal, son of Sultan Allauddin Hussain Shah of Gaur. That Sultan helped his relative in distress. He requested the fugitive to accept a jagir in Bhagalpur district and live there as king-in-exile; even issue his own currency. Hussain Shah accepted. Many of his courtiers went on to Lakhnauti and found employment in Bengal.

Kamal debated with himself: shall I stay on and remain a part of this military society even as a non-combatant, or shall I just go away?

Go away? Where to? Nishapur?

That name sounded a bit odd, now that he had started thinking of himself as a Hindustani. He was no longer a Vilayati. How could he be if he was chewing paan like a he-goat and the loyal Rajputs were picking betel leaves with him as an oath that they would die fighting for Hussain Shah? This custom was called 'beera uthana'.

This *paan*-culture was a very good culture. He was all for it, except that although he wore a sword, he didn't want to fight. This was the feudal age of constant warfare everywhere—West Asia, Europe, Russia, China, Japan. Men just loved to kill other men. Where could he go except to a Sufi retreat?

Bahlol Lodhi died in 1489. He was succeeded by his swashbuckling son, Sikander, who was proud and stern and very different from his likeable father. The Rajput chiefs of the Eastern Kingdom were loyal supporters of Hussain Shah. Led by a chieftain called Joga, they refused to pay tribute to the Lodhi government.

Sikander was a big-game hunter and sportsman. One morning, he was playing polo when the courier brought news of the Sharqi Rajputs' rebellion. He threw away his polo stick and ordered his generals to prepare themselves. "We are marching down to Jaunpur. Right away."

"Sire, you haven't had your breakfast."

"I'll have my breakfast in Jaunpur," he roared. They reached Jaunpur in record-time, ten days.

Joga, the leader of the revolt, had just bathed and was sitting down to eat in his chowka when his men brought the information that a furious Sikander was approaching the city gates. Joga stood up quickly. He put on his wet clothes and rode off in the direction of his liege lord Hussain Shah's fort in Bihar. Sikander chased poor Joga all the way and sent a note to Hussain Shah:

> *Sir,*
> *Kindly hand over this Joga character to me and oblige.*
> *Thanking you,*
>
> > *Yours truly,*
> > *Sikander R.*
> > *Camp, Somewhere in Bihar.*

Hussain Shah wrote back:

> *Please note that Joga is my servant, just as your late-lamented Abba was my servant. But he was a soldier, albeit a commoner, so I deigned to cross swords with him. You are a silly child. I will not use my sabre, I will beat you with my shoes. Get lost.*

Sultan Sikander Lodhi could not believe his eyes when he read this reply. "When a person is heading for total ruination he takes leave of his senses," he remarked ruefully.

With the help of his Hindu zamindars Hussain Shah took on Sikander in a battlefield near Chunar. Although he was defeated he still did not surrender.

Kamal could not stand more bloodshed and quietly ran away from Kohal Gunj. Hussain Shah's people supported him till his very last battles against Sikander in 1492 and 1494. He was finally vanquished in 1500 and returned to Bhagalpur, grieving for the fair city of Jaunpur which the victorious Sikander had reduced to rubble. Sikander had destroyed Jaunpur in the east and developed a new city, Agra, in the west.

Hussain Shah died in Kohal Gunj in 1505. After the fall of

Jaunpur the centre of Hindustani classical music shifted to Gwalior, though the entire region extending from Jaunpur to Qanauj, Kalpi and the Vindhyachals continued to be called the 'Hussaini Ilaqa of Melodies'.

Ali had said, "The world is as worthless as the sneeze of a goat."

Nothing makes sense any more. The contradictions of human nature have ceased to baffle me. Sultan Sikander Lodhi is a good, sensitive poet. He writes excellent ghazals under the nom de plume, Gulrukh—Roseface—not an inappropriate name, for he is stunningly handsome. The Sufis see Divine Beauty reflected in good looks, so one mystic fell in love with him. Being a stern moralist Sikander promptly sent the poor fellow to jail. He is a scholar himself and is surrounded by ulema. He is an orthodox Muslim, yet he does not wear a beard.

He is very interested in the promotion of education, yet he comes to Jaunpur and demolishes the city's famous university and its colleges. And while the colleges were being ravaged Sikander Lodhi, the educationist, sat in his headquarters discussing the new syllabus for school children with his advisors.

He has had the Rose Lake complex of palaces razed to the ground with a vengeance. Nothing left. In his frenzy he even ordered the demolition of the mosques but his ulema stopped him.

Baghdad fell once again with the fall of Jaunpur. I, Abul Mansur Kamaluddin, live to mourn its loss, just as I grieved for the holocaust of Baghdad though it happened nearly three centuries ago. I have seen the passing of a great and liberal civilisation in my own lifetime, here in India. The Mongols were heathens who sacked Baghdad, Sikander is a Muslim who devastated Jaunpur.

He is not egalitarian like his late father and has revived the pomp and grandeur of kingship. Being a puritan he has forbidden the entry of women into the shrines of saints—he says it leads to corruption. He has banned the annual Urs of Salar

Maba of Behraich as grave-worship. He has put a stop to the
worship of Seetla Devi, the goddess of smallpox. 'How can an
infectious disease be called a goddess?' he thundered and ordered the demolition of the deity's temples. It was explained
to him that smallpox was considered a manifestation of the
wrath of the goddess Kali. Sikander wouldn't listen. That was
a very unwise thing to do. Perhaps he wants to prove to his
fellow Afghans that he is not influenced by his mother, Queen
Hemavati.

Ah, Jaunpur! What a liberal city it once was. Women went
to college and to mosques which had separate galleries and
halls for female congregations, like we have in West and Central Asia. And now I hear the mullahs and pandits of Kashi are
persuading Sikander to declare Kabir Das a heretic . . .

Sikander is also a good king in a way. He has brought about
much peace and prosperity in the land and has streamlined the
administration. He has recruited a large number of diligent
Kayasthas to government offices. They are rapidly learning
Persian to run the departments of revenue, etc. Sikander has
successfully and finally vanquished his hereditary foe, and my
King, Hussain Sharqi. Sikander is not fond of music. Still, he
allows only one kind of raga to be played on the shehnai in his
royal naubat khana—Hussaini Kenra!

I think there is something for the wise to discern in that. . .

He is a patron of the learned and yet he ordered the scholars
of the Sharqi court to be presented before him, tied together
with ropes made of their "turbans of eminence". The order
was carried out. I am glad I was not among them. But should
I be glad that I ran away—leaving my seniors and my peers to
face that disgrace? Should I celebrate my cowardice and call it
my love for peace? Should I not have unsheathed my sword
and fought in the streets of Jaunpur? I came away to Patna
and sought escape in wine and music, but in the sound of the
sarangi strings I heard the rattle of death. I watched pretty
dancers and found dead women grinning.

All manner of voices, words of strange songs, complicated
sentences of dead languages created a whirlpool of din in my
head. I was a famous linguist. Now I wish to forget all lan-

guages and become wordless.

Where is my Unseen Mentor, my Guide? I recalled a Kabir song that Champa once sang— "The farewell drum of breath is beating night and day..."

He stopped writing and slapped his notebook shut. He had not written in it for long years and now he realised there was not much left to write about, anyway. He paid the rent for his room at the inn, packed up and left for the waterfront. Ships were leaving for the east and west of Patna. He could still go to Gaur and get a job in the scriptorium of the Sultan of Bengal. That king was having the *Mahabharata* and other Sanskrit works translated into Persian. "I am an unemployed translator and linguist," he could whine before the Sultan. But would he employ a renegade who had deserted his own master?

"Abay, O! Get out of the way! Can't you see we're carrying a bridal palki aloft?" Somebody elbowed him rudely from behind. The crowds pushed him till he found himself standing in front of a man selling tickets.

"Where do you want to go?" the man asked this bedraggled, miserable-looking person.

"To Nowhere. Give me the ticket and keep the purse." Kamal handed him his velvet kesa.

Some crazy qalandar. The ticket-seller returned the purse to Kamal and let him board the ship.

Kamal sat down in a corner with his travel kit which contained his unfinished *Strange Tales and Marvels of Hindustan.* Suddenly he had an urge to throw the book overboard. Then he recalled the Quranic precept—to lose all hope is kufr, denial of the existence of God. He alternately dozed and watched the colourful throng of voyagers and still did not know where he was going. The ship was on its way to Prayag, beyond the city of Kashi. Many passengers had disembarked at Patna, many more came up the gangplank. Among the new ones there were some rich young men, a group of bairagis and a saffron-clad Buddhist bhikshu who always kept aloof. Kamal had finally met some bhikshus in Bihar.

The rich young men of Patna played cards, the two merchants of Kathiawar remained engrossed in their fat ledgers,
the wedding party sang boisterously. The bride was crying.

*"Listen, Champavati, you can make your choice here and now,
if you agree to marry me. You'll get such an interesting fellow in
this life and you will be safe in the Hereafter."*

*"If my karma and sanskaras are such, I will become a Muslim
and marry you. . ."*

"Sanskaras or no sanskaras, will you wait for me?"

She laughed her silvery laugh and vanished in the moonlight.

Somebody struck the strings of a dotara. Kamal rubbed his
eyes, he had long been a victim of hallucinations and reveries.
Champa was gone. He looked up. A tall and sturdy sadhu in a
white robe loomed in front of him. He played his dotara with
his left hand for his right had no fingers. He looked more like
a Thakur than an ascetic. Maybe he was Sultan Sikander's spy.
Kamal was known to be one of Hussain Shah Nayak's trusted
officials. "Are you Maulana Kamaluddin of Jaunpur?" the sadhu
asked gruffly. That confirmed Kamal's suspicions.

He nodded, too upset to speak. He didn't want to be dragged
back into that fearful arena of tigers fighting lions.

"Don't look so scared." The bairagi sat down on a coil of
rope. "You have guessed right. I was an officer in the Lodhi
army but now I am spying for God. I fought against you chaps
in the Battle of Kalpi and lost my fingers." He spread his hand
in front of a bewildered Kamal.

"I passed with my victorious regiment through Ayodhya
where she lived. . ."

Kamal's heart sank. Like that Shaivite yogi of Shravasti did
this man also have knowledge of the unknown?

"Her non-combatant brother was killed in the war. She was all
alone in the world, she said, and she came to me. She thought I
was a Sharqi general. The foolish girl couldn't distinguish
between military uniforms and flags. She said you had promised
to come back, so she wandered in the forests looking for you.
But no swan and no dark clouds brought you her message. . .

"Then she said to me, 'Throw away this sword in the river,
soldier. Haven't you killed enough?'

"That hit me. I, a born fighter—a Thakur, a worshipper of Durga Bhavani—I became a different person. She said, go to Kashi and stay with Sant Kabir while he is still around. So I have taken sanyas and I mostly live there. And you, poor deluded man, go to Kashi too, before it is too late."

Abruptly, the former general rose to his feet and left. He never spoke to Kamal again.

The Ganga flashed on. Boats continued to sail on its gold-and-blue surface—state barges, merchantmen, galleys, fishing rafts. . . Their sails swelled in the evening wind against the setting sun and it looked as if hundreds of swans were about to fly away to the snowy north. Songs rose from dugouts and dinghies—the hymns of yogis, the chants of fakirs. Cargo ships sailed towards the country's great markets bearing cotton textiles from Gujarat and Bengal, silks and brocades from Kashi, artifacts from the Deccan. People from distant lands were voyaging on the great river. Bhikshus from Tibet and Kashmir, Arab tourists, architects from Shiraz, Javanese dancers. There was peace and prosperity in the country. Sultan Sikander ruled in Dehli and all was well with the world.

Kamal sat down next to the solitary, ochre-robed bhikshu one evening. The monk raised his eyes. It was the night of Vaisakh Purnima. Tonight, two thousand years ago, Gautam Siddhartha had been born in the remote foothills of the Himalayas. On another night of the Full Moon of Spring he had attained Knowledge. The moon rocked on the waves, its rays fell on the bhikshu's face.

"How does one liberate oneself from one's thoughts?" Kamal mused aloud.

"Thought cannot know itself, it cannot go outside itself. There is no God outside the universe, there is no universe outside God. There is no difference between Right and Wrong, but the Absolute is beyond everything. It is Silence," he replied tonelessly.

Kamal walked back to his corner, greatly dejected. The ship cast anchor alongside a picturesque hillock. A grey stone khanqah was visible through the branches of a khirni tree. Kamal picked up his bag and disembarked. He climbed the

hillock and reached the hospice. The khanqah belonged to
the Order of the Chishtis and was surrounded by green fields
where some murids were working as volunteers. They grew
food for the community kitchen. A saint's tomb and the
mosque-school were hidden behind lush creepers. It was an
immensely peaceful place, a Sufi retreat.

16. Kamal Among the Patched-smock People

Kamal recalled his mystic friends of Jaunpur who used to talk
about the Chishti Way of Love, Beauty and Melody. Inside the
khanqah, qawwali was in progress, Amir Khusro's famous *Bahut
kathin hai dagar panghat ki*—the path to the well is difficult
to tread—part of rural India's romantic lore, but in this
qawwali it had acquired spiritual meaning.

Kamal stepped in gingerly and took off his shoes. Then he
sat down on the threshold. He had always been slightly hostile to mystics although he used to say, "Some of my best
friends are Sufis!"

The ecstatic singing came to an end. The Master who presided over the lodge was a gentle, venerable old man. He welcomed the world-weary traveller affectionately and asked him
how he was. Suddenly, Kamal burst into tears.

*Sattar is one of the Ninety-nine Beautiful Names of God. He
mercifully hides the shameful or embarrassing faults and shortcomings of human beings. According to Sufi tradition, during
the Mystical Night Journey of the Lord Prophet from Jerusalem
to the highest of heavens, Allah gave him a metaphorical khirqa
or robe of spiritual authority and said, 'Bestow it on one of your
Companions who gives you this answer.' Then God whispered the
answer to the Prophet. On his return to earth Mohammed asked
his companion, Abu Bakr, what he would do if he got this khirqa.
Abu Bakr said he would spread truthfulness in the world, Omar*

said he would establish justice, Osman said he would abolish poverty. Finally Ali was asked and he gave the answer that Allah had whispered to the Prophet. He said he would hide the shameful shortcomings of individuals from their fellow-beings. He was given the robe of valayat, spiritual eminence. He passed the khirqa to his elder son, Imam Hasan, who granted it to Hasan Basri, one of the earliest mystics of Islam. From Hasan Basri the symbolic Khirqa Rehmani was transmitted to major Sufis in later centuries.

Ali is called Waliullah, Friend of God, and is regarded as the fountainhead of mysticism by most Sufi orders, especially by the Chishtis. In a silsila, or spiritual lineage, a murshid appoints one of his murids as his khalifa at the time of his death, and gives him the Khirqa-i-Iradat or the Robe of the True Disciple. The Khalifa inherits the murshid's copy of the Qoran, his prayer rug, cap or turban, rosary, his symbolic begging bowl and sandals. These objects are preserved as holy relics. Sometimes the khilafat becomes hereditary. This Chishti house was established by Makhdoom Jehanian Jehangasht, or globe-trotter, who also planted this khirni tree in the last century.

Is this the sanctuary where I can hide my guilt as a deserter?

I have been given a cell in the quadrangle. I have become a khadim of the murshid. I'll also keep jotting down the murshid's teachings in my notebook, Insha Allah. I am glad I did not throw it in the river.

Wandering dervishes keep coming and going. They wear patched clothes following the sunnat of the Lord Prophet who, because of his humility and poverty, mended and patched his clothes.

I remember what Champavati had said, that some day these people would rescue me from my delusions. . .

The inmates of the khanqah were not monks since there is no monasticism in Islam. Many of them were householders who came to stay there for a while, and the murshid was also a married man. His family lived in a tiny house attached to the tomb. The Sufis' was a speech culture, they talked and talked. They spoke about the Prophet and Ali and the great saints, they taught through parables and anecdotes. One of the murids kept taking notes which were then compiled as the murshid's *malfoozat*. Kamal read many hagiographies in the khanqah's library. He was amused to learn in *The Malfoozat of Makhdoom Jehanian Jehangasht* that after Timur's invasion, Mongol fashion had become popular in Delhi and the elite had begun sporting Chinese-style pigtails!

As a khadim or "servant" of the pir, Kamal took his turn fanning the Master. He washed the guests' hands and served them food and sometimes helped in the kitchen. Whenever a disciple was found to suffer from too much ego the murshid appointed him supervisor of the visitors' shoes. In humility, hospitality and forgiveness the murshid imitated the qualities of the Lord Prophet. The Chishtis also made Hindus their murids—the murshid and the non-Muslim together held a handkerchief in their hands and the murshid made the novice repeat after him: "From now on I will shun evil and lead a life of purity," after which the new murid was greeted by the congregation and sweets were distributed. He continued to worship in his own way.

One afternoon the murshid held a long discourse explaining the Spaniard Ibn Arabi's *Theophany*. Sheikh-ul Akbar, the Sheikh of Sheikhs, Mohiuddin Ibn Arabi, had written one hundred books on metaphysics and metapsychology. He had said that all spiritual experience has its own validity. After the lecture the murshid turned towards Kamal and said, "Go to Kashi and meet Mian Kabir before it's too late."

"Sir, a yogi I met on board the ship told me to do the same."

"I know," the murshid beamed.

This did not surprise the once sceptical Kamaluddin because clairvoyance or *roshan-zamiri*, 'luminous conscience' as it was called by the Sufis, was not an uncommon psychic phenomenon. Still, he asked a fellow disciple, "Why does the hazrat want me to go to Kashi and meet Kabir Das?"

"That may be one more step in your progress," the man answered. "Perhaps you are restless because you've lost someone. You may find some peace on this journey."

Kamal took his murshid's leave, bade goodbye to his new friends and set out once again—now towards Banaras. Walking through many villages he reached a lush forest. There he found a group of Vaishnava sadhavis from Bengal, on their way to Mathura. Sitting under a fragrant tree they were beating time with their cymbals. In the distance, yogis blew into conch-shells. Wild partridges cooed in the bushes, tuneful songs wafted up like incense from the mahua grove. Kamal sat down on the edge of a tank and listened to the sounds of the forest.

He realised he was in the Silence and the sounds he heard were the various reflections of the Silence. He was in the Sufis' World of Wonderment. This Silence was also the Absolute and he listened attentively. The Vaishnava women were singing the song of Burdwan's Jaidev Goswami in Raga Basant:

Beautiful Radha. . . all of springtime waited by the woods for Krishna. Krishna the all-forgetful. I know where Krishna tarries in these early days of spring. When every wind from the sandal woods brings fragrance on its wings, brings fragrance stolen from the thickets of cloves. In jungles where the bees hum and the koel flutes her love.

I know how Krishna passeth these hours of blue and gold. He danceth with the dancers, and of Radha thinketh none. See lady! how Krishna passed these idle hours, decked forth in folds of woven gold and crowned in forest flowers; in the company of the gopis who dance and sing and play, lies Krishna laughing, dreaming his Spring away.

Kamal loitered on the woodland paths in the company of swallows and 'mehri' birds. Then he came upon the Ganga again, gleaming through the rose-apple trees. He was looking around for Champa, in fact, she could well be one of these Vaishnava women singing the Jaidev song. Radha signified the ecstasy of the soul which has found the true meaning of Love, of which the Iranian mystic-scholar, Ruzbehan, had written—Radha was the human soul yearning to be one with the Divine, what the Sufis called Fana-fi-Allah.

"Champavati of Ayodhya?" said a villager when asked. "After the war she was left all alone. There was nobody to look after her so she joined a band of Vaishnava sanyasins and has gone away to Brindaban. Women without men become nuns, sir, men without women turn into sadhus. . ." he said in a matter-of-fact way and walked on.

Kamal had reached Banaras. There lay Shivpuri on the other side of the river, the spires of its gilded temples blazing in the sun. Myriads of temple bells rang out in unison. The air was heavy with incense, puja flowers lay strewn in narrow lanes; throngs of men and women bathed on the ghats. Kashi, the Eternal City!

There was a Muslim weavers' hamlet at the edge of the wood. A group of quaint-looking Madari qalandars passed by and Kamal mingled in with a crowd of humble people who were on their way to Mian Kabir's house.

He stayed in Kashi with the followers of the poet-saint, sang his hymns and heard his discourses. Kabir's syncretic outlook reminded Kamal of Maulana Jalaluddin Rumi who had lived in Turkey two hundred years earlier. They all say the same thing, but it doesn't help.

Stirring things were happening in Sikander Lodhi's regime. A child called Nanak was born in Punjab in a Khatri household, destined to found a new syncretic religion. The Muslims called him "Nanak Shah Faqir". "Shah" and "Sultan" in Sufi vocabulary signified spiritual elevation, faqirs or humble mystics were Kings of the Spiritual World. Like the Catholic mystics of contemporary Europe, the mystics of India were not too popular with the clerics. The pandits and maulvis of Banaras resented Kabir Das and sent petitions to Sultan Sikander to chastise this heretical weaver who was misleading the masses. Sultan Sikander requested Mian Kabir to leave Banaras.

After Kabir Das left Kamal went straight to the river-port and sailed away to Bengal because he wished to meet an eminent mystic of the Suhravardy Order at Chittagong. Kamal had become a wandering dervish. The Suhravardy missionaries had been especially successful among the lower castes of Bengal. Kamal stayed at their khanqah for a few months, then at the behest of the Suhravardy sheikh, set off on his wanderings once again.

17. Folk Singers of Bengal

Everybody seemed to be a singer in Bengal. Storytellers chanted roop-kathas; ferrymen, snake-charmers and elephant-trappers sang their ballads. They sang of Allah, Mohammed or Radha-Krishna. Vaishnavism was flourishing. Kamal rowed his boat from dargah to dargah, also singing. There were dangerous rapids in Chittagong, broad, winding rivers, mountain paths shaded with radhakali and krishnachura blossoms. Mosques and Tantric temples lay hidden in bamboo groves.

Once he came across a band of minstrels singing the Ballad of Nizam the Robber. Kamal had never heard such a strange ode to the Prophet. Its author had been a notorious highwayman of these parts a century ago. He was transformed into a man of peace by the Suhravardy Sufis and ended up as a saint himself. Kamal sat down near the singers and listened.

Had there been no Incarnation of Mohammed,
There would have been no
> *Kingdom of God in the Three Worlds.*
Hail, Hail Abdullah, Hail Blessed
Amina,
Hail the City of Medina, and
All the saints and the Lady Fatima, Mother of the world.
Now I bow down before Brindaban,
Hail Lord Krishna, the Eternal
> *Lover of sweet Lady Radhey.*
My respects to all the sects of the Mussalmans,
I bow down before the mosque of the Great Pir at Naupara
And the mosque of Hirmai to the left;
For the great saint once passed through these tracts.
Now I proceed onwards and arrive at Sita Ghat
Where I worshipfully bow before the ideal of womanly
> *virtues, Sita Debi,*
And her Lord Raghunath.
Hail, Hail, Hail. . .

Kamal smiled indulgently. This ode was certainly one of the marvels and strange tales of Hindustan, and he would have mentioned it in his travelogue but he had long stopped writing his diary, and had lost the notebooks during his wanderings.

Abul Mansur Kamaluddin of the Royal Library of Jaunpur had been forgotten. Nobody knew now who this tanned, blue-eyed man with greying hair was, who sat listening to the story of Kanchanmala from a minstrel, or who was penning a local folk-tale in Arabic. . .

He heard the folkore from Muslim village women and visualised many a scene of Bengal's fascinating Buddhist past, and the glorious days of the Pala and Sena kings. It had been a land of merchant-princes whose peacock-shaped vessels sailed on the great rivers. Right now, multitudes of worshippers of Gautam Buddha, Tara and Durga were being converted by the Sufis.

He married a Sudra girl called Sujata Debi. He couldn't see anything wrong in her being a "low caste" woman. The local maulvi who married them named her Amina Bibi. Kamal grew paddy on a fertile piece of land. The pond in front of his bamboo hut was covered with lotuses and tiny colourful fish darted over its waters. When the Bow of Indra appeared in the sky after the rains, Kamal sat on his little veranda playing the stringed instrument called *ananda lahiri*, the Wave of Bliss.

The gypsies or banjaras carried commercial goods from place to place on their bullock-carts. They told Kamal that Sultan Hussain Sharqi had died. What a man he had been, larger then life! He was of the stuff that Julius Caesar was made. Would he be remembered through his music or forgotten even in that, because in this country people do not remember artists' names? Only their work survives—who was the sculptor who made the 'Girl with the Kadam Bough' that Kamal had seen lying in a corner of the burnt-down, ancient house in Shravasti? As for himself, he had already become a nameless puthi and ballad-writer of Bengal. And he had once said that like Maulana Dawood who wrote *Chandain*, he would be remembered as Maulana Kamal, author of the mystical allegory *Champavati!*

But he never got around to writing it.

His sons, Jamal and Jalal, became architects. Amina died. Kamal had a flowing beard. Strands of grey hair fell upon his shoulders as he wrote his Murshidi and Marfati songs, sitting in his picturesque bamboo hut near Sonargaon.

In 1525 there was another upheaval in faraway Dehli. Sultan Ibrahim Lodhi, son of Sikander Lodhi, lost out to the newcomer, Zhiruddin Babur of Central Asia, who had been invited by Rana Sanga, the Rajput, to overthrow the Lodhi king. Kamal's elder son, Jalal, told him that he was going to Dehli to build for the Mughals. Kamal said nothing. He had roamed the earth and had arrived at his destination; now the world lay before his sons, the choice was theirs.

Sher Khan ousted Sultan Ghiasuddin of Bengal and occupied the throne of Gaur. This Sher Khan of Sahasram, Bihar, had also been educated in the University of Jaunpur and he, too, joined politics and decided to capture power at Dehli. So there was a terrible war between Sher Khan and Humayun, son of Babur.

Now they were called Shahenshahs, Emperors. The rulers of the Islamic world had long adopted all the pomp and splendour and titles of the vanquished Sassanian Shahenshahs of Iran and emperors of Byzantium. So the Mughal ruler was Shahenshah, King of Kings, like Darius who had proclaimed he was Lord of the Earth from Sunrise to Sunset. . .

The mighty Mughal entered Gaur and coins were struck in his august name. The Emperor was bewitched by Bengal and called Gaur, Jannatabad, the City of Paradise.

Then Kamal thought of the long-ago Persian dervish of Dehli with whom he had first come out to Jaunpur. That hermit had told him all about it—the business of change in dynasties' currencies, and place-names. Kamal had seen it all. He was a Witness. And the Moving Finger wrote on. . .

Within a year Sher Khan invaded Bengal, driving the Great Mughal back to Dehli. A fearful war raged between the Pathan Sher Shah Suri and the Mughals. (Sher Shah later turned out to be a good king, a great builder of highways and public works and an able administrator.) Kamal's elder son lost his life fighting in the streets of Gaur. One night some of Sher Shah's soldiers reached Kamal's hut. "Your architect-son Jamal has gone over to Dehli to join the Mughal government. Traitor! We are taking you to Gaur to cast you in a dungeon."

Kamal hobbled to the door, holding a lamp in his trembling hands. He regarded the rowdy soldiers, greatly puzzled, as they advanced towards him menacingly. Poor old Kamal was now eighty-five. He held fast to the door. He had grown very feeble but he stood there mustering all his physical strength. He didn't have a sword to defend himself. Slowly he tried to ponder over what these terrible men were saying. He would be taken to Gaur and gaoled, they said. He tried to think of the reason for this punishment. What had he done to be treated thus? He had no quarrel with either the Afghans or the Mughals, he merely wished to be left alone. As though the mere process of living hadn't been tiresome enough! This was his country, his children had been born here, his dear wife lay buried here. He had put all his energy into making these fields bloom, spent years beautifying the language these men were speaking. He had written songs and collected stories and he was going to continue living right here. No one had any right to call him an outsider or a traitor.

The soldiers of Sher Shah's army pushed and kicked the tottering old man and marched away laughing. Kamal fell down on the threshold. Slowly he mumbled the Qoranic Verse of the Dawn, 'Return, O soul, to Thy Lord, accepted and accepting—' Lying there in the lonely, moonless night of Amavas, he died quietly.

Dehli was called Indraprastha in the days of the *Mahabharata*, around 1000 B.C. Lord Krishna was probably a contemporary of Prophet King Dawood. How much water—how much water has flowed down since then, O Jamuna! Rai Pathora's Dilli came to be known as Tughlaqabad in the days of the Turks, today it is called Shahjahanabad. The name is creating wonder in the shoddy courts of Europe. Commerce and industry are flourishing in the Mughal regime, the nations of Christendom are vying with one another to trade with the country of the "Great Mogor".

For lack of stirrups, the Rajputs had been overcome by successive waves of horsemen from across the Khyber Pass; now, for lack of battleships, the Mughals have let the firangis slip in from the sea. Bengal has become one great bazaar of European traders. This Sultanate was annexed by Akbar and his Empire extended across the land-mass of Hindustan. When years later, the decline began, the Mughal subedars or viceroys of Bengal, called Nawab-Nazims, declared their autonomy. Prophet Sulaiman had been granted sway over land and sea by Allah. He was also the king of djinns, paris and demons, and birds and animals. He could converse with them. He was also the richest man on earth. Once he said to God, "O Allah! I wish to invite all Thy creatures to dinner at my place." God said, "Go ahead!" So an enormous feast was prepared. One fish came out of the sea and finished off the entire banquet. God said, "O Sulaiman! Only I can feed all my creatures." Now, this parable does not imply that Siraj-ud-Daulah, Nawab-Nazim of Bengal, had ever claimed to be like King Solomon. It transpired however, that the Law of Taxila's Chanakya began to operate once again. A whale called Admiral Watson came out of the sea. Siraj-ud-Daulah proved to be a small fish because Mir Jaffer, a crab, turned traitor. So Watson and Clive swallowed poor Siraj without even saying "Thank you."

Now the magnificent waterways of Bengal are crowded with Englishmen's trading vessels. They are the new overlords.

A strong wind rose and rocked the boat. The ferryman began to row with all his strength. Although this was not the season when cyclones lashed the country like Jehovah's wrath, young Cyril Ashley was perturbed. He picked up the flickering lantern and decided to help the poor old Blackamoor. He stood up and shouted, "Hello! Abdul, listen. . ."

All lower-grade Mussalmans were called Abdul by the firangis. This was one of their arrogant habits after they became victorious. They never bothered to pronounce the natives' names correctly.

A feeble manjhi was ferrying the two Sahebs across the ocean-like river Padma. He looked up.

"My name," he replied with dignity, "is Maulvi Abul Mansur Kamaluddin Ahmed."

That was certainly a long name for such a puny little creature. Cyril was amused.

"Glad to meet you, Maulvi. I say, let me help you with the oars. May I ?"

The boatman was surprised. This firangi was speaking in Bengali and was polite. Well, there are goras and goras.

"Thank you, Saheb," he answered. "Allah is my Captain, I'll manage."

Cyril was touched. "Tell me," he asked after a pause, "you are a maulvi—why are you plying a boat and in such rough weather?"

"For this," the man patted his wrinkled stomach. "After Plassey, the maktabs have been closing down rapidly."

"Oh," Cyril murmured. He had unwittingly drifted into dangerous waters. Englishmen were not at all popular with the defeated and dispossed Mussalmans of Bengal.

Abul Mansur also did not speak and concentrated on his oars.

Cyril peered under the mat roof of the boat. It contained the entire water-borne world of boatman Abul Mansur: another smoky lantern, battered pots and pans, a prayer mat, a coconut hookah hanging from the wall. The Portuguese had apparently turned all natives into tobacco-smokers. Cyril returned to his seat. His friend and business partner, Peter Jackson, was snoring. How quickly this fellow fell asleep, wherever he could. A jolly, insensitive, self-satisfied, Hogarthian character!

For a moment Cyril Ashley felt a bit peculiar. What am I doing here? A chance meeting with this fellow had scooped him out of the lanes of Cambridge and London and put him, a giant among these dark Lilliputians, in this fantasy land called Bengal. And he had lived here for the last ten years. 1797 was already on its way out. Soon we will be stepping into the nineteenth century—amazing.

The wind had dropped. The emaciated boatman broke into a soft marfati-gaan* as thanksgiving. They had safely reached the private jetty of zamindar Girish Chandra Roy, who had recently been granted the title of Raja.

18. Cyril Ashley of Sidney Sussex College, Cambridge

He was twenty-two when he received his Bachelor of Arts degree and came out of the ivied quadrangles to face the world. He had been a brillant student and a promising poet. His father was an indigent clergyman, in charge of a village parish in a remote, peaceful corner of Surrey. Cyril had been able to complete his education through a scholarship given by the lord of the manor. He intended to become a schoolmaster and devote his spare time to writing poetry, but his father advised him to take up law.

Therefore, after going down from Cambridge, Cyril Ashley joined the Middle Temple in the City of London. Here, in neighbouring Fleet Street, journalists and wits assembled in coffee houses to discuss international affairs, foreign wars, the Turks, the Russians and India. The world was opening up. There was a lot traffic—people were going to the New World and to the East. Both offered enormous opportunities to get rich quick—especially the East which was backward and politically in a shambles. Russia was busy occupying large chunks of the Ottoman's European Empire. Under the Mughals, India had become a rich industrialised country, exporting her textiles and luxury goods to Europe. But foreign trade was falling due to political troubles not only at home but in Persia and Turkey.

---

*Sufi song of East Bengal.

"The situation has become enormously beneficial to us," Cyril was told when he strolled down to his favourite coffee house to take part in the hectic discussions. "We have already made short shrift of the Frogs and the chaps from the Low Countries. After the decline of the Mughals' central authority everybody in India wants to capture power at Delhi. We have almost succeeded," a journalist said to him one evening, and introduced him to a gentleman called Peter Jackson who seemed to have come straight out of a Hogarth painting. He was portly, and in early middle-age, exuding self-confidence and success. He spread his pudgy fingers which sparkled with rings. . .

"Diamonds of Golconda!" he chuckled.

A merchant from Qasim Bazaar, Bengal, he had come home on holiday. Over cups of South American coffee he told Cyril in a gruff monotone how many thousand pounds he had made out there, trading in indigo.

"What do you intend doing now, young man?" he asked Cyril one evening.

"I would like to go to America and set up legal practice in New York."

"We have lost America, dear friend, and gained India, almost simultaneously. There is some poetic justice in that, eh? Go to Calcutta. If you use your brains you will have pots of gold at the end of the rainbow before you can say Peter Jackson!"

India! Cyril had never thought of that. "Don't the natives resent us?" he asked.

"Some do, some don't. They are terribly disunited. Many have become our allies. There are natives who will befriend us and turn against their own people if they find some personal profit in it. Bengal has become a big market-place for us—full of new towns called English Bazaar, this Bazaar, that Bazaar. . . It is the economy of the Bazaar and Dastak which is the order of the day, and we have the upper hand thanks to men like Clive and Hastings."

Peter proceeded to tell him about the dastak system and the network of Marwaris who worked as middlemen for the

English. Cyril was bewildered and couldn't understand a thing. Peter Jackson said to him, "Look, I need an intelligent and highly educated fellow like you as a partner."

"Virgil and Horace won't be of much help in your dastak business, whatever it is," Cyril responded, smiling.

"Listen, there is no money in poetry and everybody cannot become an eminent lawyer—you'll have to slog and slog for years in dingy chambers before you get anywhere."

Eventually, Mr. Jackson succeeded in persuading Cyril to come out to India with him. Law had turned out to be a terribly boring subject anyway. His new friend took him to see another friend who was a Director in the East India Company.

The Director was impressed. The following week Cyril received a letter of appointment as a Factor of the Hon'ble John Company. Came the day when Cyril Ashley bought his passage on board a gallant Indiaman and set sail from Tilbury.

When the white cliffs of Dover began to disappear over the horizon, he suddenly realised with a pang that England was left behind. He bade farewell to this other Eden where Cowper, Pope and Gray had lived and sung, and where Gainsborough and Reynolds had painted. The twilit landscapes of Turner, the primroses in country lanes, the sound of village church bells and the notes of chamber music rising from stately Georgian houses were all obliterated by time and distance.

This demi-paradise had never enjoyed such prosperity before. Palaces were being built, wealth was pouring in from Canada and Bengal and South America. New fashions were coming into vogue. The poor had become rich; the rich were richer. Everywhere there was only one thought in the minds of men—money, money, money. Cyril Ashley who had been a devotee of the Muse, was also setting out in pursuit of Mammon. The penniless scholar was going to shake the proverbial pagoda* tree and gold coins would come showering down. Or he might be killed fighting some tribal chief, only to be buried in a nameless grave in a jungle.

He shuddered when he thought of the possibility. What

---

*Name of an Indian gold coin.

did the future hold for each one of his fellow voyagers? Merchants, members of the Calcutta Council, the Chief Justice of Madras, a bunch of plain, unmarried girls of noble families who were travelling with their chaperones in the hope of finding good husbands in India? At dinner table the Captain narrated anecdotes of the wars with Hyder Ali. The English traders of Patna and Dacca were generally busy talking shop among themselves.

The boat entered the Bay of Biscay, and everyone discussed the French Revolution. 'Old India Hands' told Cyril all about the affairs of Oudh, Mysore and Arcot—all very unfamiliar names. But in no time he became quite well-versed in the history of the last three hundred years. He saw his first black people in coastal Africa. Renaissance paintings often depicted little black slaves standing in a corner. All Negroes were slaves, all Turks were ferocious. All Arabs were boorish. It takes all sorts to make the world.

Land, ahoy! The Colaba lighthouse was sighted.

Bombay!

India!

A century-and-a-half ago the customs officers of the Moghul government used to be nasty and arrogant to incoming Europeans at the port of Surat. But times had changed—now the East India Company's flag fluttered proudly on the pier. Passengers came down whistling, in high spirits, and were immediately surrounded by a throng of little black men who started carrying the firangi's heavy cabin trunks on their heads. Jackson was a well-connected person. He hired a carriage and told the hammals: "Presidency Magistrate's bungalow, Malabar Hill."

There were houses of rich Parsis on either side of the steep road. Strong-bodied Maratha women clad in purple saris walked gracefully on the sand, hawking coconuts. Malabar Hill was covered with bright tropical flowers. Rose-creepers bloomed over the red-tiled, wooden, double-storeyed bungalows of wealthy Englishmen. It had just stopped raining. The host came out to the porch to welcome them.

Raindrops fell from banana and coconut leaves while they had their tea, imported from China, in the pleasant veranda.

In the course of conversation the host said, "Some Eurasian females are very pretty indeed, but never commit the folly of marrying a black girl unless she be high born. You can take them as concubines. Some English army officers have married Moor women of rank, but everybody cannot be so lucky."

In the evenings they went out for long drives. There were vast tracts of green from Apollo Bunder to the Fort and Churchgate. Little pools of limpid water sparkled amidst clusters of coconut-palms.

The Presidency Magistrate introduced Cyril to two Parsi brothers who owned a ship-building company and spoke fluent English. The Parsis accompanied him to Surat to see the Factory. "This city used to be more prosperous than London according to visiting firangis," a Gujarati bania told him, "Shivaji Maratha sacked it twice."

They passed by an exquisite white mosque which Cyril's host, an English Factor, referred to as the Moormen's church. Then he saw a bunch of doe-eyed Gujarati women ambling along with sparkling pitchers on their heads. They were an enchanting sight.

Cyril Ashley approved of the women of India.

He returned to Bombay and waited for the next ship which was to take him to Madras. He was travelling alone, Peter Jackson would join him later in Calcutta. White domes of mosques and glittering pinnacles of temples peeped out of coconut groves surrounding the villages of Moplah Muslims, Nairs and Brahmins. They passed the Portuguese colony of Goa, then the ship cruised along the Coromandel coast. A bunch of noisy Frogs got on board at Pondicherry. They told Cyril gleefully that Tipoo Saheb had not only become a member of the Jacobin Club, he had even sent a donation to the American revolutionaries. *"Il est certainment le premier roi moderne de l'Inde."*

Cyril, who knew his Voltaire and Rousseau, was interested. but his fellow Britons on board were not amused. The Indiaman cast anchor in the port of Madras from where it was to set sail a week later. Cyril came ashore and took a room in a hotel in White Town. Then he saw the palace of Walajah, the Nawab of Arcot, and St.Thomas' Church. On the second day he lost his way and found himself in the Eurasian Town. He walked down the lane and noticed a tavern called "The Chinese Lantern". A young girl stood on its steps. She was surprisingly beautiful. She looked at him and smiled with a certain melancholy. A black woman sat on a bench, husking rice. A child came forward timidly and said to him in peculiar sounding English, "Good morning, sir, Papa says please come in and have a drink—"

Cyril had been told to avoid meeting the half-castes. He thanked the child awkwardly, and walked on. After some time he saw the winsome Eurasian wench coming out of the house. She walked briskly ahead of him, turned round and flashed her sad smile again. She had eyes as large, dark and lustrous as the eyes of the Gujarati and Malabari women he had seen. The girl was much too attractive to be ignored. He hurried on and overtook her.

"*Whither are you going, pretty fair maid?*"

He took off his hat with a flourish and recited the first line of a Cornish folk song. The gambit was successful. The girl halted and laughed. Cyril had heard this song in a country fair back home. Right now, the setting was also rustic, though tropical, and the maid was not fair but swarthy.

"*I'm going to the well, sweet sir,*" *she said.*
"*Shall I go with thee pretty, fair maid?*"
"*Do if you will, sweet sir,*" *she said.*

Instead, she asked, "Coming from London, sir?"

"How did you guess?"

"Some sailors came to my father's tavern last evening."

"Ah, indeed. We are on our way to Calcutta. Ever been there?"

"No, sir. We belong to Madras. My grandpa, he was an Englishman. He came ashore, like you, and never went back. He used to say he had come to India looking for the pagoda tree. Didn't find it—he was unlucky. Then he married a Tamil Christian woman and opened an ale-house," she spoke simply.

The story of Maria's grandfather hit him hard. He could be just as unfortunate.

"Let's sit down here, the sun is unbearable." He went over to a bench near the cathedral gate. She hesitated a little, adjusting her black lace scarf over her head, and sat down obediently. The rosary dangled from her strong dark wrist. He stood before her with great dignity and poise as behoved a true Englishman. The girl looked up at him, waiting for him to speak again. He sat down and made small talk.

Suddenly something happened to Cyril's otherwise normally functioning brain. It must have been the scorching sun (as he thought in later years). Without realising what he was saying, he blurted out: "I think you are the most exquisite creature in the world. You must come with me to Calcutta."

"Oh, but sir, it is not possible."

"Pray, why not?"

"My father, he will kill me. You are a real Englishman, and you may never like to even look at me after today. A lot of travellers like you pass through Madras," she said pensively and plucked a leaf of the tall grass surrounding the bench.

Cyril felt with utmost urgency that it was truly and positively a case of Love At First Sight. He said with intense emotion: "Listen to me, my pretty maid," while he recalled the lines of the Cornish song:

"What if I lay you down on the ground, my pretty fair maid."
"I will rise up again, sweet sir," she said.

That night he returned to the palm grove in the Eurasian Town. He came back there the next night and the night after that. On the fourth day his ship was sailing for Calcutta.

While he was getting ready to leave the White Town inn, it dawned on him that he had been unspeakably foolhardy. He couldn't possibly marry a girl called Maria Teresa of the Eurasian Town of Madras. Peter Jackson had said repeatedly, never commit the folly of marrying a black girl. He hadn't proposed to Maria yet but that stupid girl, in the manner of all Indian women, had already started considering him her lord and master. When he went to the cathedral garden to say goodbye to her, he was flabbergasted. She was waiting there with a bundle of clothes, all set to accompany him to Calcutta! Bringing forth all his powers of oratory and his poetic vocabulary, he convinced her that females were not allowed on board this particular ship, and that he would send for her as soon as he got to Calcutta. The Cornish song followed him to the sea:

"What if I do bring you with child, my pretty, fair maid."
"I will bear it, sweet sir," she said,
"What will you do for whittles for your child my pretty, fair maid?"

Yes, indeed, what would she do for whittles in case she had a child? He broke into a cold sweat for he was the son of a country parson, not a hardened sinner. He spent some restless nights on board. Then at the Captain's table he heard more terrible news of Tipoo Saheb's wars raging on the mainland. Once again the thought of getting killed in a strange country overwhelmed him. The fear of impending death helped reduce the guilt about the poor, half-caste girl he had seduced and abandoned in a palm grove in Madras.

The ship reached Diamond Harbour. Cyril hired a boat. On the evening wind wafted the faint roar of tigers and the howling of jackals in distant forests. Calcutta was still far away. Cyril shut his eyes and tried to visualise the El Dorado where he was about to arrive at last. The city of gold! London of the East! Night was falling. The magic moon of Bengal sailed alongside, and boatmen were singing plaintively in their strange language.

They approached Garden Reach. On the right bank Calcutta was bathed in clear moonlight. Banias waited for their new clients on the pier. Cyril came out of the motley throng, followed by an eager Bengali speaking pidgin English, who hired a palanquin for him and began acting as his agent. The Bengali took him to a boarding house run by an Englishwoman.

Earl of Mornington, the Marquis Wellesley, resided at Belvedere in Alipore. Cyril had his offices in Writer's Building. Indians, Portuguese, Armenians and Eurasians lived in Black Town. It did not take very long for Cyril Ashley to find his pagoda tree. He bought a pleasant bungalow overlooking the river, and started trading in indigo in the Mofussil. His Mohammedan munshee taught him Bengali and Persian and he moved in Calcutta's high society. His palanquin-bearers were dressed in red uniform, the mace-bearers carried his silver-topped canes; mashalchis ran ahead of his sedan-chair with their torches when he went out at night. A hairdresser looked after his powder, pomatum and periwig. The hookah man prepared his hubble-bubble for him after meals. His Eurasian clerk, Joseph Lawrence, and the Baboo managed his office. The Baboo bore the name of Sarkar which was Persian for 'head of works'. Many Hindu Bengalis he came across had Persian surnames indicating the designations their forefathers had held during the Mughal regime. There were Mazumdars and Taluqdars and Qanungos or 'enforcers of law'. Everything seemed to turn into a caste or sub-caste in this land.

Cyril's outhouses were full of low-caste folk—gardener, grasscutter, groom, water-carrier, washerman and chowkidar—all Hindus. His tailor, barber, butler and cook were Muslim, and his private barge was manned by Muslim oarsmen. He belonged to the superior caste of Big White Sahebs. It was the same Cyril Ashley who used to ramble in the quiet lanes of Cambridge with a volume of Blake and Donne in his hand and compose heroic couplets leaning on the Bridge of Sorrows, counting his pennies after eating mashed potatoes in dingy pubs.

The boat rocked on the turbulent waters of the Padma. This was the time of terrible cyclones. With some trepidation Cyril Ashley picked up the lantern and realised that the ferryman was rowing with some difficulty. Still he looked patient and serene for he was used to rough weather, floods, storms and all manner of natural calamities. Cyril Ashley tried to wake his friend Peter Jackson who had crawled under the mat roof and fallen asleep.

19. The Abominable Customs of the Gentoos and Mussalmans

The young Raja and his entourage and elephants awaited Cyril Ashley and Peter Jackson at the jetty. The Raja garlanded and welcomed the guests effusively. The Laat Saheb* himself had sent the two Englishmen to attend the festivities as his representatives from Calcutta. The ferryman, Abul Mansur, and his boat disappeared in the darkness of the vast river.

It was a lovely October evening. The Raja's newly built Georgian mansion faced a large tank. Tables were laid out in the spacious veranda for the Sahebs to have their repast. There were no ladies to be seen—they lived in strict purdah. Cyril plonked himself down on an easy chair and extended his legs for his khidmatgar to remove his boots. His domestic staff had already arrived by another ferry and taken up their various duties.

The fearsome chant of Hari Bol! Hari Bol! suddenly rose in the distance. Being a very still night, the words were distinctly audible. The Raja bellowed at his men: "How dare they. . . at this auspicious hour? Don't they know I am going to have a celebration? Who is it?"

"Sir, Bakshi Radhey Charan Mazumdar's son-in-law has died," the Raja's aide whispered.

It was a bad omen. The Raja was upset.

A young man came running up, shouting, "Help! Help! O, Company Bahadur!" He was panting as he came up and fell at Cyril's feet.

The Raja frowned.

"Get up. What's the matter?" Cyril asked him kindly.

"Sir, I just came to know that your honours have arrived. . . Please save my didi. . . She is about to be burnt alive. . ."

"Oh, no, not that again! What is it? What is going on out here, Raja Saheb?" Cyril turned to his host.

The Raja was about to say something when the newcomer

---

*The Governor-General

cut him short. The white man's presence had made him bold enough to interrupt the almighty Zamindar.

"Please come with me and save her life!"

"Don't do anything in a hurry. Remember Job Charnock." Peter, Cyril's friend, philospher and guide, told him gruffly. He ignored the advice and got up to go.

"Saheb! Where are you off to at this hour? The road is bad . . ." the Raja objected. Cyril elbowed him aside and rushed down the grand staircase. He got into a palanquin and told the young man to hop in. Then he ordered the kahars to run post-haste towards the village. The chant of Hari Bol! Hari Bol! was now mixed with the beating of the tom-tom.

"Yes, tell me now—what's the matter?" Cyril commanded the young man.

"My name is Prafulla Kumar, sir, I am the only son of Bakshi Radhey Charan Mazumdar. We are very poor. We are an exceptionally luckless family. My eldest sister was visited by the goddess Sitala Debi. . ."

"Visited by whom?" Cyril asked, even more puzzled. This was indeed a world full of unfathomable mysteries.

"Sir, she had smallpox," Prafulla hastened to explain.

There was a big bump. Cyril held fast to the palki's door. The kahars were running fast along the river bank. Cyril noticed that the Raja had sent his armed sepoys behind him, and they thundered ahead on horseback. A few years earlier it had been dangerous for Englishmen to travel unarmed in the countryside because of the Sanyasi insurrection. Things had cooled down a bit now but this kind of trouble was not unexpected. Cyril continued to look out of the window, lost in thought. A group of Satyapir-Satyanarayan faqirs came into view.

The boy Prafulla gazed at the river bank. He said wistfully, "My father says that on still nights like this one can sometimes see the curly-haired Satyapir*, sandalwood paste on his fore-

---

*The Bengali folk version of the Muslim mystical figure of Khwaja Khizr who, like St. Christopher, is believed to guide travellers who have lost their way. He is always dressed in green and is found walking along lonely river-banks after sunset.

head, a flute in his hand, walking along the river. My father often says that if he ever meets this particular god he will ask why he has been afflicted with all these misfortunes. But Sir," Prafulla waxed eloquent, "for me you have appeared like an avatar of Satyapir-Satyanarayan..."

Cyril felt uneasy. He was still not accustomed to Oriental exaggeration and hyperbole. A band of Muslim fakirs passed by, jingling their chains. "Allah-hoo-Allah-hoo," they chanted sombrely when they saw the Company Bahadur's procession going towards the cremation ground. To the scholar of classics from Cambridge the tall, black-robed figures appeared ominously like a Greek Chorus.

Prafulla looked in their direction and laughed sarcastically. "For the last several Thursdays they have been coming to our village. My mother can give them nothing—our jars are empty. Everybody's jars of grain are empty because of the famine," he added. "These holy men had predicted for one of my sisters that she was a Padmini and that she would soon find a rich and distinguished man! On the contrary, Sir, there is no calamity or disaster that my sisters have not faced. This eldest didi who was poxed and jinxed, she was betrothed to a cultivator. He died. Now not even a pauper is willing to marry her. There are only two alternatives—she can be married to a peepul tree or to a dying man so that the stigma of remaining a spinster is removed and she acquires the status of widowhood."

"Married to a dying man?" Cyril repeated, astonished.

Prafulla nodded. "It happens, once in a while. But my father refused both alternatives."

Cyril thought reasonably, well, we have death-bed marriages in England, too, for the sake of property. Then the Cambridge scholar and Orientalist-in-the making asked the young native, "Do the Mohammedans have such abominable customs as well?"

"I do not know, huzoor, but I'm told that amongst the Mussalman aristocrats, if they do not find a man of equal status they marry the spinster to their Holy Book."

Cyril again paused and reflected judiciously, that in Europe believers in Popery send many an unwilling girl to become the "bride" of Christ. He asked Prafulla if it was the same sister, the jinxed one. . .

"Yes. Last year a rich old man agreed to marry her but he already had two wives. He died this evening. Her stepsons want to consign her to the flames so that she gets no share in their property."

They had reached the house of mourning. A hush fell as the crowd saw the tall, young, firangi overlord step out of the palanquin. Suddenly Cyril remembered Peter Jackson's warning. Job Charnock, the founder of Calcutta, had saved a woman from the funeral pyre and had married her. So help me God, what an unholy mess I have landed myself in.

However, without a moment's hesitation, he shouted, "Stop this outrage!"

The Hari Bol! chanting and the beating of drums ended at once. The widow's eldest stepson came forward. He stood, arms akimbo, and stared defiantly at the white Saheb.

"You can't stop it, Saheb," he growled. "This is our parampara. Even Akbar and Jehangir didn't succeed when they tried to stop the rite of sati."

"Akbar and Jehangir be damned. You are living in the Company Bahadur's jurisdiction and not under your mad Nawabs and Badshahs' misrule," Cyril responded angrily.

The Raja and Peter Jackson arrived on horseback.

"You can't interfere with our religious beliefs and practices. The Mughals didn't, the Nawab-Nazims didn't. Aurangzeb banned sati and behold, his empire was lost," the man shouted back.

"Nawab-Nazims were booted out by us," Peter Jackson roared. "They got from us what they deserved. That ignoble tyrant and fool, Siraj-ud-Daulah is not around anymore, you know."

An old man who had been weeping, for his eyes were swollen, rushed out of the shadows and cried, "Saheb, don't you say a word against the Aali Jah."* He was the unfortunate widows's father.

---

*"Aali Jah Nawab-Nazim" was the Viceroy of Bengal's official title, granted by the Imperial Mughals.

"Sir, please forgive him for the disrespect he is showing to you. He held a responsible post under Nawab Siraj-ud-Daulah. The defeat at Plassey has somewhat unhinged him." Prafulla addressed the Englishmen in an abject undertone.

Confusion worse confounded. Cyril was anxious to get out as fast as he could or else he might have to do what Job Charnock did.

He heard the widow's screams. She was being dressed up as a bride to accompany her lord and master to the other world. "Baba! Ma! Baba!" she was shrieking hysterically in blood-curdling despair. It sounded like the cries of the doomed coming out of Dante's Inferno. Cyril got goose pimples. He bellowed, "I'll have your property confiscated!"

"Who are you? What authority do you have? You are not even the Collector of this district, a mere indigo planter."

The Raja hollered, "Shiril Shaheb is more important than the Collector. He has been sent here as the Laat Saheb's emissary." He waved a letter from Government House, Calcutta.

"I'll attach your lands. A new law is about to be passed against this gruesome custom!" Cyril lied. But it worked. The prestige of having a sati in the family was not worth the loss of one's assets.

The corpse had been tied with string onto a litter. The pallbearers lifted it and proceeded towards the river. The widow was discreetly left behind. The Raja's sepoys fired shots in the air, and Cyril Ashley and his entourage went back to the Raja's mansion.

20. The Confluence of Oceans

"Ah, what an adventure-filled evening it was for you, old chap," remarked Peter, sitting down at the breakfast table next morning.

Cyril remained silent. Last night's incident had saddened

him. He came from a country where order and stability were the norms of daily life. Out here there was nothing but anarchy, conflict and an irrational attachment to tradition. From where do we start the social reforms in this ocean of inequity? He heard a noise and looked out of the window. The widow's father was at the gate demanding to get in. Cyril recognised him and called out, "Send him in!"

An orderly entered the morning room. "Bakshi Radhey Charan. He is half-mad, Sir."

"Never mind. Call him."

The man hobbled in. He was attired in a moth-eaten, crumpled robe of the Mughal era, obviously dressed for the occasion as behoved a gentleman of the Old Order. It was pathetic. Cyril felt a lump form in his throat.

"I have come to thank Your Honour from the depths of my heart and soul for saving my child's life," the visitor said bowing his head.

"I am glad that I could help," Cyril replied haltingly in Bengali. He asked the visitor to sit down. The Bakshi carried a tiny embroidered folio with him which he presented ceremoniously to the young Englishman.

"Saheb, this most precious heirloom I have brought as a token of my eternal gratitude." He opened the velvet bag slowly and took out two calligraphed books. "I am told that you are deeply interested in Oriental literature, and that you have studied Sanskrit, Persian, and Urdu as well."

"Ah, yes, indeed," Cyril replied modestly. "I am also trying to compile a Bengali-English lexicon when I get some respite from my official duties."

"That is why, Sir, I know you will value these books and perhaps render them into English—Prince Dara Shikoh's Persian translation of the *Upanishads*. He translated it with the help of the pandits of Banaras. It is a rare copy. My grandfather was a calligrapher in the scriptorium of Nawab-Nazim Aliwardy Khan at Murshidabad.

"And this one, Saheb, is the Prince's famous *Majma-ul-Behrain*, the Confluence of Oceans, in which Dara Shikoh compiled the precepts of Islamic mysticsm and Vedanta. The

Prince was Emperor Shahjehan's eldest son, Sire, he belonged to the Order of Qadri Sufis and called himself a fakir."

"He did," Peter Jackson sniggered.

"Are you sure you would like to part with these books?" asked Cyril, as he turned the pages of the volumes in fascination.

"Take them," Peter whispered in an aside. "You can send them later to the British Museum." Cyril accepted the gift with genuine pleasure and gratitude. Raja Girish Chandra Roy swept in and proceeded to touch the old man's feet. Cyril was surprised.

The Raja said, "He is my guru. He taught me both Sanskrit and Persian in the village school."

"I'm told he was a soldier in Siraj-ud-Daulah's army and fought at Plassey," Cyril remarked.

"It's a long story, Saheb," the old man sighed. "I am an old fossil, a relic of times gone by. . ."

Now the Raja felt uncomfortable and wished the outspoken eccentric would leave quickly. He was fiercely loyal to the long-deposed rulers whose "salt" he had eaten. The Raja could not be rude to him because his tradition told him that a guru was like his father and a god. The Gora Sahebs could not understand these things, especially Jackson who was the typical rapacious, high-handed Company official and trader, so different from the gentle scholar, Shiril Shaheb. The Raja had joined the New Order, leaving people like Radhey Charan Mazumdar behind as the flotsam and jetsam of history. He told Cyril that as a young man his venerable guru had worked in the Military Accounts Department of Aliwardy Khan's government, and had accompanied the Nawab's grandson Siraj-ud-Daulah's army to the fateful battlefield of Plassey. The Bakshi had failed to come to terms with the Hon'ble John Company's dispensation. "I have acquired the reputation of being mad because I speak the truth and say things which people do not want to hear. Well, I may have become an eccentric, Sir, but I am not demented."

"How could you be so loyal to rulers who called you Kafirs?" asked Cyril Ashley.

"How are people like the Raja Saheb here so faithful to you, Sir, who call us heathens and treat us as inferior human beings? They didn't. We were their equals, they shared our culture. Aliwardy Khan and his court officially played Holi for seven days running. Two hundred tanks in Murshidabad were filled with coloured water. They didn't send the country's wealth out to some foreign land. We ran their administration and held the highest ranks."

"How could you remain subservient to the Mussalman for seven hundred years? The only explanation is that Indians kowtow to authority, to the powers that be."

"Aali Jah Aliwardy Khan's government consisted of a large number of Hindu ministers and generals," Radhey Charan responded.

"Yes, but then why did so many Hindu zamindars turn against him and become our allies?" asked Peter Jackson.

"Every phase of passing time has its own logic, compulsions and expediencies." The old man spoke like a sage and to nobody in particular.

Now it seemed to be a debate going on in a Fleet Street coffee house. Cyril began to enjoy it, for he and Peter were the winners and had the final word.

"The Hindu zamindars conspired against Aliwardy because of the Nawab's high taxes, didn't they?" Peter continued.

"You have made us tax-free," Radhey Charan countered sweetly. "Aliwardy Khan had to levy high taxes in order to strengthen his army and fight back the invading Marathas. You are taxing even our marriages."

"The Marathas didn't ravage your beloved Bengal in raid after raid, they didn't levy their dreaded chauth on you. . ." Peter shot back. "The mahajans and jagat seths transferred their capital across the river for fear of Maratha incursions. Large populations migrated to east and north Bengal or to Calcutta to escape their raids. That was one of the reasons that the people of Bengal turned to us for protection."

"Young Siraj exempted you from paying custom duties. You returned his kindness by heavily taxing the goods that went out of his own dominions," Radhey Charan argued. "When you began the sack of Hooghly, Siraj wrote, 'You have plundered my people. . . you who call yourselves Christian, if you remain content to reside here only as traders, I'll return to you all your concessions. Because war is disastrous. You sign peace treaties with us and break them, and you swear by the Bible. The Marathas do not have a Bible but they keep their pledges.' "

"Well, all that was settled finally in 1757. It was a famous victory," Peter said, smiling and lighted his cheroot. "We have liberated you from the Blackamoors' yoke. You are an ungrateful lot."

"Plassey was a mango orchard and the trees were in flower, at the time. Nature remains indifferent," Radhey Charan said ruefully, after a pause. "Bengal is a wilderness today. It was once the richest province of Hindustan. You have a monopoly on trade. You are taxing salt and oil and all edibles. Your cargo boats are laden with foodstuff which has disappeared from the bazaars. Famine stalks the land, prices have soared. We have nothing to eat. Why did I become so inhuman as to marry my young daughter to a man older than me? It only meant one mouth less to feed. Being Siraj-ud-Daulah's man, my lands were confiscated after Plassey. I have a little plot left to sustain us. After the closure of our textile factories, jobless artisans and weavers are flocking to the villages to work as peasant labour." The old man wiped his tears and fell silent.

The Raja turned towards Cyril and whispered, "I apologise, Sir, that you have had to hear such a rude speech from my guru. Please help his son get a job in Calcutta, it will bring him some peace of mind."

In the evening Cyril interviewed Prafulla Kumar and learned that he had been educated at the village pathshala and madrasa and knew some Sanskrit, Persian and arithmetic. Cyril asked him to come to Calcutta along with his parents and sisters, and work as a supervisor in his godown. He asked Peter Jackson to give Prafulla enough money for the family's voyage to Calcutta and settle them in the godown's outhouses.

After which Cyril Ashley devoted himself to the revelries—a session of nautch and fireworks—at the residence of Girish

Chandra Roy. The Raja knew that the young bachelor was fond of native dancing girls and had invited the best from Dacca.

To
The Editor
The Calcutta Gazette

Sir,
I read Classics at Sidney Sussex, Cambridge. Out here during the last ten years I have learnt Sanskrit and Persian. I was recently presented with a 17th century manuscript of the unfortunate Mughal Prince Dara Shikoh's Persian translation of the Upanishads. I intend rendering it into English.

So far so good. However, what this benighted country needs urgently is English education. I do not know when the Home Government and the Directors of the Hon'ble East India Company will decide to abolish Persian, and introduce English as the official language of the regions of India now occupied and governed by us. I do believe that the superiority of Europe over the Asiatics was decided for all time to come when Persia was defeated finally in her long drawn-out war against the Greeks in 470 B.C. at Salamis. The Victory of Plassey in 1757 is only a recent example. Very soon we may hear of the end of our last arch enemy . . . Tippoo Sultan of Mysore, and then all of India will be ours.

I digress. The other day, while travelling in the Mofussil I did personally come across the ghastly scene of a young widow being forcibly sent to her death by her in-laws. Luckily, I managed to intervene. There must be immediate legislation banning this abominable custom of Suttee. . . What India also needs is a Reformation of the kind we had in Europe in the 16th century. But given the complexities and very ancient roots of their superstitions, one cannot visualise it happening here. All of the Roman Empire became Christian. All over Europe Roman temples were pulled down and cathedrals built over their ruins. I do not foresee the natives giving up their religions en masse, but they should at least be given some notion of Christian ethics. . .

— A Conscientious Englishman

21. Nabob Cyril Ashley and His Bibi

The Governor-General, Lord Cornwallis, had come back to India. There was a rumour that Cyril Ashley might be sent to the Residency at Lucknow, but he was still a bachelor. After Plassey, the goddess Lakshmi had forsaken her own people and entered the homes of the firangis. During their stay in the Residencies of Murshidabad, Fyzabad and, more recently, Lucknow, English diplomats and traders had amassed great fortunes. In England they were being called 'Nabobs'. They smoked the hookah and watched the Indian nautch, attended cockfights, and maintained harems.

Cyril Ashley had saved Bakshi Radhey Charan Mazumdar's daughter from being burnt alive. She had tried to run away but her in-laws brought her back, shaved her head, gave her two white borderless saris of coarse cotton and no money, and packed her off with a group of other hapless widows to faraway Banaras. There, where these women would spend the rest of their lives telling their beads, Radhey Charan's eldest daughter was swept away by a flood. His youngest and the prettiest, Sujata, accompanied her mother and brother Prafulla Kumar to Calcutta to live in Messrs Jackson & Ashley's compound. Old Radhey Charan indignantly refused to come and stayed back in the village. One day, when Cyril Saheb came to his godown for inspection, he happened to see Sujata Debi. She had come to the office with her brother's tiffin box. Once more his romantic nature took over and he fell headlong in love with her. The following day he sent for Prafulla Kumar.

In accordance with the social norms of the time you could take a native woman as a concubine or common law wife. She was given the respectable Indian title of bibi, lady. Therefore, Cyril approached his young employee with, "I say, would your sister like to reside in my bungalow as my bibi?"

Prafulla Kumar was much too obliged to Cyril Saheb to decline the offer. He also knew that the Saheb was a gentleman and was not taking advantage of his position. He did seem to genuinely care for the Bakshi family. Sujata was starry-eyed and her mother couldn't believe her good fortune. How those Muslim fakir's predictions had come true! Sujata had found a rich and distinguished man!

The rear portion of Cyril's large bungalow was converted into a zenana. Sujata arrived in a carriage with her modest luggage to live in luxury as Cyril's common-law wife. She acquired some English, wore gowns and high-heeled shoes, and lived in semi-purdah. It was all right to have native bibis, but they were not accepted in white high society. Only pure Caucasian wives were "burra bibis", great ladies.

Cyril was a bit of a philanderer, and Sujata turned out to be a possessive mistress. There were fights. She secretly employed a tantric to ward off her rivals but black magic didn't seem to work. Cyril continued to have his flings, he even enjoyed the company of nautch girls and courtesans. Like any purdah-observing Indian wife, Sujata could do nothing about it.

Cyril knew well the kind of life the future held for Sujata's children, if she had any. What would she do for their whittles? The Cornish folk song still haunted him. He hadn't entirely forgotten Maria Teresa of Madras, and was fully aware of the fact that the offspring of such alliances were often sent to the orphanage after their white fathers died. Boys became drummers, girls obtained jobs as nannies or even turned into trollops. So would his swarthy daughter work as a nurse in an upperclass English home and sing "Baby bunting", and "Hush-a-bye" lullabies?

Betty is a lady and wears a ring.
Johnny is a drummer and drums for the King.

Ye gods. Don't we have an abominable caste system, too? So, should he marry the Honourable Eleanore Hogg-Brentwood who had arrived from England last month, hoping to find a husband here? How could these pale and insipid females be compared to the gorgeous women of this exotic land?

Sujata was so beautiful that Cyril intended commissioning some important English artist to paint her the way Thomas Hicky had painted William Hicky's bibi. There were many fashionable artists working in India at the time. Zoffany became famous for his portrait of General Claude Martin's Gorio Bibi. James Wales, Charles Smith and Franceseco Renaldi had immortalised the exquisite bibis of prominent Europeans of Fyzabad, Lucknow and Calcutta. Some day posterity might admiringly view Sujata's portrait with the caption, "The Bibi of Nabob Cyril Ashley—1797."

His life was busy and hectic. Balls at Belvedere, the Governor-General's public breakfasts, concerts at Hasting Street, feasts in the villas of Garden Reach. Performances of Otway and Sheridan at the Playhouse, evenings at the Harmonica in Lal Bazaar. Adventurous journeys into the moffusil—the riverways of Bengal were open to him. Sometimes he felt as though he were in a Russian court and the hundreds of indigo culivators were his serfs. Huge sampans carried his cargo along the Dhaleshwari, the Karnaphully and the Madhumati. The great fleet of river vessels at Dacca that once belonged to the Moghuls and the Nawab-Nazims now flew the flag of the Hon'ble East India Company's government.

Twenty-five years went by; Cyril had still not found the right Miss White. He was balding, had acquired a pot-belly and nobody to inherit his pots of gold. Even if Sujata had not remained barren, her offspring could not succeed to the Ashley millions. She had lost her looks and deteriorated into a nagging housewife. Being an honourable man he could not discard poor old Sujata, nor could he live with her. So whenever he went to Lucknow on official business he spent an evening or two in the stimulating company of Champa Jan, the celebrated demi-mondaine of that colourful city. She was witty and intelligent and sang his favourite Persian and Urdu ghazals. She made him forget his worries—at least for the time being.

He was to go to Oudh again in the summer of 1823, but peasant trouble was brewing in Nadia district and he could not leave Bengal. On a fine spring morning he reached his office feeling more depressed than ever. He had to summon an urgent meeting of his subordinate officials to discuss the holy war the Mohammedan fanatics were waging against the English. 'My cup of sorrow brimmeth over,' he said to himself, wallowing in self-pity. Then he rang the bell for he needed the latest intelligence report pertaining to the activities of the Faraidi Maulvis. His orderly appeared like a djinn. "Head Baboo," he said briefly. Another djinn stood in the doorway.

"May I come in, sir, good morning, sir."

Cyril looked up, surprised. It was a new face. "Ah. Are you the lad Mr Alcott has sent me?"

"Yes, sir. My name is G.N. Dutt, Sir. I joined duty in the forenoon, yesterday."

Smart chap. "You know your rules and regulations well! How long have you been in government service?"

"Three years, sir. I joined immediately after passing my F.A."

"Why didn't you do your B.A. first?"

"Sir, my financial circumstances were not conducive to my pursuing further studies. I support my indigent parents who live in Mymensingh."

Cyril smiled. Like all good baboos this one was also fond of speaking pompously correct English. He would go far. "Well, Dutt, you should join evening classes for your B.A. I'll speak to the Principal of Hindu College."

"Yes, sir," the young man exclaimed happily, "most kind of you, sir, thank you."

Cyril was a good judge of men. He had dealt with all manner of Indians during the thirty-six years he had spent in this country. He came to like and trust the boy, Dutt. A trunkful of documents had to be sent to the Resident at Lucknow. It could not go by ordinary dak and needed a special courier. After a few days he called the new clerk to his room and told him to book a cabin on board an Allahabad-bound ship, take the peon Ghulam Ali with him, and leave for Oudh at the earliest.

"Yes, sir, very good, sir." The young man could not believe his good fortune.

"From Allahabad's Beni Ghat you will take a stage coach to Lucknow."

"Very good, sir." He turned to leave.

"Wait. I have brought the big Johnson for you, to improve your English. You can read it during your voyage."

"Yes, sir, thank you, sir." The boy picked up the tome from the mantelpiece and left. Two subordinate Englishmen present in the room exchanged glances. The whimsical old Ashley had started patronising the baboo. The lad would go places. His former godown superviser, Prafulla Kumar, had superseded the Armenian manager of Messrs Jackson & Ashley.

Cyril lighted his cheroot and noted his junior colleagues' reaction. He remembered Cornwallis who was often irritated by his erratic tendency to fraternise with the locals. The Company had now acquired political authority, old policies had changed. Nevertheless, Cyril was a "nabob" of the old school and remembered that Indians were a subject race.

The thought of death frightened Cyril Ashley. His physician had told him to watch out, cut down on his alcohol, and worry less. So, was he going to die like General Claude Martin of Lucknow who had departed this world in 1800, leaving his considerable wealth for the education of European children? That celebrated Frenchman also had a native Muslim bibi and an adopted Muslim son (probably his own), Zulficar Martin. They were not his successors.

He closed his eyes, tiredly. Well, first things first. He must rush to Nadia to quell the Muslim peasant rebellion. Next, drown his sorrows in the French wine offered by Champa Jan in Lucknow. Then to England, to bring back a propah English bride. And what shall he do with poor Sujata Debi?

Gautam Nilambar Dutt returned to his rooms in Manektala and began packing excitedly. It was quite late in the evening when he heard a footfall and came out into the lane. A sad-faced middle-aged woman was standing before him.

"You Nilambar baboo?" she asked in broken English. She was dressed in a faded English gown and wore high-heels.

"Yes, madam," he answered politely.

"I Sujata Debi, Ashley Saheb ka Bibi."

Gautam was taken aback. He also felt a little embarrassed. He had heard that the Saheb had a very devoted bibi, who had also been exceptionally beautiful, in his zenana. Suddenly, the woman began speaking rapidly in Bengali. "I am told that Saheb has become very fond of you. Sending you to Lucknow."

He nodded, still mystified.

"Have you heard of Champa Bai?"

"Champa Bai? No. Who is she?"

"Famous vaishya of Lucknow. Saheb has been smitten by her. Spends lavishly on her when he goes there. He has become indifferent to me. I am all alone in the world. My father had a lot of personal pride. He died of shock when he heard that I was living with Cyril Saheb. My mother has died recently. My sister-in-law doesn't welcome me in her house. Where shall I go?"

She began to cry. Nilambar was unnerved. She wiped her tears and spoke again. "Tell Champa Bai: You have hundreds of admirers. Saheb could mean nothing to you but a wealthy old fool. I have nobody else in the whole world. I have served him hand and foot for twenty-five years. He knows it. The fancy Miss Sahebs he dances with in the balls—if he had married one of them she wouldn't have put up with his temper and his eccentricities for a day. I did. Now he casts me off like an old shoe. I live in his bungalow merely as a housekeeper. Champa has bewitched him. She has got black magic done against me."

"Champa. . . whoever she is. . . is not here, madam, she is far, far away in Lucknow. You need not worry," Gautam answered reasonably.

"Don't you know? Saheb is about to leave for Lucknow— on a very big post. He has told me to go back to my brother, says he has put a lot of money in the bank for my old age. I ask you, son, is money everything? And he is going to take up with Champa Bai again, even on a semi-permanent basis, when he gets there. . . Will you please tell me what you said to that harlot when you come back from Oudh? Then perhaps Saheb will still take me with him to Lucknow. I'll look after him to my dying day."

It seemed to be a hopeless situation. Gautam kept quiet. She waited for him to say something. "I'll tell her," he answered after a pause.

She went back as abruptly as she had come, leaving Gautam bewildered. Her off-white gown flickered in the darkness of the narrow lane for a moment, then she vanished round the corner. Gautam finished his packing and sat down on his reed mat to read his Shakespeare.

22. A Faery Tale Kingdom

In flat-roofed white-washed houses with painted doors, in thatched mud huts and red stone havelis, young mothers rocked their babies in their colourful cribs and sang—*So ja rajdulare, so ja, Baba tera haft hazari, data subedar.** Sleep, baby, sleep, your father is a commander of seven thousand, your grandfather a viceroy. A similar lullaby was sung in contemporary England: *Rock-a-bye baby, thy mother is a lady, thy father a knight.*

The Mughal Empire was divided into 22 provinces, and a subedar as provincial governor or viceroy was the highest rank in the realm. A commoner could become a subedar if he had proved his merit. After the death of Aurangzeb in 1707, the centre became weak; once again the provincial viceroys grew more powerful. Burhan-ul Mulk had come from Nishapur, Iran. He was appointed Subedar of Oudh in 1719, and died in 1737. Safdar Jung was his nephew and son-in-law. Emperor Ahmed Shah made him Vazir-i-Hindu—Imperial Chancellor—and Nawab Vazir of Oudh. Raja Naval Rai was appointed his deputy. In an age of harem culture Safdar Jung was an exception. Nawab Sadr Jehan was his only Begum and he had no concubines. Their son, Shuja-ud-Daulah, rose to be a strong military leader but lost out to the English at Buxar in 1764. Delhi had been ravaged by Nadir Shah Abdali—its writers, poets, artists and craftsmen flocked to Shuja-ud-Daulah's capital, Fyzabad.

---

*This song and its variations are still sung in Uttar Pradesh at childbirths and weddings.

The Nawab Vazir was also a musician and employed 12,000 instrumentalists and singers. Many of them followed him on horseback when he went out hunting. Artists of London's Royal Academy and two hundred French gun-makers lived and worked in Fyzabad, since there has never been a time in human history when fine arts have replaced the armament industry. Shuja-ud-Daulah's son and successor, Asaf-ud-Daulah, shifted the capital to Lucknow in 1787.

When the Great Famine stalked the land from Bengal to Oudh, Asaf-ud-Daulah had the great Imambara built in the city in order to provide employment to people. The construction was done at night so that impoverished gentle folk were not embarrassed to be seen working as labourers. The Imambara's architect, Kifayatullah of Delhi, built the largest pillarless hall in the world, and its mind-boggling maze of underground passages was the wonder of architecture.

The Nawab Vazirs of Oudh banned the killing of monkeys in deference to the Hindu monkey-god, Hanuman. Dussehra and Holi were officially celebrated by many Mughal kings in the Red Fort at Delhi, Holi and Basant were official festivals in Lucknow. Asaf-ud-Daulah's mother, Nawab Bahu Begum, used to come to Lucknow from Fyzabad to celebrate Holi. Sadat Ali Khan, the fifth Nawab Vazir's mother, Raj Mata Chhattar Kunwar, built the famous Hanuman temple in Ali Gunj, Lucknow, with a crescent atop its spire.

The Nawab Vazirs created a culture which combined the finest elements of the civilisations of Iran and India. It was a tension-free society of polite, fun-loving people. This chivalrous, feudal world was inhabited by scholars, poets, storytellers, musicians, scribes, knights and barons, actors, jugglers, chefs, calligraphers, embroiderers, champion swimmers, kite-fliers and cock-fighters. Extreme finesse and good taste in the minor arts became the hallmark of the craftsmen. The architecture of Lucknow reminded European visitors of Moscow, Dresden and Constantinople.

On Navroz Day, March 1823, Gautam Nilambar Dutt's stagecoach entered the city gate at Aigh Bagh. He showed his papers at the checkpost. King Ghaziuddin Hyder's guardsman

stamped Nilambar's *parvana rahdari*. The present Nawab
Vazir had become a monarch. Gautam realised with a strange
thrill that there were regions in the country which were still
ruled by native kings. His carriage entered the lush green suburbs. Double-decker camel carriages were loaded with in-com-
ing passengers. It was early morning and the splendid city was
coming alive. A log burned slowly under a peepal. An old
yogi sat in front of it, cross-legged, deep in meditation. A
thousand-year old Kali temple stood behind the tree. Nilambar
folded his hands involuntarily as his carriage passed by.

The Residency was housed in a river-side European-style
castle built by the late Nawab Vazir, Saadat Ali Khan, bought
by the English at the beginning of the century. Gautam
Nilambar was told at the guard-house that the Resident had
gone to lunch with a nobleman called Nawab Kamman at Goa
Gunj.

Abul Mansur Kamaluddin Ali Reza Bahadur had inherited
a small estate called Neelampur in one of the chaklas or districts of the Kingdom of Oudh, and lived extravagantly in the
capital. He was a good-looking married man of twenty-six.
He was also an admirer of the reigning diva, Champa Jan, but
she had not deigned to become his concubine yet. The romantic nobleman had obliquely addressed his latest ghazals
to her. A slim collection of Nawab Kamman's verse had just
been published and Champa was going to sing his ghazals
tonight. Like any budding poet or author worth his salt, Nawab
Kamman looked forward to the evening, wondering how his
latest verse would be received by the cognoscenti. Some of
these lyrics had never been recited, and he had allowed Champa
to set them to music and sing them in the soiree tonight.

After the Resident took his leave, the young host looked at
the French clock ticking away on the mantelpiece in his Regency drawing room and waited impatiently for the sun to go
down.

Gautam presented Mr. Ashley's sealed bag of papers to the
Resident at Bailey Guard in the evening.

"Do you happen to know. . . where this woman called Champa
lives?" he whispered to a native clerk the following day.

"You mean Qattala-i-Alam—the Slayer of Mankind?"

Munshi Hari Shankar smiled wryly. One would have thought this Calcutta Baboo would only be interested in English literature.

"I have an urgent message for her which I must deliver in person," Gautam replied uneasily.

"Ah! The epistle must be from Mr. Ashley. Your Saheb has also fallen victim to the arrows flung by Big-Game Hunters!"

Gautam kept quiet.

The munshi promptly despatched a *harkara* to the Street of Perfumers with the message that Calcutta government's Sikatarri Saheb had sent a letter to her through his Sikatarri. The *harkara* repeated the words to the crone at Champa's doorway. The woman relayed it to Champa—who was at that moment inside her hammam—Company Bahadur's Sikatarri had come all the way from Calcutta to meet her. So the crone brought back the courtesan's formal reply: "I wait with all my heart for his auspicious visit. Please come tonight for the soiree."

"After giving her Mr.Ashley's epistle do not come back in a hurry." Hari Shankar said, chuckling. "Stay on and enjoy her superb singing. You are lucky. She doesn't normally invite riff-raff like you and me to her mehfils."

Verily, this is a pretty kettle of fish. I am in a soup, he told himself in English—the language which gave him great clarity of thought, and being a devotee of Dr. Johnson, he could call a spade a spade.

The Street of Perfumers was flooded with the soft fragrance of summer scents. Palkis and carriages stood in the forecourt of Champa's glass-fronted, double-storeyed house. A crone welcomed him in with a toothless smile. She was the same woman (a prima donna in her own time), slightly hard of hearing, who had misquoted Gautam's message to Champa. Gautam was dressed in his formal Mughal-style chogha. The hag mistook him for one of the new Hindu merchant-princes or a zamindar from Bengal. She led him upstairs and took him straight to the masnad upon which the guest-of-honour, Nawab Kamman, was seated. He was surrounded by his cronies and friends. Gautam sat down in a corner and looked around.

Champa Jan's salon glimmered with lotus-shaped lamps. Gautam saw strange faces reflected in the tall gilt-framed Belgian mirrors. Who were they? What were they doing here? Where would they go hence? How long would the room contain this assemblage? The men were talking in soft, restrained tones discussing some complicated technicalities of Urdu ghazal. Gautam wore his best embroidered robe and a turban-like cap for he, too, belonged to a society which had been deeply influenced by Murshidabad's nawabi culture. Still, his nervousness betrayed him as an outsider. The audience politely restrained their curiosity about the newcomer.

"We have heard of the grandeur of the zamindars of Bangal," the distinguished-looking aristocrat said during the course of conversation. "In which verdant dale in that paradise of Ind is your estate located ?"

"I have no estate, sir," Gautam replied in broken Urdu. "I work for my living. I am a petty official of the Hon'ble John Company's government."

"I see." The Nawab resumed smoking his waterpipe. Gautam felt ill at ease. He was not aware of the fact that the Company's economic exploitation of Oudh had made Fort William unpopular in Lucknow. Yet the King of Oudh seemed to be on friendly terms with his English overlords.

Musicians trooped in, salaamed and stood around in a semicircle. They were followed by a dazzling woman of about thirty. She made a bow, salaamed the audience and stood in front of the musicians. Then her naqeeb, or announcer, sought the permission of the chief guest for Champa Bai to begin the performance.

Nawab Kamman nodded. It was all very formal and ceremonial.

Her diamond nose-flower sparkled as she began an ode to the Prophet, the Holy Family and the Twelve Imams. This was followed by a ghazal composed by the late Saaf-ud-Daulah. After the royal lyric was over, Champa began singing Kamal Reza Bahadur's ghazals. Every time there was a round of Wah, Wah! Subhan Allah, the young poet salaamed the audience.

"What does Subhan Allah mean?" Gautam whispered to the

poet, who by this time had become quite friendly with the Bengali visitor. "Praise be to God. We praise Allah for every good thing in life. We praise Him for the beauty and good voice he has bestowed on this singer—and," he added modestly. "the audience is also praising god for whatever talent He has given me to compose poetry."

Champa salaamed the listeners several times for their exclamations of praise. Gautam was enthralled by the heady atmosphere of the salon. This room was a hothouse of exotic plants in which Champa glowed like an incandescent magnolia.

According to custom the concert gave over just before the muezzin's call for early morning prayers. The guests departed. The room was full of dying candles and flickering flames. Gautam debated with himself—in this place, redolent with decorum, how could he be so rude as to accost Champa with Sujata Debi's message? Some other time, he decided, and began looking for his shoes.

Suddenly he was accosted by *la belle dame sans merci* herself. Lucknow's cosmopolitan society included Italian and French architects, Scottish brewers, Armenian, Jewish, Kashmiri, Iranian and Gujarati merchants, some of whom attended Champa's concerts. She had noticed the newcomer who seemed quite uncomfortable for some reason, and was now anxiously looking for his shoes in the doorway. She ordered a footman to bring his footwear, swept up to him and addressed him with ease and friendliness. "Sir, I do hope you enjoyed our Hindustani music!"

He looked up and gaped at her. Then he muttered: "Yes, I did. You sing very well indeed, madam."

"You have honoured this worthless speck of dust, sarkar." She repeated the customary phrase and salaamed gracefully. Then she added another traditional sentence—"This slave-girl shall prostrate herself if you condescend to visit this humble dwelling again."

He was rattled by the linguistic extravagance. Perhaps this woman is under the impression that I am some new-rich zamindar of Bengal, or a wealthy broker from Qasim Bazaar. I must tell her that I happen to be a mere cog in the wheel of

John Company's mighty juggernaut. Didn't Munshi Hari Shanker's courier tell her that?

Champa continued smoothly, "This bondswoman shall serve you according to your choice when you come here next, sir."

Gautam was shocked. Champa's chief musician, the sarangi-player hastened to explain, "Huzoor, in our parlance 'to serve' means to *entertain* our patrons with music and dance. Because, according to our etiquette and protocol, we can't be so presumptuous as to say that we entertain. We merely *serve*. Bai Saheba here simply wishes to tell Your Honour that she will sing the ragas of your choice for you."

The cocky citizens of Lucknow considered the rest of the world to be uncivilised. Champa was enjoying this encounter with the attractive, limpid-eyed barbarian. He said a hurried goodbye and rushed back to the sanctuary of the Residency whose sprawling complex of ballrooms, banquet halls, hospital and gardens was a few acres of Regency England in the middle of latter-day Haroun-al-Rashid's Baghdad.

Gautam had never seen a woman like Champa Jan. In Calcutta, upper class women lived in strict purdah. When a Hindu lady went to take a holy dip in the Ganga her palanquin was lowered into the water. Of trollops there was no dearth in this city. They belonged to all races—Jewish, Eurasian, Armenian. He had seen them from a distance. Champa was a vaishya in the classical mould and she seemed to relish her power over men.

Slowly, he got to know Lucknow. He went to the kingdom's famous Prime Minister, Agha Mir's, office. He saw His Majesty the King in his Durbar when he accompanied the Resident as a courier from Fort William. He was surprised to hear the King speaking fluent English—not Gautam's idea of an opium-eating Oriental despot.

The women of Lucknow were witty and fun-loving. Even aristocratic ladies were not entirely secluded behind the walls of their mahals. They went on purdah picnics and participated in festivals. Still, this was not a mixed society, and like the geishas of Japan, tawaifs were the sophisticated entertainers of gentlemen.

Gautam began to ponder: why don't our women have the same freedom that Englishwomen enjoy? For instance, why don't they go horseback riding, like the Mems do? He asked this of Hari Shankar one morning while they were on their way to Ramna.

"Of course they did—once," Hari Shankar answered stoutly. "Rani Karnavati, Durgavati, Razia Sultan, Chand Sultana— they wore armour and led their armies into battle."

"Oh, but they were queens. Why doesn't your wife go horsebackriding in Dilkusha?"

Hari Shankar looked offended. "Purdah is a symbol of status, only working women do not live in seclusion. We have our cavalries of Turk and Negro women who guard the royal harems, you can see them parading in front of Machhi Bhavan. in the mornings. My patni is a purdah-observing housewife. Grih-Lakshmi. . ." It seemed Hari didn't even like the idea of his wife being mentioned in the course of conversation. "*Na stri swatantram*—there should be no freedom for women. Thus spake Manu Maharaj," he said with finality.

Gautam persisted, "How have American women become so bold and courageous that they cross the Pacific and come all the way to Calcutta to teach our native females?"

"They have an ulterior motive," Hari Shankar replied piously. "They want us to become kristaans. Look at Bishop Heber and the rest who visit Lucknow from time to time."

"Right. But think of the misery of our young widows. I don't blame them if some of them want to become Christian," Gautam argued back vehemently.

"Ha-ha—here comes our Champa Jan. She does not burn herself, she sets men afire with a mere glance!" Hari Shankar remarked jovially. They were ferrying across the Gomti. His Majesty was coming to Ramna, the royal wildlife sanctuary, in order to watch a ram fight. All Lucknow seemed to be afloat on all manner of colourful boats, on their way to Ramna. It was like a fiesta on water. Gorgeously attired tawaifs came sailing in their own pleasure boats.

"*Dohai hai Company Bahadur ki!*" Champa shouted gleefully from a mermaid-shaped *bajra*. She was standing near the prow like a Roman statue draped in white. Her muslin dupatta was fluttering in the river wind.

"Ah, good morning, Miss Jan, we were talking about you just now. . ." Gautam doffed his hat and shouted back gallantly.

"Call her Bi Saheba, that's how courtesans of rank are addressed over here," Hari Shankar whispered to him. "She sings for royalty. She owns an elephant, and Nawab Kamman has gifted her an orchard outside the city in which she keeps rabbits and a few deer. I think she would like to add you to her zoo," Hari Shankar continued in a jovial undertone.

Champa Jan ordered her crew to bring her boat alongside the Company scribes' canoe. Then she said, "Come on, Sikatarri Saheb, don't be bashful. Hop in. Munshiji, give him your hand. . ."

The two men jumped over to her ornate barge. Gautam grew more nervous. Here were two degenerate Lucknowites trying to ensnare a morally upright young man. Champa winked conspiratorially at Hari Shankar, who looked pleased as punch. Both of them were enjoying themselves hugely.

It became obvious to Gautam that Champa was Amrapali, Delilah, Salome and Theodora, all rolled into one. She looked frankly interested in him. Being a connossieur of men she knew how to pick and choose. She was certainly the kind of courtesan Damodar Gupt had written about in his treatise.

"Why didn't you come again after that evening?" she asked Gautam, playfully removing a lock of hair which had fallen across his brow. He wore his hair in Regency fashion and was dressed in coat and trousers.

Before he could think of an answer, the barge touched the Ramna landing-stage. "Hurry up, His Majesty has already arrived," she said and went ashore, followed by her maids. Champa walked quickly for spectators had to reach the arena before the King took his seat in his balcony. Gautam realised that here was his chance to deliver Sujata Debi's message to her. He broke into a run and overtook her. Then he said urgently, "Madam, I mean, Bi Saheba, I have to tell you something very important."

"Come over tomorrow evening. This is no place for amorous declarations."

"I beg your pardon!" he retorted, "I have no room in my life for. . . for. . ." he stopped himself from saying something rude. The crowd of citizens was swelling around them on the river bank. "Do you know Cyril Saheb?" Gautam caught up with her and asked, panting.

"Yes, I do indeed," she replied sharply. Her mood had changed and she looked angry. She did not like to be rebuffed.

"Do you know that he has a wife?"

"Either you are very naive or a plain damn fool, Sikatarri Baboo. All the gentlemen who come to see me have wives. So? Is that what you wanted to tell me urgently? Don't waste my time!" she said imperiously and walked rapidly towards the arena.

23. *Farewell to Camelot*

Gautam was contrite. He must apologise to her and he must tell her about Sujata Debi.

Being a man-eater, Champa was going to be the ruination of poor Cyril Ashley. He was fond of his Saheb and should try and save him. At the Residency he had learnt that Mr. Ashley was due to come here, probably as the next Resident. He decided to confide in Nawab Kamman. The young nobleman already knew that Cyril Ashley was his rival.

Gautam went to see his friend one afternoon. "You know, Nawab Saheb, if you don't act now, Cyril Saheb may take over." He told Kamal Reza Bahadur about Sujata. The young man thought for some moments then said, "I'll ask Champa to give us a concert in her garden house next week. There, you can talk to her undisturbed."

Kamman sent for his pen and ink-stand. The servant came back. "Huzoor, I can't find a fresh quill, you have rubbed them all off, writing your ghazals."

"Get a fresh stock from the stationers at once." The fellow left hastily.

Gautam Nilambar grinned. "Nawab Saheb, for want of a pen you may lose Champa Jan. We have a saying in English about how for want of a nail a kingdom was lost—"

"For want of a chair a kingdom was *gained* over here, Nilambar Mian! We are not losers." Kamal Reza laughed. Chobdar brought fresh hookahs. Gautam was becoming quite a fop of Lucknow, he was even wearing a muslin angarkha and dopalli topi. After that unpleasant encounter with Champa on the way to Ramna, he had decided to indulge himself. Why not? And he could plant his feet in two boats simultaneously— one Indian, one English.

"Nawab Saheb, how for want of a chair did you gain a kingdom?" he asked munching a paan.

"See, uptil now the rulers of Oudh were officially designated the prime ministers of India—Nawab Vazirs. They owed nominal allegiance to the weak Mughal Emperors at Delhi. From Jehangir's time the English ambassadors had to stand in audience before the Mughal Emperor in the Diwan-e-Khas at Agra and Delhi. They were not considered worthy enough in rank to sit on a chair like subedars, generals and other dignitaries of the Empire. After your East India Company became the virtual ruler of the land, Lord Myra the Governor-General expected to get a chair in the Durbar but Akbar Shah made him stand as usual. Lord Myra was furious. He asked the Court of Directors to elevate the Nawab-Vazir of Oudh to the status of a full-fledged monarch in order to cut the poor powerless Mughal Emperor to size. Now our Ghaziuddin Hyder is His Majesty the King of Oudh, so we have two kingy-wingies— one at Delhi, one at Lucknow. . ."

The servant brought a fresh quill.

"Now, I ask you, Gautam Mian—as Betaal used to ask Vikram at the end of each story—you being a budding thinker, was it chance or fate or foolishness and arrogance or hurt pride on the part of the poor figurehead Akbar Shah II, or the cleverness of the English, or the good fortune of our Ghaziuddin Hyder, that all this came to pass?"

Gautam thought for a while then replied. "A combination of all."

"Right!" Kamman scribbled a note to Champa asking her to arrange a musical evening in her garden house on a certain date.

Gautam met her after the garden-house soiree was over and repeated the rather tiresome story of Sujata Debi.

She listened carefully, then said, "Tell me, even if I do not meet Cyril Saheb, how would it help since he has lost interest in her? I know men. They are by nature promiscuous. Some get a chance to be unfaithful to their wives, some don't. And that poor woman is not even legally married to him." Champa sighed sympathetically and offered him a betel-leaf, indicating that she had dismissed the subject.

Gautam saw her several times again in the garden house. They talked for long hours for she was a brilliant conversationalist. He sought out intelligent, educated females and had found one in Lucknow. She never enticed him to sleep with her. "Ours is a Platonic friendship," he told her loftily.

"Platonic, my foot," she retorted. "It is a foolish kind of friendship, basically because you are a coward. But so be it."

Then he stopped seeing her altogether, there was no point. It was one of those absurdities of life—we meet the right people in the wrong places. "So be it," she had said stoically while feeding her rabbits.

The monsoons were about to set in and Gautam Nilambar got ready to return to Bengal. All his friends in the Residency came to the gate to see him off. A maidservant tied a little velvet band on his left arm entrusting him to the safe-keeping of the Twelfth Imam. He was to take the ship from Cawnpore.

He bade adieu to Lucknow with a heavy heart. When the horse-carriage reached the Naka, he suddenly said to his coachman, "Let's go to Chowk first. I would like to buy some perfumes to take home with me."

Gunga Din understood. He drove to the Street of Perfumemakers, but stopped in front of Champa Jan's house.

She was amazed to see him. "You've come!" she exclaimed.

"No, I'm going away, and I'm in a hurry."

"All men are in a hurry. I don't know what they want to achieve."

"I just came to say goodbye, it was nice meeting you."

"Kind of you to say so." She salaamed politely.

"And I apologise again for my occasional rudeness."

"That's all right. I, too, have realised that, after all, I am a mere singing woman. I liked you because you were different. Novelty is always attractive!"

"I was merely a fake Englishman."

"No matter. We have a fake English king. He dresses up like William IV and marries Englishwomen. He even has his tazias made in England."

Gautam looked at her in silence. What an exceptionally intelligent, sensible young woman she was. He was going to leave her here, alone with her thoughts in this room full of silver lamps and damask curtains, and return to his dreary little hole in Manektala, to be alone with his thoughts.

"You say you are a phoney firangi."

"Yes, and you meet real ones. . . That reminds me, I request you once again to keep Sujata Debi's plight in mind when you see Mr. Ashley next."

"Oh, not that boring topic again! Have a heart! Who keeps my plight in mind when they see me?"

"Are you unhappy? I thought you were on top of the world, as Lucknow's prima donna."

"Are you happy as a successful young man? I have always seen you in a pensive mood."

"Well, I have my problems. I am trying to build up my life, find a place for myself in the sun, as they say."

"Indeed! Even if you think you are master of your destiny, it is ultimately Fate which decides your life."

She crossed over to the balcony and looked out. A wedding procession was passing by, a comic play was being enacted on a float, jugglers displayed their tricks in its wake. An orchestra played merry tunes upon another "mobile throne" and was followed by the bride's lavishly decorated palki.

"Lucky girl," Champa mused aloud. After a few minutes she turned towards him.

"Well, sir," she resumed the formal stance of the day she had first met him. "You must not delay your departure. You don't belong here. You must reach Calcutta before the rivers are in spate. And may God give you no other sorrow except the sorrow for Hussain. This is how we bless one another in this city but I repeated this phrase out of sheer habit, for you know neither Hussain nor sorrow. So, goodbye!"

She made a bow with a faint smile and disappeared behind a damask curtain.

Gunga Din drove back to the main road. Gautam looked out at the busy street scene. Gallants swaggered in the lanes, officers of the Negro women's platoon marched past. Female crooks loitered in the alleys, opium-eaters had assembled in front of their dens. How fascinating the world was! Shakespeare had called it a stage, Bhartrihari, too.

They came out of the bazaar. The highway was full of camel-carriages, horses, elephants and sedan-chairs. The old yogi still sat under the tree outside the city gate. A log was burning in front of him. Gautam got down from the carriage and walked up to the shrine of the goddess. So far he had known her in the form of Kali, now she had shown herself as Jog Maya, Illusion, as well.

The yogi addressed him, "Going away too soon, traveller!"

"It is foolish to linger on the shores of a mirage, baba. Your city is an illusion. Jog Maya extended her ten arms to ensnare me, but she let me go. I am returning intact."

"None of us is intact, son," the ascetic said. "We are clay dolls made by the Potter and we keep breaking all the time. Do not be so sure of your strength." He picked up a little earth. "Look how fragrant it is. Take this handful of earth with you and place it in Jog Maya's temple in Cuttack. . ."

Gautam hesitated. Perhaps this fellow was a Tantric, and he was rapidly losing faith in his ancestral religion anyway.

"Take it, this is the dust of Lucknow, carry it with you. For the spell of this city is such that it keeps haunting you forever. You think you have come out of the Imambara Asafi's maze, but you are mistaken. Go. . ."

The coachman told him, "This yogi baba was a general in

Ali Janab Shuja-ud-Daulah's army. He took sanyas after our defeat at Buxar. . ."

Here was another strange custom of this country. After the Indian allies' defeat at Buxar, Nawab Mir Qasim of Bengal had put on the garb of a fakir. How did that help? Gautam wondered.

At nightfall they stopped at a serai which had been built by Raja Taket Rai, Asaf-ud-Daulah's famous Minister of Finance. The armed sepoys in Company uniform provoked much comment at the inn. "A baboo on his way to Fort William. Ask him, when is the Company Bahadur reducing our taxes? He would know."

They surrounded him in the courtyard. Most of them were peasants on their way to Lucknow, carrying their petitions. How innocent and good these people were. He felt sorry that he was leaving Oudh.

Torches flickered in the wind. Gautam was confused. He tried to reflect and analyse. Had there been lawlessness in India before the British came, commerce and industry wouldn't have flourished to such an extent that it attracted the European powers. True, we had no Roman Law, but did the English abide by the book when they broke their treaties with native rulers?

Neem leaves rustled in the gateway as Gautam lay awake on his cot. The inn-keeper's sharp-tongued wife was busy cooking for the night-runners of the King of Oudh who had arrived with the royal mail and were on their way to Delhi. Gautam had learned in Lucknow that Shuja-ud-Daulah's despatches used to reach the Peshwa's Court from Fyzabad to Poona in one week—well they were not as benighted and inefficient as the English claimed.

Why, why did we go down?

Because we are fatalists. King and commoner, ascetic and courtesan, all resigned to their fate. The night-runners' shadows were moving about on the quadrangle's walls. The point is that the Europeans have become devotees of Reason. We are still medieval and emotional. The English are surprised and say that the natives were happier under their mad kings than they are now. But perhaps these kings were not all that mad, really. . .

He felt a pang of sadness when he realised that this Faery Kingdom of Oudh, this Camelot, was probably not going to last long knowing, as he did, the might and shrewdness of the government he worked for in Fort William. After the death of Saadat Ali Khan the present-day Sultanate of Oudh was a sham and a farce. But this kingdom's candles burned at both ends and they gave out a lovely light. . .

24. The Pagoda Tree

12th September 1825

Honoured Sir,

I beg to state that I am Maria Teresa Thomas, licencee of "Pagoda Tree", Armenian Street, and I am pleased to inform you that I have now opened Tea Rooms in Ranee Mundy Galee, wherein the best Chinese beverage is served to August Personages of Calcutta. I am sending this epistle and the humble gifts to your office in Fort Willian so as not to cause unnecessary Annoyance, Suspicion and Speculation in the lofty mind of Lady Ashley, who I am told is in the family way, a delicate condition indeed.

As they say, once bitten twice shy. When I first came to Calcutta twenty-five years ago and sent you a letter through a harkaru, *your native Bibi bribed him and took the letter from him. Obviously she never gave the said epistle to you. Later I sent letters by Dawk. She intercepted them and through her native spies threatened me with Dire Consquences. Being a worshipper of Kalee, quoth she, she would get me eliminated through her sorcerers if I ever tried to contact you again. I gave up. No disrespect to you, Sir, but I thought it was not worth it. I mean Your Honour were not worth getting murdered for.*

I came to this City from Madras when my Annabella was full 10 years old. My Papa had died, also my only brother (in the war against Tipoo Saheb in Seringapatam). After the death of my mother, my father's Armenian partner sold our tavern and we shifted to Calcutta. Uncle Aratoon Aram Artoon opened an alehouse in Armenian Street and called it "The Pagoda Tree". Then we opened a punch house in Bow Bazaar Road and also employed a number of chee chee girls to entertain the Jacks. I did not marry as per the Force of Circumstances and led a Loose Life. Annabella is a Beauty. I did not want her to grow up in the bawdy house. (She is your daughter, Sire, but I do not press the point because you may not believe it.) However, I put her in the Convent of the Holy Cross in the French Territory of Chandernagore. In Calcutta I have not told a soul about you. As for poor Uncle Aratoon, he knew the whole story. He went to Dacca on business and died there. But Annabella I did inform, and she never evinced any desire to meet you. Being of a deeply religious bent of mind, she was more interested in the Holy Family. Eventually she took the veil and at the age of thirty-five, as Sister Eliza of the Holy Cross, she looked a sad old woman when I went to see her last year. She is shut up in the nunnery, cut off from the Vile World which usually ill-treats us Females. Annabella prays to the Virgin for your salvation. Being a Protestant you should have little hope of Salvation, anyway, but even a wicked man like you may be forgiven because your saintly, though illegitimate, daughter is praying for you day and night.

Now, why I am writing this letter is due to a happy occasion. The other day some journalists who frequent my Tea Rooms were discussing with much gusto and excitement your recent knighthood and also your marriage to a horsey aristocratic lady (no offence meant, Sir, I am only repeating what the above-mentioned journalists guffawed), and that you had safely come back to Calcutta and may soon be sent as Resident at the Court of the King of Oude. So, in order to congratulate you and in celebration of these Good Things happening to you (including your native Bibi's demise by snake-bite—served her right—pardon me, Sir), I herewith forward to you (you need not send me a thank-you note) a box of the best Assam tea and bottles of Scotch Whiskey.

Arise Sir Cyril, ha, ha.

Yours faithfully,
Maria Teresa
of " The Pagoda Tree."

Cyril finished reading the letter, took off his glasses and had a momentary blackout. He felt dizzy and his hands trembled as he tore the note-paper into bits. He bent his head and sat very still, as if in deep meditation, although he had never prayed. For him the Bank of England had long been more important than the Church of England.

He stood up, walked about in the room, stopped before the mirror of the hat-rack and looked at himself. Then he hissed aloud—"Rat!" The orderly on duty outside rushed in with a stick.

"Where is it, huzoor?"

"What?"

"The rat."

Saheb, who shot tigers, had become so scared of a mouse that he was trembling. The orderly looked under the table and all around the vast, high-ceilinged room.

"Come out, you susra!" he hollered in Bihari Urdu, beating the floor with his stick.

Meanwhile, Cyril took control of himself and said, "Never mind, Abdul, it came out for a moment but it's vanished again."

"Huzoor, we need a new office cat. Tom has become too old."

"Yes, yes. You can go now, Abdul."

The chaprasi left, still quite perturbed.

Cyril went back to his chair and closed his eyes. Now he had terrifying visions of Maria Teresa sending out copies of her letter to the Calcutta press. She had chosen the right time to appear, after thirty-six years, in order to blackmail him. He felt his heart sinking.

Abdul went straight to the Saheb's Man Friday, Joseph Lawrence.

"Saheb is behaving strangely, Sir. I think he is not well at all."

Jo, the old faithful, hurried to his boss's office and caught sight of Maria's gift basket placed upon the mantelpiece. Then he noticed the torn letter lying on the table. He grasped the situation in a moment. He had learnt about Maria Teresa recently when she shifted to the respectable tea-shop in Rani Mundi Gully. He had met her and, being a fellow Eurasian, also sympathised with her. She had said calmly: "It was my destiny that I suffer. Why did I allow myself to be seduced by him? Now I know that all men are like Cyril Ashley—why blame him?"

At Joseph Lawrence's request she had kept her story a dead secret. He realised that she was a thoroughly decent woman and would not dream of blackmailing Sir Cyril. Her servant had brought the hamper and letter to him in the morning. Now he wished he had told Cyril about her earlier and saved him this massive shock. Anyway, right now, what the boss needed was a good strong drink. Lawrence took out a bottle of Scotch from the beribboned basket, while the newly created knight stared at him blankly.

It did not take him long to announce, "Joseph, I am drunk like a lord," after which he passed out.

Joseph Lawrence felt his pulse. It seemed normal. He sent for Fort William's chief physician, Dr. McGregor.

Old McGregor arrived driving his buggy at top speed. He was a jovial and expansive Pickwickian character let loose in Fort William. He examined the great man who was still in a stupor and had been carried to the sofa.

"Sir Cyril is fine. Just overwork, needs complete rest," he told Lawrence and eyed the bottle of good cheer freshly imported frae bonnie Scotia.

In a few minutes Sir Cyril came to and said, "Oh, hello, doc, good afternoon. Have a drink. Joseph, take out the glasses and join us. Bandobast. Ek dum. Juldee."

They had a boisterous office party.

Cyril climbed up on his table and began singing a Cornish folksong at the top of his voice.

"What if I lay you down on the ground, my purty maid?"
"I'll rise up again, sweet Sir," she said.

McGregor took up the refrain zestfully,

"Sir," she said, "Sir," she said.
"I'll rise up again, sweet Sir," she said.

"They are celebrating Burra Saheb's Knighthood," two baboos remarked as they passed by in the corridor.

Cyril jumped down and began dancing a jig.

Hot cross buns
One a penny, two a penny
Hot cross buns.
If your daughter doesn't like them
Give them to your son. . .

He proceeded to make up his own rhyme:

My daughter is a holy
Holy Cross nun,
She can't like a hot cross bun.
Her Mammy is wanton, runs a den,
One a penny, two a penny. . .

Tears rolled down his face and he sat down. McGregor was busy drinking and did not notice his anguish. Cyril continued crying silently. He would never meet his first love, Maria, never see his daughter, a sad, middle-aged woman shut off from the world. And soon his high-born wife was going to produce for him a much desired, thorough-bred heir or heiress.

He wiped his face, placed his pince-nez on the tip of his nose like a preacher, and addressed his audience.

"Please turn to page number 0,0,0."

"Yes, Your Grace," his drunken congregation of two answered in unison, "0,0,0."

Cyril stood up and made up his own lullaby:

Rock-a-bye Baby
On Pagoda's tree
Your cradle is White
Your future is Bright
Your mother is a Lady
Your father a Knight. . .

Doctor and clerk sang the chorus. Suddenly, Cyril threw up his hands and implored, "Sister Eliza of the Holy Cross, pray for us sinners. . . ." Then he staggered to the sofa and plonked himself down on it.

Lady Ashley gave birth to a son. The Bishop of Calcutta baptised him Cyril Edwin Derek Ashley, and the Governor-General of India and his lady were his godparents.

After some time Gautam Nilambar resigned from his government job. He had acquired a Bachelor of Arts degree and became a teacher in a Brahmo Samaj school. One evening as Gautam sat in the Samaj office going through the day's newspapers, he came across a headline announcing Sir Cyril Ashley's sad demise at the age of 65. Gautam was overcome with grief. Cyril was a rare human being, they didn't come like him anymore.

Death came to Cyril Ashley in a lonely circuit house in a remote corner of Bihar. He had returned on horseback after inspecting his indigo plantations. His orderly had taken off his riding boots, he had bathed and changed for dinner and was awaiting his usual sundowner in the drawing room when, all of a sudden, he felt he was going to die.

He stammered and could not call out, Koi Hai— he had had a massive stroke, and died quietly in his armchair.

Sir Cyril Ashley was buried in a small European cemetery in the nearby district headquarters. He had retired a few years earlier from the Company's service and had spent most of his time reading Persian and Sanskrit classics. Something seemed to have snapped within him after that fateful Morning of Revelations in Fort William on September 14, 1825. His friends and subordinates attributed his unhappiness to his bad marriage.

Upcountry papers carried long articles eulogising the deceased. He was one of the Empire builders, a noted Orientalist and an immensely likeable person. The Royal Asiatic Society of Bengal and Fort William College were closed for a day, and special church services were held in Calcutta and Lucknow.

His unpleasant wife sailed back to England with little Edwin Derek Ashley.

25. The Waterway of Tears

In Lucknow, Ghaziuddin Hyder was succeeded by an equally flamboyant Nasiruddin Hyder. An opera titled *The Barber of Lucknow* could be written about the King's French coiffeur, de Russett, because he was as unscrupulous as Figaro, hero of the French opera, *The Barber of Seville*. Nasiruddin Hyder's maid, Dhania Mehri, had also become very influential. The King had bestowed upon her husband the title of Raja Mehra. Many noblemen of the Court went to England, some became Freemasons. Lucknow had a modern racecourse and tennis courts called gend-khanas. Nasiruddin's successors, Mohammad Ali and Amjad Ali, were lack-lustre and pious.

Vajid Ali Shah, the tenth ruler of Oudh, became a legend in his lifetime. He endeared himself to the people as Akhtar Piya, or Jan-i-Alam—life and soul of the world. Like Hussain Shah Nayak of Jaunpur and Sultan Baz Bahadur of Malwa, he was an accomplished musician. He composed thumris and dadras, perfected the dance style of kathak and created the ballet called Ras Lila or Rahas in which he danced as Krishna. In the annual Jogia Mela or Spring Festival held at Qaiser Bagh everybody wore yellow, signifying the colour of mustard. Vajid Ali Shah wore the ochre robes of a yogi, and his favourite dancer was dressed as a jogan.

There was fun and frolic all year round. People loved Jan-i-Alam. When he went out, two officers rode ahead with boxes in which the commoners put their petitions. The King attended to the petitions himself.

In January 1856 Sir James Outram, the new Resident, arrived in Lucknow and told Vajid Ali Shah to quit because he was no good. The Company's army was given seven hours to sack Lucknow if the King did not agree to step down. The King's mother, Malika Kishwar, argued forcibly with Outram. No way—Vajid Ali had to go. Most people in Britain felt that the forced abdication was unfair. Jan-i-Alam's advisors asked him to take his case to London. The Hindu populace made a *kabat*: *Hazrat jatey hain London, Kirpa karo Raghu Nandan*

—the venerable King is going to London, come to his aid, O Lord Rama.

He was to be banished to Calcutta. The grief-stricken populace cried and wailed when the ex-King climbed on to his carriage called Bad-i-Bahari, Breeze of Spring, and left for Cawnpore. The city was plunged in gloom. Muddabir-ud-Daulah, Raja Jwala Parshad and Mir Munshi Raja Daulat Rai Shauq insisted on accompanying him. He asked them to stay back in Lucknow because they were too old to travel. Mir Hasan "Londoni" had brought an English wife from Britain who had written a book about Lucknow which had become a bestseller in England. Mir Hasan also stayed back due to his infirmity, but a large number of royal relatives, courtiers and servants went with the King to Calcutta.

After the abdication Revenue Minister, Mushir-ud-Daulah, Moin-ul Mulk Maharaja Balkrishan Jasarat Jung and others went to the Residency and were placed in charge of the English officers. The King's property and valuables were auctioned, his elephants, horses and cattle sold. When his tuskers were being auctioned some of them scooped up dust in their trunks and squirted it upon their heads. They shed tears, too. The Sahebs asked if they had sore eyes—the mahouts replied that they had never seen the elephants behave like this.

The ex-King was taken on a steamer from Cawnpore to Allahabad. His traditionally faithful ally, Kashi Naresh Maharaja Ishwari Parshad Narain Singh, requested him to break journey and stay in Banaras for a few days. When he arrived there the Maharaja observed all the protocol as of old. He stayed there for fourteen days. On May 13 the mournful caravan reached Calcutta. A Kothi belonging to the Maharaja of Burdwan in Garden Reach was rented for him.

Akhtar Piya had not fully recovered from the trauma of his forced exile. The hardships of the journey by steamer, train and coach from Lucknow to Calcutta made him physically ill. He gave up the idea of going to England. But his mother Malika Kishwar, widow of King Amjad Ali Shah, was a politically astute and strong woman; she decided to proceed to Britain herself, present the case of unlawful dispossession before Parliament, and meet Queen Victoria herself.

Much earlier, Asaf-ud-Daulah's mother, Nawab Bahu Begum, had defied Warren Hastings. She was also a good poet. About tears she had once written—*Tari ki raah se jata hai qafala dil kae*—a convoy of sorrows has come out on the waterway.

The royal party prepared to leave. Her Majesty, Badshah Bahu Malika Kishwar Nawab Taj Ara Begum was accompanied by her younger son, General Sikander Hashmat, Prince Hamid Ali, son of the ex-King, Vakil Masihuddin Khan and a number of noblemen, ladies-in-waiting and servants. One hundred and ten men and women boarded the *S.S. Bengal* at midnight, June 18, 1856. There was a heartening send-off, crowds at the pier broke down and wept. Everyone had very little hope of getting any justice from the East India Company's Court of Directors.

When the ship passed by the Kothi of Matia Burj the 37-year-old ex-King stood on the upper-floor veranda and waved a tearful goodbye to his mother, younger brother and son.

It was a sad journey. The Queen Mother, Malika Kishwar, and her ladies-in-waiting stayed in seclusion in the staterooms. Sometimes they held majlises in which the *soz-khwan* women recited the dirges for Imam Hussain in classical ragas. The English crew thought they were singing melancholy songs. The box containing the Queen Mother's priceless jewels fell overboard at Suez and was never retrieved. Perhaps it was stolen. The voyage seemed to be jinxed.

From Suez, Malika Kishwar's party travelled to Cairo where they rented the villa of Ibrahim Pasha. On the tenth day, they left Cairo by train in the morning and reached Alexandria the same evening. Hormuzjee Parsi, Royal Treasurer, joined them in Alexandria. Then they boarded the *S.S. Indus*. The boat cast anchor in Southampton harbour on August 20, and the party was accorded a royal reception by the Mayor. The Queen Mother disembarked in her gold-and-silver palki, the carpeted pathway to the coach curtained on either side. H.M. Malika Kishwar was escorted by *khwaja saras*, the royal eunuchs. Major Bird, a personal friend of Vajid Ali Shah who had preceded the royal entourage, was present at the pier. He requested Her Majesty to shake hands with the Mayor through the venetian blinds of the coach. Thousands of spectators cheered and shouted, "Hurray, hurray!"

The entourage included a court jester, cooks, footmen, maids and the royal sweeper, Mansa. There were five hundred trunks, some of which contained raw foodstuff and spices to prepare Indian meals in England. The party was taken to the Royal Park Hotel. Crowds had assembled in front of the hotel as well. Major Bird was back on the soil of liberal England. He addressed the public and made an impassioned speech.

"Ladies and gentlemen," he said, "The Queen Mother of Oudh is sixty. In her old age she has undertaken this long voyage in order to seek justice in Britain. As an honest Englishman, I must tell you that her son was our loyal friend. He helped the Hon'ble John Company with enormous loans which the Company never paid back. Tell me, if the Emperor of France or another monarch mightier than Queen Victoria breaks his pledges and forcibly dethrones Her Majesty, would you be happy?"

"No! No!" shouted the crowd.

On August 22 a throng of lords and ladies of Albion came to the hotel. The Princes held their durbar in the ballroom, Majors Brendon and Rogers acted as interpreters. On August 30 the party reached London by train. Harley House was rented to accommodate them.

The Queen Mother's arrival was officially ignored in London, perhaps because Major Bird's Southampton speech was not to the government's liking. Londoners were fairminded, and they would not have approved of the high-handed manner in which the King of Oudh had been deposed. On October 11, 1856, General Mirza Sikander Hashmat met Queen Victoria in Crystal Palace.

On January 16, 1857 the Princes, accompanied by Mashiuddin Khan and Major Bird and others, went in a procession of five coaches to India House. Spectators thronged the pavements. The delegation was received by English officials who doffed their hats. The Princes were taken to see the

Indian Museum and meet the Directors of the East India Company. During the banquet Masihuddin Khan told them to prove the charges levied by the former Resident of Oudh, General Sleeman, against Vajid Ali Shah. "If he is found not guilty and you still justify the annexation, we will take the case to your Parliament."

The Directors made no reply.

On January 21, 1857, the Great Sahebs came to a lavish dinner at Harley House the Princes hosted. Money was running out. The Queen Mother sold a necklace for two lakh rupees to a lord, who bought it for his bride.

H.M. Malika Kishwar went to meet Queen Victoria. She was received by eight Englishwomen who had lived in India and could speak Urdu. Malika Kishwar wore a simple Egyptian dress she had bought in Cairo. She was accompanied by her son and grandson and the envoy, Mashiuddin Khan. Queen Victoria shook hands with the Princes and asked the Malika about her voyage. The Queen Mother said, "We had never sailed in a boat on our sweet little stream called the Gomti. Now we have crossed the seven seas to seek justice for our son."

Queen Victoria was probably not amused, though she expressed her sympathy for the hardships experienced by Queen Mother Kishwar during her journey. Then she changed the subject and said, "We have ten children, some of whom are still in their cribs. The eldest, the Prince of Wales, is thirteen years old. Will you allow him to come in?"

Malika Kishwar said, "Yes, indeed. We would love to see him."

The Prince of Wales was called in with his governess. Malika Kishwar graciously made him sit near her and, according to Eastern royal custom, took off her diamond necklace and put it round the British heir's neck. The ornament's pendant contained a phial of rare perfume. Victoria asked about it. Malika Kishwar said, "In our country when a guest leaves, he is given a phial of perfume."

The interpreter did not translate this correctly and Queen Victoria thought Malika wished to leave. She said to the Indian queen, "Perhaps you are very tired. Do take a little rest over here before you go. We'll meet again and talk at leisure some other time."

The case was presented in Parliament. Lord Dalhousie who had come home after his annexation of Indian states, expressed his inability to attend Parliament and answer the questions put by the Members, due to indisposition. Most Members of the House of Commons said the annexation of Oudh was unlawful. Unfortunately, the Sepoy Mutiny broke out in Meerut Cantonment on May 9, 1857, and this totally altered the situation.

In Matia Burj, Calcutta, the ex-King had just finished his early morning prayers when he was arrested and jailed in Fort William. His former people said, "Joseph of Canaan is imprisoned in Pharaoh's Egypt."

Telegraphic news from India, of English men and women being massacred by the mutineers enraged the British. Public opinion turned against the royal visitors—according to them it was these very people who had instigated the rebellion in India. Malika Kishwar realised that the situation was now hopeless and dangerous. She left for France from where she planned to go to Mecca via Egypt. In Paris she fell ill and died.

There was no love lost between France and England because the British had ousted the French from India. The government of France telegraphed the British Foreign Office: 'La Majeste died on French soil. She was our guest. We will give her a state funeral'. No satisfactory reply was received from Whitehall. The French gave a fitting farewell to the poor queen who had died of a broken heart. Sikander Hashmat was too grief-stricken to walk along with the cortege, so the French Prime Minister made him sit in his coach. Multitudes wore mourning dress and accompanied the procession, thousands of Frenchwomen waved black kerchiefs from their balconies. Malika Kishwar was buried with full state honours in the compound of the Turkish embassy.

The shock of his mother's sudden death proved fatal for General Sikander Hashmat who had been ailing for some time. He died in February 1858. He was also given a state funeral, and was buried in the mosque yard of the Ottoman Embassy. It was uncanny—the Prince's four-year-old daughter also died, and followed her father and grandmother to the grave.

Eight months earlier, Malika Kishwar's fearless daughter-in-law, Queen Hazrat Mahal, had indeed declared war on the Company's government in Lucknow. She had instigated and inspired the entire population of Oudh to take up arms against the British.

26. *The Queen and Her Knights*

It was a pleasant afternoon in the winter of 1868. Two elegant men in their late sixties sat on a lakeside bench in Calcutta, conversing slowly. The older man wore an embroidered Kashmiri choga, his friend was rather nattily dressed in tweeds. He looked the kind of person Britons sneeringly referred to as a WOG—a Westernised Oriental Gentleman. The two friends had met a few days ago after nearly forty-five years. It was a chance meeting at a mehfil of Hindustani music held in the house of the nominal Nawab Bahadur of Murshidabad.

"When Sultan-i-Alam was exiled from Lucknow I was away in Iraq and Turkish Arabia on pilgrimage. In Medina I read in an Egyptian newspaper about Her Majesty Malika Kishwar's departure for Inglistan from Alexandria. I had enough money with me, so I rushed to Alexandria and took the next ship to Southampton. In October '58 I returned from Europe and found that Lucknow had changed. My house had disappeared, too." The man in the gray Kashmiri robe continued, "They had demolished a large part of the city and laid seven wide roads to help quick troop movement. They had engineers, sappers and miners. The latest armaments. Telegraphic communication, tinned food for soldiers and a network of our own men who spied for them. . .

"Begum Hazrat Mahal's massive lashkar had a lot of patri

otic fervour, little training and less organisation. They had antiquated guns. And yet, and yet, within a month they liberated Oudh with sheer guts.

"On his way to Calcutta Jan-i-Alam had stopped over in Banaras at the request of Kashi Naresh Maharaja Ishwari Parshad Narain Singh. The Maharaja scattered rose petals on the pathway and walked alongside the royal carriage as he escorted the ex-King to the palace. He presented the customary nazar. Sultan-i-Alam touched it and said, 'Keep it. I can't give you the usual gifts.'

"Sultan-i-Alam Vajid Ali Shah's chief queen, Begum Hazrat Mahal, had stayed back in Lucknow and she and her military advisors held their meetings in the House of Virgins."

"House of ?" Gautam asked, bewildered.

"Virgins, *achhutis*—pure women. King Nasiruddin Hyder's stepmother, Badshah Begum, had appointed a bunch of highborn spinsters to look after the rituals of Moharrum in her Imambara. These women were supposed to be impeccable—*achhutis*. Lucknow was crawling with British spies. Nasiruddin Hyder was a clever fellow—he had an underwater house built for his secret cabinet meetings, probably near Chhattar Manzil*, because he was anxious to get rid of British domination. He let it be known that the house was built for the inaccessible *achhutis*. The ruse worked. He met the scholars and vazirs and held discussions in this hide-out in absolute secrecy.

"This King died young. He has been defamed as a sod and an imbecile, but he set up a modern observatory and hospital, an English school and a printing press, and he sailed a steamboat in the Gomti."

The Bengali gentleman stroked his grey moustache in amazement.

"Begum Hazrat Mahal also used this inaccessible place for her cabinet sessions."

"Well, there are more things in heaven and earth than. . ." the learned Babu murmured.

The nawab continued: "The Mutiny broke out in the sec-

---

*After 1947 a labyrinth of underground passages was excavated near Chhattar Manzil. These tunnels probably led to the underwater house.

ond week of May and the Queen's troops defeated the English at Chinhat near Lucknow on the 30th of June. The English took refuge in the Residency, where they were held under siege for 140 days."

"Ah! The Residency!" the Bengali gentleman repeated nostalgically. As a young clerk he had worked there for a few months in 1823. And at Chinhat where the nawab once had his garden house. Whatever happened to Champa Jan and Munshi Shankar? He didn't want to think.

The nobleman went on, "Begum Hazrat Mahal's 14 year-old son Birjees Qadr was enthroned as Wali in the absence of his deposed father. The Begum became his Regent, Maharaja Balkrishan was reappointed Finance Minister.

"To the traditional slogan of *Khalque Khuda ki, Mulk Badshah ka*, the words *Hukum Company Bahadur ka* had been added ever since the time the English gained political authority in north India. Now the town-criers and drummers dropped the second—Company Bahadur's hukum had been abolished.

"The exiled Peshwa Baji Rao II died in Bethur near Cawnpore, in 1851. His adopted son, Nana Rao, sent his vakil to England with a petition asking for a pension. The vakil, Azimullah, was a remarkable fellow, entirely self-made. They say his mother was an ayah and that he himself had worked as a butler. He learnt to speak and write fluent French and English and became a school teacher in Cawnpore. Handsome and suave, he was lionised by the ladies of English aristocracy in London. But he failed in his mission—Nana Saheb's petition was turned down by the Court of Directors. Azimullah Khan returned to Cawnpore and English women continued to send him love-letters.

"Now Nana Saheb also declared his independence and assumed the title of Peshwa Bahadur. Hindu Criminal Law was introduced according to which offenders' limbs were mutilated. Nana Rao's soldiers besieged the English in the city, Azimullah Khan led the revolt. He had met French and Russian statesmen in Europe and studied the war strategies of the Ottomans in Constantinople; he became the Mutiny leader, Danka Shah's advisor.

"Cawnpore was re-taken by the English, Nana Saheb's palace and temples were blown up. He took his family to the garhi of the local chowdhary at Fatehpur Chowrassi, midway between Cawnpore and Allahabad. The Queen Regent sent her Minister of War, Raja Jailal Singh Nusrat Jung to escort him to Lucknow, and saw to the re-decoration of Sheesh Mahal for the Peshwa herself. On his arrival he was given an eleven-gun salute, but he said perhaps it could have been 21 guns."

Gautam smiled sardonically.

The nawab continued: "Her Majesty said 21 guns are reserved for visiting monarchs. Twenty-five thousand rupees were spent on the feast for him. I am told Begum Hazrat Mahal sent him a robe of honour, a sword, jewels and a caparisoned elephant with a silver howdah. . ."

Gautam listened, wide-eyed. Then he said, "Couldn't this extravagance be curtailed in war-time?"

"This was Lukhnavi wazadari, Nilambar Mian."

"No wonder you chaps lost the war," the babu commented. The nawab opened his silver betel-case and took out a betel-leaf. His friend lighted his cheroot. The nawab began again.

"Birjees Qadr's birthday was celebrated with great fanfare. Some Englishwomen who had been taken prisoners-of-war, wore Lukhnavi dress and dyed their palms with henna. . ."

"I thought all of them were languishing in the besieged Residency?"

"Not all, Nilambar Mian. Truth is the first victim, etc. . . . .

"On the 16th of September Colin Campbell, Lord Clyde, entered Lucknow with his army. The Queen had summoned the feudal barons to her aid, and swashbuckling knights arrived on their charges from all sides.

"Raja Debi Baksh Singh of Gonda, Raja Sukh Darshan, Lal Madho Singh of Amethi, Rana Beni Madho Singh Bahadur of Beswara, Raja Man Singh of Shahgunj, Raja Hanwant Singh of Kalakankar, Raja Gulab Singh, and many more. It was a galaxy of the descendants of the Sun and the Moon," Nawab Kamman waxed eloquent, "and the Pathan and Sheikh taluqdars of Nanpara, Malihabad, Sandila, Mahmudabad, Bhatwamau, etc.

"The Begum visited the front lines on elephant and palki. Our men fought valiantly in defence of the city. On the 25th of February 1858, in the fierce battle of Alam Bagh, the Begum again rode out on elephant and took part in the action. Raja Man Singh of Shahgunj showed such valour in Alam Bagh that Begum Hazrat Mahal called him her son and gave him her own dupatta, along with the robe of honour.

"And the Brahmin-zadi Laxmi Bai died fighting like a man in the field of honour in Gwalior.

"There was this jolly Frenchman who used to be a confectioner in Lucknow. He sought me out in Paris and narrated to me the story of the two valiant queens, Laxmi Bai and Hazrat Mahal. 'Laxmi Bai was like Jean d'Arc—just like Jean d'Arc,' he said in wonder. Henri also told me that a French priest, Father Joseph, had become a murid of Maulvi Ahmadullah Shah and was called Yusuf Ali Shah.

"The Goras pounded Qaiser Bagh with cannon-balls. General James Outram had come back to India and was campaigning in Lucknow along with Lord Clyde, Commander-in-Chief. He sent word to the royal ladies to vacate the palace because he was going to have his breakfast there at 10 a.m. the next day. When she saw that the fall of Lucknow was imminent, the Queen dressed Birjees Qadr in the ritual green garment of a fakir of Imam Hussain. The women bared their heads, let down their hair and stood under the midnight sky, crying, 'Ya Ali, Ya Hussain'. This is a rite followed in extreme distress, Nilambar Mian."

"The pity of it, Iago, the pity of it," the learned Mr. Dutt sighed.

"Abyssinian women soldiers died fighting in the battle of Sikandar Bagh. The Queen was in Begum Kothi. Her advisors requested her to leave the city, and she left Lucknow on the 21st of March, 1858, in a palki, escorted by Rana Beni Madho Singh. Her entourage and soldiers followed. The British captured Lucknow when the Jallad-i-Falak Mirrikh[1] was on the ascent. Throughout the time of the Mutiny, Mars had glowed

---

[1]"The Killer Planet", Mars.

in the night skies like a red-hot coal or a blood-shot eye. You must have seen it too, Nilambar Mian.

"Half the town followed the Queen—it was a stupendous exodus. When Her Majesty reached Bondi in Behraich district, the place turned into a miniature peacetime Lucknow. The Begum stayed in Bondi for eleven months. Meanwhile General Clyde planned to trap the royalists in Behraich. The knights continued to fight back in the countryside, and Maulvi Ahmadullah Shah was killed in Shahjehanpur on the 5th of June, 1858. His body was torn to pieces and burnt in the local kerbala where tazias are buried on the tenth day of Moharrum. His severed head was hung from the gates of the kotwali.

"Ahmadullah Shah was the only warrior who twice confounded Lord Clyde's strategies. Even English generals admitted that he was a true patriot and a true soldier—he never killed an innocent person.

"Raja Beni Madho Singh had reached his castle in Shankarpur. He told Lord Clyde that he would surrender his fort because it was his property, but he would not give himself up because his person belonged to his Sovereign. Meanwhile, Nana Rao and others had regrouped in the forest fort of Nanpara. Lord Clyde marched up to the fort, they vanished. He chased them up and down the region, blowing up forts. It was like the English sport of hares and hounds that I had seen in their own country, where they rode out wearing red coats and their hounds hunted poor, helpless vixen. Here Lord Clyde was Master of the Hunt, followed by his Redcoats, but there were no hares. They were confronted by lion-hearted men.

"The Begum did not accept defeat. Queen Victoria's famous Proclamation was published on the 1st of November, 1858. Our own Queen issued a counter-proclamation in which she logically challenged the British Empress' statements point by point."

The nawab cleared his throat, paused, then continued, "In the Firman she wrote, 'The Proclamation says that all contracts and agreements entered into by the Company will be accepted by Queen Victoria. Let the people carefully observe this ruse. The Company has seized the whole of Hindustan and if this arrangement be accepted, what then is new in it? The Company called the young Raja of Bharatpur a son, then took his territory. The Raja of Punjab was carried off to London.

" 'They expelled Peshwa Baji Rao from Poona and interned him for life in Cawnpore. Their breach of faith with Sultan Tipu is well known. The Raja of Banaras they imprisoned in Agra. On one side they hanged Nawab Shamsuddin of Ferozepur, Jharka, on the other they took off their hats and salaamed him.'

"That reminds me, Nilambar Mian, Outram had come home on leave while we were in London. I was told that one day he turned up at Harley House in mufti, carrying a rolled umbrella like any average Londoner. He said to General Sikander Hashmat, 'I am Outram who took Lucknow from you, I have come to pay you a visit.' The Prince asked him to take a seat. He kept standing, according to protocol, because Sikander Hashmat was a prince of royal blood. . . so, what was I saying?"

"The Begum's Firman."

"Ah, yes. So Her Majesty wrote that these are old affairs, but recently in defiance of treaties and oaths and despite the fact that they owed us millions of rupees, and on the pretext of misgovernment and the discontent of our people, they took our country. If our people were discontented with Vajid Ali Shah, how is it they are content with us? And no ruler ever experienced such loyalty and devotion of life and goods as we have done in recent months!

"Queen Victoria's Proclamation says that the Christian religion alone is true. What has the administration of justice to do with the truth or falsehood of a religion? asked the Begum. She ended her Firman adding that the English promised no better employment for Hindustanis than making roads and digging canals. If people cannot clearly see what this means, there is no help for them."

Gautam was astounded. He had never heard of this counter-proclamation. The nawab had come to the end of his unhappy narration.

"The Queen's knights continued their battle in the countryside", he said. "Ultimately Rana Beno Madho Singh, Nana Rao, Bala Saheb, Jwala Parshad, Khan Bahadur Khan, Mammu Khan, all of them were pushed out by Lord Clyde to the Nepal border. They crossed the Rapti and went into Nepal, but Rana Jung Bahadur refused to help them because he had become loyal to the British Crown. Raja Jailal Singh, the Begum's Minister of War, and Jwala Parshad were executed.

"With his seal of 'Peshwa Bahadur', Nana Saheb wrote from Deogarh in Urdu to Maj. Richardson that he would rather die with honour than accept the terms of surrender. He dated his letter 22nd Ramzan, 1275 A.H.

"Rana Beni Madho Singh was also camping with his womenfolk at Deogarh. He told them, 'I am leaving. Don't desert the Begum, stay with her.' Then he made a heap of the jewels and money he had brought with him. He told his soldiers, 'Those of you who want wealth, take it and go away. Those who want death with honour, come with me.' Two hundred and fifty men stayed back with him. They fought the Gurkhas and were killed, the Rana was taken unawares and shot in the back.

"The glamorous French-speaking Azimullah Khan, Nana Rao, his brother Bala Saheb, all succumbed to malaria in the rain-forests of the Terai. This is precisely what General Clyde had planned.

"The Begum was given asylum in Nepal and still lives there. Now eminent Englishmen admire her courage and her charisma—how all of Oudh took up arms on her call."

Nawab Kamman fell silent and gazed at his turquoise ring. The precious stone, feroze, signified victory.

27. Bakht Khan, Lord Governor-General

A workman passed by carrying a step-ladder, on his way to

light the gas lamps. The two old men watched him in silence. After a long pause Nawab Kamman resumed his dolorous saga.

"And the significant thing is, that despite their total victory, they are still afraid of Sultan-i-Alam's immense popularity. Why, they recently demolished a pavilion in Qaiser Bagh where he used to preside over his Jogia Mela, dressed in yellow. This Basant festival was open to the general public. The people of Lucknow gathered at the pavilion and wept, remembering him. Now the authorities are maligning him as a debauch. I assure you, Nilambar Mian, he is no rake, he has never missed a single early morning prayer."

Gautam kept quiet. These were sensitive matters involving one's faith and intense personal loyalties. Then he said haltingly, "Nawab Saheb, our customs of polygamy and harems seem odd to westerners."

"They are hypocrites! Over there they have mistresses and bastard children. Here, even a dasi-putra has a certain right of inheritance.

"Anyway, they occupied Lucknow, and Sikhs, Gurkhas and 93rd Highlanders sacked the city. Begum Kothi and the Imambaras were plundered, the colossal chandeliers of Imambara Hussainabad now lighted the new girjaghars of Lucknow. In their frenzy the English razed half the city. The Imambara Asafi was turned into military barracks, the royalists were disarmed and the troops of Raja Hanuwant Singh of Hardoi laid down their arms. But, like Beni Madho Singh, Raja Hanuwant Singh refused to accept defeat. 'My men owed allegiance to me, they have given up. I owe allegiance to my Raj Mata Hazrat Mahal, I will not surrender. You can kill me.' He was immediately shot by the firing squad." The nawab wiped a tear and added proudly, "These men were Surajvanshi and Chandervanshi Rajputs of Oudh."

Dutt Babu pursed his lips, then said with some hesitation, "Nawab Saheb, you must have heard of Mr Charles Darwin—"

"Yes, I have, indeed," the nawab replied somewhat sharply. "Descent from sun and moon is a metaphor, all mythology is a metaphor of eternal verities, mon cher ami.

"I had gone to France with Malika Kishwar's party feeling

utterly miserable. Owing to the Sepoy War my Rastogi* had not sent me any *hundis* from Lucknow. The fugitive royals had enough troubles of their own, so I found myself down and out on the streets of Paris.

"Henri, who used to once cater for my chai-pani parties in Lucknow, now introduced me to some young Frenchmen who were studying at L'Ecole Orientale. I started giving them private tuition in Persian. One of the students booked a passage for me on board a French ship and that's how I got back to Lucknow, via Pondicherry. As I told you earlier, the city was lying in ruins. I wandered in a daze in desolate lanes, looking for my next-of-kin. One evening I sat down exhausted amidst broken columns and fallen arches and recalled Mirza Rafi Sauda's dirge. After the sack of Delhi by Abdali, he had lamented:

> *Owls hoot where once we heard Raga Hindol,*
> *At night you only see the light*
> *Of the torch-like, flaming eyes of ghouls*†

"Eventually, I found out that my family had joined the Great Exodus after the departure of Begum Hazrat Mahal and managed to reach our tiny garhi in Neelampur. I went there and after some time, brought them to Matia Burj.

"Now, wherever I see an ancient banyan and its beards, I avert my eyes. They remind me of corpses dangling from roadside trees. When I came back to India the hanging mela was in full swing. Twenty-seven thousand Muslims were hanged in Delhi. Thousands of Hindus and Muslims were sent to the gallows in Cawnpore, Allahabad and other places. In Lucknow they installed the gallows in a row on a roadside. Forty to fifty persons per day was usual for the hangmen, and the corpses were kept dangling till the next batch was brought. Many were executed on the mere suspicion of being rebels and lots of

---

*Till recent times the Rastogi banias of Lucknow managed the spendthrift Muslim elite's financial affairs.

†*Ghol-i-biyabani*, or *agiya baital*, who are supposed to be invisible on dark nights except for their fiery eyes.

distinguished men were tied to cannons and blown up.

"They hanged a few old women, too, for good measure and a young courtesan, Azizan Bai, who had fought as a soldier in Cawnpore. Urdu poet Imam Bakhsh Sehbai and his sons were shot. Maj. Hodson even presented two Mughal princes' severed heads on a platter to the old King." The nawab's voice quivered.

His friend was distressed. What can I say to him? I can't even begin to gauge the depth of his anguish. He has lost an entire civilisation, and yet he is in the dock as the culprit.

Gautam was well-acquainted with the version of the Mutiny which the English press of India had published. The Siege of the Lucknow Residency had already become a literary legend in England and Anglo-India. The heroism of British generals and soldiers, the bravery of European students of Lucknow's La Martiniere College, the massacre of English families all over north India, the treacherous drowning of boats carrying English women and children in the Ganges off Cawnpore—all of which was true, too.

In the crowded reading rooms of Calcutta's public libraries Gautam had gone through the English ladies' diaries published in the magazines of London during '57–58. Bookshelves were full of novels, poems and general reminiscences coming out from England. In the smoking rooms of exclusive clubs, in drawing rooms of the Civil Lines across the country, in the mess bars in cantonments, civilians and war veterans narrated their horrible experiences. They talked of the loyalty and bravery of their native subordinates, domestic servants and sepoys, and the brutality of the rebels. After Hyder Ali and Tipu, Tantiya Tope, Kunwar Singh and Danka Shah were the new bogeymen in the nurseries of Anglo-India.

How much can one know? The nawab had quoted Sauda. How would Gautam know about the Urdu poets Sauda, Mir, Nazir and Insha and the overtly political poetry they had written after the rise of British power in India? Or Mus-hafi, who had openly said in a couplet: "How cunningly the Firangis have taken away the glory and wealth of Hindustan!" Who had heard of them in Britain? Lord Byron could sing of the

Isles of Greece, stir the West and go off to fight the Terrible Turk. The Greeks were admired for their War of Independence, but 1857 was condemned as the native rebels' mutiny.

The nawab drew the string of his tiny purse and took out a pinch of chewing tobacco.

Today in 1868, who knew of the anti-British native press of pre-Mutiny years? On May 31, 1857, *Dehli Urdu Akhbar* had challenged two English newspapers: "Where are the boastful *Englishman* and *The Friend of India*? Now they should see how the so-called stupid and incompetent natives have routed the high and mighty Britons."

The native Christian compositors of the English *Delhi Gazette* were slain while they were typesetting the news of the outbreak of insurgency at Meerut. The office was destroyed, the paper closed down. In June 1857 the leaders at Delhi drafted a democratic constitution using English terminology. General Mohammad Bakht Khan, C-in-C, was appointed "Lord Governor General Bahadur". His High Command included General Talyar Khan, Brig. Sheo Charan Singh, General Thakur, Brig. Jeo Ram, Brig. Misra, General Sidhari Singh, Brigade Major Hira Singh and Maj. Gauri Shankar. An order was issued from the C-in-C's office to all units to attend the general parade at 4 p.m. on August 14, 1857.

One Urdu paper wrote: "Our soldiers should not loiter in the capital because Hazrat Dehli's water induces lethargy. Once you take a stroll in Chandni Chowk-Jama Masjid-Dariba area and taste the laddoo and qalaqand of Ghantewallah halwai, you begin to take it easy.

". . . Mirza Birjees Qadr, the boy king of Oudh, and Maulvi Ahmadullah, alias Danka Shah, have ordered the Chakladar of Gorakhpur and all administrators to courteously bring the Sikh queen, mother of the deposed Maharaja Dalip Singh of Punjab, from her exile in Nepal and re-install her on the Khalsa gaddi of Lahore." (The plan was foiled by Rana Jung Bahadur.)

Sirajul Akhbar proudly carried the Court Circular from the Red Fort and reported the daily engagements of an active and conscientious monarch. In July '57 the paper's title was changed to *Akhbarul Zafar*—News of Victory. On July 12 it carried the following: "Some Englishmen disguised themselves as lehnga-clad females and got into a bullock cart (at Jhajjar). How are the mighty fallen! These were the people who did not even nod in acknowledgement when a native salaamed them. . ."

The populace could not hate the firangis enough—they were arrogant and insulting. And they had tried to subvert their faith by greasing the sepoys' cartridges with cow's fat and pig's lard. The sepoys were ordered to cut these with their teeth. That, of course, was what ignited the uprising but there were other reasons as well. Economic exploitation, high taxation, dethroning kings and chieftains which made for general unemployment, the missionaries' insensitive verbal attacks on the religions of the people. . . The resentment had been building up over the years. The pent-up anger exploded in the macabre catastrophe of 1857—it all boiled down to 'Kill the Firangi and save your Din and Dharma'. In Dehli an elderly woman rider in green fought alongside men, shouting "Din! Din!" The Urdu press reported that the king awarded her another horse.

Maulvi Mohammed Baqar was the editor of *Dehli Urdu Akhbar*. Principal Taylor of Delhi College sought shelter in the editor's house, and Maulvi Baqar made Taylor disguise himself as an Indian woman when the mob arrived to lynch him. Before he escaped through the back door, he gave Baqar a bundle of papers and said, "If Delhi is re-taken by us, give these papers to the first Briton you meet."

The mob got to him and beat him to death.

During those months of independence, the dak system was excellently maintained between Delhi and Lucknow. Urdu news weeklies were being published regularly. Begum Hazrat Mahal sent her Vakil with one lakh fifty thousand rupees, a crown and jewels to his Majesty Bahadur Shah II in Delhi.

The Urdu papers printed fairly accurate reports from all the battle-fronts, gleefully publishing the news of the murder of Englishmen and the burning of their bungalows and establishments. When the rebels' occupation of Agra was celebrated in the Red Fort, Indian musicians also played an orchestra of western instruments, but the euphoria and excitement did not last long.

After a fierce battle Dehli was recaptured by the English in March, 1858.

Maulvi Baqar kept his word and gave the bundle left by the late Taylor to an English colonel. He read Taylor's note scribbled in Latin—*Maulvi Mohammed Baqar did not try to save my life*. Baqar was summarily shot by a firing squad. His son, Mohammed Husain Azad, lived to become the author of the famous history of Urdu literature entitled *Aab-i-Hayat, The Waters of Life*.

Lord Canning, the first Viceroy of British India, told his Council that the indigenous press had been inciting the people to mutiny before 1857. Heavy censorship was imposed on the vernacular papers, but some poignant poems lamenting the destruction of Dehli and Lucknow were published in Urdu. The erstwhile Mughal capital was now called *Dehli-i-marhoom*, the late lamented Dehli. The two deposed kings, Bahadur Shah and Vajid Ali Shah, wrote heartrending ghazals and mahavis. Mirza Ghalib wrote of his deep sorrow in his letters to friends.

But some Urdu poets began penning odes to governors and viceroys. Human nature would never change, men would continue to hate and kill one another, thought Gautam. Men at war turn into wild beasts, and in this war religion and race rule on both sides. After the English defeat at Chinhat, Lucknow, Lord Clyde had said, "It is a matter of great shame, as all Christiandom is watching us."

The mutiny had begun in the Bengal army, but the bhadralok and new zamindars of Bengal remained loyal to the British. Gautam Nilambar Dutt was among the eminent bhadralok of Calcutta, convinced that the uprising was quixotic. All these queens and kings had only wanted to regain their lost thrones, though for the populace they symbolised independence and became the leaders of a full-scale patriotic war.

The solid fact remains, thought Gautam, that after 1857 the English ushered India into the modern age.

Some of the stories of native brutality against Englishwomen and children later proved to be false or vastly exaggerated, but the savagery of the English revenge was mind-boggling. Even as an Anglophile Gautam couldn't justify what the English did during those terrible days. They indiscriminately executed whomever they could even before the natives began slaying them; now the British authorities were saying that the Muslims went to the gallows with pride and derision and the Hindus looked indifferent, as though they were going on a long journey.

Gautam stole a glance at his friend who sat motionless, lost in thought. It was all very well for the English press to publish cartoons of General Bakht Khan and laugh at his title of "Lord Governor-General"—but wasn't his defeat extremely heartbreaking? For the first time Gautam felt he understood the native rebels' feelings, and the point of view and trauma of people like Nawab Kamaluddin Ali Reza Bahadur of Neelampur.

Dusk fell, it had become chilly. The nawab rose to his feet and said, "Khuda hafiz, Nilambar Mian. Next time we meet, I'll tell you about the two years I spent in England and France. And I must tell you something—the English are a fine people in their own country, they become a different species as soon as they cross the Suez."

He got into his buggy and drove away towards Matia Burj, where poor Vajid Ali Shah had created another miniature Lucknow in a house he had named Radha Manzil. Gautam watched the tiny carriage disappear in the gathering mist. Highland pipers passed by playing Gautam's favourite Scottish air. Soon Calcutta would start getting ready for its famous Christmas season. Pax Britannica! How swiftly law and order had been restored in India! Peace! It is so wonderful. It also proved the new Darwinian theory of Survival of the Fittest !!!

28. Champabai, Chowdhrain of Lucknow, Photograph by Mashkoor-ud-Daulah, 1868

Upon returning home from a meeting one day, Babu Gautam Nilambar Dutt was told by his gardener that Nawab Kamman Saheb had come from Matia Burj, waited a while, and just left. Dutt Babu rushed out of his gate and looked up and down the street. A very old man was walking away slowly, bent over his stick. He was dressed in spotless white muslin and wore a dainty little embroidered muslin skull-cap. His carriage stood at the street corner. Dutt Babu hastened to call him back.

The old man halted. "Ah, Nilambar Mian! It's good to see you," he said, "this may be our last meeting, for all you know."

"Why, Nawab Saheb? As it is, we see each other very rarely, I'm so dreadfully busy all the time." He led the august visitor back to the double-storeyed Dutt House.

"My friend," the nobleman entered the chintzy, wall-papered drawing-room, "I came to say goodbye. I would like to go to Kerbala again and die there, but I hate to desert my King-in-exile."

Gautam pulled the silk cord to ring the bell. A servant came in. "Tea," the master said briefly. His daughter played an English music-hall tune on the piano upstairs.

"Nawab Saheb, you will be glad to know that my son, Manoranjan, is going to Lucknow's Canning College as lecturer in law," Gautam informed him.

"Masha Allah! Masha Allah! How wonderful." They chatted for a while.

After a pause Nawab Saheb said, "Here, I have brought something for you as a memento of lost times." Slowly he took out a small sepia photograph from his angarkha pocket and gave it to Dutt Babu. The host put on his rimless glasses. He couldn't recognise the face, so turned the tiny picture over and read at the back: *Champa Bai, Chowdhrain. Photograph by Mashkoor-ud-Daulah, Qaiser Bagh, Lucknow, 1868.*

Gautam looked at the photo again—a dignified old lady in an elaborate gharara sat on a plush chair, smoking a water-pipe.

Nawab Kamman noticed the immense sadness on his friend's face. "Yes, Nilamber Mian, that's it. This is what Time the Old Crook does to pretty women."

"What does 'Chowdhrain' mean?" Gautam asked sombrely.

"Well, in her middle age, she became the head or chairwoman, so to speak, of the tawaifs of Lucknow. It is a very prestigious position in their society. The Chowdhrain solves their problems and settles their disputes, and her decrees and decisions are binding on them. Champa Jan also had access to the Royal Court and was received there with courtesy. Then came the catastrophe. During the Mutiny her house was looted, her wealthy patrons killed. She rented a small room and went to seed. She could not cope with the trauma of the destruction of Lucknow, so she hit the bottle.

"The new British administration of the city ordered all courtesans to have themselves registered and obtain a license from the municipality. They were made to get themselves photographed, attach a copy each with their licenses, and display their ages and rates on their doors. This was outrageous and they found it extremely insulting, because most of them were not whores—they were highly respected performing artistes. Anyway, they had to obey orders and so they had themselves photographed in Mashkoor-ud-Daulah's studios.

"Poor Champa Jan was no longer in that category but she was the Chowdhrain. She got herself photographed and gave a copy to a friend of mine who was coming to Calcutta. She said, 'Give it to Babu Saheb with my humble salaams.'

"She could not remember your name, she was suffering from memory lapses as well. My friend gave me this picture thinking I might know who she meant."

Gautam looked shaken.

"Like many courtesans, the poor woman has come to a bad end," Nawab Kamman continued ruefully. "I am told her hangers-on and relatives fleeced her of every last penny she had. After she gave up drinking she got addicted to opium and, eventually, she became a beggar."

"Beggar?" Gautam repeated in horror.

"Yes, Nilambar Mian. Some courtesans become queens,

some mendicants. This is kismet."

There was a short silence.

"Is she alive?" Gautam asked.

"Oh, yes. I'm told she is seen with other beggars at Char Bagh Railway Station. Earlier, they said she used to wait anxiously for the train arriving from Calcutta and peer at every passenger's face. Now she has become almost senile and does not do that. Well, that was the last news I had of her from my cousins from Lucknow." He sighed deeply. "I would have brought this photograph to you earlier but I read in the papers that you were away for quite some time in England." Nawab Kamman sighed again. "If you go to Lucknow, don't try to seek her out—let your dreams remain intact. Now, I must take your leave. Khuda Hafiz, Nilambar Mian."

The host accompanied the Nawab to his carriage and returned to the parlour. He put Champa Bai's photograph behind a shelf and looked around, not knowing what to do next. He had acquired a place in the sun, as he told Champa he would on the day he departed from Lucknow in 1823. He had become a prosperous printer and publisher. His wife belonged to one of the best Brahmo families of Calcutta and he had fine children. He was a prominent member of the anglicised bhadralok society. What more could life offer him?

He walked around the room. The walls were lined with book-racks. Books and more books, newspaper files, law magazines and folios, reports and resolutions of various committees and conferences. Everywhere there were problems—and he had found their solutions.

Had he found their solutions. . .? He felt suffocated in the stuffy room. Gas lamps shone dimly in the streets. He stepped out into the garden. These are the nights when one can hear the swish of unhappy ghosts flying by, he thought. A dog slept soundly by the edge of the tank. If Gautam had believed in the transmigration of souls he would have thought the dog was someone's condemned spirit. He went in again. From a revolving almirah he took out Toru Dutt's *Poems* and read:

O echo whose repose I mar
With my regrets and mournful cries

He comes. . . I hear his voice afar,
Or is it thine that thus replied?
Peace! hark he calls!—in vain, in vain.
The loved and lost, comes not again.

He shut the book and took up a report of the Joint Select Committee of the House of Commons.

A few weeks later he read in the newspaper that Nawab Kamaluddin Ali Reza Bahadur of Matia Burj had passed away peacefully in his sleep.

29. Sunset and Sunrise Over the Gomti

A 'suited-booted natoo juntulman' stepped out of the inter-class compartment, carrying a carpet-bag. A coolie went in and picked up his luggage. A few English and white-skinned Eurasian families alighted from I and II class "Europeans Only" bogies. A row of fully covered palkis stood on the platform with their kahars, to carry purdah ladies from the zenana compartments. Eurasian guards and ticket-checkers walked to and fro on the crowded platform. The coolie led the passenger, Mr. G. N. Dutt, to the gharry-stand outside. Then he shouted, "Hey, come along, Lachhman."

An old man kept sitting on the coachbox of a phaeton while a youngster jumped down and salaamed the new arrival with great courtesy. "Huzoor?"

Mr. G. N. Dutt took out a trans-Gomti address. His son Manoranjan Dutt, taught law at Canning College Aminabad, and lived across the river. Lachhman clambered up to the coachbox again.

"Babuji coming from Allahabad?" The new capital of the north western province was full of such Bengali babus who worked in the government.

"No, Calcutta."

"Who is it?" the old man asked Lachhman with an air of secrecy.

"Juntulman from Calcutta," Lachhman replied.

"May I speak to him?"

Lachhman turned around and said, "Huzoor, Gunga Din Chacha here begs permission to have a word with you. He is quite deaf. You'll have to shout."

Gunga Din! The name rang a faint bell. But Gautam Nilambar recalled that it used to be a common name among the shagird-pesha, the servant class of Lucknow.

"Yes, of course," he replied. "Ask him if he ever drove a carriage in Ghaziuddin Hyder's time."

Lachhman relayed the question to the old man.

"No, sarkar, I was a mehra, a palki-bardar, at Farah Bakhsh, then in Qaiser Bagh. After the Bad-i-Bahari left the garden, autumn set in—"

Lachhman gave the reins to his aged companion and explained, "Huzoor, old Chacha here means to say that after Sultan-i-Alam left Lucknow in his carriage called the Breeze of Spring—"

"Yes, yes. I understand," Mr. Dutt said a bit impatiently. He had heard all of this melodrama and poetry from his weepy friend, Nawab Kamman, till the old aristocrat died. Gautam knew that even the unlettered commoners of Lucknow spoke a literary language, but he was surprised that the bloodbath of 1857 had not changed them. Then he felt uneasy as he realised that, like Nawab Kamman, old Gunga Din was also crying silently. Gautam had been a devotee of Reason all his life. Trained by Englishmen he had come to believe that in order to survive and win, you must be strong. Look at all the East—wallowing in tears and sentimentality. He pursed his lips, as was his wont.

Gunga Din straightened his back and said in formal Urdu, "My lord, send me to Calcutta, kindly. On account of my King lives there."

Lachhman laughed. "Sir, don't you worry about old father Gunga Din's plea. He makes the same request to everybody who arrives at the railway station from Calcutta."

"Does he often cry like this?" Gautam asked the lad.

"Sometimes. The city is full of such old fogeys. This is nothing, sir. We have these touring actors who stage *Inder Sabha* from village to village and the audiences shed tears, remembering Akhtar Piya. I was very small when the disaster struck so I don't remember anything, except that when the Sahebs blew up Machhi Bhavan all Lucknow was shaken by the explosions, and I trembled like a puppy and howled and howled. Amma says that many pregnant women aborted their babies, and a lot of people died of heart failure."

Gautam shuddered. "Is the King alive, sir?" Lachhman asked. Gautam nodded. He was very much alive and writing doleful poetry in Matia Burj, though poor Hazrat Mahal had died in Nepal in 1869.

The phaeton was coming out of the railway station compound when it stopped with a jerk. The coachman yelled: "Why don't you get out of my way, you bag-of-bones?" An old woman hobbled up and stretched out her gnarled hands. Wrapped in a thin, tattered *dulai* she started droning mechanically—"Give us a pice for the sweet sake of Ali. May you never know any other sorrow except the sorrow for Hussain. . ." The beggar woman repeated the common form of blessing prevalent in Shia-oriented Lucknow—"May God give you no other grief except the grief for Hussain. . . One pice, only one pice."

Gautam Nilambar froze. The late Nawab Kamman had told him about Champa Jan who had become a beggar at the railway station and waited for passengers from Calcutta. He shivered as it struck him that this mendicant could be Champa. Was she? He adjusted his glasses and peered out. She stood on the roadside like a shadow.

"Don't you give her a pice, my lord," Lachhman leaned sideways and whispered to him from the coachbox. "She's addicted to opium and she pesters all railway passengers like this. Spends her alms on the stuff."

Gautam took out a fistful of Victoria coins from his purse.

She opened her eyes very wide at the sudden sight of sparkling silver. Then she regarded the old Brown Saheb sitting in the carriage. A destitute, toothless woman had been waiting unreasonably at the railway station for an old man to come back. She did not recognise the eminent, elderly gentleman who looked much younger than his age because he was wealthy and had no personal worries. Life had treated him kindly.

She shook her head. "I don't need so much, just a little for my daily dose."

He gave her a rupee. She clenched her fist tight and whined: "My lord! May you celebrate your great-grandchildren's weddings. I have been ruined by the Mutiny. O, you patron of the lowly. . . During the Royal regime, I rode out on my own elephant. May Allah bless you."

Lachhman whipped the horse and the carriage moved forward. He guffawed. "She owned an elephant! Excellent excuse some people have made out of the Mutiny. All kinds of riff-raff claim to have been people of consequence before 1858."

Champa stared at the rupee in the gloom of the evening. Then she sneaked into a by-lane and stopped before an opium den where addicts sat in dim corners with their heads between their knees.

Gautam Nilambar looked back once and saw her standing under the street lamp. She was still gazing at the coin. Her hair shone like a lot of silver and her face was covered with deep furrows. The skin of her arms sagged. She wore a patched gharara and her quilted stole was full of holes.

He leaned against the cushions and closed his eyes. Where does Beauty go after it slides off the face of a lovely woman? Does old age turn women into a different species? Why are old men venerated and women ridiculed as hags? Why didn't I run after her and ask her to sit next to me in this carriage and take her home? Why did I leave her standing all by herself under a gas lamp? Despite his learning and wisdom and worldly experience, Gautam realised he had no satisfactory answers to these questions. He felt extremely agitated and gasped for breath. The victoria proceeded smoothly on its way to Badshah Bagh. The signboards on the new, gaslit roads bore the names of British generals who had conquered Lucknow twenty years ago.

Singharewali Kothi or Water Chestnut House loomed on the other bank of the Gomti. Babu Manoranjan Dutt lived on the ground floor, as a tenant; the landlords, called Raizadas, lived upstairs. They were the descendants of Rai Mehtab Chand, a nobleman in the court of Nawab Saadat Ali Khan, the fourth ruler of Oudh. Nilambar Dutt's phaeton crossed the bridge and turned towards the kutcha river-bank road. After a few minutes the carriage entered the gates of the quaint-looking mansion whose three small turrets had given it the name of the three-cornered water chestnut. Gautam had not informed his son that he was coming—he wanted to give them a surprise.

That night, after Manoranjan Dutt and his wife and children had gone to bed, Gautam Nilambar came out of his room and watched the river. After a while he walked down the mud track. The temple of the monkey god Hanuman was visible through the arches of the bridge. Monkeys slept on the trees above. Fiery-eyed *agiya betals* followed him, the ghosts of his memories. He had witnessed so much. What else was there left to see? The river was flowing. Houses stood on its banks. These houses had names and there were people sleeping inside. The people had names, too. Some houses were built of stone, stones also lay scattered on the shore. Time was flowing, time was arrested in the stones. Flames rose from the burning ground. Who knows how many persons had died tonight?

Gautam kept on walking, the cremation grounds were in front of him. Kali danced on the Burning Ghat, Kali who gathered the entire universe into herself at the end of its cycle. Only those who had annihilated desire could worship her fearlessly, or so said the red-robed priests of Kalighat.

"All desires are burnt to ashes in the charnel field. Kali, who is beyond intellect and speech, turned the Universe into Nothingness, void into Puran. Puran which is Light and Peace. . .

"Kali, whose dress is space, is space herself, for she is infinite. Her powers are infinite, she is higher than Maya for she created the world by becoming Maya herself.

"In the Burning Ground she stood on the white body of Shiva. Shiva was white for he was Swaroop, and destroyed the demons of Maya and self. He didn't move, for he was above change. Kali was the Manifestation of his change. Shiva didn't change but was present within every change. Kali danced in the smoke of the flames. She was Durga, and Tara, and Dhumvati. The Burning Ground was the ultimate reality of life," said the red-robed priests of Kalighat.

Gautam had been a Brahmo for long years. He could not get rid of Kali. And nobody had answered his questions. He stood at the bridge watching the dim flames of the funeral pyres. Then he returned to Singharewali Kothi.

30. The Bridge

When it struck five in the morning the lady of the house got up and woke the maidservant who was asleep on a mat near the bedroom door. The lady of the house said, "Hurry up. Nirmal Bitiya's school re-opens today, her motor lorry will be here soon." The mehri rubbed her eyes and rose to her feet. She wound her long hair into a coil and waddled like a goose towards the tap. Now she would fill brass pails with water and place them in the bathrooms, lay out his shaving things for the master and Hari Shankar Bhaiya, and proceed to make tea. Another day had dawned.

Birds had begun to twitter in the weedy garden. A bullock-cart passed by. The milkman came along, aluminum buckets dangling from his bicycle handle. The lady of the house went into the Thakurdwara in the eastern tower. The room was air-less and warm with the peculiar stuffiness of the rainy season. Lord Krishna stood in his formal stance, holding his little brass flute inside the little brass temple upon the altar.

Singharewali Kothi, the double-storeyed mansion of the Raizadas of Ibrahimpur, had seen better days. Now it looked bare and unkempt. Several cots lay along the wall of the upper floor veranda. A large china vase with a tulsi plant stood on the adjoining roof of the river-side portico. Two teen-aged girls slept soundly under the photograph of a shaven-headed, rotund high-priest of Gorakhnath.

A young man of about nineteen was fast asleep in the third tower facing Moti Mahal. A table fan buzzed on the bedside table. All four windows of the tower were open and a pleasant breeze filled the congested room. Its built-in shelves were stacked with English, Persian and Urdu books. Urdu and English journals were scattered on the threadbare cotton duree, *Penguin New Writing* and art quarterlies which came out from Calcutta lay in a corner. Neckties were trailing down from the tennis rackets; socks were stuffed in a box of tennis balls. A portrait of a young and handsome Jawaharlal Nehru adorned the cornice. The walls displayed group photographs of the University Union, 1938–39, 1939–40. Then there was the youngster holding a trophy, playing Macbeth, rowing in the University Regatta. High above the mantelpiece hung a faded group photograph of the staff and students of the Law Faculty of Canning College (now called the University of Lucknow). The young man's father was present in the back row, wearing the long coat and black round velvet cap worn by Hindu gentlemen. It was called the Babu cap. He had funny, drooping moustaches, and stood behind his teacher, the late Manoranjan Dutt, son of the well-known social reformer, G.N. Dutt of Calcutta. With his hands upon the silver top of his cane, Dutt Babu stared hard into the camera. He had also been a tenant of Singharewali Kothi. The photograph was taken in 1898 when Dutt Babu retired from his illustrious teaching job.

Munshi Mehtab Chand, the Raizada ancestor, glowed dimly in oils in the drawing room downstairs. He sat on a gilt chair with stylised plush curtains in the background. He wore the robe of honour of the Court of Nawab-Vazir Saadat Ali Khan.

The third tower was used as a music-room.

This house was the centre of the universe for its inmates. From here loved ones were carried out in the form of corpses, and bridal palanquins were brought in. Festivals were celebrated, children were born, people quarrelled and made up, laughed and wept. All this happens in every household. The dwelling watches the spectacle in silence and nobody listens to its wordless story. It is forever competing with Time. Let's see how far you can come with me, continue being my witness, says Time. The House keeps quiet. Years pass. The seasons return again and again. The House remains anchored like a brave little ship in the river of time. Often it is carried away by a strong current and is lost forever.

Singharewali Kothi had been built by Munshi Mehtab Chand who was awarded the title of Rai and was one of the pay masters or Bakshis of the army in the government of Nawab Saadat Ali Khan. Now his great-grandson, a barrister of less than average monthly income, lived in it. The barrister had one son, Hari Shankar, and two daughters, Laj and Nirmala. He spent most of his time on Congress politics, attended mushairas and wrote learned articles on Urdu poetry. In his spare time he also visited the law courts. There was some income from the agricultural land he owned in a nearby district. The family had not prospered in modern times; still they carried their hereditary nawabi title of Raizada with a certain aplomb.

At this moment he was sleeping under a mosquito net on the open roof of the riverside portico adjoining the back veranda. The sound of his wife's wooden sandals woke him up. This was the only troublesome habit his dear spouse had. Early in the morning she disturbed everybody's sleep with her numerous noisy activities of opening the almirahs, closing the pantry, walking back and forth from one room to another on her wooden sandals. Then she would enter the Thakurdwara and start reciting the holy book aloud, and that woke everyone up properly.

Trilochan, the water-man, got ready to sweep the rooms. The beddings were folded. "Get up, Bitiya, you are going to have morning classes from today," Jamuna Mehri, the maid servant said to the younger girl who sprang up like a jack-in-the-box. She took out a wrist-watch from under her pillow. "Golly, it's five o'clock," she exclaimed in an English-school accent.

The older sister, Lajwati, turned in her bed, languidly opened her eyes and looked at the river. She was about eighteen and went to Isabella Thoburn College, which reopened later.

Their brother Hari Shankar emerged from his tower-room, dragging his slippers dopily, and looked at the river and the bridge. The bridge connected the private world of this house and the river with the larger world outside. That other world was also his own. He stretched his arms and yawned. Then he picked up a towel from a chair and went to his bathroom, humming a Pahari Sanyal song. The younger sister, Nirmala, came out dressed in her school uniform of white blouse, navy blue tunic and red belt. Jamuna Mehri handed her a glass of milk and an apple. The La Martiniere Girls High School's "motor lorry" honked its horn. The vehicle was mostly fully of ruddy-faced English girls. Laj appeared on the balcony. An Indian teenager popped out her curly head and shouted, "Hellow, Didi. I'll come in the evening."

After the school bus left, Jamuna Mehri handed another glass of milk and two bananas to the son and heir, Hari Shankar, who drank the milk, threw away the bananas and dashed out like a runner clearing the hurdles. He hung his notebooks with a flourish on the handle of his bicycle and darted off in the direction of the University. The domes and turrets of the palatial red-stone buildings of the campus were slowly emerging from the early morning mist.

31. *Shahzada Gulfam of Badshah Bagh*

"In the evening when the sun went down behind the rose-apple trees, my victoria arrived at the Moti Mahal bridge. This was the time I returned after my classes at Marris College of Hindustani Music. Then Gunga Din, the coachman, would sometimes turn around and ask, 'Bitiya, would you like to go to Singharewali Kothi?'

"I am narrating this story from this point on," said Talat as she recounted her family saga to her friends of a winter evening. They sat in front of a log fire in a flat in St. John's Wood in London. The time was 1954. "There are many ways of telling a dastan," she said. "How shall I begin? I don't know which characters are more important. Where did this story start? What was the climax? Who was the heroine? How should she have ended up? And who was the hero? Who is the listener of this story, and who is the narrator? My older brother, Kamal, used to say that one day he will sit down and decide about all this. But he hasn't even been able to decide about himself. 'Yes, I'll go', I would tell Gunga Din. He turned the victoria around and descended onto the kutcha road that branched off from the end of the bridge. This uneven track was grandly called Riverbank Road. It used to be very quiet. The shamshan ghat lay some distance away. The river reflected the silver palace called Moti Mahal and the golden-domed Chattar Manzil and the Imambara of Shah Najaf. The river flowed politely under the stairs of these royal buildings. Once in a while a canoe would go past in this green, liquid silence. There was a Hanuman temple under the bridge and the place was crawling with playful holy monkeys. At a little distance there stood Singharewali Kothi, so called because of its three turrets. The steps of this house also descended to the river.

"One evening when I reached Water Chestnut House I found Laj's wedding lehnga being stitched by her aunts. One of them asked me, 'And when is your sister getting married?' I got flustered because my elder sister Tehmina's forthcoming marriage to our cousin, Amir Reza, had run into rough weather.

"Now I pass the candle to my brother Kamal, who will tell you the story of . . ."

"Amir Reza's dad, Sir Zaki Reza was my father's first cousin. Amir was an only child," Kamal took up the narration.

"After the First World War, a lot of Central European and White Russian refugees were floating around in India. Madame Nina, who was engaged as Amir's governess, was one of them. She had abandoned her husband. As it happened, a few months after Madame Nina's employment as Cousin Amir's nanny, Lady Reza passed away. No foul play was suspected because our Fatima Chachi died of typhoid, too. Amir was brought to our house, Gulfishan, in Lucknow.

"He was seven years old and inconsolable. Sir Zaki took him to Switzerland for his schooling—our Chacha thought a total change of environment would help the child forget his mother. Not surprisingly, Madame Nina continued to work, now ostensibly as Uncle Zaki's secretary, in Allahabad. He wouldn't have married her anyway, though he trusted her completely. In any case, she was a Roman Catholic and could not get a divorce from her estranged Russian husband. Uncle Zaki left the house in charge of Madame whenever he went to Europe to meet his son. In the summer of 1935, while he was in Switzerland, he died of a stroke. In Allahabad, Madame Nina decamped with most of his valuables, and couldn't be traced again.

"In 1936, Amir Reza returned to India. He was now a stunningly handsome young man of eighteen. My parents travelled to Bombay to receive him at Ballard's Pier. When he arrived at Gulfishan he took me and Talat in his arms and wept. He kissed Tehmina lightly on her cheeks, as relatives do in the West, and he was surprised to see her blush.

"Anyway, all of us became very fond of him and did our best not to make him feel that he was not a homeless orphan. He was a very rich orphan, indeed, because he jointly owned a great deal of common Reza property. Being the elder son of the family he was called Bhaiya Saheb—I was merely 'Bhaiya'. Uncle Zaki had no real brothers or sisters. His house in Allahabad had long been locked up. His loyal coachman, Gunga Din, had come down to Lucknow with his victoria to work for us. When he touched his young master's feet, Amir recoiled.

"He was a European boy, and as days went by he felt more alienated in his Indian surroundings, but he never spoke about his uneasiness. He couldn't understand the emphasis we placed on family relationships, and above all he simply could not accept arranged marriages. When he learnt that his late parents and mine had decided that Tehmina would marry him when they grew up, he felt too embarrassed to say no—probably because he was living with us.

"Gradually he withdrew into his shell. His mother's death, his long formative years in exile, the way Madame Nina had robbed his trusting father, his unwanted betrothal, all this was enough to make him an introvert. He grieved quietly for his Dad who lay buried in a snow-covered Lutheran cemetery in the Alps.

"Once Amir visited his mother's grave in Kalyanpur. He said to me that he now realised how important it was to die in one's own country and find a plot in one's own graveyard. One would not feel lonely in the Hereafter—he had discovered some sort of nationalism via dolorosa.

"He joined La Martiniere College which both Hari and I also attended. La Mart was established in Lucknow in 1848 by General Claude Martin's Trust for the education of European boys. The children of the Indian elite also studied there. I had no older brother, so I hero-worshipped Cousin Amir, even proudly wore his hand-me-downs. He spoke English with a French accent and he was a born lady-killer. However, his only friend and confidant was the loyal coachman Gunga Din, perhaps because the humble servant was the last remaining link with his father's ruined household, and Amir's childhood.

"My sister Tehmina knew he didn't much care for her, and was too proud to let him see that she was quite genuinely in love with him—for, wasn't he going to be her husband in the near future?

"Tehmina attended La Martiniere Girls' High School. Perched up on a green hillock across the river, the school was housed in a medieval-looking 'English' castle surrounded by a moat. The castle was called Khurshid Manzil and had been built by the Anglicised Nawab Saadat Ali Khan for his queen, Khurshid Zadi. I often saw Tehmina standing in one of the castle windows talking to some classmate. It all somehow reminded me of Byron and Walter Scott.

"Then Amir Reza reached the University. The campus was known as Badshah Bagh, King's Garden—for it had been laid out by King Nasiruddin Hyder in 1828— and Amir was known as 'Shahzada Gulfam of Badshah Bagh.'

"Let's face it, he was no intellectual giant. The main aim of

his life was to become Triple Blue of the University. I continued to be his ADC till I grew up and replaced him with
Jawaharlal Nehru.

"Then Champa Baji entered the scene and complicated our
unruffled lives. Amir Reza was engaged to my sister, Tehmina,
but fell in love with Champa Ahmed. He graduated from Canning College and joined the Royal Indian Navy. He was too
glamorous to have become a civilian or a boxwallah. Now if
you put Charles Boyer in uniform the result would be devastating. Champa too responded to Cousin Amir's subtle over-
tures. Slowly, the plot thickened. Now, whenever she was mentioned, Tehmina laughed hollowly and Hari Shankar looked
foolish and lit a cigarette. Champa Baji was the interloper.

"This Hari was a rascal. He was well aware of my calf-love
for Champa. He would tell Amir darkly, 'You have made your
conquest, sir, but some people I know have the delusion that
they can also attract Champa Baji's attention.' Then he would
proceed dutifully to tell Amir that girls like Champa came to
the University by the dozen, how could she be compared to
our Tehmina? Hari was concerned about Tehmina who was
his rakhi sister. See, both Hari and I belonged to rural areas
where these traditions and old values were very strong.

"Champa was not one of us. We all came from the same
background. Hari Shankar's family and my people had been
friends for generations. Champa had come from Banaras and
joined the Isabella Thoburn College for her B.A. in 1941.

"In 1944, Tehmina did her M.A. It was the fateful summer
when her 'childhood engagement' with Amir was broken.

"I am wondering whether I can ever give you the complete
picture of the time when all this happened? There are so many
things. . . the royal gate-house in King's Garden which was
now the University post office, the malins passing by, jingling
their anklets. Queen Qudsia Mahal used to live in Badshah
Bagh and her chief malin carried a khurpi with a bejewelled
handle.

"Mir* said:

---

*Mohammed Taqi Mir (1722–1810), one of the Four Greats of Urdu
poetry.

Kaha main ne, gul ka hai kitna sabaat ?
Kali ne ye sun ke tabassum kiya.

'I asked how long the rose would last. The rose-bud heard me and smiled.'

"Sorry, I digressed. Where was I? I was going to tell you about our convocation. You see no one can convey to others a particular atmosphere with all its associations and overtones. No artist, no painter, no writer can do so. Consider these very insignificant details: at night a humble lantern burned in a niche of the historic gateway of Badshah Bagh. An old woman who wore a red lehnga picked up fallen tamarinds on Faizabad Road on hot summer afternoons—she was killed by a passing train near the railway crossing. Our old cook, Noor Ali, looked like Ali Baba and recited the *Khalif Bari Sarjan Haar* although he was illiterate.

"Look, here I am sitting on a high balcony of Bennet Hall giving you a running commentary of the Convocation. The green lawns are hedged with red and yellow canna flowers, the shadows of the red-stone buildings, colourful saris, the gold embroidered gowns of the faculty have all mingled in a sunny haze. Time is flying, I can hear the swish of its wings.

"The boy in charge of recorded music has put on Pahari Sanyal's New Theatre song on the loud speaker—*Whose voice do I hear in the depth of my heart as the caravan leaves.* This ghazal is being played especially in honour of the famous singer-actor from Calcutta. Clad in a silk kurta and white Bengali style dhoti he is sitting in the front row, busy talking to his friends from the faculty of Marris College. The song resounds—

Yeh cooch ke waqt kaisi awaz
Dil ke kanon mein a rahi hai—

Caravan after caravan of young hopefuls arrives to receive their degrees before entering the market-place of life.

"Now I hand over the microphone to my comrade, Hari Shankar. . . Hello. . . hello. . . Little Sir Echo, how do you do, hello. . . hello. . ."

Hari Shankar replies: "Hello. . . This is Hari Shankar, Hari

Shankar Raizada, Kamal's double and alter-ego. The only
brother of Laj and Nirmala, Champa Baji's stooge. But I'm
quite a significant character, too, playing so many roles. How
shall I begin, where shall I enter? All this is very confusing.

"Th"e new graduates of Isabella Thoburn College arrive,
led by their Principal and the American faculty. They are all
wearing caps and gowns and look very elegant, indeed.

"Now Vice-Chancellor Habibullah arrives, accompanied by
senior professors who have already become living legends in
India's academic world.

"In front of me," Hari Shankar continued, "the panorama
of the Convocation is bathed in soft winter sunshine. Tehmina
looks radiant in her cap and gown. Soon it will be evening,
the girls will stroll down to Hazarat Ganj and have their photographs taken at C. Mull's studio. That was also an annual
ritual. Year after year, throngs of young women in their caps
and gowns trooped down to C. Mull's for their photographs.
All year round, tall and handsome Mr. Mull could be seen
standing in his doorway. He was always impeccably dressed in
a black suit with a carnation in his collar. He stood at his
plate-glass portal in such style as though it were a studio in
Paris. Mind you, Lucknow was called the Paris of India, anyway. The Mulls were as old as Whiteways of Hazrat Ganj, the
former abode of Begum Hazrat Mahal.

"Kamal's sister, Tehmina, was a close friend of my sister,
Laj. They often ganged up to persecute us. Allah! Please, Hari
Shankar, get us tickets for Sadhana Bose's dance at the Mayfair;
take us to see *Waterloo Bridge*; get my library card renewed. . .

"I remember one evening I was about to leave for Hazrat
Ganj when I noticed these two sitting on our riverside terrace.
They also saw me and one of them promptly shouted, 'Hey,
Hari, take us Ganjing too. We would like to see *Gaslight*.'

" 'Forget it,' I yelled back. 'I have an important appointment to keep in the coffee-house.' 'And my pink sari from the
dyers,' Laj added. 'Just make a detour to Aminabad.'

" 'Big deal! Pipe down, bye!' I climbed on to my bike. Then
a certain sadness overtook me. There they sat on the balus-

trade, dangling their feet, looking so fragile and vulnerable despite their bravado and New Woman stance.

" 'Go on. Shout at her,' said Tehmina reproachfully. 'The poor thing is a guest in your house for two more months'. Then in an over-dramatic manner, she broke into Amir Khusro's* wedding song—

Kahey ko biyahi bides, sun Babul mora.

'Why did you send me to an alien land, O Father mine.' For the last six hundred years this song has been tearfully sung in north India at the time of the bride's departure from her parental home.

"Tehmina continued to sing: 'Father, O Father, we are birds of your courtyard who fly away. We are cows of your field only to be driven off whenever you say.'

"Laj wiped a tear.

"Father, O Father, you gave double-storeyed mansions to my brothers; an alien land to me.'

"I pedalled off briskly, feeling very emotional myself. The song followed me as I came out of the gate. Tehmina was perhaps thinking of her own uncertain future because of Champa Baji's sudden intrusion in her fiancé's life.

"Laj was married in 1943 and went away to Delhi. Now we had to run errands for Tehmina, Talat and Nirmal.

"Often Talat stopped by our house in the evenings when she returned from Marris College. I sat in the window of my turret and watched her carriage descending the slope. At this particular moment all used to be perfectly still and sad and fragrant. The silent music of the river reached my ears, and my heart sank. Mir Anis described the violet hour as the time when the river stopped flowing:

Jhut-puta waqt hai, behta huwa darya thehra.†

"My alter-ego, Kamal, sometimes said that sunsets depressed

---

*Amir Khusro, 14th century Sufi poet and musician. He was the chief disciple of Hazrat Nizamuddin Aulia, the patron saint of Delhi.
†Urdu poet Mir Anis (1805–1874).

him too. He was ultra-sensitive, too much beauty made him nervous. I knew what he meant."

Kamal started to speak again. "When we returned to Lucknow from our fun trips, the train stopped first at nearby Sandila in the cool, early morning haze, and we heard the familiar cries of the vendors selling the famous laddus of Sandila. Country gentlemen dressed in snow-white, very wide pajamas and dhotis, white angarkhas and dopalli topis strolled to and fro, waiting for the next train. The platform was covered with the bright red bajri of finely ground bricks. A number of palkis always stood by in a row for purdah ladies. The railway station was surrounded by flowering trees and mango orchards and it was utterly peaceful, interrupted only by the cries of laddu-sellers.

"In July '44 when we were returning from Mussoorie, the train halted at Sandila as usual. A laddu-seller appeared in the compartment's window. 'Huzoor! These laddus are waiting to be tasted by your honour.'

" 'Are they fresh?' asked Shankar teasingly.

" 'Upon my honour, your honour. This is Sandila, sire,' he said with such pride as though this was the very heaven! We bought a clay handi covered with red tissue-paper. The train moved. A village bride was ambling down towards the gate, crying profusely. The rustic bridegroom grinned from ear to ear. He was dressed in turmeric yellow, followed by jovial baratis.

" 'Hope Nirmal gets married soon, like Laj did,' remarked Hari Shankar lightly. 'Now she has taken over from Laj—don't chase girls, don't smoke. Don't do this. Don't do that.'

" 'You ought to be ashamed of yourself,' I replied remorsefully. 'You want even Nirmal to go away soon so that you can have the time of your life, with nobody to check or disapprove.' "

Hari Shankar said, "We have an ancient folk belief in our country, that if you stand under a tree at twilight or at high noon, you may be 'captured' by the sprite resident in that tree. Also, according to a Muslim folk belief, a good-looking young man can be 'touched' by a passing fairy and lose his reason.

Or if a virgin goes up to the roof to dry her hair after her bath a wayward jinn could fall in love with her and 'possess' her. . .

"In Agha Hasan Amanat's Urdu opera *Inder Sabha*, 'Prince Gulfam of India' was asleep on the roof of his palace in Akhtar Nagar, which was the poetic name for Lucknow, capital of Vajid Ali Shah 'Akhtar'. Subz Pari of Raja Inder's celestial court happened to fly past. She fell in love with Gulfam and had him 'abducted'. Raja Inder was furious. He banished her from his court. The Prince was cast in a well in the Caucasus Mountains. She put on an ochre robe and became a jogan. There was a happy ending.

"Raja Inder was played by Vajid Ali Shah himself. Handsome men came to be called Gulfam, Rose-face. Our Cousin Amir was also referred to as Prince Gulfam of Badshah Bagh or Gulfam of Gulfishan.

"Amir played tennis against the top players of India, Ghaus Mohammed and Miss Khanum Haji. He was captain of the Boat Club. He also joined the Forward Bloc for a short while then left it. He was groping for an emotional anchor which he probably found in Champa Ahmed. It was promptly said in India Coffee House in Hazrat Ganj that Gulfam had been abducted by Subz Pari."

Now Kamal resumed speaking: "Sorry, I was telling you about Amir and Tehmina. Hari and I had been urgently called home from Mussoorie to persuade Tehmina to say 'yes'. The Doon Express was now reaching the pleasant suburbs of Lucknow, and the long miles of Alam Bagh rolled out beside the running train. Railway lines glistened in the rain as the train slowly steamed in at Char Bagh Junction. My heart always sank a little when the train entered Char Bagh—we had come home.

"Hari Shankar said from his berth, 'We have this rehearsal at the radio station tomorrow—go along today to Champa Baji's cottage and give her the script.' Then after a pause he asked, 'Why has Tehmina done this? I mean why did she refuse to marry Bhaiya Saheb?'

"I looked at him in anger. Whatever I thought somehow reached his mind through some kind of telepathy. I just couldn't get rid of this fellow. He was like my invisible other self. My *humzad*. My heart sank.

"Qadeer was waiting for us in my D.K.W. motor car outside in the portico. I dropped Hari Shankar at Water Chestnut House, and went home."

Silence fell, as though the memory-candle had been blown out. Slowly the black-out lifted and Kamal began speaking again: "I reached Gulfishan and wandered from room to room in the strangely silent house. I didn't know how to ask Tehmina the reason for her refusal. I knew the reason. As did everybody else.

"I took the radio script and made for Champa Baji's cottage in Chand Bagh. I found her sitting under a garden umbrella on the tiny front lawn.

"My cousin Amir sat on a cane stool and he rose to his feet when he saw me coming. 'Hello, Kamal! When did you come? Just now, eh? I must scoot. Have to go somewhere.' Quickly he crossed over to the gate, got into his red sports car and drove away. He looked quite shaken. Obviously, something terrible had happened at Gulfishan.

"I sat down awkwardly. 'Baji, this is your part.' I gave her the papers of the humorous Hawapur University programme we used to write and broadcast over AIR, Lucknow, every now and then.

" 'Who thought of this title?' she asked curtly.

" 'Talat. She is the budding writer locally, as you know.'

" 'Very apt. You people are so windy,' she said with scorn.

" 'You mean windbags, ma'am.'

" 'Well, my English is not good. No La Martiniere, no nothing. Besides, you all think you are the cat's whiskers—correct? That's the phrase I have picked up from you baba-log only,' she continued in her Indian English. She looked furious, so I had no choice but to take her leave.

"Talat's friend Gyanwati Bhatnagar was singing over the radio. Her voice poured out from the house and undulated in the sun. Were there still some certainties left in life, and peace and some kind of hope?"

Talat resumed speaking and picked up her own thread:

"The carriage descended on the slope of the kutcha road

and entered the compound of Water Chestnut House." She paused, and said, "Don't you see, this is so useless? My past is important only to myself. Others can find little meaning in it," she said to Kamal.

"Like pious thieves we evoked our special gods but they betrayed us," said Talat. "Our Thieves' Kitchen has closed down. I tiptoe up to the confluence of light and darkness thinking of new names for things—like the golden, architect-god Prajapati, or like Adam and Eve."

"Now I remember nothing," said Kamal Reza, raising his face. "Passing years float around me like soap bubbles. Lights glisten on rain-filled streets of the night. The moon is rolling over sleeping chimneys, slipping away towards the sea. Sharp winds whistle tipsily over southern moors. Birds of the night are circling over the oily waters of heaving harbours.

"Crowds pass by. Canoes sail on shaded streams. I am on the shore.

"I have to search for a ship. A ship whose lights have gone out, which will quietly enter the dark ocean. A ship which is going towards a place where, I have this gut feeling, there is nobody to say, 'Welcome home, Kamal Reza. . .' "

32. A Spray of Roses

Lucknow, July 1939.

Lanterns lit up the boats passing under the bridge. Sitting in the porch of Water Chestnut House, Talat and Nirmala were now discussing their music lessons. Master Suraj Baksh was about to come and Nirmala had not yet practiced her lakshan geet. Trilochan came upstairs, grinning. "Surdas-ji is here," he announced.

Master Suraj Baksh came upstairs with firm, confident steps. He was a young, sightless graduate of Marris College who always wore a checked coat. He came all the way from Baroodkhana to Nirmala's house on foot, for his tuition. When he walked his head moved from side to side as though he was witnessing scenes hidden from the sighted. He entered the veranda. Nirmal touched his feet. He enquired pleasantly of Talat what she had learnt that evening in the music college. She replied, took his leave, wished everybody goodnight and ran downstairs.

Gunga Din sat on the chabutara, contentedly smoking his bidi. When he finished he threw the butt away and climbed onto the coachbox. As the phaeton moved out of the gate Nirmala's and Master Suraj Baksh's voices rose alternately in the stillness of the evening. Teacher and disciple were repeating the phrase *Aad anant, ant, nit, bhed naad ke*—Everlasting are the mysteries of sound. . .

Gulfishan stood midway between Isabella Thoburn and Karamat Hussain. Its garden had a profusion of flowers and the house's name, in Persian, meant a spray of roses.

From the front gate a little canal ran all along the compound wall till it reached the back garden where it joined up with the cement cubicle of the tube-well motor. Close by was a doll house made of bricks. Originally built for Tehmina, who was now an undergraduate, it had been "inherited" by Talat and survived the vandalism of the young hooligans, Kamal and Hari. Talat and Nirmala had only recently given up playing with dolls; when they played "house-house" Nirmala's dolls came over as guests. Last time Talat hosted a "hundkulia party" the two ruffians turned up and proceeded to demolish the little chulha, scattering the miniature pots and pans. "Why have you wrecked my kitchen?" Talat asked tearfully.

"Just for the heck of it!" Hari replied.

Tehmina rushed out shouting, "You bullies, aren't you ashamed of yourselves, terrorising helpless little girls?" and chased them out with a hockey stick.

The two schoolboys ran off, laughing. Both Kamal and Hari had been thoroughly spoilt by their doting mothers and thought they owned the world. They would raid guava orchards and compensation money would promptly be sent to the owner the very next day by fond parents. One night they removed the detachable name-plates of the neighbourhood bungalows and put them on the wrong gates, another time they went "Ganjing" on camel back. Now they had joined the University and their high spirits found a legitimate channel in Inquilab, Zindabad!

The phaeton entered the porch of Gulfishan. A servant quickly appeared and carried Talat's tamboura inside.

Kamal sat on the back veranda doing his homework. Begum Reza and her widowed sister-in-law squatted on the prayer takht under an arch, telling their beads. Water-pitchers covered with jasmine garlands stood in a row on their stands in a corner. Refrigerators had not arrived in most Indian homes yet.

Tehmina passed through the corridor linking the house with the pantry and kitchen. Hussaini the cook followed her, carrying a wooden pail of ice-cream.

It was an utterly peaceful domestic scene. Kamal was unusually quiet too, concentrating on his maths. Talat went up to him and said hesitantly, "You look very serious—what are you up to?"

"Get lost," he replied.

"Let the poor boy study," admonished her mother.

"Yeah. And get me some ice-cream," Kamal ordered his sibling.

A tonga arrived in the portico. Out-of-station cousins trooped in, bag and baggage. Joyful greetings followed and soon everybody proceeded to the dining-room. Then they would sleep outside, ladies on the back chabutara, men on the front lawn, all under white mosquito nets. Surahis of cool water covered with Moradabadi katoras would be placed at each bedside. If it rained servants would materialise at once to carry the cots and bedding onto the verandas.

Life was safe and secure, with no uncertainties.

Relatives kept drifting in and out all the time or stayed with the family for months together. Across the back lawn stood a neat little cottage inhabited by Qadeer, the chauffeur, and his wife. The adjoining outhouses contained the cook, the bearer, the syce, gardener and maid-servants of all ages and temperaments. The service area had been screened off by a row of mulberry trees. Sometimes Ram Autar, the gardener, stuck his sickle in the trunk of a tree and looked at the sky thoughtfully or produced strange guttural noises to scare the parrots away from the mango and guava trees.

Washermen lived outside at the back of the compound, and a betel-leaf seller's kiosk and a temple stood at a distance. On Sunday mornings the 'native Christian' girls of Isabella Thoburn College visited the washermen's houses and distributed toffees and holy pictures, and sang Methodist hymns in Urdu, set to English tunes.

There were many houses like Gulfishan down the road. The same kind of exceedingly refined people lived in them. They all had motor cars and their daughters went to convent schools and I.T. College and their sons studied for the competitive examinations of the Imperial Covenanted Services.

Gulfishan's cook was called Hussaini—most cooks were called that. Washermen were known as Nathu; all bearers answered to the name of Abdul. Syces were usually Gunga Din. Night-club violinists were known as Tony, fathers had such names as Syed Taqi Reza Bahadur or Aftab Chand Raizada. (Fathers in novels as well as in real life—that is why they say that novels portray our lives. Otherwise one could write any number of fantasies, don't you think?)

Qadeer, the chauffeur, hailed from the eastern-most district of Mirzapur. Once he had a brainwave of buying a camera. He collected a lot of English photography magazines and pestered everyone in Gulfishan to read out the price lists. It was his secret ambition to own a camera and he had been saving up for one religiously over the years. One day he finally did it. He bought a camera for one hundred and fifty rupees complete with tripod, a backdrop and other such stuff. Husband and wife set up a little 'studio' in their bamboo-walled courtyard and began photographing furiously. Qadeer took countless pictures of Tehmina and Amir and Kamal and Talat and every other resident of Gulfishan, including the cat. He had a romantic bent and nobody dared disagree with his ideas. Tehmina playing the sitar against the crudely painted back-

drop of a palace with full moon, peacocks, swans and fountains; Tehmina in a thoughtful mood, holding a pen; Kamal
standing with his cups and trophies which he had won in college debates; Amir looking decorative with his tennis racket.
Mother and Aunt Zubeida reclining on sofas; Laj and Nirmala
dressed up as Radha and Krishna; Hari Shankar gravely reading a fat book.

These post-card size pictures cost Qadeer eight annas each
and were bought enthusiastically by their models at treble their
cost. The couple spent all their spare time in the dark-room
in their cottage. On hot summer days when everybody was
fast asleep, one could hear Qadeer's voice rise from his cottage
singing the ballad of Alha-and-Udal. He sat on the threshold
of his room beating time on an empty petrol tin, singing away
happily. Qamrun, his wife, sat in a corner, crocheting. As soon
as she spotted someone from the bungalow coming down to
pay them a visit, she covered her face with her sari in case the
visitor was a male, and began preparing a betel-leaf. Fair and
attractive, she belonged to the same district of eastern
U.P. as Nirmala's mother. She was often invited to Water Chestnut House. Whenever Mrs. Raizada came to Gulfishan,
Qamrun was immediately sent for from her cottage. Dressed
in a coloured sari of coarse cotton she would gracefully ascend
the terrace and her silver anklets would announce from afar
that Qamrun Nissa had arrived. Then Mrs. Raizada and
Qamrun would spend hours chatting happily in their Bhojpuri
dialect.

Qadeer and Qamrun were children of peasants. Before he
became a chauffeur, Qadeer was an ardent Kisan Sabha worker
and preached the use of the spinning wheel in his village. This
was when young Jawaharlal, the Cambridge-educated son of
Motilal Nehru, was bent upon uprooting the landlord-peas-
ant system and travelled from village to village making speeches.
Who knew the evils of the zamindari system better than Qadeer
who had suffered under it for years?

So, when Kamal and his comrades held elaborate discussions on the lawns of Gulfishan, Qadeer hovered around on
the pretext of fixing the table-fan or serving cold drinks, and

tried to understand these learned arguments. His father had been beaten to death by the zamindar's men, when he failed to pay the land revenue permanently fixed by Lord Cornwallis a hundred and fifty years ago. The rest of the family had been ejected from the land, so Qadeer had gone to Calcutta where he had become a cleaner in a motor garage and later got a job as a driver. Back in the village his family continued to starve.

The Indian National Congress launched the No Tax Movement and it caught on like wildfire in the villages. The landlords were on the government's side against the peasants and the Congress. Qadeer couldn't understand the goings-on in big cities. Kamal and his friends maintained that the real reason for people's restlessness and disintegration was economic. The government gave it a Hindu-Muslim twist so that the masses could be diverted from the root cause. Qadeer understood.

Qamrun came to the bungalow after lunch, carrying her little son on her waist, and joined the long and langorous gossip session in the begum's bedroom. Talat's mother would be lying on the divan reading an Urdu women's magazine, Aunt Zubeida and a visiting female relative, if any, might be reclining on the prayer settee or the four-poster. The massive paandan of filigree silver would be lying open in front of them.

"Aha, Driver's Wife! Do sit down," one of the ladies would greet her.

She would salaam gracefully and squat on the carpet. One of them would offer her a betel-leaf.

At four, Kamal, Tehmina and Talat returned from their classes and suddenly the drowsy house came to life. Tea cups jingled in the dining-room, and one was also handed to Qamrun. At about this time Qadeer brought Taqi Reza Bahadur from the Chief Court which he attended almost every day. Litigation against fellow landowners or members of their extended families was a favourite pastime with zamindars. At the sound of the car Qamrun pulled the sari over her face, picked up her sleeping son and ambled back to her cottage.

Apart from Mrs. Raizada, Qamrun had another dear friend in Ram Daiya, the gardener's little wife. Ram Daiya was not

blasé like the city-bred maid-servants of Gulfishan. She didn't
sing filmi songs like Talat's ayah Susan did, she was of the Mali
caste and also belonged to Qamrun's part of the province.
Like Qamrun, she had been married at the age of twelve and
her husband, Ram Autar the gardener, was a full twenty years
older than her. When he brought her from his village she had
alighted from the ekka wrapped in a red Japanese-silk sari and
weeping copiously; she was taken into the bungalow and presented before the ladies in order to bow low and say bandagi.
Later, Qamrun had gone to the outhouses and begun talking
to her in Purbi to put her at ease.

Gunga Din, the coachman, was a middle-aged widower. He
loved his victoria and looked down upon Qadeer's silver-grey
Chevrolet. His was one of the few surviving victorias in
Lucknow, the last of the old leisurely order. Gunga Din suddenly acquired enormous importance when the war broke out
and petrol was rationed. Now he teased Qadeer good-
humouredly: "Why don't you drive your wonderful motor-
garry now, Mister? Look at me—I don't bother about the Ger-
man-wallah. No Hitler-Phitler can affect my Typhoon."

33. Warren Hastings Bahadur's Haveli

A few days before the seventh standard annual examination
Talat came down with double pneumonia. She was heartbro-
ken at the thought of losing a year, but during her convales-
cence she leaned against the bolster and queened it over everyone. Kamal procured a rickety film projector and clips of
ancient silent movies from somewhere for her amusement.
Shadows of dead years flickered on the screen, but Jean
Harlow-Charlie Chaplin-Zubeida-Sulochana failed to entertain her. Hari Shankar was a clown and tried out his mimicry,
but she was not amused.

One morning Hari jumped in through the French windows

of the morning room and spoke in the manner of the European Ward nurses of King George's Medical College.

"And how are we today?"

"Bad," Talat sniffed.

"Tut, tut."

"Hari, why are you grinning like a Cheshire cat?" she asked suspiciously.

"Instead of losing one year we are gaining *three*. We are going to Master Saheb's School in July '40, and appearing for Japani matric as a private candidate. And, hey presto! I.T. College in July '41. . ."

Talat blinked. "Tatterwalla School on Barrow Road?" She hopped off the divan bed and danced in sheer joy. Then she stopped. "Hey, knowing you as I do, is there a catch in it?" she demanded.

"No catch, cross my heart and hope to die," he said like a schoolboy and jumped out of the same windows.

Pre-war Japan flooded British India's markets with cheap goods, including silks and georgettes. Inexpensive things were referred to as 'Japanese', and high school without matriculation for girls was also called 'Japani'.

Master Saheb was an old-world Kayasth teacher who had opened his school a year earlier in the quiet and elegant residential area of Barrow Road, Lal Bagh. As soon as Nirmala heard that Talat was soon going to join I.T. College via a short cut, she declared war on her family. Therefore, she was also withdrawn from La Martiniere School and sent off to do her Japani matric.

In Lucknow, history is yesterday. La Martiniere College is housed in General Claude Martin's palace, 'Constantia'; La Martiniere Girls' High School is still called Khurshid Manzil. King Nasiruddin Hyder's Observatory is now a bank. These European-style buildings connect with the era when English notables received grandiose titles from latter-day monarchs in Delhi and Lucknow, who could do little else. Nawab Cornwallis Azimulshan Madarul Maham Sarkar Company Angrez Bahadur. Saiful Mulk General Martin. Embadul Daulah Afzalul Mulk John Bailey Saheb Bahadur Arsalan Jung. Ashraful Omra Lord Myra. . .

Warren Hastings Jasarat Jung, Nawab Governor-General Bahadur of Fort William-in-Bengal was popularly known as "Hastan Bahadur, Firangi Subedar Bengal". He was later tried in England for his misdeeds. Nawab Sade Jehan, mother of Shuja-ud Daulah and his widow, Nawab Bahu Begum, mother of Asaf-ud Daulah, were remarkable women. Nawab Bahu Begum had established a Department of Higher Studies in her palace in Fyzabad. Hastings extorted millions of rupees from Begums who had sided with Maharajah Chait Singh of Banaras against him. The ladies had summoned their zamindars and rajahs for assistance when they confronted the Governor-General. His troops persecuted the Begums' own battalion, flogged the Urdu-beginis—women soldiers—and forced them to surrender the treasure.

Master Saheb belonged to Nawab Bahu Begum's Fyzabad. He heard from his elders that Hastings had interned the formidable royal ladies in this very haveli in Lucknow, so he rented this now dilapidated stately home from its present owners for his school. Master Saheb coached his flock for the matriculation examination of Banaras University, where girls could be offered Hindustani music or botany instead of mathematics. A bamboo lattice covered with a dense creeper of morning glory served as the compound wall and accorded the name, Tatterwalla School, to this delightful institution.

On the 1st of July 1940, Talat picked up a very excited Nirmala from Singharewali Kothi and was driven by coachman Gunga Din to their new school. Master Saheb was a thin man of about forty who limped a little and was held in great esteem and affection by his pupils and their parents. His wife taught botany. Before school began the girls assembled in a big room in the gatehouse and sang Iqbal's *Sare jahan se achha Hindustan hamara*. Master Saheb stood in one corner and listened to the song with a solemn expression on his face. A sincere and staunch Congressman, he was a representative of mainstream Gandhian nationalism.

There was yet another aspect of the new nationalist movement that was making its presence felt—some people had openly begun talking of Ancient Hindu Culture and the Glory-that-was-Islam. How was Indian culture to be defined? Was it a ruse for Hindus to enslave the Muslims? Could 'real' Indians only be Hindus? Were Muslims unholy intruders who should be treated as such?

Nobody had ever asked Mirzapur's Qamrun Nissa and Ram Daiya their opinion on these matters. The ancient Hindu-Buddhist-Jain, the intermediary Turco-Mughal-Iranian and the latter-day British feaures of Indian civilization were so intermingled that it was impossible to separate the warp and woof of the rich fabric. The jingoistic attempts of chauvinists to 'purify' this culture were creating bad blood and confusion. In Lucknow, however, communal harmony was taken for granted—it could not have been otherwise.

Talat and Nirmala had been brought up in the hybrid Indo-British culture of the upper-middle classes. They merged in the homely Hindustani-Oudhi atmosphere of Master Saheb's school with the same ease with which they had mingled in the pucca English set-up of La Martiniere. Nor did Master Saheb's Persian-Urdu culture clash with his orthodox Hindu religion. One Kayastha girl still came in a curtained tonga. On Vishwakarma, when Hindus of different castes worshipped the tools of their various trades, the Kayasthas continued to worship their qalamdans—pen-and-ink stands which had always been the tool of their profession.

Thirteen-year-old frock-clad Talat was the youngest of thirty girls from the old families of Lucknow. Half the students were Muslim but most of them did not observe purdah, and had taken up classical music as a subject. Times were changing fast. Master Suraj Baksh taught music, Talat strummed the tamboura.

The Urdu-Persian Maulvi Saheb was a tottering gentleman of Old Lucknow. He held the degree of Maulvi Fazil—maulvi meaning a scholar, not a priest. This maulvi was a Kashmiri pandit whose forefathers had come to Lucknow from Kashmir in the early years of the nineteenth century, attracted by the nawabs' patronage. His community had produced many famous Urdu poets, novelists, lawyers and doctors.

Maulvi Kaul taught the Urdu course prepared by Maulvi

Mahesh Parshad, head of the Department of Urdu and Persian, Banaras Hindu University. When Maulvi Kaul fell ill Master Saheb asked Hari Shankar to teach in his place. (Hari Shankar was now doing his M.A. in Persian.) After a few days he began teaching with great solemnity and was officially known as Chhotey or Junior Maulvi Saheb. He overawed the girls with his bad temper and discipline.

Amidst the row of 'English' shops on the Mall in Hazrat Ganj, an ancient gate leads to Maqbara Compound. Inside its vast quadrangle stands the mausoleum or maqbara of Amjad Ali Shah, father of Vajid Ali Shah. The Imambara had temporarily been converted into a church when General Outram conquered the city in 1857, and Lord Cannon attended divine service in its precincts. After some time it was given back to the Muslims to resume their dirge for Imam Hussain, to which now was added a silent mourning for their lost kingdom. Many Christian converts had occupied the compound while the Imambara was being used as a church and their descendants, as well as new Christian tenants, continued to live in the outhouses of the quadrangle.

During Moharrum big 'majlises' were held in the Imambara. The events of the martyrdom of the Prophet's grandson Hussain were recounted and elegies recited. Indigent Christians lived in the basement rooms and the women did brisk business during the Forty Days of Mourning, looking after the mourners' shoes and collecting charity. A white-skinned Anglo-Indian community also flourished in Lal Bagh and had their own club in Hazrat Ganj. A number of blonde Eurasian girls were professional Kathak dancers—Vajid Ali Shah's culture still held sway in Lucknow—and one of them, called Rosie, lived with her parents in a bungalow near Tatterwalla School.

In the monsoons when the students sang Gaur Malhar in the music class above the gate-house, and the greenery outside was drenched in rain, the world seemed to be full of liquid music. The easterly wind brought the sound of Rosie's ghungroos to the tower-room as she practiced in her bungalow. Her teacher was a shishya of Shambhu Maharaj of the House of Vajid Ali Shah's Kalka Binda Din.

The matric candidates left for Banaras in March 1941. Kamal and Hari Shankar came to Char Bagh to see their sisters off. "You go ahead," said Kamal gleefully, "we'll join you there for sight-seeing as soon as our own exams are over. We have always wanted to visit Sarnath."

"I am told, on reliable authority, that some absolutely stunning females study in the colleges of Banaras," observed Hari Shankar with a wink.

"What would your poor students think if they overheard their Junior Maulvi Saheb talking like this!" Nirmala admonished her older brother.

Thereupon Hari Shankar turned towards his students gathered on the platform, and solemnly began explaining some important points about Mirza Ghalib's poetry for their Urdu paper.

34. The Maharajah's Rolls Royce

Champa Ahmed looked out of the window of Besant College's library. It was a hot and dusty April morning and a whirlwind was dancing in the distance. Yellow laburnum leaves flitted about in the compound. Mrs. Annie Besant smiled soulfully out of her oil portrait which hung right above the head of the frowning and harassed librarian.

Bye-bye, Mrs. Besant, if I get a first class I won't be coming here again, Champa said quietly and quickly sent up a little prayer: 'Please, Allah Mian, give me a first division in my intermediate arts exam for the sweet sake of Mohammed and the Children of Mohammed. Amen.' Then she hastily added— 'My mother's name is Nafisa Begum.' She had always been told that the angels who convey the prayers On High only require the name of the supplicant's mother.

Her friend, Lila Bhargava, returned her books and said to her as they went downstairs, "My cousin Kusum has come from Lucknow for her high school exam. She has studied in that quaint place called Master Saheb's Tatterwalla School. Let's go to the University and meet her."

Upon a huge, canopied terrace girl students of the Theory of Music paper were softly humming their answers before writing them down. The humming could be heard outside where Champa and Lila stood under a flowering mango tree, waiting for Kusum Kumari Bhargava. The sun became more intense. "This is the time when lucky people go to Mussoorie," Lila remarked wistfully. Champa said nothing. She had learnt to accept her lot. Year after year she had spent summer in the same heat and dust, in the same congested mohalla of the city of Banaras.

Kusum walked towards the canopy.

Champa's parents belonged to the genteel white-collar class. Her father was a briefless lawyer. He came from the western district of Moradabad, and had set up his legal practice in his wife's home-town. Her mother's people were comparatively better off. Champa was an only child and her father had already received several proposals for her marriage. But she had not been to a convent school and she did not know how to roller-skate. Champa's father took a mild interest in Muslim League politics and especially went to meet Amir Ahmed Khan, Raja of Mahmudabad, when he visited Banaras. The Raja was financing the new Pakistan Movement.

Banaras was also the centre of Hindu revivalism. Champa's ambitious mother was not concerned with politics—her plan was to send her daughter to Lucknow's Isabella Thoburn. A girl's social status was elevated overnight by attending this American missionary college, and upper-class girls from all over India came here to study. Champa's father wanted her to join the Muslim Girls' College, Aligarh, but Nafisa Begum put her little foot down firmly. "No," she said, "my bitiya will go to I.T. College like the daughters of Rani Phool Kunwar and the Begum Saheb of Bilari."

Kashi Naresh's white Rolls Royce glided by soundlessly like the Chariot of the Sun. Two beaming young men stepped out and glanced around blithely. One of them was of medium height, the other tall and very fair with curly hair. Both were highly presentable and seemed much pleased with themselves. Obviously, strangers to the campus. The Fair One stuck his thumbs in his trouser pockets and whistled softly, not unlike an English youth. Then they noticed the pretty girl in a white sari who lingered under the mango tree. The Fair One stopped whistling. Both of them realized that she was also observing them intently and looked away, embarrassed. The girl was amused and smiled faintly. Another young woman came along, fanning herself with a notebook.

The young men covered their very high-class noses with their handkerchiefs in order to protect themselves from wind-blown dust. Two lanky, frock-clad kids bounced down the staircase of the canopied terrace and ran towards them. One of them shouted breathlessly, "Bhaiya, Bhaiya, can you imagine an examination hall where everybody was humming away to glory while doing their papers?" This child was pale and thin and resembled the dusky youth who addressed her as Nirmala. The rose-pink one with wavy hair seemed to be the sister of the Fair One. All four were speaking rapidly in English and in very pucca tones. The liveried chauffeur kow-towed before the girls and opened the royal limousine's door.

The Sun-Chariot vanished in the shining noonday haze. Lila had come back after briefly meeting Kusum and had taken a long, hard look at the boys.

"His Highness doesn't have sons or nephews of that age, so who were they?" she wondered aloud.

"Loafers," answered Champa primly.

"So carefree and happy, as though they owned the world."

"The Rolls Royce has done it. If they had come here on an ekka you wouldn't have thought twice about them," Champa told her friend sternly.

These two students of English literature had just finished their Bernard Shaw. Lila continued, "They stood there with such aplomb and poise—like Caesar and Antony."

"Listen, Cleopatra, the sun has affected your mind. They were merely a pair of snooty young Brown Sahebs who thought they had arrived in a native pathshala by mistake."

"And the kids were so bright and chirpy," Lila remarked.

"They were just a bunch of spoilt brats, all four of them. Educated in English schools in the hills, a different breed altogether. No concern of ours. Stop envying them."

Lila changed the topic. "Listen, Champa, this cousin of mine, Kusum, has invited us for the musical play that the Tatterwalla Lucknow gang is going to stage at the place they are staying. Kusum is also going to join Marris College in Lucknow."

Champa frowned. Marris College of Hindustani Music. Colvin Taluqdar's College. La Martiniere. Canning College. Loretto Convent, Isabella Thoburn. Karamat Hussain Muslim Girls College—the Golden Circle. The magic world of Lucknow, inhabited by such Charming People as she had just seen. Suddenly she was struck by a wave of resentment and frustration, annoyed with her friend Lila, a poor schoolteacher's daughter, carried away by the glimpse she had caught of those enchanting creatures.

On her way home, however, as her rickety tonga passed through noisy bazaars, she found herself comparing her own lowly existence with the grandeur of the denizens of Quality Street. The tonga entered a lane and stopped before a modest homestead. This is where I live, she told herself resignedly. Those two uppity lads who were stunned by her looks, if they were to see her in this depressing petit bourgeois locality, how disappointed they would be! Who were they? She could lecture a guileless Lila on the futility of being envious, but she secretly yearned for all the good things of life herself.

35. The Last Song of Vajid Ali Shah

In Banaras, Master Saheb's flock was staying in an ornate threestoreyed red-brick mansion, surrounded by a neglected garden. Its windows were heavily grilled, its balconies and spiral stairs made of wrought iron. A pair of wooden dwarpals with saucer-like eyes and fiercely pointed jet-black moustaches 'guarded' the main entrance. They wore sola topis and their quaint uniforms were painted a garish blue. They held wooden guns in their hands and were typical of post-1857 Indian kitsch.

The landlady was a pious Brahmin widow who lived on the third floor and was popularly known as the Panditayin. When, in 1856, Sultan-i-Alam Vajid Ali Shah was being taken to Calcutta, he stopped over in Banaras and gave a large sum of money to his host, Maharaja Ishari Parsad Narain Singh, for a specific purpose. The shehnai players of the city were traditionally Muslim and were often employed by temple priests to play their wind instruments in the morning for the ritual of 'waking up' the deities. The deposed king set up a trust for the shehnai players to play in the main temple of Kashi every morning—the parting gesture of a monarch whose predecessors had created an exquisite composite culture during the 166 years of their reign over this land.

Students of Hindustani classical music used to sit under a tamarind tree in the garden and practice for their examination. One morning the tiny Panditayin strolled down and handed Talat an old copy book. "See, bitiya, when Jaan-i-Alam came here he gave some of his rare compositions, his thumris, to my grandfather who was an acharya of Shastriya sangeet."

Talat was thrilled. She opened the tattered book gingerly. It had a few lines scribbled in it in Hindi and Urdu. "We have kept it safely, it is so precious," the Panditayin said. She retrieved the book from Talat and trotted back to the house.

At meal times a dining-cloth was spread on the floor in a hall. A fat Brahmin cook trundled in, followed by his thin assistant who carried a brass pail full of curd. The chief Misra ladled out curd and poured it into the girls' brass cups from a great height so that he was not polluted, for the girls belonged to all manner of castes and creeds. Vegetarian food was served on banana leaves.

When the examinations began Master Saheb's wife gravely posted herself at the exit every morning and observed the propitiating ceremony of Oil-and-Lentil, and Fish-and-Curd. These customs, signifying good omen, were followed by Hindus and Muslims alike. Passing through the door on her way to the examination hall, each girl looked at her reflection in the pot of oil, and a drop of curd was applied to her forehead. The words "curd and fish" were repeated by everyone. Fish was a symbol of good fortune and adorned the royal crest of the Nawabs of Oudh—the gates of their buildings displayed a pair of fish facing each other in bas-relief.

Kamal and Hari Shankar turned up on the morning of the Theory of Music exam. When Talat and Nirmala came out of the canopied terrace, they saw the two jokers standing before a sparkling Rolls Royce. They were looking in the direction of a mango tree and the object of their appreciative attention was, of course, a senior girl in a white cotton sari. She had a golden brown complexion and was very pretty indeed. The schoolgirls gave her a quick once-over and ran towards the limousine.

Kamal and Hari were staying with the chief minister or diwan of a princely state across the Ganga. They had come to the University in one of the royal motor cars to take their kid sisters to the estate for lunch. The Diwan Bahadur was distantly related to the Reza family.

"I have to buy a Banarasi sari and lots of bangles for Qamrun," said Talat as they reached the bridge-of-boats. "For Hussain's wife, Ram Daiya, and Susan also. Give us some dough."

"Are you under the impression that we are tycoons? That we operate some kind of a private bank? We are two destitute bachelor-students who subsist on charity ourselves," said Hari Shankar piously.

"But in spite of our poverty we can be large-hearted like nawabs," added Kamal. "If you tell us who that vision was that we saw in the fragrant arbour, we will buy all the bangles of Banaras for you two."

"What's that?" asked Talat. "What vision? Where is the fragrant arbour? Give us some dough, quick."

"Only if you find out about her first," Hari Shankar haggled.

They spent the day behind the khas screens of the Diwan's large bungalow, and gossiped with his daughters who had come down from their convent school in Nainital. Though still a student, 20-year-old Hari was a prize bachelor. The chief minister's begum was in her element suggesting suitable matches for him. "There are so many Rajas in Poorab Des with marriageable daughters, but they are all Thakurs. We'll find a nice Kayastha girl for you, daughter of some ICS official. . ." The Kayasthas had retained the tradition of their caste, and now manned the British administration.

After the examinations were over the girls, escorted by Master Saheb and Didi, shopped in the mysterious by-lanes of the old city. At nightfall they went boating on the Ganga, the next day they visited Sarnath in the blazing sun. Little brass lamps shone their light on the marble floor of a newly built Buddhist temple, and row upon row of golden statues of Prince Gautam Siddhartha glittered in the semi-darkness of the hall.

"How peaceful. Shanti. Buddha's Shanti," remarked Talat thoughtfully. They were sitting on the cold marble floor.

"Ahem. . .," Bano nodded and smiled wisely, for now she was about to reveal the truth: "We have come in here after roaming in the hot sun; we are bound to feel restful. And the hall is so cool." Suddenly Talat got up and started to dance, and the other girls joined in.

A day before their departure for Lucknow, a tiny stage was set up in the courtyard of the Panditayin's house and decorated with plantain leaves. Cotton carpets were spread on the floor for spectators to sit on and a printed calico hung as a backdrop. There was no time to produce a regular play, so it was decided to present the story of Mira Bai. Instead of dialogue, the plot could unfold through the 16th century mystic-princess's famous bhajans. The girls knew the popular story so well that they could ad lib. Shahida was playing the role of Mira's stern husband, the Rana, who was against his wife's total devotion to Krishna. From time to time, her moustache fell off. Kusum was the Emperor Akbar, though her untimely laughter spoilt the scene a little, and consequently was thoroughly enjoyed by the audience. Gyanvati Bhatnagar was a famous radio artist and an accomplished singer—naturally, she played Mira Bai.

Talat was director and general handyman, and would ascend the stage whenever there was an unforeseen shortage of actors. In one scene she was Akbar's prime minister, in another, Mira's friend and confidante. In the scene where Mira Bai was married to the Rana, she borrowed Akbar the Great's white moustache and, as a pandit, entered the 'wedding canopy' uttering some supposedly learned mumbo-jumbo. In the grand finale the gopis sang and danced around Bano who stood in the classical pose of Krishna, the Divine Flute Player. Farida, whose face had been decorated with little dots of toothpaste, made a very demure Radha. The audience sat under a starlit sky, Kamal and Hari squatted in the last row. They did not see Champa who was sitting in the front, near the stage.

Champa's prayers were answered. She obtained a first division in her intermediate arts examination and promptly got a coveted seat in Isabella Thoburn College, Lucknow. A well-to-do relative in Lucknow was informed of her forthcoming arrival on July 13. She started packing, but there was nothing much to take apart from the half dozen new cotton saris her mother had bought for her, costing three or four rupees each. One evening while her father was talking to a client in the room facing the lane, her mother came to her room and handed her an envelope. "Evening mail," she said and returned to the kitchen.

Champa opened the square, grey-blue, very classy envelope post-marked Mussoorie. The letter was in English. She was addressed informally as 'My dear Champa'. It read: 'I am glad to learn that you are going to join our college this year.' This was followed by detailed information about Chand Bagh. She was told that depending on her interest, the following clubs would welcome her. If she was an outdoor girl she ought to meet the Sports Director, Jaimala Appaswamy. The Tennis Secretary, Radha Shrinagesh, would love to have her in the Tennis Club in case she played that game. The Drama Society was waiting for her eagerly if she liked to pace the boards, etc. Also that she had been placed in the charge of the writer of the letter who was a student of B.A. final, and would be her official advisor in the coming year. Therefore, when she reached the college on July 14, 8 a.m., she would be met by the writer at the steps of Florence Nicholas Hall and the writer would try to solve all her problems. The letter was signed: Tehmina Reza, Oakland Hall, Mussoorie.

Champa was flabbergasted. Who was this Tehmina Reza and how had she obtained her address? This was straight out of a story-book. Such mysterious epistles arrived in romantic Urdu novels written by upper-middle-class ladies of an earlier era. Then she remembered a volume of Irish fairy-tales she had once bought for four annas in a second-hand book shop. It had belonged to some English girl student of St. Mary's Convent, Banaras, and was titled *A Password to Fairyland*. Was this stranger Tehmina Reza's letter such a password? She couldn't quite believe that she was going to enter the fabled world of The Elite. She may even become one of them some day, if God was on her side.

36. The Moon Garden

"Pledge we our faith dear Chand Bagh to thee, through years that onward roll. . ."

The college song was set to the tune of 'Drink to me only with thine eyes' and was sung with gusto by the students while the pianist, Mrs 'Music' Jordan, sat ramrod straight on the stool and gravely pounded the keyboard. She also played the organ in the college chapel. She pinned her anchal neatly to her left shoulder with a brooch and wore her sari four inches above floor level. Both Mrs 'Music' Jordan and her sister-in-law, Mrs 'Economics' Jordan, were Lucknowites. Then there were two Bengali Brahmo ladies, two olde-worlde, courteous gentlemen who taught Urdu and Persian, and a kindly Hindi-Sanskrit panditji. Mrs Constance Das was the college's first Indian Principal and had recently taken over from the American, Dr Mary Shannon, who had retired.

Mrs Das was gracious and handsome, a very high-caste, upper-class Indian Christian. She was the younger sister of Lady Maharaj Singh—Sir Maharaj belonged to the Christian branch of Kapurthala's Sikh royal family. Vice Principal, Miss Sarah Chacko, was from Kerala. Indian society was a cocktail or pot-pourri, cheerful co-existence was the norm.

The rest of the college staff was white American, except for the ever-smiling Miss Downs who was a Black nurse, in charge of the King's Daughter's Infirmary. A Methodist missionary, Miss Isabella Thoburn had come from Ohio in 1862 and founded this college in Aminabad. It became a degree college in 1895 and was shifted to Chand Bagh across the Gomti in 1922.

Isabella Thoburn College was popularly known as Chand Bagh. Before 1857, Chand Bagh was part of Ramna, or royal parkland, where deer and bison were kept and where the rulers of Oudh came to watch elephant and ram fights. In Lucknow, various localities were known as Baghs or gardens, laid out by the Nawab Vazir and later kings. The residential areas were called Ganj or treasure-houses.

With its magnificent buildings, beautifully furnished drawing rooms, well-tended playing fields and gardens, Chand Bagh looked like a college campus, Anywhere, U.S.A. All the buildings were inter-connected through long, gleaming corridors. The eucalyptus grove was called the Forest of Arden. The three college hostels were named Nishat Mahal, Maunihal Manzil and Maitri Bhavan. Hindu and Muslim boarders jointly celebrated the festivals of Id and Diwali. Some Hindu girls wore ghararas and solemnly lighted joss sticks on the occasion of Milad Sharif, the Prophet's birthday.

The American teachers of Chand Bagh were the finest emissaries the U.S.A. could have sent to India in its period of isolation. The Americans were aliens and steered clear of Indian politics. Still, instead of the British governor and his lady, they often invited personages such as Sarojini Naidu, leading Urdu poets and Pandit Jawaharlal Nehru to address the girls on non-political subjects. The college was affiliated to the University of Lucknow: the method of teaching was Ameri-

can. Sociologically, however, the term 'Americanization' was
unknown. The continent of America had not really been discovered by Indians yet, except by those Punjabi farmers who
had settled in California in the Twenties.

On the morning of July 14, 1941, Champa Ahmed of
Banaras was taken by surprise when she counted 40 Muslim
names on the list of 250 students displayed on the notice board.
The tall and statuesque Meher Taj, daughter of the Frontier
Gandhi, Khan Abdul Ghaffar Khan, who looked like the Statue
of Liberty was a student there, and so was Chandralekha Pandit,
niece of Jawaharlal Nehru.

As an educated class, Indian women were slowly emerging
from their seclusion. Lucknow had two middle-aged Muslim
sisters, Miss Shah Jehan Begum and Miss Roshan Jehan Begum,
who had graduated from Chand Bagh in the 1920s. Both were
"England-returned": Miss Roshan Jehan Begum was Principal of Karamat Hussain Muslim Girls' College down the road,
(a purdah college whose sprawling campus was hidden behind
high walls). Both sisters were spinsters and were often seen
bicycling back and forth on Fyzabad Road. Bicycles were the
preferred mode of transport for modern college women in
Lucknow, and had somehow become the symbol of female
emancipation here, just as they had been in England and
America in earlier times. Doe-eyed Miss Noor Jehan Yusuf must
have been a beauty as a young woman. She was Inspectress of
Schools and also lived on Fyzabad Road. When she went to
England for higher studies her sister went with her as a chaperone and they, too, were spinsters.

By 1941, when Champa joined Chand Bagh, women had
acquired greater self-confidence and society was also generally
more liberal. Still, Chand Bagh remained a conservative college. Hostel rules were strict, junior girls could go to Hazrat
Ganj only with seniors as chaperones. The city was out of
bounds and 'dating' was unknown.

Chand Bagh was also a great social leveller. Daughters of
ruling princes and commoners all wore simple saris, for the
missionaries, being American, did not have the class snobbery
of the British.

As the stranger Tehmina Reza had promised in her letter, on the morning of July 14, at 8 a.m. sharp, with American precision a slim Plain Jane met a slightly bewildered and nervous Champa Ahmed on the steps of Florence Nicholas Hall, the neo-classical porch of Isabella Thoburn College.

"Hello. Are you Champa?" she asked pleasantly.

Champa nodded, tongue-tied.

"I am Tehmina Reza, your advisor for one year. Come along."

Champa was disappointed. She was expecting to meet some glamorous princess who had written to her from Oakland Hall, Mussoorie. This was a homely, good-natured student of B.A. final, who told her that the college office sent the addresses of newly admitted girls to some of the senior students to write letters of welcome. Along with one faculty member, the seniors acted as advisors to new girls during their first year in Chand Bagh. Tehmina's younger sister, Talat, had joined as a freshman. She said to Champa, "Omigosh, Champa Baji, we saw you in Banaras in April, didn't we, Nirmala?"

Champa was invited by her 'advisor' to Gulfishan.

It was a Saturday afternoon. She sat on the back lawn near the roses, talking to Tehmina, when she saw Kamal and Hari strolling down towards them. Their eyes met. All three were momentarily taken aback, then all of them broke into merry, youthful laughter.

"Have you met these rascals before, Champa?" Tehmina asked her.

"Well, not really. Saw them riding a Rolls Royce and wondered about them," Champa answered smoothly. As one of the have-nots she had trained herself to hold her head high in all situations. Here she was amidst the Chosen Few and she was not going to reveal her deep sense of insecurity and inferiority. She was as good as any of them, and would take them in stride. Besides, she had an address in Lucknow: the rich relative's bungalow on Sir Wazir Hasan Road. She needn't worry, they would never go to the congested mohalla in Banaras to see where she actually lived.

Kamal and Hari gaped at her as she continued talking to them in a patronising manner. They also realised that she was a few years older than them so, of course, romance was out. And she was Elder Sister Tehmina's friend and, as such, had to be respected.

Talat called her Champa Baji, so Kamal and Hari also began to address her as Baji. But they wondered why a girl of twenty-three was still doing her B.A. (previous). It was a personal question which nobody could ask—she couldn't have told them that she had begun her education late because of her father's financial difficulties.

"We, the zamindars of Poorab, are very orthodox—I couldn't go to school till my grandfather died," she volunteered the 'information' herself.

Unwittingly, Champa Ahmed had embarked upon a career of spinning yarns in order to keep up with the Joneses.

Tehmina had asked Champa to stay back for dinner. Amir spotted her in the crowd of guests on the lawn, and with his killer instinct walked over and introduced himself in a most charming manner. Gallantly he brought her food from the buffet tables and managed to remain by her side all evening. He was clearly smitten. Still, he *was* her mentor's fiancé—the plot of the women's serial romance had thickened much too fast. Inside, in the drawing-room, poor Tehmina was dreamily playing Strebbog's *Faery Waltz* on her cottage Steinway. A full moon shone in a black velvet sky and the garden was flooded with the heady scent of raat-ki-rani.

The dinner guests began to leave.

Amir asked Champa quietly, "May I see you tomorrow?"

"No."

"Why?"

"For obvious reasons."

"Damn the reasons. We are only born once, etc.," he said masterfully. He was willing to take risks. Besides he seemed to be the kind who was in control of situations.

The next evening he drove down to Chand Bagh and sent in his name as Miss T. Reza's cousin.

Now, 'cousins' was a special term for visitors to women's

hostels, but Lieut. Reza, everybody knew, was a genuine relative. Champa came to the Visitors' Room—

"I am your chaperone for the evening," he grinned, and signed the register.

He whisked her off in his scarlet sports car to Mohammed Bagh Club in the cantonment. Being a Services Club it was not frequented by civilians. They had coffee, and he brought her back much before the gates closed. Had she been late she would have been 'gated' and not allowed out again for a certain period of time.

Amir was on a month's leave and he took Champa out every other evening. They went deep into the countryside, well beyond Chinhat or Bakhshi ka Talab, two favourite picnic spots near Lucknow. It was all strictly honourable. They did not even hold hands, just talked. He told her about his childhood, his terrible governess Nina, his 'compulsory' engagement to Tehmina. He was an unhappy young man. "How can you and I not hurt poor Tim? I'm really at sea. . . that reminds me. . . I may be sent to the war front soon. Promise you'll wait for me— we'll find some way out of this tricky situation, don't worry."

Both Amir and Champa thought they had been discreet about their secret meetings, but one day Pandit Jawaharlal Nehru inadvertently let the cat out of the bag. He was at Chand Bagh to talk about his "discovery of India". Standing on the stage in the Assembly Hall, he looked down benignly at the girls as though they were all members of his own extended family. He was affectionate and informal. During the course of his lecture in which he discussed pre-historic Indian geography, he said, "If you wished to go to Mussoorie you would have had to board a ship and cross a sea to reach the Himalayas."

The following day Tehmina took Champa along to India Coffee House—Hari, Kamal, Laj, Nirmala and Talat had invaded Hazrat Ganj, as usual, on their bicycles. Tehmina and Laj began to discuss Panditji's visit.

"He is cho chweet," Nirmala exclaimed.

"Oh, he is tweeet. . ." Talat said even more emphatically.

Kamal and Hari Shankar groaned.

"Yes, but he revealed his class affiliations when he talked about going to Mussoorie. . ." Tehmina objected. She was extremely left-wing.

"Come on, Tim," said Hari judiciously. "Panditji was talking to Chand Bagh girls, he wasn't addressing farmers of the Kisan Sabha. Don't you agree, Champa Baji?"

"Oh, I didn't attend his lecture. I was in the library, studying for my test," Champa replied nonchalantly.

Tehmina, Laj, Talat and Nirmala exchanged meaningful glances. Tehmina was obviously very upset. All of them kept quiet. On the way back as they were descending the slope of Monkey Bridge, Tehmina shot ahead of the rest and asked Champa to follow her. She went straight to Chand Bagh.

"Let's go to the swimming pool for a chat," she said grimly.

The pool was deserted. Autumn had arrived, auburn leaves lay in heaps under the trees. Champa sat down rather weakly on a diving-board, Tehmina kept standing. "Look, Champa, never tell lies," she said, raising her voice. "There was no need for you to say you were in the library yesterday when Pandit Nehru came. The library is closed for the week, for renovation. You could have said you had gone out.

"See, we're no small-town fuddy-duddies, but it is a close-knit society and everybody knows everybody else. You have often gone out in your parrot-green sari with Amir. Perhaps you know that his sports car is known as Prince Gulfam's Flying Carpet? Now the University wags are saying that the Sabz Pari of Chand Bagh has abducted Gulfishan's Shahzada Gulfam.

"A few girls get talked about every year in Chand Bagh and Badshah Bagh. We wouldn't like you to be one of them."

An ominous silence followed the outburst. Suddenly something happened to Champa. 'She is yelling at me as though I am her ayah, Susan. Would she speak so harshly if I were the daughter of a high court judge or a taluqdar? Despite her leftist pretensions she is like the rest of them. . .' Tehmina had sensed Champa's financial status. She had only one 'party' sari, a parrot-green georgette, which she often wore when she went out and because of which she was called Sabz Pari, the heroine of the Urdu opera *Inder Sabha*. Quite often Tehmina lent her

her own super-fine clothes for special occasions, and now this indigent scholarship-holder had the cheek to steal her fiancé.

"I didn't know you were such a cheapster, or could be so ungrateful," she shouted.

Champa trembled with rage. Ungrateful! I've been eating her salt and wearing her clothes, like a hanger-on of her patrician family.

She stood up and said defiantly, "I am no Jezebel, but if you want me to make Miss Shah Jehan Begum and Miss Roshan Jehan Begum my models, you are sadly mistaken. I will not give you the satisfaction twenty years hence, of seeing me cycling up and down Fyzabad Road as a bespectacled old maid with a shingle bob."

Tehmina stared at her in disbelief. After her conquest of Amir, Champa had discovered the power of her sexuality. Instead of being ill at ease in her new surroundings, she now made other women feel insecure and envious. In their frustration they could only call her "cheap". And Amir, the uncrowned prince, was willing to alienate his almighty family for her sake. The assurance made her bolder.

"Chances are that *you* will turn into a battle-axe, leading processions down Monkey Bridge as a bogus revolutionary," she added, before she started running across the green towards her hostel.

Amir continued to meet Champa whenever he came home on leave, Hari and Kamal remained ardent admirers. She was invited, as usual, though less frequently to Gulfishan and Water Chestnut House for parties. Tehmina learned to hold her peace. It would have been too undignified and commonplace to break off with her—like an Indian film with two women, the goody-goody heroine and the scheming vamp, fighting over the chocolate-cream hero. Ugh. Tehmina remained coolly cordial with Champa through the years that onward rolled. . .

37. Over the Waves

"I am convinced Champa Baba has fed him owl's meat," Hussain's wife said gravely. She was doing petit-point embroidery with silver thread on Tehmina's red chiffon dupatta. Like many working-class Muslim women of Lucknow, she was an expert needlewoman who did silver-thread kamdani as well as cotton-thread chikan embroidery in her spare time. She had learned the craft from her mother, now her ten-year-old was watching her carefully. The driver's wife was busy crocheting petticoat lace for Tehmina Bitiya, and Ram Daiya was helping them as a kind of assistant. The women sat on rush mats spread under the mulberry tree outside the servants' quarters. Tehmina's trousseau was added to every year, all year round, ever since she had been a schoolgirl. And now, this disaster.

"Owl's meat. . ." Hussain's wife repeated.

Although a rare bird, you could find a good owl for black magic in the celebrated fowl market of Nakhas. Of course, it was expensive, but if you had special mantras recited over it and mixed its meat in a kebab and gave it to the man you wanted to enslave for life, he became as stupid as an ulloo. An ancient tried and tested recipe.

". . .otherwise how could Bhaiya Saheb have given up our pearl-like Bitiya? Champa Bibi is a dark enchantress of men. A kali jadoogarni of Poorab Des.

"If they were not such Angrezi-fashion people, I would have asked Begum Saheb to get a tawiz from Dargah Shah Mina Saheb for Tehmina Bitiya as an antidote."

"She must have got the jadoo done last Diwali," Ram Daiya put in, "and again this Diwali."

"Yes, of course," Susan, the ayah, agreed. She was also very concerned about Bitiya for she had often seen her crying quietly in her room. . .

Diwali had come and gone. Laj and Nirmala had made rangoli in their courtyard to welcome the goddess Lakshmi. Ram Autar and Gunga Din had gone out to gamble—if you don't indulge in the game of dice on Diwali night you'll be reborn as a doormouse in your next life. Even Qadeer gambled a little to attract good fortune.

On the moonless nights of the festival, Mrs Raizada and the Begum of Gulfishan had always told their children not to stir out of the house for fear of the black magic done by the devotees of Loona Chamari, the sorceress of yore. All manner of weird, dangerous things happened on these dark nights. *Mooth bans*—flying cooking pots—were despatched to hit and kill the enemy, little clay bowls filled with 'Black Magic' sweets were kept at the crossroads to transfer the evil spirits to unsuspecting passers-by.

"Don't sit on the grass, rain-serpents may still be lurking in it," Aunt Zubeida used to say. "The snakes slide away to hibernate after they have licked the burnt-out Diwali lamps."

The sacred month of Ramzan had also come and gone. This month had a presence of its own, a mystique and sense of holiness. People fasted and prayed, but it was also loads of fun. Everybody woke up in the early hours of the morning and had the sehri before first light. Cooking for iftar began in the afternoon for breaking the fast at sundown—a lavish repast was laid out on the table. Canons went off in the city to announce the exact moment for breaking the fast.

In city streets bands of volunteers went about tunefully announcing, "Wake up and have your sehri." Every evening Hussaini or Qadeer bicycled down piously to the nearest mosque, carrying tiffin boxes full of iftari. The snacks were sent from various households to the poor, to wayfarers and to the mosque's mullah for them to break their fast with. Heaps of edibles from various households were piled up in the illuminated mosques during the month of Ramzan.

Iftar parties were the done thing and on the last evening of the fast, the excitement of sighting the crescent moon of Id was electric. Then the festival itself: new clothes, Id cards, presents, feasts, varieties of sweet vermicelli. Everybody, rich and poor alike, wore new clothes and new shoes. As children Kamal and Talat had been so excited about their new shoes that they kept them under their pillows!

Menfolk went to the Idgah for congregational prayers and

came back greeting everybody with joyous shouts of "Id Mubarak!" Bhaiya Saheb would go for prayers with Kamal and Father, dressed in a cream-coloured sherwani, white churidars and Salimshahi shoes. He looked like a Mughal prince. On this Id he was away in the western seas infested with German submarines. Everybody in Gulfishan prayed for his safe return. They loved him. Why was he behaving so foolishly about Champa?

It had shocked Talat to discover that feminine beauty was so highly prized, that for men Body was more important than Brains. She lay in a corner of the back lawn, plucked a blade of three-petalled bitter-sweet grass and munched it reflectively. She could hear the faint, sad murmur of women in the out-houses. Perhaps they, too, were talking about Tehmina's tragedy as they stitched her clothes for the Hopeless Chest.

Then there was silence.

Talat blinked at the intense blue of the sky. A shining still-ness throbbed everywhere. She put her ears against the cool, peaceful earth. I am lying on the earth with my ears flapping, like Yajooj and Majooj. She stretched her hand and plucked another blade of khat-mithi ghass and continued nibbling it unhappily.

Kamal and Hari Shankar were strolling on a quiet road in Dehra Dun. An Englishman of their acquaintance had become a sadhu, and Kamal and Hari Shankar had been asked by his friends to tail the runaway during the holidays and bring him back. They had fruitlessly combed a few caves and temples in the foothills near Haridwar, and then one day they ran into him near Jog Maya's temple outside Rishikesh. He pleaded with them to be left alone, jumped over a little stream and disappeared into the pines.

Now the two young men walked down a fragrant road in Dalanwalla, the Rispana flowing in front of them.

"Hari Shankar. . . yaar," Kamal mused aloud.

"Yep."

"Come to think of it, this chap is dead right. We ourselves are in a goddamn bloody awful mess, pardon my language."

That evening they pondered a good deal over the philosophy of renunciation and uttered great profundities.

"All this seems to be a great cosmic misunderstanding," Kamal observed.

"Let's read the bungalows' names. . ." responded Hari Shankar and read out the names.

"Ashiana ! Aha."

"Cloud's End. I say, that's a lovely one."

"We're living on the edge of a cloud, we shall never build a house. For *the falcon doth not make a nest*," Kamal quoted Iqbal.

"To think that people have built houses, lovely houses of all kinds. The world is full of houses."

"Yes, isn't it strange."

"I had an urge just now to change some of these detachable name-plates as we did once on Fyzabad Road, Lucknow, but I realised that we are not young hooligans any more. We're only being philosophical."

"Come to think of it, that was a rather philosophical act of ours," observed Kamal, "because the houses remain the same, only their owners' names change. . ."

They sat down on a little Chinese bridge which connected Kamal's own house, Khyaban, with the avenue, and resumed their thinking. The Englishman's renunciation had upset them. He just gave up and went off to the woods. Why?

The English sadhu slept peacefully on a rock by the Rispana.

38. Inquilab, Zindabad!

In the first week of September, 1943, Kamal was about to leave for Calcutta for famine relief work when he received a letter from Laj's husband who was a central government officer in New Delhi. Laj's parents were now trying to find a suitable match for their younger daughter, Nirmala. He wrote:

You are off to Calcutta, I hear. Sir Deep Narain Nilambar's son, Gautam, is also there these days. We're thinking of proposing Nirmala to him. We hear he is also busy in this famine relief work—apart from producing Marxist plays for the Indian People's Theatre, that is. All rather alarming, I'm afraid. He is reported to be connected with the fine arts in some dubious way and lives soulfully at Santiniketan. Make it a point to track him down in Calcutta and find out all about him—is he a responsible young man or another vagabond like yourself and Hari Shankar? Give me the lowdown at the earliest.

This was followed by relevant details about the boy's family.

Kamal pocketed the letter and groaned. Thousands are dying of hunger, the country is heading for total disaster, and what is Jeejaji doing? He's busy match-making. Kamal was a fire-eating student worker. Also, ever since the fiasco around his own sister Tehmina's engagement, any talk of weddings made him see red. "Should I be carrying corpses in the streets of Calcutta," he said to Talat crossly, "or go around husband-hunting for Miss Nirmala?"

Still, as a matter of duty he carefully noted down this fellow's address and left for Bengal with a large contingent of boys and girls from his university. They sang, argued or dozed during the long and tedious journey. Kamal watched the green cornfields roll by as the train hurtled along towards the east. He kept thinking: This is my unhappy country, this is my starving country. The urge for revolution created an upsurge of intense and painful emotions in his young heart. He leaned back against the hard wooden wall of the compartment. He was not used to travelling third class but he did not want to open his holdall and lie down on his expensive bedding. His peers would call him a sissy. He closed his eyes and tried to analyse his class affiliations and the fountainhead of his intense patriotism. His father had recently joined the Muslim League and he could find no simple explanation for the happenings of the recent past—wheels within wheels within wheels. . .

Like everybody else he also had his personal India. It was made up of so many things. The picturesque village Neelampur, the vast, ancient family graveyard surrounded by banyan trees.

A clear brook ran through the burial ground like the Biblical "living waters". There was a tiny dargah adjoining the cemetery, inhabited by quaint-looking harmless dervishes. Sometimes in the dead of night you could hear one of them shouting, "Allah—hoo!" None could fathom the mysteries of those silent nights and those lonely cries—what the Sufis called the *flight of the alone to the alone.*

There was another mysterious-looking gray building in his village, the matth of an ancient sanyasi order, which he had once visited as a boy with his father. A thick-set young man in ochre robes sat placidly upon a wooden settee in a bare room. The young man was a university graduate and had recently succeeded to the gaddi of the matth. He had remained silent and given Kamal an orange.

Well, he also has one kind of life to lead, thought Kamal, in an area of human experience of which I know nothing.

Outside, the monastery's garden was full of marigolds and plantains. Red lotuses bloomed in a tank, a koel sang in the mango trees.

So, how was this country to be defined? India was Qadeer's old mother, clad in a yellow sari of rough cotton. She was a career woman, as it were, warder of the district jail's female wing. She had come to the railway station at Mirzapur once and given Kamal clay toys. The quiet avenues of Civil Lines where the dog-boys of the Angrez Sahebs took out their pets, were also India. In rural areas chicken-pox and small-pox were simply called 'Mata' and considered a manifestation of the wrath of the goddess Sitala. Their old cook, Basharat Hussain, belonged to a village in the district of Ghazipur. He looked like Ali Baba with his long white beard.

As a small boy Kamal had come down with chicken-pox, and one fine morning old Basharat Hussain tiptoed into the sick-room. He put on his muslin skull cap, stood on one leg, folded his hands and implored the folk 'spirit': "Sitala Mata, leave Kamman Bhaiya alone and go away. I beg of you, I fold my hands before you!"

This khansama was also India.

1857 still haunted his grandparents' generation. Even

Englishmen had recorded that they had sewn Hindus and Muslims alive in cow-hide and pigskin, as punishment.

Kamal's adventurous great-grandfather, Kamaluddin Ali Reza Bahadur, alias Nawab Kamman, had gone to England in the fateful year 1856. On his return two years later, he had found Lucknow lying in ruins and had shifted to Calcutta. His descendants had moved back to the north.

The Muslims have an emotional problem. Once an English friend at Oxford asked Maulana Mohammed Ali to suggest a caption for a photograph he had taken of a beggar woman in a ragged burqa, sitting on the steps of Delhi's Jama Masjid. Mohammed Ali scribbled underneath—*Her father built it.*

In 1901, two puny taluqdars of the Terai region travelled to Delhi, both descendants of Queen Hazrat Mahal's knights. The Two Gentleman of the Terai were Kamal and Hari Shankar's grandfathers, proudly come to attend the Delhi Durbar celebrating Queen Victoria's Diamond Jubilee.

Akbar Allahabadi, the satirist, wrote:

How shall I tell you what I saw
In the Empire's pomp and show,
Jamuna-ji was flowing past
The highest of the mighty Laats,
The famous Duke Connaught.
Elephants and horsemen, canons and camps and military bands,
Worthies jostling in the throng
To get close to the seat of power.
In the high noon of the Raj
I even saw Curzon Maharaj.
The Mehfil and the Saqi are theirs.
Lady Curzon danced till dawn
In Shahjahan's marble hall.
The Ball was like Inder Sabha, I hear,
For how could I go there?
The view from a distance is my share.
Only the eyes are mine, the rest is theirs.

Kamal sat up and started reciting the poem, then leaned back again.

"Mad, yaar," his friends said, grinning. He closed his eyes and resumed his own journey. Passing through the poverty-stricken districts of eastern U.P., Kamal recalled some events of his childhood. In 1934 the Congress leader, Rafi Ahmad Kidwai, had started the No Rent Movement and the peasants of U.P. stopped paying land revenue. Both Kamal's father and uncle, Sir Zaki, were furious. Asad Mamoon was jubilant. Asad Mian was a visionary nationalist, a cousin of Kamal's mother. He had named his daughter, Khalida, after the Turkish writer, Khalida Adib Khanum, Minister of Education in the new Republic of Turkey. He used to come out with unusual bits of information: When Khalida Khanum visited Bombay in 1934 she gave the dancer Annette the name Azurie. The Mangalorian dancer had performed at Begum Atiya Fyzee's Three Arts Circle on Malabar Hill. According to data collected by the government in 1921, more Muslim girls attended schools in U.P. than their Hindu counterparts.

So why is this community becoming backward?

Indians had rejoiced at Japan's victory over Russia in 1905 but could not celebrate the heroes of 1857. They found their heroes in Turkey, Italy and Ireland. Novels were written in Urdu about the Turco-Russian War of 1878, Muslims named their new-born sons after the heroes of the Balkan Wars and World War I. In the University of Lucknow there were two brothers, Midhat Kamal Kidwai and his sibling, Anwar Jamal, who had been named after the Generals Midhat and Enver Pashas. Kamal was fondly called Kamal Pasha, after Kamal Ataturk, founder of modern Turkey. . .

The train crossed into Bihar. Kamal thought of Qadeer's shrivelled mother. . .

Badrun Nissa belonged to Monghyr district, and like many old women, was a fund of legends and little-known stories of her region. Like the one about Gul and Sanober, children of Nawab Mir Qasim, Nazim of Bengal, Bihar and Orissa. Brother and sister would cover themselves with tiger-skins and bring food to their father who was hiding in a forest somewhere in Bihar, after the defeat of Buxar. They were shot down one night by an English officer who mistook them for tigers lurking in the bush.

Kamal kept gazing out of the window. So the British were again the villains of the piece. Yet the indisputable fact remains that they created modern India. Even Maha Guru Karl Marx said so. He ducked his head—a particle of windblown coal had got into his eye.

As children we read books published by Father Tuck, London EC4, but also heard stories told by Nani and our old aunts and nurses—Hakim Luqman's fables, *The Arabian Nights*, epics of Iran and Arabia. Allusions from the *Ramayana* have become part of Urdu proverbs. Then there are the dastaans of Aamir Hamza, *The Stories of the Prophet*, anecdotes of the Sufi saints, events from the reigns of sultans and queens. Tana Shah, a seventeenth-century Sultan of Deccan was a gentle and over-refined aesthete. When a sweepress passed by furlongs away, he is said to have fainted. "Tana Shah" had become synonymous with sensitivity.

The Indo-Muslim life-style is made up of the Persian-Turki-Mughal and regional Rajput Hindu cultures. So, what is this Indianness which the Muslim League has started questioning? Could there be an alternate India? Why?

Indian liberals were influenced by the liberalism of nineteenth century England, and in the 1920s two Englishmen, Pratt and Bradley, organised the Communist Party of India.

There is no colonial power like British colonial power.

Indians have become victims of urban middle-class politics. Life in the villages is different. Here everybody is referred to as bhaiya, chacha, dada—a big self-contained joint-family, subdivided on the basis of caste. Muslims are merely another caste. There is no inter-dining, but this taboo is considered part of tradition. No religious rancour. Upper caste Hindus do not dine with the lower castes of their own community, either.

Had Zaki Chacha been alive today he would also have become a Muslim League leader.

Asad Mamoo told us stirring tales of Maulana Obeidullah Sindhi, Raja Mahender Pratap, their Free India Government, their underground "Red Kerchief Movement". They stitched secret messages inside the linings of the couriers' coats. Their leader, Maulana Mahmoodul Hasan, Rector of the Seminary of Deoband, was arrested and deported to Malta. Many revolutionaries lived in poverty in exile in Europe, or died in penury at home. And the legendary Firangi Mahal, the seventeenth-century college of theologians—after 1857 its Rector Maulana had not eaten sugar or ice made in English factories and had not used English blankets. He was the first boycotter of British goods.

Traversing the parched countryside of Bihar, Kamal suddenly remembered Raja Ram Narain Mauzan's couplet that Asad Mamoo often recited:

Ghazalen, tum to waqif ho, kaho Majnun ke marney ki
Diwana mar gaya, akhir ko, veerany pe kya guzri.

Gazelles of the desert! You know how Majnun died.
What happened to the wilderness once he was gone?

The Raja was an Urdu poet of Patna. He also happened to be the Naib Nazim of Bengal, Bihar and Orissa in Siraj-ud-Daulah's government. When he heard of Siraj's defeat at Plassey the Raja spontaneously uttered this *sher*, then tore off his clothes and ran towards the forests. The Raja took sanyas and was never seen again.

Both Siraj and the Raja were India.

And the long-forgotten Umar Sobhani, the Cotton King of Bombay, who financed the Indian National Congress. As punishment, the British government brought down the price of Lancashire cotton and made him a pauper overnight. He died in 1926.

Comrade Mahmud-uz Zafar's father was a Pathan aristocrat of Rampur. His cousins, Uzra and Zohra, had gone to Germany to learn modern dance, and at the age of six, Mahmud was sent to England for schooling. He could hardly speak Urdu. They had an immense Tudor-style mansion in Dehra Dun with its own waterfall, parkland and zoo. We children used to go there from Khyaban to play. His sister, Hamida, is an eye-surgeon and they donated their stately home to the Party. True communists.

Sir Wazir and Lady Hasan's son, Sajjad Zaheer. In 1931 he came from Oxford to India for six months and published

Angarey, rebellious short stories in Urdu. Dr. Rashid Jahan was a contributor who married Mahmud-uz Zafar. Her parents, Sheikh and Begum Abdullah, founded the Muslim Girls' School in Aligarh in 1907, now a famous college for women. The Abdullah's daughters studied in England, something unheard of at that time. One of them, Khursheed, joined another band of pioneers—Devika Rani and Himanshu Roy. She is Renuka Devi, the star of Bombay Talkies. Then there was Lady Saheb Singh Sokhey who became Maneka, the dancer. Amazing, yaar.

The U.P. government banned *Angarey*. In 1935 Sajjad Zaheer and his comrades in London launched the Indian Progressive Writers Association, and its Manifesto was written by Dr. Jyoti Ghosh, Dr. Mulk Raj Anand, Promod Sen Gupta, Dr. Muhammad Deen Taseer and Sajjad Zaheer.

Calcutta, Lahore, Lucknow and the Muslim University, Aligarh, were among the major centres of Leftist activity.

In 1937 two important things happened in Lucknow: the revival of the All India Muslim League and the establishment of Congress rule. According to Asad Mamoo the revival came about largely because of the personal rivalry between two local politicians, Chowdhry Khaliq-uz Zaman and Syed Ali Zaheer.

One day, as Kamal was passing by the Council Chamber whistling softly, he saw Mrs. Vijaylaxmi Pandit step out of her black limousine. Beautiful lady with an aura of romance. Kamal had heard from his elders that her father's very good-looking private secretary had fallen in love with her. But he belonged to another community and was hastily banished to America. She then married a Maharashtrian Brahmin.

Begum Jahan Ara Shahnawaz was the other gracious lady Kamal happened to see the same day that winter. A well-known political leader she, like Mrs. Pandit, represented an upper-class political family. She had come from Lahore to attend the historic session of the All India Muslim League.

And the Shahzadis of Hyderabad, Durr-i-Shahwar and Nilofer. Sad-faced Turkish beauties of Blood Royal, the last glow of the Ottomon Sultanate, whose portraits were hung in many middle-class Muslim homes. The Padshah of the Deccan was an emotional substitute for the last Mughal emperor.

"The imperialist allies wrecked the Ottoman Sultanate," Asad Mamoo thundered. "How could an eastern race remain masters of half of Europe? Call them Terrible Turks. Only Christian whites can be the master race." Asad Mamoo said to Tim, "Women's Urdu magazines used to publish the pictures of all those beauties—Mrs. Pandit, Queen Suraiyya of Iran, the Maharanis of Cooch Behar, Kapurthala and Baroda. These magazines also proudly flashed the pictures of the Urdu short-story writer, Hijab Imtiaz Ali of Madras and Lahore who had become a pilot. In 1936! We were sitting in the veranda of Khyaban when this women's weekly arrived, *Tehzil Niswan*, with her picture on the cover, goggles and all, sitting in the cockpit!"

The Baradari of Qaiser Bagh was Vajid Ali Shah's Xanadu. Masters of Kathak like Achchan and Shambhu Maharaj dance there, ragas float out of Marris College, there is continuum in the sound of music.

There was this Ustad they say, who, through his rendering of certain ragas, could cure any ailment, and another who could conjure the psychic forms of ragas and raginis through his singing. When a Maharashtrian pandit of Shastriya Sangeet sings and an Ustad gives a concert, do they belong to two different civilizations? Now this new business of Culture is being redefined as "pure Hindu" or "pure Muslim" by the Mahasabha and the Muslim League.

Begum Shahnawaz wore a silk sari and her long ear-rings flashed as she spoke in front of the microphone in Qaiser Bagh. The All India Muslim League was revived at that session by M.A. Jinnah and Amir Mohammed Khan, the youthful Raja of Mahmudabad.

He is young, and he is an idealist, said Kamal's father. The Raja is financing the new Pakistan Movement. Mr. Jinnah had been a Congressman, once called the Ambassador of Hindu-Muslim Unity. His wife, Ratibai, was the exquisite daughter of a Parsi baronet, Sir Dinshaw Petit. The Jinnahs were High Society. When Mrs. Jinnah died, her photograph was published in a magazine with the caption 'Alas! This beautiful face is vanished forever!'

In 1938 an industrial exhibition was held on the banks of the Gomti. Kamal sat on the steps of Gulfishan as film songs played on loudspeakers in the evening wind. One of the songs wafted: *Kaya ek gharonda hai.* The body is a house of clay. . . house of clay. . ., sung by a film actor called Ashraf Khan. Like the Jews in America, a disproportionately large number of Muslim men and women belonged to the entertainment industry and were among the leading performing artistes of the country. Innumerable gharanas had maintained the traditions of Hindustani classical music. The Muslim thread was present in every pattern of Indian tapestry—was all this going to be erased by the demand for Pakistan? The thought disturbed old nationalists like Asad Mamoo. Young people had dreams of their own of a socialist India.

The Urdu press called Sarojini Naidu Bulbul-i-Hind— Nightingale of India. The Nizam's government had done a lot for women's education—Sarojini Naidu was one of those sent to England on a state scholarship. She became a firebrand Congress leader, but at the same time was emotionally loyal to the Nizam—so how could India be defined in general terms? Human allegiance is complex and unfathomable.

No Hindu-Muslim rift in the princely states—the problem is characteristic of post-1857 British India. Jaipur and Gwalior, both Hindu states, have the most spectacular Moharrum celebrations, patronised by the Maharajas. "So shall we vote for feudalism?" Tehmina had argued fiercely with a relative who had just returned from Hyderabad. "Why do you choose to ignore the peasants of Telengana?"

The Congress government resigned in 1939, the Muslim League observed a Day of Deliverance. Kamal's father said: "The Muslims have had a foretaste of majority rule. A little common sense and the Congress need not have alienated them. You mark my words, Asad Mian, the League movement is now going to snowball."

The Muslim slogan—"You've done the rounds with your begging bowls/If you are a Muslim join the League."

Kamal thought he was a socialist, yet when he went to see the illuminations of Shah Najaf on the 8th of Moharrum and

read *His Majesty King Ghaziuddin Hyder* emblazoned across
the imposing facade of the Imambara, it brought tears to his
eyes. The staff at the Imambara wore the uniform of the erstwhile kingdom as they marched in the spectacular Mehndi procession. This was an extravaganza introduced by the Shia kings
of Lucknow. Young Qasim, son of Imam Hussain, was betrothed to his cousin on the eve of his martyrdom and, according to Indian Muslim custom, gaily decorated trays full of
henna and gifts were sent to the bride's home. This procession was part of the many grand rituals enacted to enhance the
high drama and tragedy of Kerbala. A colossal black Chup Tazia
was taken out in utter, awesome silence on the 40th day of
mourning. Hindu officers and men of the U.P. Police Cavalry
dismounted as a mark of respect to Imam Hussain, as they
accompanied the Chup Tazia. This was what India and Indian
culture were all about.

The graduating batch of 1937-39 included Anwar Jamal
Kidwai, Sardar Jafri, D.P. Dhar, Ali Jawad Zaidi, the Abbasi
brothers and Shankar Dayal Sharma. The exceptionally good-
looking Mustafa Hyder was simply referred to as T.D.H.—
tall, dark and handsome—by the Badshah Bagh-Chand Bagh
girls. When he contested the election for the presidentship of
the Union, the girls distributed pink leaflets announcing,
Indira Nehru says: Vote for Mustafa Hyder.

Hari Shankar and I joined Canning College in 1939 as young
hopefuls and admired the galaxy of brilliant young women at
the University—Tazeen Habibullah, Maya Sarkar, Shakuntala
Jaspal, Sakina Ali Zaheer, Rita Dey, Nishat Ghulam Hasan, the
graceful Minhaj sisters, Sultana, Amina and Khadija.

Even a traditional demi-mondaine, a tawaif in the mould of
Umrao Jan Ada, became a Party sympathiser. Some comrades
held their underground meetings at her house in Chowk, and
she was called Comrade Hasni.

In his elegies on the Battle of Kerbala, Mir Anis had turned
the Euphrates into the Gomti. In 1878 the Urdu novelist
Pundit Ratan Nath Sarshar sent his hero, Azad, to fight alongside the Turks in the Turco-Russian War and promptly transported the city of Lucknow to the banks of the Danube. Now

the comrades had brought about the confluence of the mighty Volga with our good old Gomti which flowed politely through the City of Gardens.

Majaz, Sardar Jafri, Wamiq Jaunpuri and Kaifi Azmi recite their poems in the coffee house. On the morning of New Year's Day young men and women telephone one another, quoting Sardar Jafri's latest poem:

> *Yeh kis ne phone per disasal-i-nau ki tahniat mujh ko,*
> *Tamanna raqs karti hai, takhyyul gungunata hai,*
> *Musarrat ke jawan mallah kashti leke nikle hain,*
> *Ghamon ke na-khudaon ka safina dagmagata hai.*

Who rang to greet me on New Year's Day?
Wishes dance, fancy sings out with joy.
Young gondoliers of bliss
Have taken out their boats,
There rock the barges of the Captains of Gloom.

Inquilab, Zindabad!—Long Live Revolution!—the Urdu phrase scrawled in English all over, as the new Writing on the Wall has become the war-cry of young people all over India. . .

During the train's long and tedious journey, Kamal's thoughts kept changing track. He argued with his friends or dozed till they crossed into Bengal at midnight. He was asleep when the train stopped at a small railway station. A number of English officers paced to and fro on the platform. The convoy train had no lights and it was all a bit frightening. A Eurasian guard told the students from Lucknow, "Go back to sleep, men. This blooming train won't budge till the army moves on. *This is the Army, Mr. Jones."* He began humming a popular war-time song: *This is the Army, Mr. Jones, you had your breakfast in bed before, Now you won't have it there any more, tra-la-la.*

The Eurasian guard strode to the end of the long platform where a little crowd had collected around a dead body. An English captain alighted from the military train to have a dekko.

"What's the problem, men, get lost," the Eurasian guard shouted at the crowd.

"A man has breathed his last, sir," a railway babu answered

gravely. "Hungry man. Before he expired he told me his name was Abul Mansur. Said he could not keep body and soul together, so he was returning his soul to Almighty Allah with thanks."

The English captain suppressed a smile.

"Further, the late mortal said, sir, that his wife Amina Bibi who lives in a hamlet yonder, may kindly be informed that he, on account of his untimely demise, could not reach Calcutta and that she should accept it as God's Will and eat roots. He further said he had two issues, they have already died of starvation. And he is happy that his spouse shall die soon and they'll all meet by the Fountain of Eternal Bliss in Heaven."

"Good Lord!" the young Englishman exclaimed in distress. He was used to the killing fields of the Western Front but had never seen death by starvation.

"Now, sir, I must hand over these mortal remains to the Mohammedan constable of the railway police, who shall have the needful done, burial, etc. Before the late Abul Mansur expired he. . ."

The Englishman moved away, feeling sick.

"Sir, Indians don't die, they expire. . ." the Eurasian guard explained apologetically. The convoy was about to leave. The English officer sighed, "Oh, well. Let's proceed on our way to expire in the jungles of Burma. Goodbye, gentlemen."

The military train snaked its way into the dark night. The good-hearted babu placed a lantern near the corpse of peasant Abul Mansur and began his wait for the police constable. As the Howrah-bound train passed along the dark end of the platform, the boys noticed an eerie, silent, red railway lantern burning near a dead body covered with a torn chadar.

Kamal was awakened by a friend. He sprang up like a jack-in-the-box and felt his coat pocket, then yelled, "Good Heavens!! I've lost the letter and that bloke's address. What's his name. . . that bloke. . .?"

39. Gautam Nilamber of Santiniketan

Members of the Indian People's Theatre Association and Communist Party workers were assembled in a local student leader's house on Syed Amir Ali Avenue. IPTA's Lucknow Squad had arrived, and rehearsals for the Famine Relief Fund Variety Programme were in full swing. A budding artist stood before an easel, putting the finishing touches to a portrait in water colour. It was to be auctioned at the end of the play. The host's sister came dancing towards him and stopped. . .

"Dada. . ."

"Kee?" he asked dreamily.

"Go and look after the U.P. Squad." She flitted past, shouting multifarious orders.

He put his brush down and glided to the corner of the hall in his flowing Bengali-style dhoti. Kamal and party were practising a Hindustani chorus song, dressed in white kurta-pyjamas of handloom cotton, Nehru jackets and cream-coloured shawls of raw silk—the elegant attire of the middle-class Leftist avantgarde youth of the country. The painter folded his arms and leaned against the wall, trying to look bored and aesthetic.

Everyone was speaking vociferously in Bengali, and the singing added to the general din. At last the chorus trailed to an end and the lead singer looked up. The artist said, "*Adaab arz karta hoon*," in lilting Urdu and added in very pucca English, "You the chaps from L.K.O.?"

"Ah! Adaab. . . Tasleem! Yes. Kamal Reza of Canning College at your service."

"Gautam Nilambar of Santiniketan."

They shook hands.

"The upward brush and the downward brush and the Duality of the Soul?" Kamal chuckled, noting the artist's somewhat contrived personality. Ringlets fell to his shoulders, he had a goatee beard on the tip of his chin and a faraway look in his eyes. He nodded and smiled conspiratorially.

So this was the Gautam Nilambar who was to be sought out in Calcutta and presto! here he was! As Jeejaji had already informed Kamal, he was the son of a high court judge in Allahabad and was visiting Bengal for the sake of his Soul. His father was a pillar of the British Empire, a self-made man who had been knighted by the British government. It stood to reason that his only son should join the I.C.S., the world's most prestigious civil service. The lad, like his peers, fancied himself a rebel, so he refused and chose Santiniketan instead. He had been there for a year and had come down to Calcutta with other students to work at famine relief. He was of medium height, with intense eyes, looking both a bit self-conscious and pleased with himself in Bengali garb. Kamal tried to hide his excitement.

"I have sung myself silly and need some tea, yaar," Kamal said to his new friend as he accompanied the artist to the make-shift studio. They established an instant rapport, as young people usually do.

"Have you heard of Hari Shankar Raizada by any chance?" Kamal asked cryptically.

"Who is he?" Gautam shook his head, carrying a cigarette to his lips like Robert Taylor.

"Childhood pal of mine. Star debater, just like yours truly."

"Call him here," Gautam said majestically, like a nawab.

"He's at home in Lucknow at the moment. He is our boat club captain. Fell overboard—ha—ha—and hurt his leg."

"Why do you all live in Lucknow?"

"Where else should we live? In a one-horse town like Allahabad? Look, you've drawn the nose all wrong."

"It is very difficult to draw lips."

"You can be irreverent."

"Have a cigarette."

"Are you an artist?"

"No. A *ghasiaru*." Gautam used the word 'grass-cut' with the typical U.P. mannerism. He will do, he is quite mad, like us. Kamal beamed at him approvingly.

"Jeejaji has written to me about you. . ."

"Who is Jeejaji?"

"Our Laj's husband."

"And who, pray, is 'our Laj'?"

"Stop showing off, Jeejaji knows all about you."

"A lot of people know about me."

Kamal regarded him intently. Then he grinned. This fellow appeared to be masses of fun. He was gleefully playing the role of a bearded bohemian (minus a French beret) and spoke English with a public school accent. Probably Nainital or Doon School, and he seemed somewhat unreal.

"You are vain, too." Kamal remarked.

"Yes, of course. Aren't you?"

"Yes."

Gautam picked up a brush and began adding stroke after stroke to the flaming background of the Santhal girl's head.

"If you stay on in Santiniketan for another five or six years you might succeed in becoming a painter of sorts. At the moment there is very little hope," observed Kamal gravely. "But you'll turn into an honorary Bong all right."

"I am going down south as well, in order to learn Bharat Natyam from Ram Gopal. *Na dir dam, tana di re na—Na dir dam. . .*"

"I intended joining Uday Shankar's Cultural Centre at Almora but my sisters hooted me out of my resolve. As a matter of fact, girls are quite bogus, they simply haven't the capacity to understand a man's real self. Do you have sisters?"

"No."

"Then, I was momentarily attracted by Shunyavad."

"Are you chaps Buddhists in Lucknow?"

"When my younger sister went to Banaras for her exams I visited Sarnath. And over there I experienced a sort of inner peace, you know what I mean. . ."

"No, I don't."

"Anyway, so I thought there must be something to Buddhism. Then it occurred to me that it was extremely hot outside and the Buddhist Centre's hall was cold and dark and peaceful so I felt peaceful, too. The so-called mysteries can easily be explained likewise. Are you in the Party?"

"No."

"I thought as much. You don't look like a tremendous revolutionary to me, anyway."

Gautam glared at Kamal.

"Do you know what Mahatma Gandhi said to your Gurudev . . .? That your house is on fire and you are busy listening to birdsong, or something to that effect," Kamal added. "You must meet Bhaiya Saheb as well, Syed Amir Reza, my cousin. As a youngster he showed great promise and painted a lot of water colours. But he is much too good-looking—long, curly eyelashes and so on—so he gave it up."

"Why?"

"He thought people might take him to be a queer."

"Is he?"

"Good heavens, no! But he is a loner, can't relate to people easily. At the moment he is somewhere in the Pacific, fighting the Fascists as a naval officer. I hope the sea brings him out of his shell. Ho! Ho! Now, tell me something. I believe in having very clear-cut views on everything."

"Shoot."

"What do you think about the class struggle? Do you believe in the Glorious Future of the Proletariat?"

"Yes." They shook hands again.

"If you're convinced that feudal society will soon die a natural death, then half the battle is won. Let's have some coffee at Firpo's."

They rushed out and hailed a cab, two scions of affluent families on a spree in good ole Cal.

40. Quality Street

Shanta, wrote Gautam leisurely,
autumn has arrived in the lush woodlands of Oudh. The gardener's daughter is passing by, jingling her anklets. Yellow flowers droop from delicate branches, straight out of a Chinese water-colour. On Sunday mornings sophisticated university women turn into Ravi Varma and Abdul

Rehman Chughtai paintings. They spread mats on the floor, tune their tambouras and sing classical melodies. I am writing to you from one of these young ladies' homes called 'The Raizadas' Singhare-wali Kothi'. Friend Kamal Reza lives in 'Gulfishan,' not far from here. I met this bloke in Calcutta recently, and thereby hangs this tale—because now I strongly suspect that Kumari Nirmala Raizada's father and my Dad ganged up to scoop me out of Santiniketan. Dad got me a job as a weekly columnist with this newspaper, for which Winston Churchill worked as a young man! Dad even fixed P.G. accommodation for me on Clyde Road. It's all happened so fast that I am quite bewildered.

Upon my arrival in Lucknow I rang up Kamal Reza. The following day he brought me here to meet Hari Shankar and his sister, Nirmala. I don't think she knows about this 'conspiracy.' Anyway, she is too busy talking her head off to take any serious notice of me as her prospective pati-devta. At least that's what I think. She's a great girl, vivacious and genuine, like her friend Talat. Her family is also steeped in Old Lucknow Culture. All fine and dandy, the only snag is that I am in no hurry to tie the knot, even after a year and a half when Nirmala graduates.

Nirmala and Talat are real buddies. Their gang also includes a dreamy young woman called Champa Begum. It's an evocative name, reminds one of a Mughal miniature of a fine lady, Persian-style, in peshwaz, standing under a magnolia tree.

Don't smile, I'm not being soppy. Santiniketan does this to me.

Anyway, so this Champa Begum is part of Kamal's crowd, yet seems a bit of an outsider, an onlooker. You know what I mean.

Last evening I saw an excellent open-air performance of Quality Street. *The venue was the eucalyptus grove, called the Forest of Arden, in Isabella Thoburn College. Chandralekha Pandit played Phoebe, Ranjana Sidhanta was the 'hero'. The cast included Nirmala, Talat and her elder sister, Tehmina. All of them are themselves residents of Qual-*

ity Street. Right now, as I'm sitting on the steps of Nirmala's house facing the river, they are all busy discussing Communist Party politics inside, so I thought I'd scribble a few lines to you. . .

"Have you finished writing your column?" Nirmala demanded as she jumped over the balustrade. Talat followed her. "Lemme have a dekko, what's the topic? Talat also wants to become a journalist."

Gautam quickly slipped the unfinished letter into his briefcase and mumbled, "I was writing to a relative. . ."

"Well," Nirmala declared, "there are two types of letters one writes from a new place: a) Wish you were here, and b) There's nothing to write home about. Which kind is it?"

"Nirmala, don't be nosy," Talat rebuked her and added in the same breath, "Cousin Amir went horseback riding at 3 p.m. He phoned from Dilkusha Club—he'll be here at 4.30 for tea."

Kamal emerged from the house and explained to the slightly baffled newcomer, "Our cousin, the dashing naval officer. I told you about him in Calcutta, didn't I?"

"Ah, so you all are the huntin', shootin', fishin' types. Being solid middle class, I am overawed!"

As though on cue, Amir Reza arrived on the scene like Peter Pan. It was uncanny.

"This is naval precision! He said he will be here on the dot of 4.30 and he is," said Talat proudly. "Adaab, Bhaiya Saheb."

Jamuna Mehri brought tea.

"Adaab, Bhaiya Saheb!" There was a chorus. Everybody called him Bhaiya Saheb—a colloquial term of respect in U.P.— everybody except Champa. Gautam noticed that she seated herself coyly on the rush mat and poured tea for the handsome young man. She had suddenly become very self-conscious.

Aha! So this is what it is. Alas, alas—Gautam thought as he watched Peter Pan flash his smile, surrounded by the cast of Arcadia.

Kamal sat down on the bench near Champa. After a few moments of silence he quoted the eighteenth-century Urdu poet, Mir:

Le saans bhi aahista
Ke nazuk hai bohat kaam,
Aafaq ki is kargah-i-
Sheesha-gari ka.

(Breathe softly, for the task of the Universe's workshop of glassblowers is extremely delicate.)

"Old Mir Saheb was talking about human relationships."

"I am aware of that," she answered dryly.

"Are you? In that case why did you deceive poor, harmless Tehmina? Have you any idea how much you have humiliated my good-natured sister? She has become the spurned, rejected fiancé. You are the victorious femme fatale."

"You are being melodramatic, Kamal. I did not deliberately humiliate her. She shouted at me that day near the swimming pool as though I were her ayah Susan, and now you are insulting me." She was coldly furious.

Kamal ignored her protest. "I put it to you, Champa Baji," he said in a court-room voice, "would you have fallen head over heels in love and encouraged Amir Reza if he had been a clerk living in a slum in Nakhas?"

She stared at him, speechless.

"Mind you, I still think the world of you, but I believe in being truthful. That's why I keep telling Gautam that he is a bit of a charlatan. Look, Amir is a playboy, he may let you down."

"I seem to be surrounded by well-wishers, but I can look after myself, thank you. Earlier you were all hell-bent on turning me into a Party sympathiser, now you're trying to sort out my emotional life for me. Why can't you leave me alone?"

"Champa Baji," Kamal went on peaceably, "your sole aim in life should not be to become a decorative ballroom dancer. Do something creative, apart from mooning around Chand Bagh."

"For instance?"

"Paint, the way Saulat Rehman and Talat do. Dance, go to

Almora and join Uday Shankar's Cultural Centre. Go along with Kamala and Vimala."

"And?"

"Well. . . write. Discipline yourself a little, attain inner balance. . ."

"Life is so chaotic, how can you organise it? Besides, are writers very balanced people? I think neither Gautam nor Talat are quite all there. She is writing very stupid short stories, and they're not honest either. The other day I read Gautam's column titled 'These Charming People' in which he has obliquely called you all sextons of Time's graveyard, dressed in coat-tails. And he's added that you all depend on your attractiveness to remain alive. He pretends to be your friend, but makes fun of you in his articles."

"Talat is still a kid, and Gautam is a journalist. He has the freedom to write what he likes. Anyway, he is not far wrong—despite our concern for the masses we are, as a class, mournful undertakers of the Past. And Cousin Amir Reza's passport to success in life are his ravishing good looks.

"Writers, including my kid sister, may not be all there, but they do achieve a kind of inner equilibrium during the creative process. Just try to bring about an equation between intellect and emotions, then half the battle is won."

"I don't believe in high falutin' theories."

"Ah, Champa Baji, beware of experiments! There is a Danger Zone Ahead!" He rose to his feet, stuck his thumbs in his coat pockets and strode back to Water Chestnut House.

41. Inder Sabha

Amir Reza had gone to Mussoorie to meet a friend. On his return to Lucknow he visited Water Chestnut House to say goodbye to the Raizadas—he was leaving for the Eastern Front the following day.

He found Gautam, Champa, Talat and Kamal as usual, sitting on the terrace facing the river. Gautam was smoking thoughtfully, Champa was knitting, also thoughtfully. The rest were discussing dialectic materialism. Amir Reza greeted them and sat down on the steps near Gautam. M.N. Roy and Trotsky continued to be thrashed out by Hari, Kamal and Talat.

"Pipe down, yaar," said Gautam after a while. "Contemplate the river. This is that time of evening for which Mir Anis has said *Jhuppata waqt hai, behta hua darya thehra*—Dusk falls. The river has stopped flowing."

Kamal looked at him and observed gravely: "Your ringlets made you look such a pseud. I'm glad you cut them before coming to Lucknow."

"No personal attacks please," Talat raised her hands.

"And Gautam Nilambar," Kamal continued, "if, from the dawn of recorded history, prophets and philosophers and rishis and Sufis hadn't *talked*, there would have been horses stabled in the libraries of the world. You should be grateful to god that we talk and you listen. A time shall come when you'll yearn to hear our voices."

"You believe that Time is fatal?"

"That's pretty obvious," Kamal replied.

The sun went down in the river, Chattar Manzil's golden domes turned amber, a boat sailed past.

"Do you believe in the mystery of symbols?" Gautam asked Kamal. "That boat which is passing by, it has a lot of significance."

Kamal smiled. Gautam dramatised trivia, making whatever he said seem terribly profound. It had become an attractive mannerism and most people liked his affectations. Good old Gautam.

"The river is time, flowing," Gautam went on as he picked up a pebble. "The stone is the symbol of Timeless Become, and the end of the world is as certain and as unimportant as the death of a mouse. In the Upanishads. . ."

"What does 'Timeless Become' mean?" asked Talat. "For goodness sake, don't be pompous, Gautam Mashter."

Amir rose to his feet and said, "Quite right. Let's go to

Mohammed Bagh Club for dinner. And Champa Begum, I'll teach you the Old Waltz—come along."

Talat took him aside and said, "Bhaiya Saheb, Nirmala's folks have arranged a grand dawat for Gautam. They've got Hussaini and his wife over to cook. They couldn't invite you because you were not in town, now please stay back."

"Nirmala's engagement?" Amir Reza cried jubilantly. "That calls for pink champagne." He strode in and telephoned Mohammed Bagh Club. In a short while a liveried bearer arrived in a jeep with a basketful of scotch, red claret and liqueur.

Barrister Raizada looked enormously pleased when he saw the bearer arranging a temporary bar in the veranda under Amir's supervision, with Hari's eager help.

"God bless you, sonny," he said to Amir. He was an old colleague of Amir's late-lamented barrister father, Sir Zaki. "As a true Kayastha I love to booze, but can't afford it any more. I am overwhelmed by your gesture."

"My duty, sir," Amir said, bowing. "My sister Nirmala is getting engaged." (By this time he had become sufficiently Indianised to call Nirmala his sister.) A bottle of champagne was opened, followed quickly by whisky.

The atmosphere became emotion-charged. Gautam began to feel uncomfortable, but he joined the old gentleman, Amir and Hari for a round of whisky. Kamal didn't drink. He sat with the girls on the river steps.

Mrs Raizada welcomed them in to the large dining room on the ground floor. The Club bearer properly poured white wine between courses.

Gautam continued to feel miserable.

Hari was boisterous. "Hussaini, zindabad!" he shouted and turned to Gautam. "You know, Hussain's ancestors cooked for King Vajid Ali Shah."

Now Talat spoke. "Like Bhaiya Saheb, he has only done his duty. I dunno about your Behraich, Gautam, but in our region when somebody's daughter gets married, the entire village pitches in to help the bride-to-be's father. It's a kind of sacred duty. Hussaini is also very excited that Nirmala Bitiya. . ."

Kamal was sitting next to her and gave her a kick under the

table. Gautam was acutely embarrassed. Hastily he asked Talat, "Why hasn't Tehmina come for this dinner?"

"Because of that horrid woman. She telephoned and I told her that both of them are here—Tim knows about the goings-on, old waltz, etc.," she answered in an undertone. Kamal gave her another nudge.

"Why are you crushing my toe, Kim?" she asked aloud.

Kamal felt like fleeing. By this time he had realised that Gautam was not interested in Nirmala. He looked at the radiant faces of the young girl, her parents and brother, and thought it was heart-breaking. All my bloody fault. Why the hell did I have to dabble in match-making?

Dinner over, they came back to the terrace. The bearer served liqueur, the old barrister excused himself and went upstairs, feeling quite groggy.

"This house is floating away like a ship, Admiral," Gautam said tipsily and saluted Amir Reza. "And the Gomti is flowing backward." A boat passed. The boatman was singing a ghazal from *Inder Sabha*.

"This is Lucknow, Gautam Mashter," said Talat with much feeling, "where even today the common people remember and sing *Inder Sabha*. . ."

"Let's go and see it," Gautam got up enthusiastically.

"See what?" asked Kamal soberly.

"*Inder Sabha*. It is being staged Out There. Let's go and catch shadows in our nets!"

They piled into Amir's station wagon and drove out in the moonlight till they reached a bridge. They heard voices and looked below. A procession of quaintly shaped barges glided past with people in glittering costumes. Their voices were inaudible. Sometimes they twittered like birds, at others they screeched like off-key violins. Across the river in the woods, dogs barked and jackals howled. The wood on the burning ghat snapped and splintered as it burned.

The light of the moon became intense with their own faces looking white and blank in its blaze. Faces with no features.

"Bridges—they have built bridges all over, like houses," Gautam murmured angrily. They proceeded towards the cantonment. The station wagon stopped with a jerk. La Martiniere College loomed in front of them across the glassy lake.

"What books, what knowledge, what wisdom they taught me in these noble halls. . ." said Kamal, Hari Shankar and Amir Reza in unison.

"Why do you read?" they turned to Gautam and asked crossly.

"It's no use explaining to him," said Nirmala, "he is nuts."

They approached the Italian Renaissance building and peeped in. The classrooms were dark and hazy. When morning comes students will read there again. The pink, green and blue of the Italian bas-relief on the ceiling gleamed in the half-light of the moon which trickled in through tall windows.

Zoffany's portrait of Sally Begum, also called Gori Bibi, the Indian ward of General Claude Martin, hung in a classroom. The General's adopted son, Zulfiqar Martin, stood by her side. Talat pressed her nose against the window-pane and looked at the portrait. The others walked back to the lake.

She followed them.

"Come here, please."

Talat turned round. Gori Bibi stood near the water and beckoned to Talat. "Talk to me please," she was saying, "all day long there is such a lot of noise here. Droves of people chatting and reading books and delivering lectures. No one even so much as looks at me." She started to cry. Talat was upset.

"Listen to me, Sally Begum," she tried to be philosophical in accordance with the gravity of the situation. "You go right on concentrating on the point of eternity. These different patterns of time are in fact—I mean—" she grew more confused and stopped, foolishly. Then she remembered something. "Listen, I always wanted to know. Are you—were you General Martin's wife or the 'daughter' he adopted during the great famine?"

"Keep guessing," Gori Bibi replied. "That's one good thing about the Past, it so easily becomes a Mystery!" Then she vanished.

"Promise that you will never read again," Kamal was yelling

at Gautam on the lakeside. "A young Englishman, our professor of chemistry, gave up and ran away to the Himalayas. Absconded. Just like that." He snapped his fingers. "I wonder if he is still alive or whether some man-eater of Kumaon gobbled him up. Or if birds build their nests in his beard while he listens to Narad Muni's celestial music. . ."

Om. Om. Om. The sound boomed and resounded in the open moonlit spaces. Hari. Hari. They walked on the shaded path. Champa extended her hand and touched the branch of a kadamb tree. A leaf floated down to the path.

Vishnu who is in the falling of a leaf. Hari, Hari, Gautam repeated. The General lay asleep in his marble vault. The world passed over him. A large owl flew past. Words emerged from the library and spread all over. Their meanings leered like will-o-the-wisps. They climbed the cannon and sat dangling their pencil-thin black legs. The cannon thundered: *I was named Lord Cornwallis and accompanied General Claude Martin to Seringapatam. I fired at Tipu Sultan. Now they have invented new weapons. . .*

Kamal who had abruptly left them on the way and disappeared, returned and joined them near the gate of Dilkusha Garden.

"Where have you been?" Gautam asked, still very indignant.

"Went across to Farah Baksh and saw the King, then I met the English Resident on the way back. He sat in a palanquin, wearing Indian court dress, pugree and all. I salaamed and he told me that he was going to attend the King's Coronation.

" 'Which King?' I asked. 'I have just seen one in Farah Baksh.' "

" 'Oh, that one'?" the Resident said, 'He is dead. His son is now going to ascend the Throne.'

"How funny. Isn't it funny, Hari Shankar? These kings die, too. . ." Kamal finished speaking sadly.

They entered Dilkusha Gardens. The trees were painted a lustrous yellow. A light blue wind rose, stirring champa leaves, a peacock slept on the grass. They walked down towards the graves of British officers who fell during the Siege of Dilkusha in 1857. They parted the nettle branches and read the tombstones. Lieut. Paul of the 4th Punjab Rifles, Capt. Macdonald of the 93rd Highlanders, Lieut. Charles Dashwood.

"Hello. How do you do!" said Lieut. Dashwood, popping up from behind the brambles where he had been playing bridge with his dead comrades.

"Hello, Charlie," Gautam offered him a cigarette.

Nawab Qudsia Mahal emerged from the daisies.

"Nasiruddin Hyder's queen—she did herself in," Champa-Beatrice told Gautam. The Queen sat down on a stone and spread her dazzling silk farshi pajama on the grass.

"Once a Frenchman brought his balloon out here in these gardens," the Queen made small talk in order to entertain her visitors. "Such a multitude had assembled here to watch the flight. It was great fun! And the Frenchman went up in this balloon and descended twelve miles outside the city. Have you ever been up in a balloon, like this. . ." she rose in the air and vanished.

In the great moonlight-filled hollow of the roofless Dilkusha Palace, English wives of King Nasiruddin Hyder danced a mazurka. Champa sat down on the stairs. A seedy European was standing in front, singing the Ballad of Dead Ladies.

But where are the snows
Of yesteryear !

He stopped abruptly and said, "Remember, beautiful women die twice. So get ready to face your first death which will come soon. I am de Russet, King Nasiruddin Hyder's favourite coiffeur," he announced. "I, the Barber of Paris, once virtually ruled this kingdom, now nobody even remembers my name. Therefore, be grateful for the time that is still yours." He vanished.

Amir Reza came up to her and said, "Let's go to Chattar Manzil Club and I'll teach you the Old Waltz."

They drove out on to Castle Road and turned towards Qaiser Bagh.

"The Silver Pavilion!" Champa exclaimed to Gautam: "They *are* staging *Inder Sabha* out here. You were right!"

They tiptoed into the Baradari. Inside, the silver floor and silver pillars shimmered fiercely in the light of Belgian chandeliers. King Vajid Ali Shah was playing Raja Inder. The Diamond Fairy sang in the Court of Inder:

The pearls in her ears
Against her raven hair
Are like drops of rain
In monsoon clouds.

The Black Giant roared:

I've brought this Prince from the land of Ind.

Prince Gulfam sang:

Dawn is here,
Sing Bhairvin, love,
Before the fantasy fades.

Outside, illuminations twinkled on the Mermaid's Gate and in the Chinese Garden. Now His Majesty King Vajid Ali Shah was dressed as Krishna and 'Milkmaids' danced the Ras Lila in the arbour. Fountains splashed perfumed water. The Autumn Fair continued in full swing.

They came out of Qaiser Bagh and made for Chattar Manzil. A large number of cars were parked in front of this "European" club. It was Saturday night. "The Governor is here. I saw Capt. Frazer going in just now," Kamal observed. On the last step of the staircase which descended to the river sat King Ghaziuddin Hyder, barefoot. He threw one of his shoes in the water and when it sailed out dancing, he clapped his hands to summon a page-boy. But no page-boy appeared. Only the sound of western dance music and laughter continued to stream out of the ballroom. So he bent over the water and picked up the wet shoe himself. Then he threw the other shoe into the river. Gautam respectfully offered him a cigarette.

"No. We only smoke the 'gurguri'. Who are you?" the King frowned.

"Just . . . I . . ." replied Gautam confusedly.

They left His Majesty playing with his golden shoes by the river and drove towards the Old City, beyond King George's Medical College (where men were dying and being born incessantly). They went around town and came back to Badshah Bagh.

The modern building of Tagore Library hovered massively over King Nasiruddin Hyder's Canal.

'Come inside,' the building seemed to be saying. 'Drown your sorrows in the ocean of books.'

"Nonsense," said Kamal, "I know better."

Hussainabad Clock Tower struck one in the distance. The waves rippled. An owl flew out against the moon.

Gautam opened his left eye lazily and looked at the river. He was lying on the steps of Nirmala's residence. Champa, Talat and Nirmala sat on the balustrade dangling their feet in the water. The boat passed. *Inder Sabha's* ghazal faded in the distance.

"Did I pass out?" Gautam asked, rubbing his eyes.

"Yes, you did," the cast of *Inder Sabha-Quality Street* replied in unison.

42. The Sage's Grove

Professor Bannerjee was an economist of international repute. His bungalow on campus remained enveloped in romantic gloom. When, in the afternoons, his students dropped by they would find the old professor sitting under the seemal, deep in thought. His disciples would sit in a semicircle on the grass while he spoke to them in a soft, sad voice. Gautam Nilambar and Champa were frequent visitors.

India was moving from crisis to crisis. As if the Bengal famine were not enough, communal politics had snowballed. One Sunday afternoon the students' gathering was larger than usual. That day the newspapers had published Mr Jinnah's two-nation theory in detail. Kamal turned towards Champa. "I hear, Champa Baji, that you have also become a follower of Mr. Jinnah?"

"No," Champa replied coolly, "when I was a student in

Banaras, I heard of Vir Savarkar and Mr. Jinnah. I was once told that I had no claim on Kashi because I did not put the caste mark on my forehead and my mother said her prayers to Allah in Arabic instead of worshipping Lord Shiva. And therefore it followed that my culture and my loyalties were different. I countered by asking, 'Have you read Ghalib's Persian *Ode to Banaras?*' I was told that Persian was a foreign language. This was very heart-breaking. So I could have said to myself, why not Pakistan. . .? But I didn't. Frankly, I am quite confused about all this.

"I used to sing *Jana Gana Mana* under the tricolour at Besant College, and I often felt that I was considered an outsider under that flag."

"Have you ever realised," Professor Bannerjee mused as he watched a little sparrow sitting on a branch of the seemal, "that Hindu-Muslim riots were unknown before the arrival of the English? There used to be big, full-dress wars, but they were waged by rival political powers who happened to be either Hindu or Muslim. Of all the Mughal Emperors, Aurangzeb had the largest number of Hindu generals in his army."

"Sir, in my district the peasants still sing the ballad of Rana Beni Madho Singh, who died fighting for his queen and country. The queen in his case was Begum Hazrat Mahal. As a child, I remember seeing his great-grandson who would come riding on an elephant from his garhi to ours. He always spoke in dialect and was a quaint relic of the past. Special food was cooked by a Brahmin rasoia and he ate separately in our mardan-khana. All that was a part of peaceful co-existence," Kamal said sombrely.

"The British learnt one important lesson from the Mutiny of 1857—never allow the Indians to remain united. The result is there for us to see today," Prof Bannerjee continued.

"Indians are the most excitable lot in the world. Look at the explosion today—they can go to any extreme in the name of religion," said Champa.

"The English also stitched alive rebel noblemen in pigskin and cowhide in 1857, as punishment," Kamal reminded her.

The Professor smiled. "Only a few Englishmen were guilty

of that dreadful atrocity. The first thing we students did when we set foot in Britain was to have our shoes polished by a bootblack in Piccadilly. I did that, too."

"We can have a multinational state like the Soviet Union," Kamal put in.

"This is the trouble with you—all your arguments eventually lead to Moscow," Champa retorted.

"Champa Baji, I don't want religion. India needs peace, and bread."

"Are you a very staunch nationalist, Kamal?" she asked him in awe.

"Yes, every honest person should be a nationalist," he answered. "How is it that all the great Muslim intellectuals and scholars and theologians of India are nationalists? Have they sold their souls to the devil? Have a heart, Champa Baji!"

They got up and began strolling on the lawn. "For you, India only means the cities. You don't even know that there is no communal tension in the villages," Kamal went on. "Tell me, does His Highness the Aga Khan represent Muslim peasants and artisans? How is he different from Birla and Dalmia?"

Talat crossed over and joined them. "Did you read today's newspaper?" she asked her brother quietly.

"Yes, I know, he replied, suddenly very crestfallen.

"What happened?" asked Champa.

"My father, Khan Bahadur Syed Taqi Reza of Neelampur has joined the Muslim League, basically because the Congress is against the landlords," he said.

"Kamal, if your father thinks the Muslims' salvation lies in the establishment of Pakistan, you should have no quarrel with him at all. Don't you believe in freedom of thought?" said Champa.

"You cannot discard your motherland like an old coat," Kamal shot back.

"Come on, girls, let's go for rehearsals," Feroze called out from the gate. They took the Professor's leave and made for their hostel. Gautam and Kamal watched them sadly as they moved off. How many more evenings were they going to spend here in the sage's grove? The world was falling apart.

43. The Forest of Arden

The University women were staging their annual play in Lady Kailash Hostel. Feroze was the dialogue coach and chief prompter, Kamala was Anarkali, Talat, Dilaram and Enid Rae, Prince Salim. The Vice Chancellor and senior faculty members sat in the front rows, and the radio station orchestra played background music. Now Nirmala was singing in Akbar's Palace, now Enid stood at the trellised window looking out at the river, singing, 'O happy boatman of the Ravi. . .' Anarkali was saying, 'The Crown Prince of India and in love with a servant-girl. . . How very funny!' All this passed like a dream, then the curtain fell. The audience came out onto the driveway.

Gautam said to Champa, "Are you angry with Kamal? He was quite rude to you that evening at the Professor's place. I apologise on his behalf. Why are you so quiet?"

"I am merely studying the various attitudes to living," she said curtly.

"Shall I throw some light on the subject?" Talat piped in, joining them near the banyan tree. She was still wearing Dilaram's costume and hadn't removed her make-up. "Tonight I was praised so lavishly for my acting that I wondered what kind of expression I should wear on my face while receiving compliments—dignity, cheerfulness. . .? The trouble is that humility can be taken for an inferiority complex. If one is not modest, one is accused of being arrogant; if you talk to everyone pleasantly, you are flippant and flighty; if you remain cool and poised, you are either a bore or conceited."

Outside the warden's bungalow the Vice Chancellor was talking to the hostel's new warden, Dr Paranjoti. Talat continued, "Now take this good lady from down south. On hot summer days, when she goes out she wears a sola topi with her sari. She doesn't mind if people think she's eccentric. She knows she is not—she just finds a sola topi is better than a fancy umbrella. So, I've come to the conclusion, Champa Baji, that one ought to remain oneself. One should not endeavour to be

what one is not. For instance, look at our dear old Gautam. . .
When he speaks you feel you are in the market-place of Plato's
Athens, or that Kahlil Gibran is walking under the cedars of
Lebanon. . . No, Champa Baji, just be yourself. Goodnight."
She ran back towards the hostel.

Gautam laughed. "Isn't this kid a magpie!" he remarked
affectionately. They came out of the gate and began walking
on University Road. Champa stopped at the Chand Bagh crossing. "No, Gautam," she said, "I am not angry with Kamal.
You know I am not very popular with the Reza family and,
anyway, I have no right to be angry with anyone."

"You want to be a martyr, too! Avoid self-pity, Champa,
your problem is very personal. You are in love with Amir Reza,
the rest is incidental. And your other problem is words," he
added darkly in his usual sage-like tone.

"Words!" she repeated. "Talat was right. Here is a phoney
prophet sermonising under the laburnums of Badshah Bagh."

"Champa Begum, shall we discuss all this over a nice hot
cup of coffee at your place?" he suggested amicably.

Champa lived in a cottage outside the I.T. College compound. They walked along the campus wall and heard the college soprano Cynthia's voice rising out of the eucalyptus grove.

Under the Greenwood tree
Who loves to lie with me—

"Here, in the Forest of Arden, they are rehearsing *As You
Like It*," Champa told him.

"Ah! A few minutes ago we were in the make-believe world
of Akbar and the Fort of Lahore, now we are in the Elizabethan age. . ." Gautam remarked. "And both were contemporaries!"

"Who?" Champa asked absently while she unlocked the door
of her cottage.

"Akbar and Elizabeth." Gautam sat down on a cane chair in
the veranda and began listening to the tuneful song. Champa
went in and, after a few minutes, came back with coffee. The
full moon sailed in the blue waters of the college swimming
pool across the guava grove.

"It's all so spell-binding," said Gautam after Cynthia finished her song. "You share this place with a colleague?"

"Yes, Sita Dixit. She is also a teacher. Her brother is Amir's fellow officer in the navy."

Amir again. Gautam lit his pipe. The fact was, he realised with some alarm, that he had begun to resent Lieut. Amir Reza, R.I.N.

"And you would go to the club and play golf if you became Begum Amir Reza?" he asked with feigned innocence.

"Yes, why not?" she snapped back.

He stood up, walked over to the hat-rack and looked at himself in the mirror. "Would any young woman fall so deeply in love with me? Come to think of it, I ain't bad looking either!" he said jovially.

"Doesn't Shanta care for you as much?"

Gautam was taken aback. "How do you know about her?" he growled.

"Ah! A little bird from the western ghats told me. Uma Bhalekar, class-fellow of mine at Chand Bagh. She knew Shanta . . . you are in love with her but she is your first cousin's wife."

Gautam quickly recovered from the impact of her revelation.

"Yes. She was also a status-seeker. Very beautiful and a fairly well-known novelist in Marathi. She married my prosaic cousin who is in the Indian Civil Service and is posted in Maratha country. I saw her after her wedding and realised we should have met earlier. There is no divorce in Hindu law. She is a very liberated, bohemian sort of person and wouldn't have minded having an affair with me, but I am solid, middle class and conservative. I don't like women who smoke and drink and sleep around. . ." Champa had somehow compelled him to confess. "And she enjoys being an I.C.S. officer's lady," he finished.

"Well. So Shanta is out. But you won't even marry poor Nirmala! You would rather dwindle into an eccentric, jaded, phoney brahmachari-guru. You have the makings of a guru under that facade of bogus humility, the indulgent smile— Oh, Gautam, I feel so tired, and I must admit that despite your play-acting, or because of it, I find you very attractive. Ah! now you'll think I'm not a one-man woman. Perhaps I'm not, I don't know. Like Shanta I can't marry you either—and both you and I have seen through each other. Your gang takes great pride in being brutally frank—Kamal calls his circle the 'Thieves' Kitchen'. You all think that only philistines are hypocrites, although nobody can be totally truthful except a lunatic. But now I also know that we are all exposed in the fierce light of one another's perceptions. You'll never find that half-light in which you can hide yourself. That fierce light is beating down upon me, as well, and you are seeing through me and I am seeing through you, that is why I know. . ."

". . .that I am seeing through you!" Gautam threw up his hands and burst out laughing. "O.K. I must rush home and write my column which will include a rave review of Talat's *Anarkali*. And remember, vis-a-vis Amir Reza, that Salim's fixation for Anarkali spelled disaster for both. Goodnight!"

He jumped down from the veranda and disappeared.

Merry laughter rose from the Forest of Arden. They had finished their rehearsal of *As You Like It*.

The War in Europe was in its last phase.

Lucknow's fashionable shopping mall, Hazrat Ganj, was full of Indian and Eurasian WAC (I) girls. High Society had become more vibrant with the presence of smart young Indian officers of His Majesty's armed forces. Coffee houses were buzzing with ardent young men discussing the latest political situation. Tehmina was doing her law, Champa had passed her M.A. and found a teaching job. The year was 1945.

Lieutenant Commander Amir Reza had come home on leave and went to meet Champa in her cottage near Chand Bagh. She was on her way to Tagore Library, but got off her bicycle and started walking with him. Amir said to her, conversationally, "Would you like to live in a nice, airy flat in Colaba, Bombay, as Mrs Reza?"

Champa blushed.

There is a little demon inside every intelligent human being which makes them do what it likes. Was it a demon or her conscience with a capital C? She couldn't quite decide. Whoever it was, it whispered in her ear, 'Say no'. She had also realised that all of them, despite being great leftists, were feudal at heart. They had all thought she was a social climber. She recollected with anger how Kamal had taunted her once for having fallen for Amir because he was upper-class, and how Gautam had called her a status-seeker. It also occurred to her that she had found Gautam Nilambar more attractive, the dark, brooding type. Amir's flashy halo had somehow lost its shine.

She remained silent for a few moments and then said, "No."

"Then why did you lead me up the garden path?"

"Which garden path? Sorry, my English is not very good."

He was astonished. "Can you honestly say you did not flirt with me on the quiet, knowing well that I was to be married to your friend Tehmina?"

"You can't equate ethics with impulses. It was a passing phase, mere infatuation."

"After all that hoo-ha about our romance, how can you be so cynical," he fumed. They had reached the Badshah Bagh Gate. "You've turned out to be quite commonplace and you have no moral courage. I also hear rumours about Gautam and a rich restaurant owner called Shahid Mirza. It's disgusting."

Being a man of few words he did not argue with her and this was a public place. Everybody knew him. He had been called Shahzada Gulfam of Badshah Bagh. He waited for her to say something, but she kept quiet. He uttered an emotionless goodbye, almost like a smart salute, as though she were a battleship soon to sail out to some other war zone. Then he did an equally smart about-turn and marched down purposefully towards Gulfishan. Back home he began packing furiously.

Tehmina had just returned from the University after doing her final law paper. Hectic family conferences took place in the house because she had now finished her education. Amir Reza had still not proposed. He left in the evening.

Everyone got into a terrible temper at Gulfishan, and Kamal and Hari Shankar avoided Tehmina. Summer vacations had begun, Champa returned to Banaras and Tehmina's family proceeded to Nainital. Hari Shankar and Kamal went off to Mussoorie for the roller-skating championships season.

In July the elite returned from the hills, and the doors of Gulfishan were re-opened. Trees rustled in the moisture-laden breeze. One day, Amir Reza turned up unexpectedly and went straight into his aunt's room. "Congratulations," he said, "Tehmina Begum has become a lawyer."

Begum Taqi Reza remained silent.

"I think it's time she got married," he continued.

"To whom?"

"To me, of course."

"Aren't you ashamed of yourself, sonny? You ditched your own cousin for that. . . that. . . slut!"

"I beg your pardon, Chachi-jan!" he retorted in a shocked voice.

"Listen, beta," the aunt tried to control herself, "last December when you came, Susan and Gulabia went to your room to clean it, and Susan found Champa Begum's sari in your wardrobe. We had all seen her wearing it off and on. How could you do this to us—and so brazenly?" Begum Reza broke down.

Amir was flabbergasted. Why had the stupid woman left her sari in his room, of all places? And how had she gone back to her hostel without a sari, for goodness' sake? He felt giddy. Then he remembered in a flash: one winter month the entire family, including most of the servants, had gone to Kalyanpur for a wedding. The coast was clear. He had taken Champa boating down-river; she had brought a change of clothes in a bag because he had said he would at least teach her how to float.

The water had been too cold and she began to shiver and sneeze. Amir brought her back to Gulfishan, she changed hurriedly in his room, and left her wet sari behind in her nervousness because she had spotted somebody coming towards the house. Amir narrated the incident to his aunt but she was not convinced. Still, his lapse was forgiven and Tehmina was told that Amir wanted to marry her straightaway. There was this nice, airy flat in Colaba waiting for her. Tehmina was furious. No, she shouted, enough was enough.

Kamal returned from Mussoorie along with Hari Shankar while Amir was still in Lucknow. When he reached home from Char Bagh he was told that Tehmina had said her final and emphatic "No" to Amir's long-awaited proposal of marriage. Everybody in the house was very subdued. In order to escape the mournful atmosphere he decided to take the "Hawapur University" radio script to Champa. He found her sitting under a garden umbrella on her tiny lawn. Cousin Amir was also there. He had gone there to tell her about the sari disaster, but left as soon as he saw Kamal.

Champa was petrified. Now if she agreed to marry Amir, it would only prove that she had been sleeping with him. Life was so absurd. She was not willing to lose her reputation, whatever was left of it. These people of the upper middle class and middle-level feudal society had as strict a moral code as her own petit bourgeoisie. She was already being counted among the three or four 'fast' girls on campus.

The following day Kamal heard about the Case of the Hidden Sari, and was asked to persuade his dear sister Tim to change her mind.

Tehmina didn't say "Yes" once she had said her mighty "No".

Champa continued meeting them. They were too civilized to mention the sari episode, but Talat and Nirmala remained very agitated. One cloudy afternoon, all of them were having their tea on the back lawn of Gulfishan. In the far corner of the lawn a tall, Chinese champa tree stood in solitary splendour. A carpet of its tiny, yellow flowers covered the grass.

"Whenever I look at this tree, Champa Baji, I think what a lovely, fragrant name you have!" said Kamal with great sincerity. How these stupid men still admire the sorceress, thought Talat indignantly.

Gulabia, the sweepress, passed by. She gave Talat a knowing, mischievous look. That made up the young lady's mind. She blurted out, "Listen, Champa Baji. Now that the cat is out of the bag, let's not continue with this farce of good manners. It's getting on my nerves. Did you or didn't you? Just say yes or no."

There was a shocked silence. Champa turned pale like a fallen champa flower.

Tehmina glared at her younger sister. Kamal and Hari looked away, acutely embarrassed.

"No," Champa answered coldly.

"That's okay, Champa Baji," Kamal apologised. "Please don't mind Talat. You know she's a nut."

"Your great and glorious cousin Amir told me that he had told you all about how I left that controversial sari in his room. Also, kindly note that he proposed marriage to me again. I refused, again for dear Tehmina's sake. I BEG YOUR PARDON!" she almost screamed, and rose from her chair.

"Talat, you horrid creature! You're a spoilt brat but you have no right to insult your guest. Say you're sorry!" Tehmina cried. "Champa, you know she's quite mad. Please, don't go."

But by this time Champa had already run across the lawn and got on to her bicycle.

Nobody spoke. The amaltas leaves rustled overhead, the Chinese champa continued to spread its fragrance. Talat was unrepentant. She grumbled, "I'll be judge and I'll be jury, said the cunning old Fury."

"Shut up," Tehmina rebuked her crossly.

"We have all discovered during the last few years, that she tells fibs, and also fancies herself as a femme fatale," Talat replied.

"Come on, yaar, she's no Chhappan Chhuri,"* said Hari Shankar peaceably.

"Says you! She thinks she is Marlene Dietrich," Nirmala piped in. "She is cunning, a designing woman, a so-and-so. . ." They were very loyal to Tehmina, and Champa had become the traditional vamp of Hindi movies.

Tehmina got up and walked back to the house. Hari and Kamal admonished the younger girls.

"Don't you realise how much you're hurting poor Tim by

---

*Janaki Bai, a famous gramophone singer of Allahabad of the 1920s was stabbed fifty-six times by a spurned lover, survived, and was known as Chhappan Chhuri, 'Fifty-six knives'.

raking up this Sordid Sari Sequence?" said Kamal. "Sorry for
the alliteration."

"All right. But don't you go on defending The Wicked
Lady," Talat growled. They had seen this British film the previous evening.

"No, you must give her the benefit of the doubt," Hari
Shankar got up. "The court is hereby adjourned."

44. Miss Champa Ahmed
(Graduation Portrait by C. Mull,
Hazrat Ganj, Lucknow)

Professor Bannerjee's youngest daughter got married a few
days after Partition. It was a subdued affair. The Professor belonged to Dacca and his relatives could not come because of
the riots. They had also decided to stay back in Dacca as Pakistanis. Things were happening too fast and much too violently,
and the world seemed to have gone quite mad.

The Bannerjee house was overflowing with people who had
come for the wedding lunch. The senior Rezas and Raizadas
had already arrived. Champa, who did not wish to be seen by
them, hid herself behind the youthful crowd surrounding the
bridal couple. All of a sudden a young Bengali addressed her
loudly : "Hellow, there! How is Mr Jinnah? How is it that he
has gone away to Karachi and left you behind?"

Champa was completely taken aback. Who was this stranger?
How had he guessed that she was a Muslim? Was it written on
her face? Was this how Muslims were going to be sneered at in
the future? The man was immediately rebuked in Bengali by
someone else and Champa slipped out of the room quickly.

On the way back to her cottage she saw Talat and Nirmala,
dressed in wedding finery, ambling along in the direction of
the campus bungalows. They did not notice Champa because
they were talking urgently to each other.

"Honestly, I don't feel like running away to England at a time like this, when the country is plunged in total disaster. But higher education is necessary, too, for rebuilding India. Although right now it would be a kind of bourgeois opportunism, don't you think?" Talat was saying.

"Quite right," replied Nirmala gravely. "But it is so difficult to get admission into Cambridge. I've managed only because my father studied there." She fell silent. Gautam had not even hinted that he would marry her, but her parents were hopeful because he was going to England, too.

The girls flitted by and mingled with the moving crowd of wedding guests.

Now Kamal was approaching Champa.

"Champa Baji, congratulations! Your Pakistan has come into being, after all." Intense bitterness, irony and heartbreak lent an edge to his voice. Champa was aghast. She half expected him to deliver another fiery speech but he was strangely quiet, as if this was no time to get worked up and lose one's temper. The era of debates was over; now a real world waited for action. Kamal stood still for a while, gazing at the royal gatehouse of Badshah Bagh. After that he also went his way.

On Thursday evening Champa ran into Talat at the radio station in the studio of programme producer, Begum Saeeda Reza (no relation of the Gulfishan family). The radio station was a cosy place, like India Coffee House, frequented by the inhabitants of Lucknow's Bloomsbury and Belgravia. That evening when Champa entered Begum Saeeda Reza's room, Akhtari Bai Fyzabadi's transformation was being discussed by a few women. Akhtari had been India's Dame Melba, but after her recent marriage to a barrister she was respectfully addressed as Begum Akhtar. . . and she had turned extremely pious.

"She wore a patched cotton gharara," said Mrs. Maya Jameel to Talat. "When I asked her, she said it is Sunnat-i-Rasool—the Lord Prophet usually mended and patched his clothes because of his poverty."

"Ah! So that's why some dervishes wear patched smocks! Anyway, Akhtari Bai may have changed, but some people don't!" Talat had bitched, throwing a glance at Champa—who had deceived Tehmina and Nirmala and waylaid Amir and Gautam in rapid succession. Champa was a maha-thugnee and unforgivable.

Then Talat had added darkly. "Okay, I must rush, Saeeda Apa, my cousin Amir has come home on leave and he is taking us to Mohammed Bagh Club for dinner. Would you like to come along, Champa Baji, for a bit of old waltz, for old times' sake?"

Everybody in the room kept a poker face. Champa fumed.

Now, three days later in the cloudy silence of Badshah Bagh, Champa recalled Talat's insult at the radio station. She had done so once before in her own house after the sari episode. Champa ground her teeth with sudden resolve. I'll show her, the bloody, snooty bitch. . .

Of course Amir still cared for her. He had written from the high seas, said he would look her up when he visited Lucknow. She made a snap decision. She would go to him and say: Here I am, the time of troubles is over, we shall have rest and tranquility. Let others tear their hair and eat dust in the valley of sorrow. A day shall come when they will tire and try to find some refuge, their haughty heads bent low. But they are shameless hypocrites. They were all anti-British leftists and now they are making a bee-line for England, deserting the toiling masses for whom their hearts used to bleed. Damn them.

She reached University Road and continued walking till she stopped at the gates of Gulfishan. With much bravado she called out to Ram Autar who was busy switching off the tube-well motor. Gunga Din stood near him, smoking a bidi. He quickly threw it away when he saw her. "Salaam, Bitiya," he said.

"Is Bhaiya Saheb in? Tell him to come out and meet me," she ordered in a firm voice. Who were they, after all? Mere servants. Was she going to be intimidated even by the gardeners and coachmen of Gulfishan? She closed her eyes for an instant and felt she was growing to her full size and, like Alice, had realised that all these creatures of Wonderland were just a pack of playing cards. But she woke up with a snap when she heard Gunga Din answering her gruffly, "Bhaiya Saheb left early this morning for Pakistan, and everybody else has gone to Badshah Bagh for the wedding."

He looked at her morosely and saw that the news had shaken her. He spoke slowly, "Yes, Bitiya, I am very sorry, too. I've known him since his infancy, he was very fond of me. He would play with me, and I took him out in the buggy every evening for fresh air. He was only four years old when Lady Saheb went to Heaven. He came running to me and cried: 'Gunga Din! Gunga Din! Mummy is asleep and they're taking her away in a very strange manner, on a bed sort of thing. Why isn't she going in your buggy? Run after them and bring her back!"

Gunga Din wiped his wrinkled eyelids and continued hoarsely, "He hated his governess, Nina Memsaheb. I am sure that firangi poisoned Lady Saheb." He paused and sighed deeply. "Now in my old age he has deserted me for good. I have a feeling everybody will leave for Pakistan, we'll be left all alone over here. The earth has slipped from under my feet, Bitiya. . ."

Ram Autar's reaction was somewhat different. He was frowning. Being literate he read Hindi newspapers, and he recollected the editorial in his newspaper that morning in which all Indian Muslims were described as traitors and potential Pakistanis. He informed Champa, "He has gone to Bombay where the navy is being divided into Hindu ships and Muslim ships. He will take his Muslim ships with him and sail off to Karachi, Qadeer was saying. Ho! . . la! . . ." he emitted a deep and angry sound from his throat to scare away the parrots and threw a stone at the guava trees.

Gunga Din kept very quiet.

Champa was dumbstruck. Ram Autar and Gunga Din remained lost in thought. She turned away like a defeated long-distance runner. Amir Reza had left because, apart from horses, sports cars and pretty women he now had a fresh interest in life: a brand new country, promotions, greater opportunities and challenges. Men have an entirely separate world.

And I wasted so much time on this person. . .

It was about to rain. Suddenly something strange happened. Champa felt an inexplicable elation. There was freedom in the wind, joyous contentment was palpable in the rustling of the leaves. Did others also experience this sense of liberation? Poor

Tehmina, for instance or foolish Gautam, who was in love with his cousin's wife, Shanta?

Ha. . . ha. . . how funny, she laughed to herself, and began to run. Wide, wet, sweet-smelling earth was spread all around her. She jumped over a crystal-clear brook and ran round the compound of Gulfishan until she came upon the lattice which stood in front of the outhouses. She caught a glimpse of Qamrun's turmeric yellow sari through the mulberry trees.

"Salaam, Bitiya. What is it, you all right?" Qamrun addressed her, coming out of the grove.

"Salaam. I'm fine, Driver's Wife," she replied, panting.

Qamrun looked at her in silence.

"May I sit down here, Driver's Wife?"

"Certainly, Bitiya, do come in. It's going to rain any minute."

Champa entered the veranda. Its floor was intensely cool. Pot and pans glimmered on the railing, Qadeer's black felt cap hung from a nail on the wall, pappad lay drying on a printed bedsheet on a cot.

"One doesn't get a wee bit of sun these days to dry them," Qamrun made polite conversation. She was aware that something was amiss. Then she began abruptly: "Bitiya, you do not know what men are. We do. They are happy as long as you go on adoring them, and they want enormous sacrifices from us. Otherwise they're unhappy. How can I explain to Tehmina Bitiya that girls are always in a weaker position? Why did she say no to him in the first place? Now that he has gone away for good, she's crying her eyes out."

Champa didn't reply.

"What is a mere woman, after all," Qamrun continued sadly. "She is a man's personal servant as a wife, and even as a mother. In her youth she is tormented by her in-laws, in her old age she is bullied by her daughter-in-law, as a widow, if she is poor she is ignored by everyone. All her life she has to serve, serve, serve. And even then men are not satisfied. What do they want? Complete submission, like God." Qamrun knew all about Champa and Amir. "Are you also going to Vilayat?" she concluded.

"He is not the only man in the world, there are thousands

of others. All men are not alike, Driver's Wife," Champa said weakly. In a gush of easterly wind a shower of rain fell on the lemon trees.

"They are all alike, Bitiya, whether they live in bungalows or servants' quarters. Even in Vilayat they are probably no different. My father used to work as a cook for English Saheb-log, and some of them were wife-beaters. Shall I make a paan for you, Bitiya?"

"No thanks, Driver's Wife, I must go. Khuda hafiz, Ram Daiya." She rose from the charpayi and walked away.

"Why don't the Bitiya-log understand. . .?" Qamrun asked Ram Daiya ruefully.

"They are scared, they think they know everything because they have read a little English," Ram Daiya replied, shaking her head. "They are no better than us after all."

Champa walked briskly back to her cottage, another resolve forming slowly. She had half-heartedly applied for a scholar-ship advertised by the new Ministry of Education, for inter-preters. They were to be sent to Paris. She had taken some evening classes in French during the golden days of her ro-mance with Amir Reza. She must get that scholarship. She thought of all the Beautiful People who were about to leave the shores of Ind—Atiya Habibullah, Ranjana Sidhanta, Feroze, Talat, Nirmala, AIR's handsome announcer, Aley Hasan. Even Gauhar Sultan, the AIR singer, was going. Both Amala Roy and Hari Shankar had joined the new Indian Foreign Service. (Only poor Tehmina was staying back like the drab Phoebe of Quality Street.) If she, Champa Ahmed, got the scholarship—well, it would be the password to the real fairyland, the West-ern World. . .

The Exodus from India had begun.

She entered the sitting room of her tiny bungalow in Chand Bagh and flopped down, exhausted, on the settee. She had just run a marathon against Time. Unwittingly she looked up at her graduation photograph adorning the cornice. She had retained her small-town habit of displaying one's own pictures in the drawing-room with flower vases on either side. Her graduation portrait was by the famous society photographer,

C. Mull, taken in 1943 when she, too, had performed the exciting 'ritual' of going down to Hazrat Ganj with fellow graduates of I.T. College. They wore their best saris and had on their caps and gowns, scrolls in their bags and stars in their eyes when they were greeted by the suave photographer. That was four years ago, and in 1945 another picture had been taken of her with her M.A., L.L.B. degree. Also by C. Mull.

Now, for the last couple of years, she had been a lecturer. She was thirty—Talat and Nirmala were ten whole years younger than her. She must hurry up and stop fooling around. No more going to the India Coffee House with the local long-haired, pipe-smoking fraternity. She was called the Intellectuals' Moll. When she went out with Ahmed Hashim, the play-boy-owner of the ritzy Hazrat Ganj restaurant, Rose of Sharon, they began to refer to her as the Countess of Sharon. What was she to do? Desert her poor unsuspecting parents for the time being, and go away.

I.T. was run by missionaries who probably belonged to the Bible Belt of America. Here, junior girls could not go out without a chaperone—Champa was considered too flighty even by the standards of this institution. So be it. Bye-bye, folks.

45. The Broken Tanpura of Sultan Hussain Shah Nayak of Jaunpur

Talat picked up her tanpura and came out onto the veranda. 'Come home this monsoon,' she tried to sing the melody in Raga Malhar but her voice stuck in her throat. Amir had come home from the wars and gone away for good, gone to Pakistan. Tehmina was sitting inside, making a new blouse on the sewing machine. Talat went in. Amir Reza must be in Karachi at this moment. It was almost as if he had never been here, never lived in Gulfishan. The First Act had come to a close, as it were, with his departure. How could he stay back here, weather our storms and fight our battles? She sat down near her older sister and began turning the handle of the machine.

Tehmina raised her head and regarded Talat. The table-fan continued whirring. Inanimate things often have near-human expressions. A table-fan turning mechanically from side to side somehow looked so foolish, thought Talat.

Outside a koel was crying koo-hoo, koo-hoo. Ram Autar was shouting in the distance. Suddenly she regained her self-confidence and began speaking, "Actually, Tim, emotions are unreliable. Intellectual empathy and personal equations also don't mean a thing. In the ultimate analysis, one is utterly alone," she ended profoundly.

"There you go again," said Tehmina and looked at her, amused. "Are you also hoping to become a Cambridge don some day?" she asked.

Talat was hurt. "Do you think I am an ass?" she asked sadly.

"Not at all, you are very intelligent. But you also happen to be a woman, silly billy."

Talat was shocked. "Tim, you are a revolutionary. I say, go ahead, fight, struggle. Work for the equality of men and women. You encouraged Bhaiya Saheb to acquire such a high opinion of himself—you ought to have thrown a shoe at his Greek nose!"

"Talat! Don't be rude."

"Oh yes, now defend him, too. So, what's the difference between you and Ram Daiya? She is beaten regularly by Ram Autar and accepts it meekly. The other day when Hussaini's wife took her aside and scolded him, the idiot yelled: 'Don't you dare say anything to my man.'" Talat broke off as she was on the verge of tears.

She dashed out of the room, climbed onto her bicycle and pedalled furiously in the direction of Water Chestnut House. She found Kamal, Hari and Nirmala on the riverside steps playing "Kot-peece", and cheating as usual. That cheered her up considerably and she joined in. Gautam arrived, like another disturbing thought. Nirmala was visibly upset, her brother and childhood friends looked away.

Gautam sat down next to them and lit a cigarette. He seemed

excited about his impending departure for America. "I'm leaving next week," he gushed.

"From now on a Washington-based journalist, eh?" Kamal remarked sombrely. "Hazrat Ganj will miss you."

"I'm sure it will. I was such an interesting fellow. . .Say," he asked after a while, "where has Champa disappeared?"

"Haven't the foggiest," Talat said dryly.

"Her cottage was locked. I thought I would say bye to her, too." He tried to sound casual.

"She's very secretive. May have gone home—she has got a scholarship to France, you know," Kamal informed him.

"Wow!" said Gautam. "I say, girls, let's have some tea— *thora cha, ekdum, jaldi, bandobast*. . .as Bhaiya Saheb used to say, Col. Blimp style."

Talat and Nirmala rose to their feet and ambled away towards the kitchen. Jamuna was not around. Nirmala put the kettle on the brick-built cooking range and burnt some waste paper to ignite the coals. Then she wiped her eyes.

"Is it smoke or are you really crying?" asked Talat good-humouredly.

"Both."

"What a fool you are. I think he's either confused or too philosophical about you. You know how he loves to reduce everything to metaphysical concepts."

"My foot."

"Or he intends to remain a confirmed bachelor and is aspiring to gurudom. Acharya Gautamdeva—something of that sort."

"My left toe."

"Still, I'm sure one day he will turn up in England and take you round the sacred fire."

"And then keep comparing me to Champa Baji so that I live in her shadow thereafter. No thank you." She cried some more.

"Don't be such a weeping willow, *yaar*. Men forget their previous infatuations once they get married, that's what I've noticed," Talat said wisely.

"I feel so humiliated," Nirmala replied and burst into tears again.

Tehmina went across to the window after Talat had left. The First Act is over, she said to herself. If someone wrote a play about this my character would be described thus: Tehmina Begum, M.A. , L.L.B. Homely, sensitive; does her best to hide her unhappiness. Courteous and humble. Proud. Strong.

Some children of visiting relatives were playing "Kora Jamal Shahi" on the back lawn. Susan was hanging rainbow-coloured dupattas on the clothesline. Kamal returned from Water Chestnut House and began playing with the kids. One child chased the other outside a circle of sitting players. He would drop the whip behind a sitting player and thrash him if he was caught unawares. Kamal began running around. "Hello, Tim," he yelled. Then he took up the refrain of the game, *"Kora Jamal Shahi—Kora. . .peechhey dekha, maar khai."*

Tehmina leaned against the railing and watched him. He shouted *"Kora Jamal Shahi. . . Even Champa Baji is going away . . . peechhe dekha maar khai. Kora Jamal. . ."*

"Karachi?" Tehmina shouted back indifferently.

"Paris! *Kora Jamal Shahi. . ."* he thrashed a little girl with the 'whip'. She began chasing him in her turn.

"How . . .?" asked Tehmina.

"She's a go-getter, isn't she? And Gautam has invited you to his farewell party, Saturday." Kamal began running faster till he dropped the 'whip' behind another child and then, thrusting his thumbs in his coat pockets, trotted off towards the motor garage.

India Coffee House was buzzing with animated conversation. Along with the regulars there were many newcomers—Hindu and Sikh refugees—well-dressed young men and women from across the new border. The citizens of Lucknow had never heard of Hindu Pathans who were now wandering the lanes of Aminabad, uprooted from the North West Frontier Province. There were rich refugees and poor refugees, but their influx had not altered the peaceful atmosphere of the city. There was no tension in Hazrat Ganj, only new faces.

Half of Coffee House was occupied by Gautam's friends. Some Urdu poets had been invited there to meet Louis

MacNiece. "If you have a poet as Governor of U.P., this is bound to happen. Day after day she holds mushairas at Raj Bhavan. With her Hyderabadi-Urdu culture and graciousness Mrs. Naidu specially asked me to recite my poem to Mr. MacNiece," a young Urdu poet announced proudly.

"He has come to India to write about flies settled on corpses," said Tehmina with disdain.

"Well, we do have flies settled on thousands of corpses at the moment in the country," responded a journalist. "Lahore is burning, Delhi is burning."

"The West had millions of dead bodies littered over half the world till only two years ago. We are not the only savages," Tehmina argued vehemently.

"Good old Tim is back in form," Talat whispered to Nirmala. "She'll be all right."

"This year the rains have been the heaviest," the Urdu poet continued, "the Monsoon of Blood. It pours from the skies. There is blood on flowers, blood on our hands. People have bloodshot eyes..."

"Not in Lucknow," Kamal said smugly. "At least you should be thankful that the culture created by our ancestors has proved more powerful than the present insanity."

"Culture, culture everywhere, and not a drop to drink," the Urdu poet addressed the host. "Gautam, are you taking us to Kapoor's Bar after this Gandhian meeting?"

"No," Gautam spoke for the first time. He was chain-smoking and very quiet.

"Instead of riots we have a spate of mushairas in Lucknow in aid of the refugees," Talat remarked.

"I hate to be called a refugee." A young former lecturer from Government College, Lahore, said unhappily. "Do you know what it means to us, to be driven out of our home-town, Lahore—the most beautiful city in the world?" There were tears in his eyes.

"I was tuning my tanpura for my riaz in the morning to sing Khayal Jaunpuri, and one string snapped. Gautam, there's symbolism for you. Hussain Shah's tanpura broken into two," said Talat ruefully.

"The instrument is all right, you probably tuned it too tightly, or the string wasn't strong enough," Gautam was cryptic.

"Who was Hussain Shah?" someone asked Talat.

"Never mind."

"Vajid Ali Shah and Sultan Baz Bahadur and Hussain Shah—they're all irrelevant today," commented someone else.

"Did Beethoven become irrelevant in Europe during the recent war?" Tehmina shot back.

"Hear, hear," said Nirmala loyally.

"Secularism is enshrined in the philosophy of the Congress," Tehmina continued in her university-union manner. "Pandit Nehru made a derelict old lady, a direct descendant of Bahadur Shah Zafar, sit next to him on the ramparts at Red Fort on the 15th of August."

"How sweet!" Talat exclaimed. Hari and Kamal groaned.

"Pandit Nehru has a sense of history, and this was a touching symbolic gesture." Tehmina concluded her little speech. Suddenly Talat had visions of Tehmina Reza turning into one of the leaders of new India. No, she won't be a willing wall-flower. The same thought had struck the Urdu poet.

"You can become another Begum Aizaz Rasooi*. . ." he said aloud.

"I beg your pardon?" Tehmina was enraged.

"I mean another woman leader like Begum Aizaz Rasooi."

"Then she may be made a governor or an ambassador some day and cock a snook at Bhaiya Saheb," Nirmala whispered to Talat approvingly.

"Here is tomorrow's India on the anvil, political ambitions in the making," S.P. Kaushal remarked cynically. He wrote abstract poetry in English and was in charge of English programmes at the radio station.

"I have no political ambitions," Tehmina replied sharply. "I'll merely work for the Party as a sympathiser."

On the other side of the table they were discussing life's new, expanding horizons.

---

*A flamboyant leader of that era, wife of a taluqdar of Sandila.

"They already have television in London."

"And Gautam is going all the way to America by air," another friend commented. Talat interrupted him as a grim reminder: "Have you read Faiz Ahmed Faiz's latest poem. *The Morning of Freedom? Yeh daag daag ujala, yeh shab-gazida sahar.* . ." She went on to recite the poem. The audience became very still.

Pothan Abraham, the Malayali who worked for *The Pioneer*, broke the silence. "Now translate it into pidgin English, I couldn't understand a word."

"Translate Urdu poetry into English? How can you render *jigar ki aag* as the liver's fire?"

"Try," said Abraham, smoking his pipe dreamily.

Talat pondered a while, then began, "Okay—This blighted dawn, this darkened sun. This is not the morn we waited for. We went forth in the desert of heaven, hoping to reach our destination of stars. We hoped that, somewhere, we would come ashore from the placid river of the night, that the barge of sorrow would end its cruise. Whence came the early morning breeze, where did it go? The wayside lamp does not know. The night's burden has not diminished, the hour of deliverance for eye and heart has not arrived. Face forward! For our destination is not yet in sight."

There was gloomy silence again.

Meanwhile, Malcolm got busy with his pen and sketchbook. He was a jovial young man from Lal Bagh, a talented artist who used to sit in the Coffee House and sketch the pretty girls who came in.

Now he drew a victoria with a winged horse, and Talat inside it with her broken tanpura. The victoria was taking off from Monkey Bridge, heading west.

Talat looked at the sketch intently and said, "Malcolm, kindly mend the tanpura, it cannot be broken forever."

"Perhaps it is, dear lady, perhaps it is," said Kaushal soberly.

"You mean Humpty can never be put together again?" asked Talat, raising an eyebrow.

"Talat!" Tehmina admonished her as usual. "From Faiz Ahmed Faiz you descend to Humpty-Dumpty—grow up!"

46. The Hon'ble Cyril Ashley of Sidney Sussex College

The Hon'ble Cyril Derek Edwin Howard Ashley looked at the time again as he paced up and down under the international clock in the tube station at Piccadilly. He had invited Champa Ahmed to see "Waters of the Moon" tonight. He opened the latest *New Statesman and Nation* and began scanning its pages. The weekly magazine carried a fiery letter to the Editor by one Gautam Nilambar, on the subject of India's Partition and world peace. Cyril was keen on going to the Indian dancer, Surekha's, place to meet this person and thrash out the issue with him. But Surekha had told him that Nilambar, who had just been transferred from Moscow to India House, had left for Bonn.

Cyril was the younger son of Lord Barnfield of Barnfield Hall, Surrey. His grandfather, Lord George Thomas Ashley, had controlled considerable interests in the jute and rubber trade in the City. Cyril's great-grandfather, Cyril Ashley, the son of a poor village parson, had gone out to India in the eighteenth century as a factor in the East India Company. He traded in indigo in Bengal and Bihar and had also acquired great wealth at the Court of the King of Oudh. After his death, his widow had returned to England with their little son who, on growing up, had started his business in rubber. He bought a number of villages, was created a hereditary peer and sat in the House of Lords. His son served his country in far-flung outposts of the Empire as a suave and shrewd diplomat. He was an expert on Near Eastern affairs and knew how to deal with the troublesome Afghans and the arrogant Ottomans. In India he tolerated a few upper class Mohammedans because they were very refined and cultured. He met the Anglicised Hindu-Bengali elite in Calcutta's Great Eastern Hotel, and north Indian wogs in Delhi's Imperial Hotel whenever he visited India. His grandfather, Sir Cyril Ashley, must have been a very romantic person indeed. A portrait, "Nabob Cyril Ashley and his Bibi" by a Royal Academy artist hung in the main draw-ing-room of the Manor in Surrey.

Lord George died in 1940. He was survived by two sons, Lord David and the Hon'ble Cyril Ashley. Cyril had been a child during the Roaring Twenties and grew up in the Thir-ties. Many artists and writers came to his town house in South Kensington to meet his avant-garde stepmother, Lady Ellen, who smoked, painted weird canvasses and read *The Daily Worker*. Bloomsbury was anti-fascist, Auden and Spender were the leaders of progressive thinking, Unity Theatre produced communist plays and the Group Theatre was staging plays written by Louis MacNiece, Auden and Isherwood. It was fash-ionable to talk of the Spanish Civil War and be a Leftist.

The East was being intellectually rediscovered—Eliot and Ezra Pound were quoting from Sanskrit and classical Chinese. With the family's age-old India connection it was quite natu-ral that Cyril be interested in that country's history and ar-chaeology. From Winchester he went to Sidney Sussex, Cam-bridge, where he read Indian History. Soon the War broke out and he joined the Royal Air Force. In 1945 he returned to Cambridge and resumed reading about the wars the British had waged in the East. He was specialising in the East India Company's problems of governance in India.

The Barnfield family was past its prime. Communists lurked in the Barnfield rubber plantations in Malaya, and the Mau Mau had appeared in Kenya. Lord David still had his tea gar-dens in Sylhet, which was now in East Pakistan. He opened his Manor to the public every Sunday, but financial worries had made the peer an old man while still in his forties. And he was still a bachelor.

Cyril continued his studies at Cambridge, indifferent to the material problems of worldly existence. He married a middle class Jewish girl, Rose Lyn, whom he had met at a bottle-party in Chelsea. She was a potter by profession, but not a success-ful one. That was why Cyril was attracted to her—he didn't like terribly accomplished women. His wife worked in a ce-ramics factory in Staffordshire. Every now and then he looked with surprise at the gold ring on his left-hand finger, then remembered that he was married and had a very understanding wife. Once or twice a month they spent the weekend in the country or came down to London, where she had a basement flat in Swiss Cottage.

Once he bought a shilling ticket along with the Sunday crowds and went sight-seeing to his own home in Surrey. His brother was away on the Continent, and the new guide did not recognise Master Cyril. He toured the house, went from room to room and wondered. . . It's funny, I was born here.

The Manor stood beside a little lake. Its oldest wing was built in the early fifteenth century and had real blown-glass windows, as well as a lady chapel. A new wing was added in the eighteenth century, the Age of Prosperity. Outside, there were Italian statues and marble fountains, even a sad-eyed Buddha who sat on a pedestal in the rock garden—a silent reminder of the days of the Barnfields' Oriental glory.

As a young boy Cyril used to stroll in the park, and often walked down to the two open graves which belonged to the Middle Ages. They turned into tiny pools after the rains, and Cyril would sit on the rough grey edges and ponder the mysteries of life and death. For outsiders the place was redolent of high romance. Cyril could find nothing romantic about it, not even story-book material in the fabulous personality of his ancestor, 'Nabob' Sir Cyril Ashley. Who knows, he must have plundered a lot of Indians to become what he had become.

In 1700, Mirza Abu Talib Istahani of Calcutta discovered the library and valuables of Murshidabad's Nawab Sher Jung in the house of an English judge in London. In the 1930s Cyril Ashley could not possibly know who the real owners of the Mughal curios he saw in his own house, were. He thought that only a fool would deny that all life was absurd. Therefore when he entered his Manor as a stranger he experienced a curious sense of satisfaction. This must be Nirvana, he chuckled to himself.

Cyril Ashley was a modern man, prey to all the disillusions and betrayals and emotional and spiritual doubts of the age. Living in mid-century Britain he, too, revelled in Sartre, and even read the local thinker, Colin Wilson. Michael and Denis were his only friends at the University. (Michael was Jewish and a Zionist. Denis, like Michael, was middle class, and wrote abstract poetry.) Apart from these two there were lots of others, black boys and brown boys.

And girls.

Cyril was never greatly attracted to the women of his own race, they were all so irritatingly alike. The post-war period was a great and golden era in which humanity was entering a new age of International Understanding, Goodwill and Cultural Amity. All manner of females came from all over the globe to study in England's cloistered universities. Yellow, black, brown. Among his friends, June Carter was his compatriot. She fitted the Angus Wilsonian description of a British university woman. She wore horn-rimmed glasses, had fuzzy hair and studied Slavonic languages. Then there was his dear Rose— he had married her and discovered that she was good-hearted, but a dreadful bore. She spoke in a monotone which was nerve-racking. Slowly Rose and Cyril drifted apart.

In the University Union he heard the fiery speeches of two new speakers: Kamal Reza and Nirmala Srivastava who had recently arrived from faraway Lucknow. That name rang a bell. His ancestor, Nabob Cyril, had lived in Lucknow and made a fortune there. In his research Cyril had not yet reached Oudh, he was still at the Battle of Plassey.

As a socialist, Cyril tried his best to hide the fact that he was the son of a peer. He avoided meeting the newly-arrived brownies for some time. At the University he knew only one Black Girl in Search of God, with whom he talked at length about Indian philosophy when he met her. She turned out to be a Pakistani. Her name was Roshan Kazmi, a quiet person with a disturbingly intellectual face.

During a weekend visit to London, he accompanied the Indophiles, Denis and Michael, to an exhibition of Tagore's pen-and-ink drawings at India House. A long-haired Bengali acquaintance asked them to come along to Exeter Street for a cultural programme celebrating Tagore Week in London.

The cosy little hall of the Indian Students' Centre was already packed to capacity when they reached. Everybody squatted on the floor like yogis. Cyril and his friends found a place near the low dais but Cyril was worried about the crease of his trousers. Joss sticks burned in front of a portrait of Tagore who somehow looked like God the Father. A harmonium was placed on a table. The compère ascended the dais and made her announcements in nasal English.

She was stunning. Eyes enlarged with kohl, a big coil of hair adorned with flowers, flaming red sari of Murshidabad silk with a contrasting bright green blouse. This was the New Ajanta Look adopted by post-Independence Indian women who had come out West. The young lady had a golden brown complexion and a fantastic figure.

"Wow," whispered Denis.

"Yes, wow," agreed Michael wholeheartedly. Cyril tried to contemplate Nothingness instead of gaping at her. Then he reflected on the greatness of the Great Sage. The trouble was that these days he was a bit turned off by the East. His ship was sailing towards Byzantium—he had become a believer in the supremacy of Western European Christian Civilization.

"Shrimati Shunila Mukerji—the great exponent of Rabindra Sangeet," the seductive M.C. announced.

Everything Indian is great—why are they so fond of hyperbole? Cyril wondered. A middle-aged lady with puffy cheeks and lustrous eyes ascended the stage and smiled dreamily. She began playing the harmonium and sang lilting Bengali songs while the compere read out the translations in florid English. Then she announced: "Shrimati Surekha Devi, the great exponent of Bharatanatyam."

Sarong-clad south Indian drummers trooped in, followed by the dancer who arrived like a shaft of lightning. She also had elongated eyes and arched eyebrows. The little darkies in white sarongs began a majestic chant in Telugu and played the mridangam. The music seemed to be emanating from some other sphere of the cosmos, and the dance was other-worldly, too. Cyril Ashley was mesmerised.

The programme came to an end, the flamboyant compere disappeared, and the crowd dispersed. Mrs Shunila Mukerji was talking to William Craig, the publisher, near the exit.

"You ought to meet Shunila Debi," the long-haired Bengali who had brought them here gushed importantly. "She is a Theosophist, a fast-vanishing breed. She has helped many a migratory Indian Lame Duck—a species to be found increasingly on this island. And she is the high-priestess of expatriate intellectuals. She has lived through the blitz which killed her eminent barrister husband, and she is taking us home for drinks, fish curry and TV. Come along."

Cyril Ashley suppressed a smile. These people were so funny.

"That sexy wench will turn up there, hopefully," Denis whispered.

"Let's go." They marched down with the others to the tube station.

In no time Cyril found himself in a luxury flat in Chelsea. The arty drawing-room was filled with cigarette smoke and loud conversation. The hostess lighted candles in front of an antique Nepalese Buddha and intoned a short prayer in Pali. The soulful effect was marred by the appearance of Patricia Kirkwood on the tiny black-and-white screen of the television set. Drinks were served by a Polish refugee maid.

Surekha Devi had come from Lahore to Delhi as a refugee in 1947. Her husband was studying at the London School of Economics, and her real name was Avinash. She was an unassuming Punjabi girl, surprisingly bereft of the airs and mannerisms of a celebrated dancer. Mrs. Mukerji introduced her with a flourish as India's Anna Pavlova.

"There is more to that statement than meets the eye," the Long-haired One informed the three friends from Cambridge. They were sitting on an ottoman in a far corner. "Surekha Devi's husband is an orthodox man, yet he has allowed her to be the partner of this famous male dancer because he is—well—like Nijinsky. . ."

"Who is like Nijinsky—the husband or the male dancer?" asked Denis with a poker face.

"The latter, of course. That," the Long-haired One pointed towards two portraits, "is the late Mr Mukherjee K.C., and this is his son, Ashutosh, an artist living in Paris."

The hostess sat down under a Tibetan thangka and recounted anecdotes of her friends—Thambimuttoo, Editor, *Poetry London*, Dr Mulk Raj Anand, Krishna Menon, and fellow Bengali, Mrs Ella Reid.

"And what do you do at Cambridge, young man?" Mrs Mukerji turned towards Cyril.

"East India Company's administration, Ma'am," he answered briefly. Somehow he was feeling cheated. The sultry siren hadn't come after all.

"Oh!" Shunila Debi cried, "in that case you must see the documents I have—land deeds, etc., that John Company gave to my husband's family in Rajshahi district, in East Bengal. They might be of some interest to you."

Well, one could ignore the Pali prayer bit, the lady was transparently sincere. She may even tell him the whereabouts of the enchantress in red.

The next time Cyril came to London he realised he had lost Mrs. Mukerji's phone number, but he decided to take a chance and call on her.

"The lady has gone to Paris to meet her son," said Mr Jenkins, the janitor and jovial one-armed ex-soldier. "She will also go to the Low Countries to see the Little Mustess—whoever they are!" And then it happened. The Ajanta painting (which now also looked somewhat like a Matisse), materialised then and there. Stepped out of the lift—as simple as that.

"Ah! Here comes the Maharani!" Mr Jenkins exclaimed. Those were the days when every well-dressed, sari-clad woman was taken to be an Indian princess. She beamed at Cyril in recognition, for she had seen him sitting uncomfortably on the floor at the Students' Centre. They introduced themselves to each other informally, as students do.

"I came to see my friend, Kamala, of the Indian Foreign Service. She also lives in this building," she informed him.

"You didn't accompany us here that memorable evening."

"I was in a hurry to go back to Paris—I'm studying at the Sorbonne," she lied, compulsively.

Cyril detected a note of indifference in her voice, probably because she had noticed the plain gold ring on his finger.

"None of the Indian girls drank at Mrs Mukerji's place. Still very conservative, aren't you, so I can't ask you to have a drink with me before you leave."

"I wouldn't mind, but I'm afraid I'm in a hurry again. Some other time!" she answered politely. They walked to the Underground, she said goodbye and disappeared into the crowd.

A self-assured, modern young woman, and she wouldn't mind a drink or two with friends. Must be Paris that does it. She'll have to be chased, and she might even ignore the plain gold ring on his finger.

He went to Paris but couldn't locate her at the Sorbonne. Ashutosh Mukherjee was of little help, but Cyril did find her eventually in Mrs Shunila Mukerji's salon in Chelsea one evening, and met her several times again over the year at Surekha Devi's flat in St. John's Wood.

He got to know Kamal Reza and the U.S. based Hari Shankar. Gautam Nilambar, the third of the trinity, had recently been transferred to Britain from Moscow, but Cyril had not met him yet. In his letter to Kingsley Martin this character had blamed the Muslim League entirely for Partition. Cyril Ashley did not agree.

He continued loitering under the international clock feeling rather foolish, and wondered idly if he had fallen in love with the exotic Champa of the Tropics.

47. *Young Indians in Mid-century England*

Nirmala was on her way to Fitzwilliam Library when she caught sight of Gautam.

"Nirmala! I have been looking for you everywhere. . . how are you?" he exclaimed, rushing down the road towards her. "I met a most formidable female professor in your college who was thoroughly unhelpful in tracking you down. How are you, Nirmal?"

She closed her eyes for an instant. This *was* Gautam who stood before her, talking to her excitedly.

"How do you happen to be here?" she asked.

"I've come from London to see you."

"I believe you are in regular foreign service now."

"That's right."

"Enjoying life?"

"Hmm. . ."

The conversation came to an abrupt end. Gautam noted that Nirmala was no longer a chatterbox—she had become serious, sober, quiet. "Come along, Kamal told me he would meet us at the Koh-i-Noor," he said.

Students in flapping black gowns were passing by. She gestured towards them, saying "That's Denis. . . That one is Cyril, the good-looking blond fellow, he's the son of a lord and Champa Baji's new boyfriend. She often comes here from London to meet him. They're referred to as Nabob Cyril and his Bibi after the famous painting of his ancestor and his Indian common-law wife."

Gautam looked shocked. After a pause he asked, "So has she found love and happiness at last?"

Nirmala gave a short laugh. "I remember there was an English or American movie called *It's Love I'm After*—we went to see it at the Plaza in Hazrat Ganj. Boys at the University used to give new year titles to the girls, and that year Champa Baji was given the title: '*It's Love I'm After*'! Once she even became a sort of jogan. She let her hair fall over her shoulders and wore an ochre sari—that phase lasted a couple of months."

Gautam remained silent.

"I have a feeling," Nirmala was saying, "that Champa Baji will eventually become like Mrs. Shunila Mukerji. Do you know Mrs.Mukerji?"

"Yes, I do."

"Time cheats us outright and goes on cheating us," said Nirmala. "Shunila Debi must have been an unusually attractive woman twenty years ago. Men used to consider it a privilege if she spoke a few words to them; now she's a lonely old lady who rounds up young men and takes them home for fish curry. Time betrayed her."

A drop of rain fell on her eyes. She wiped her face with her handkerchief and continued: "For Champa Baji, this is the era of the Hon'ble Cyril Ashley, son of Lord Barnfield. Just as you were the son of Sir Deep Narain, and Amir of Sir Zaki Reza."

"Nirmal, you're being very unfair to Champa," Gautam said quietly.

"No, Gautam, this is a fact. Champa Baji has been disappointed and she has disappointed us, too. The other day Kamal was saying, how is it that Champa has slowly lost her magic? And Talat said rightly, Champa Baji is the same, we have grown up."

Gautam looked at her ruefully. Nirmal continued, "She was in Paris and left whatever she was doing to come here. Now she's trying to get into Girton. She can't seem to decide anything about herself. I think she's one of those people who need some kind of emotional support."

The sound of a trumpet rose from Jesus Lane. Gautam stopped walking.

"I don't know who it is," said Nirmala, "he often plays very sad tunes." A shower of rain had made her hair wet. "Amir is also in London, has come here as a Pakistani diplomat. Nowadays he's busy showing his water colours to Roshan Ara."

They had reached Koh-i-Noor. "Gautam," Nirmal asked thoughtfully, "why are people so second rate?" He kept quiet. A group of undergrads passed by.

"Nirmal," Gautam stopped again.

"Yes?"

"Will you marry me?"

"No."

"Why? Nirmal—" The words choked in his throat.

"Because," she said in a very clear and deep voice, "you are second rate, too. Come, let's go inside."

Nirmal had really grown up. They entered the restaurant.

Roshan Ara Kazmi met Commander Amir Reza on a bright and sunny Id day on the lawns of Woking Mosque. The place was swarming with the small Muslim community that lived in and around London, mostly from India and Pakistan. A few English girls who had married Muslim students were dressed self-consciously in bright saris or shalwar-kameez. There was that special happiness in the air which Muslims experience in abundance on no other festival as they do on Id-ul-Fitr. Roshan had come from Cambridge with her friends and was introduced to Amir Reza by a common acquaintance. Amir was elegantly dressed in a grey suit and black lambskin qaraquli called a Jinnah cap. Jawaharlal Nehru, who was a product of U.P.'s Indo-Muslim feudal culture, had made the black sherwani and white churidar pajama (basically the formal upper-class Muslim dress) the Indian diplomats' attire. The Pakistanis had to be different—therefore they continued to wear western dress.

Roshan had acquired a string of Commonwealth scholarships and was tipped to become a formidable professor in the future. However, she was instantly captivated by Amir Reza, and then her intellect was of no help. While she was talking to him Talat came along, her Lukhnawi gharara rustling on the English grass.

"Adab, Bhaiya Saheb, Id mubarak," she said zestfully. Kamal followed her. Both of them had met Roshan in Cambridge. There was an exchange of pleasantries and small talk.

"Oh, Sir Feroze Khan Noon and Lady Afternoon are here! Must go and say Id mubarak to them. Excuse me," Amir Reza walked away hurriedly.

"And pray who is Lady Afternoon?" asked Aley Hasan of the BBC Hindi Section, who had joined them.

"Sir Feroze's second wife, Austrian lady," Talat informed him. "Sir Feroze Khan Noon said in a speech the other day in London, that we Muslims produced such great men as Chengiz Khan and Halaku Khan. The poor fellow doesn't know that they were not Muslim!"

Kamal and Aley Hasan laughed.

Roshan didn't like the leader of her country and his wife being ridiculed by Indians. She kept quiet. But she was puzzled by the abrupt departure of the fabulous Commander.

"Why did he leave in such a hurry?" she asked Talat.

Talat grinned. "See, we are Bharatis, and he belongs to Pakistan's armed forces, therefore he avoids us if he can."

"Why should he do that? You wouldn't try to steal defence secrets from him, would you?"

"Roshan—do you have a divided family? I mean, close relatives who are divided between India and Pakistan?"

"No, I am a native of Lahore."

"So you won't understand this dilemma, and anyway we belong to Nehru's India. We give a sort of complex to people like Cousin Amir," Talat added loftily.

"Oof, this is the kind of holier-than-thou attitude of you Indians that we resent," Roshan Kazmi said, frowning. She ambled away, crossed the lawn and joined the little group which had surrounded Sir Feroze and Lady Noon. Amir led her gallantly towards the tea stalls.

Talat laughed. "Kamman, do you see what I see?"

"Yeah."

"I think she will do. He is getting on and he needs a doting wife. She was absolutely goggle-eyed."

"Don't start match-making, for god's sake."

"Nothing could be more auspicious than today for this," Talat replied cheerily.

Champa was sharing a broken-down flat with Comrades June Carter and Neil Brigg, both of whom had been introduced to her by Cyril. June was teaching some obscure Slavonic language at the University, Neil was an engineer. Both were members of the Communist Party of Great Britain. On weekends the comrades got together at Feroze's or Surekha's place and talked till the early hours of the morning. Champa didn't meet Gautam anywhere—she heard that he had become an important person and was always extremely busy. Kamal was at Cambridge, Hari Shankar was posted to New York.

On the first day of her job as reader in a small publishing house, she woke up at six in the morning and quickly got ready. The ever-helpful Mrs. Shunila Mukerji had found her this job.

After gulping down a cup of tea she dashed out and boarded a bus for Maida Vale. She had met Bill Craig several times but had never seen Shanta. Mrs. Nilambar, too, had surfaced in London—she had left her husband, come to Britain to get her novel published and was living with Bill because divorce was not yet allowed by Hindu law.

A massive sandalwood Ganapati sat on the mantelpiece in William Craig's drawing-room in his house on Warwick Avenue. Bill was sprawled on the sofa, absorbed in *The Times*, a stocky, balding man in early middle-age. "Do you know how to proof-read? It's quite easy." He placed a bundle of yellow papers in front of her, got up and sauntered towards the kitchen. Clad in a brown-and-yellow sari of rich south Indian silk, Shanta came downstairs. Tall, sturdy and handsome, a blue-eyed Chitpawan, she crossed over to a corner table and began typing briskly.

"Bonjour, Madame!" Champa tried to impress her.

"Hello. I have heard a lot about you from Gautam. How do you do," she said casually, still typing away at great speed. She certainly had very superior airs. Successful Indo-Anglian novelist and business partner of a noted British publisher. She didn't bother to speak to Champa again.

Bill brought her a cup of coffee. He was good-natured, and also had a glad eye. Shanta didn't accompany them to the office. She was leaving for Paris in the afternoon.

"What is your programme in life?" Bill asked his new employee during lunch break. He used to proof-read people, too.

"Haven't a clue."

"Are you very confused?"

"Yes."

"Are you also caught in the Net?"

"Yes."

Bill reverted to gloomy silence. They were all caught in the Net. Himself, and Cyril Ashley and all other Western European intellectuals. The representatives of New Asia living in the West were suspended in mid-air, between diverse hells. Their Christian and Jewish and Muslim and Hindu and Buddhist souls were suffering all kinds of agonies. Arnold Toynbee had written ten fat books about them and still hadn't come to a satisfactory conclusion. Bill was a trader in words. He believed in their might and muddle, and their hollowness.

Shanta was also entangled in the Net. Their private hells, individual catacombs and separate universes were all the more painful as there was no way out, except for those who had become Marxists and thought they had found the Final Answer.

"We have recently lost our Indian Empire and there's going to be a great demand for nostalgic novels about the Raj. You write, I'll build you up as the modern Flora Annie Steele."

"Who was Flora Annie Steele?"

"Never mind. You begin a novel about Lucknow, right away."

They began to eat. He said, "Mulk Raj Anand is old hat, we need young people like you. You write a novel about Old Lucknow—you must know somebody from the ex-royal family of Oudh?"

"I myself belong to the ex-royal family of Oudh," she answered recklessly.

"Jolly good!" he exclaimed. "My father is an Old India Hand, he was an indigo planter in eastern U.P. Germany developed the chemical blue dye and Britain's indigo trade came to an end. Father sold his estate in Ghazipur district to a Muslim zamindar and returned to England. I was schooling in Mussoorie. We came back to our damp and cold house in Cobham, Surrey. Father still lives there. He would love to help you in your writing with his reminiscences. For instance, he can tell you about Sir Harcourt Butler and his favourite singer, Zohra Bai of Lucknow. Sir Harcourt was Lieutenant-Governor of the United Provinces in the 1920s, and was called the last of the Nabobs.

"I can take you to Cobham to meet Dad off and on. Shanta will be away in France for nearly a month. Let's meet at the Writers' and Artists' Club in Haymarket tomorrow evening, and we'll discuss this project in some detail."

"Princess Champa of India!" Bill Craig gravely introduced her to his friends in the Club.

"No titles please, we're a democracy," she said modestly. She had realised with acute anxiety that Bill knew the Lucknow Gang—her fantasising had gone too far. In Paris she had told the Frogs that she was a niece of the Nizam of Hyderabad—then she ran into some Hyderabadis and immediately stopped being a royal niece.

In the Club an English journalist looked at her in absolute fascination. "You know something, Princess," he gushed, "the beautiful Maharani of a Punjab state who died here recently, was called the Rose of India. I think you are lovelier than her. What should we call you?"

"I'll ask Dad the botanical name of this flower. Let's go to Cobham, Saturday week," said Bill with a glint in his eye.

48. Lala Rukh

"Sorry, couldn't make it earlier, had to rush off to Russia. Here is a little souvenir for you from Moscow," he said, placing a parcel on the table.

She opened it eagerly and took out a gypsy shawl. "Oh, Gautam, how *sweet*!" she cried as though she was still in Water Chestnut House.

Tenderly he wrapped the stole round her shoulders. She blushed. "Some day I'll take you to Outer Mongolia. You very much want to go there, don't you?" he said.

Nirmala nodded vigorously. "And Alma Ata."

"And Alma Ata. And Samarkand-o-Bukhara. The works. Do you remember Thomas Moore's *Lala Rukh*?" He ordered lunch. The owner of Koh-i-Noor was a fellow Kayastha, a Mathur from Old Delhi.

"Lala Rukh," he resumed, "was Aurangzeb's daughter. She set forth in a caravan for Kashmir where she was to wed the

King of Bokhara, and her barge sailed on the Indus. Say, *hoon, hoon,* that's the tradition, when you listen to a story you keep saying *hoon.*"

"Yes. But Talat's mother once told us that if you heard a story in the day time, travellers lost their way," she answered, luxuriating in the warmth of the colourful shawl.

A fair and lanky girl came in. She had a long nose and wore ballerina glasses. Smoking a black cigarette, she smiled myopically at Nirmala and sat down at a corner table.

Although the unusual-looking undergraduate was beyond earshot, Nirmala whispered to Gautam: "Light from Pureland . . ."

"Light—let me think: Roshni?"

"Roshan," Nirmala responded in a more confidential undertone: "Subject: Philosophy. Current interest: A. R. of the Holy Navy."

Gautam burst out laughing, feeling immensely relieved. No, old buddy Nim hadn't changed—there was still hope for him.

"Have you ever met him in London?" she asked.

"At diplomatic receptions, yes. He was correctly cordial with me. So was I."

"Although I have noticed that Pakis are more friendly with H's."

"You mean they don't drop their aitches—ha—ha—"

"Yeah. But they avoid fellow M's from India. And vice versa. Anyway. So A.R. has also become very F.O.N.D. of R.O.S.H.A.N. And she is positively ga-ga—"

"Honey," he cut her short, laughing. "You would be a complete flop if you joined M.I.5."

"And Bhaiya Saheb has started painting once again. Even made her portrait. Although, let's face it, she's no oil painting." She winked at Gautam and giggled, the way she used to all those years ago in Lucknow. It seemed that in an instant they had crossed the razor-thin bridge of time.

Nirmala continued. "When B.S. showed Talat that portrait she said its caption ought to be, Think and Be Sad."

She fell silent. Gautam was left standing alone on that invisible and fragile bridge. Frightened by his loneliness he said with great urgency, "Nirmal, can you still change your mind about me?"

In a flash she recollected the smoke-filled kitchen of Water Chestnut House when Talat had predicted—some day he will land up in England and take you round the sacred fire. Good old Talat.

Last time she had said no in a huff. She wouldn't now, but she kept quiet all the same.

"You know they say khamoshi means neem-raza, half-consent. Shall I take it as that?"

Students were drifting in and out of the door.

"Hello!" Michael called out and came towards them. Gautam had met him at Surekha's place. They shook hands, and Gautam fished out a tiny gift bottle of vodka and presented it to him.

"Oh! Thanks. Now I'll get drunk like a lord. Which reminds me—the future Lord Ashley is giving a bottle-party tonight. Would you care to join us? It's a sort of celebration."

"Thank you, but I must leave right after lunch. What's the celebration for?"

"Cyril has received a grant to work on Anglo-French relations in eighteenth century India, post-Plassey—1756 and all that!"

"1066 and all that!" Gautam responded cheerily.

"Yes, and he has engaged Miss Champa Ahmed as his research assistant for the project! Soon she'll be leaving Bill Craig's office to come here. She has a diploma in French from Paris, you know. Cyril has found just the person to go through French documents, etc."

Michael returned to his table, and for some reason Gautam became very tense. There was silence. The food arrived and they began to eat. Then he said reflectively, "I was sorry to hear what you told me about Champa last time. I'm sure she is more sinned against than sinning."

Nirmala tried to fight back sudden tears. He was still thinking about Champa. This man had just proposed to her again and was still thinking about Champa.

"I personally think that we shouldn't discuss Champa Baji any more—the topic has become really boring," she said and tried to look busy finding something in her handbag. "For you Champa Baji is a paragon, but perhaps you forget, Gautam Mashter, that we have known her from childhood, almost."

"This is very funny!" Gautam was peeved. "Why do all of you keep harping upon your childhood? Those who don't happen to know you or Champa Ahmed from their infancy, are they donkeys?"

Now he had come in the range of a powerful arc lamp. Just as she found herself in that bright light confronting Gautam, so this relentless critic of human weaknesses, the guru, considers a fraud like Champa to be a paragon.

"See, you started narrating a dastaan in the day time and you lost your way," she commented sadly.

"I did not," he replied emphatically. "Let me finish the story . . ." He took a deep breath. "So, there was this poet Framroze in Lala Rukh's entourage, and she fell in love with him. Therefore she banished him from the royal caravan because she was on her way to marry the King of Bokhara, remember?"

"*Hoon.*"

"When she reached Kashmir she discovered that Framroze was her royal fiancé in disguise. Therefore, Nim, do not banish the poor poet in a hurry."

"Was he, is he, also in love with her?"

"Yes."

"Are you sure?"

"Yes, I am quite sure."

"*Hoon.*"

"Nirmal! Don't misunderstand me, I have nothing to do with Champa. You were right in calling me second rate. Please try to understand me. . ." Now he sounded like the hero of a trashy Hindi film.

"Oh, Nirmala. . ." He slipped into the dark once again. He was a mere schoolboy. Who says men are wise and all-knowing? Sitting at that table in front of him, Nirmala felt she was growing like a flowering creeper, like a tree, like mercury inside a barometer. She was attaining Knowledge. Now she too would switch off the artificial lights and slip into Darkness. That state of being in the Darkness, is the highest of all states.

She would sit there and peer out. From now on she would put on the Cap of Solomon* whose fable Qadeer had narrated to her, once, in the outhouse of Gulfishan.

"Everybody cannot find the Cap of Solomon. I am grateful to you, Gautam, that you helped me grow up and showed me how to find this magical cap."

"Finish your cup, Nirmala," he said gently.

She was playing with her coffee spoon. "I was merely being Eliotonian, Gautam Mashter," she replied gravely.

"May I come to see you next week?" he asked.

"Yes, if you like." She carefully placed three coffee spoons in a row. "That makes a fairly short measurement. . ." she remarked, smiling wanly, ". . . of one's life! Doesn't it?"

49. The Revolutionaries

A Red Indian sat upon a log sending out smoke signals under a full spring moon.

"Hey, you make excellent rings," Talat said as she strolled by. The smoking Red Indian jumped down and joined the group winding its way to the dining hall. They began to sing, *"We'll make Lady Astor wash dishes when the Red Revolution comes/ We'll make Mr Churchill smoke woodbine when the Red. . ."*

They had rented a farmhouse in a village for the annual conference of the Federation of Indian Students Unions of Great Britain. The Cold War was at its height. Inside, some Red Indians were making fierce anti-American speeches. A Scottish comrade was playing his guitar and belting out a ballad in praise of Joseph Stalin. Talat and Feroze walked across to the lounge where Professor Hyman Levy sat on a leather sofa surrounded by ardent young men and women. Talat spotted Roshan Kazmi

---

*According to Muslim lore, if one wore that cap one became invisible but could still see others.

in the gathering and greeted her warmly. Outside, around the bonfire, a group was singing:

One great vision unites us
Though remote be the lands of our birth,
Foes may threaten and smite us
We shall bring peace to the world. . .

A mixed crowd of English, Welsh, Scottish and East Pakistani students had been invited to attend the conference. The host Indians were Reds of many hues, most of them, like Talat and Kamal, Nehruites. Faiz Ahmed Faiz, who was in jail in Pakistan, was their hero as well. Both West Bengal and East Pakistan were united in their devotion to the revolutionary poet, Qazi Nazrul Islam. Most young progressives in England believed that Pakistan would soon have a red revolution because conditions there were as bad as those in pre-1917 Russia. And India would shine like a beacon for the rest of humanity.

The students had also invited a few pro-India socialist M.P.s and Left intellectuals like Professor Hyman Levy, author of *Literature in the Age of Science.* He had come all the way from Scotland. With his shock of white hair, Semitic nose and intense yet benign look, he was the model left-wing Jewish intellectual. London School of Economics was full of them, all friends of India.

"I am ashamed of the way my country treated you for two hundred years," he was saying to the young people sitting in a semi-circle before him. Roshan passed a little note to Talat— "Point for reflection—Britain is his country, Israel is his country, too. . ." Talat glared at her.

He turned towards Roshan, "I'm thrilled to see so many brilliant young Indian women gathered here tonight. . ."

Roshan pursed her lips.

Talat saved the awkward moment. "We must have been a great disappointment to you, sir, the way we behaved in 1947. All the humanism of the humanists could not save us."

Talat was quite unpredictable. That hot afternoon in April 1941, she had suddenly got up and started dancing in front of the row of glistening Buddhas in Sarnath. Now she stood up and declaimed as though she was on the stage of the Old Vic, taking part in *Murder in the Cathedral*.

> *Clear the air! Clean the sky! Wash the wind, take stone*
> *From stone and wash them.*
> *The land is foul, the water is foul, our beasts and*
> *Ourselves are defiled with blood.*
> *A rain of blood has blinded my eyes.*
> *I wander in a land of barren boughs: if I break them they Bleed,*
> *I wander in a land of dry stones: if I touch them they bleed.*
> *How can I ever return to the soft quiet seasons?*

She sat down again, as abruptiy as she had stood up.

How do I return to the soft quiet seasons? he repeated to himself, smoking furtively. He wore a pork-pie hat, his face was half-hidden in the upturned collar of his overcoat and he looked like a shadowy figure in a Cold War spy novel.

"Didi, an American agent!" a youthful Bengali whispered to Talat. "I noticed him lurking out there while you were reciting that reactionary Royalist's poem—I'll go and see. Come on, comrades!"

"Don't behave like a schoolboy," Talat scolded him and peeped out. She recognised the profile of her cousin Amir, and grasped the situation in an instant. He had come here to haul up poor Roshan and didn't want to be seen by the Bharatis. A delicate and dangerous mission, indeed! She felt a surge of affection for him and slipped out of the lounge. Then she accosted him merrily.

He looked embarrassed.

"Bhaiya Saheb! Adaab! Do come in. There are so many of your countrymen here attending this conference. And look, you are a diplomat. I've seen your High Commissioner and his Begum hobnobbing with Krishna Menon at so many parties, so don't make life difficult for yourself. Come in! You must have gone to Cambridge to see Roshan and were told that she is here—right?"

He smiled and patted her head, "My clever little sis!" he said with some emotion.

Talat was touched. He had never been demonstrative with

his family—Bhaiya Saheb must be growing old, he has become wiser and sadder, she decided and led him to a secluded corner of the barn. He sat down on a bench. "I'll ask Zarina to get you a cup of hot coffee. Relax." She ran off, came back and perched like a monkey on a haystack. "Remember, Bhaiya Saheb, you used to be in the Forward Bloc in Lucknow. Most of these people will probably also get over all this when their student days are over. It's a necessary phase in young adulthood."

"Yes, Dadi Jan. You have always been the Wise One of the clan."

Zarina brought him coffee and left, and gradually he relaxed. He felt he was back in the barnyard at Kalyanpur.

"How is my rakhi-sister, Nirmala?" he asked. "I don't see her here."

"She is not well—admitted to the University Hospital for a check-up."

Talat reminded him painfully of Gulfishan and Tehmina and Champa. How could life be so pitiless that it had turned Champa into a tramp? Did this self-righteous slip of a girl know that she had over-simplified matters by adhering to mercurial political ideologies? How could intelligent people divide life into black and white?

He had been an Indian student himself fifteen years ago, organising similar conferences. Tonight he was a different person, inhabiting a separate world. A very different person indeed, in the spring of 1953. And he was dreadfully tired. How can I return to the soft quiet seasons once again?

"Now take this tamasha, for instance," he continued, "you are like a bunch of Salvation Army people."

Talat promptly broke into, "*Onward Christian soldiers, marching on to war.*"

"It will only create intense nostalgia when you recall these evenings and faces in the future. Every moment, every season brings with it the memory of times past. Still, you hold conferences and sing community songs, and you are always organising."

Talat blinked.

"You never see the inner drama," he went on, "you do not acknowledge what is really happening. You're simply not looking, all you do is to keep plotting, keep setting traps. But I'll still escape. You," he added after a pause, "cannot waylay me. I shall always be separate, and always be wandering. Now please go and call Roshan, I feel responsible for her and it is getting late."

Talat left. He lit another cigarette and listened to the song they were singing in the hall—*Way down upon the Swanee River, far, far away/That's where my heart is turning ever, that's where the Old Folks stay.* He used to sing this haunting American slave song around the bonfire at La Martiniere. Unwittingly, he joined in the refrain—

All the world is sad and weary, everywhere I roam.
Take me back to my old. . .

Suddenly he noticed Talat standing in front, looking at him in wonderment. She literally couldn't believe her ears. He stopped, sheepishly. Roshan came forward, carrying her overnight bag, and they said goodnight to Talat and left.

Advancing towards his car he said gruffly, "Do you realise that a report has been sent against you to the Educational Advisor? Remember, you are here on a prestigious government scholarship."

"You," she said defiantly, "have the moral outrage of someone who has found me in a den of iniquity. Who do you think you are—Senator McCarthy? There are many East Pakistanis here also, attending the conference as observers."

"Yeah, but they are Bengalis."

"What do you mean? Aren't they Pakistanis like you and me?"

"Sure, but they are Bengalis," he replied obstinately and opened the limousine door for her.

50. The BBC Canteen

On the way to London from the Fedin Conference Talat discovered that she had broken a sandal. She got off the train, dived into a shoe shop and after acquiring a new pair, caught a bus to St. John's Wood. The moment she entered her flat the telephone rang.

It was Chacha from BBC. Sajida Begum, an eminent educationist, had to be interviewed right away. "She has come to England after attending some conferences in western Europe and is due to go back home." With the exuberance and boundless energy of a 24-year-old, Talat ran out again to do his bidding.

The BBC canteen on Oxford Street was full of cheerful din as usual. Members of the Middle Eastern and Eastern Services were floating in and out of the hall. Indians and Pakistanis usually sat together because most of them belonged to the pre-Partition All India Radio. The Urdu Section included Siddique Ahmad Siddiqui, affectionately called Chacha or Uncle, Taqi Saiyid and Yawar Abbas, Attiya Hosain and Hamraz Fyzabadi. Ejaz Hussain Batalvi, Zarina, Feroze and Talat were frequent broadcasters.

The canteen had no teaspoons. "Since it probably had no teaspoons during the war, it shall never have any—the British are great believers in tradition," Chacha had once said dryly.

A rotund, prosaic, bespectacled lady sat in a corner, stirring sugar in her cup with a fork. She was talking to Feroze who had come a day earlier from Cambridgeshire. Talat joined them.

"No spoons," the lady complained.

"British tradition, ma'am," Talat replied dutifully.

Sajida Begum resumed her conversation with Feroze. "In Copenhagen I was interviewed over Denmark's BBC," she said, continuing to ignore Talat. Feroze who had known her in Aligarh before she migrated to the new country, introduced her to Talat. Sajida Begum was also a novelist.

"Feroze tells me you work in the telegraph office," she said patronisingly.

"Yes, ma'am. Right now I am on leave for a fortnight."

"Then you will go back to delivering telegrams door-to-door?"

"No, ma'am, I'm a cub-reporter on Fleet Street."

"She got a by-line for her very first story," Feroze tried to rescue Talat.

"You write stories, too? Romantic or progressive?"

Feroze gave up—then grinned: "She is going to write a novella about her cousin, Comdr. Amir Reza. *The Life and Times of a— of— a—*"

Talat got the hint. "Its title is going to be *Romance de la Rose* because our house in Lucknow is called Gulfishan and he used to speak in French."

Sajida Begum's eyes gleamed behind her spectacles. Her attitude towards Talat changed instantly.

"Do you often see him over here?"

"No. When he is not flirting with upper-class English girls, he goes to Cambridge singing, 'Lydia, O Lydia, O Encyclopaedia'."

"Why?"

"Have you heard of Miss Roshan Kazmi? That's why. . ."

Sajida Begum looked worried. "Well, I have no ulterior motive nor any vested interest in him," she said in the dreary monotone of bores. "My brother knows him and has asked him to look after me while I am here. Being so young and inexperienced, you see, I do feel lost sometimes."

On the way down to the basement studios Feroze whispered to Talat, "You know how ancient she is? Thirty-five! Almost Attiya and Champa Baji's age."

"St. John's Wood is becoming curiouser and curiouser. Sajida Apa has also rented a flatlet over there because she was told that all writers and artists live in that mohalla. Now she's busy cultivating Bill Craig and Shanta because she wants them to publish her new novel," Talat informed her friends in the BBC canteen a few days later.

On a Sunday morning Sajida Begum dropped by at Greville Place and said to Talat darkly, "This Champa Ahmed seems to be the number two person in Bill's office—Shanta is not around. I suspect there's more to it than meets the eye. Talat, you must warn Shanta—let's meet her this evening. A stitch in time saves nine. . . ."

"Yes, and strike while the iron is hot. But it is none of my business, Sajida Apa. Besides, I'm going to interview Mr and Mrs Max Factor for the Women's Page this evening. They're here from Hollywood and are staying at the Dorchester."

"You must be joking! Max Factor is a lipstick, not a human being. Tomorrow you'll say you are going to see Mr Lipton or Miss Brooke Bond! Don't take me to be such a simpleton, Talat Reza."

Dusk fell on Park Lane. Footmen stood at the entrance to the Dorchester Hotel, announcing the arrival of guests. Famous film stars, leading fashion columnists, debutantes, people who inhabited the glossy pages of *The Tatler* and *Country Life*. Countless diamonds glittered on Mrs Max Factor's mink coat as she glided into the Blue Room.

'. . . Father, Jewish immigrant from Balkans, started shop small back-room Hollywood. Max Factor, Empire at present. . .' Talat jotted down rapidly. Mrs Max Factor spoke to her for a full twenty minutes in an exclusive interview—Talat's Conjeevaram sari did the trick.

Talat happened to be one of the two women from the subcontinent who had found temporary work as a journalist on Fleet Street—the other was a Keralite married to an Englishman. Talat had come to be known as 'the sari reporter', her sari a kind of press card which gave her easy access to celebrities.

The following week Talat received an excited call from Sajida Begum. "I met Amir Reza again. He is more handsome than Girigiri Peck, isn't he? You and Kamal do not stop talking, but he is so quiet one wonders what he's thinking about."

"Nothing much, Sajida Apa, nothing much."

"Well, to me he appeared ever so thoughtful and a little sad when we dined at Istamboul last evening."

"And a Hungarian violinist played *Night in a Spanish Garden* especially for you."

"How did you know?"

"I guessed, Sajida Apa. So, my no-good cousin is taking

you to fancy restaurants!"

"You see, it happened like this—I met him at a party and somebody said, let's go to Istamboul. Amir asked me if I would like to go along. I thought they were going to Turkey, so I said Yes! How was Mrs Max Factor? A real person? Listen, that reminds me, you told me about an English goldsmith the other day who pierced the Queen's ears for the Women's Page . . ."

"For the Coronation," Talat corrected her.

Sajida Begum paused awhile then said, "And then you interviewed the Queen's beautician?"

"Yes, Mrs Henry Holland—she's Oscar Wilde's daughter-in-law."

"She must be very expensive."

"I should imagine so, although she gave me a free facial in her beauty parlour on Bond Street," Talat added nonchalantly.

Sajida Begum disappeared from the scene for a while. "I'm leaving for a six-week study tour of Britain," she said before going underground. "Study tour" was a rather dubious term, anyway.

A reasonably slim lady wearing fashionable goggles and the latest 'sheath' dress over her shalwar entered the BBC canteen one afternoon. Nobody could recognise her—she had been transformed by Oscar Wilde's daughter-in-law!

"The importance of being earnest in the pursuit of you-know-who," said Talat in an aside.

"Hear, hear! how witty some people have become around here," said Feroze meanly and blinked. She still could not believe her eyes.

However, Sajida Begum in her new incarnation failed to cheer them up, for a few days earlier Nirmala had been diagnosed with tuberculosis of the lungs in Cambridge. Kamal had made a frantic call to Amir Reza and both of them had accompanied a very scared Nirmala to the Chest Hospital in London. Hari Shankar was not available on the phone in New York.

Sajida Begum was waiting to be complimented on her new urchin cut, which did not suit her. Then, suddenly realising why they were so quiet, she sighed. "Very sad. I rang up Capt. Reza to congratulate him on his promotion and he told me. I hope it is not galloping T.B."

"Don't be ghoulish, Sajida Apa," said Talat angrily, "Nirmala is okay. She'll soon be taken to Lidhurst Sanatorium, for full recovery."

"An aunt of mine had T.B., she died in Bhawali Sanatorium," Sajida Begum responded smugly.

"*Thoo— thoo*, Sajida Apa, that must have been in 1853. T.B. is completely curable today."

Sajida Begum persisted, "Heroines of old Urdu novels always died of tuberculosis of the lungs. French novels, even. . . remember Camille?"

"Shoo—shoo, Sajida Apa!" the girls chorused furiously. Placidly, she moved on to another table and was greeted by the members of the Urdu unit.

"Capt. Reza told Mummy that Nirmal would be out of the woods in no time," said Zarina. "He came to see us yesterday."

They carried their cups of coffee from the counter and Zarina said to Surekha and Feroze, "My father began legal practice as Sir Zaki Reza's junior in Allahabad and Lady Reza was a friend of Mummy's. After her death, Mummy says, Reza used to come to our place with his governess, Nina, but he hated her. He's still a little orphan, deep within. He comes to 'The Laurels' for solace and advice, which he gets in plenty from Mummy."

Zarina's mother was an expansive and warm-hearted English-woman, everybody's refuge in trouble. Gautam also went to see her whenever he needed to, and his barrister father had also been a friend of Sir Zaki's in Allahabad.

"Now Capt. Reza is very worried about you, Talat, because these two McCarthy characters have been sent to witch-hunt in the BBC."

"The BBC has refused to be witch-hunted, if that's the correct expression," Talat replied.

"Yeah. . . And he is distressed about Roshan. She went off to Rumania even though he had told her not to. 'Stupid woman', he growled, 'sacrificing her chance of a Fulbright for the sake of dancing about in a one horse-town like Bucharest.'

" 'Aye, aye, sir,' I said.

" 'And she is here on a government scholarship and her father is a senior army officer. And do you know what she told me? That she went to the youth festival because she wanted to psychoanalyse the Commies! And she travelled on fake travel papers which the Rumanians had issued. Was it an honourable thing to do?' he thundered.

" 'Aye, aye, sir,' I agreed. It was not an honourable thing to do. Oh, he was livid. After he left, Mummy said Roshan should be mothering this Little Boy Blue instead of behaving like an Independent Brainy Woman. Men don't like it. Still, the frequency of their quarrels is increasing, which means they'll get married soon. Mummy said Nirmal will be out of the hospital and we'll all go to the Woking Mosque for the Kazmi-Reza wedding sooner than you expect. Insha Allah."

51. John and Mary's Painting Book

"Do you remember that painting book, Talat," asked Kamal, "in which two English children roam the countryside in a tiny red car?"

"Yes, I do. They stop at a road-house marked 'Teas', and John fills the car's tank with a toy petrol tin. . . and they pluck bright red apples from a very green tree. It was just like this place," said Talat looking around, "and there was a blue stream and a china white motor-boat and a windmill and horse-carts, and cottages of pre-war England. I even remember the names of the colours we used—cobalt blue, crimson lake, viridian. We used to get loads of such books on our birthdays, published by some mysterious 'Father Tuck, London E.C.4.' They're still there, in Khyaban."

The waitress brought the bill. "There has been a terrible world war but England's countryside is still the same, spread out like John and Mary's painting book," Talat continued.

"We are the same, too, we carry all of our past with us wherever we go," said Kamal.

Gautam was listening to their conversation in silence. He understood the importance of their childhood for these people, including Nirmala, and recalled with a pang how irritated he had been when she had mentioned hers that morning in the Koh-i-Noor. After that, he was meeting her again for the first time, a T.B. patient now, because he had been away on the Continent. If he had married her in Lucknow her life could have been very different, she may not have been lying in a sanatorium hovering between hope and despair. Half of Nirmala's lungs were soon to be removed. Had intellectual flirtation with Champa been so important to him? What is it that a man really wants?

Hari Shankar, who had flown in from New York, was absorbed in studying the willow pattern on the crockery. "This is so typically English," he remarked.

"Let's go," said Kamal abruptly, rising from his chair. Quietly, they walked down towards Gautam's sleek American limousine.

The sanatorium sprawled over a low hill, surrounded by magnificent parkland. Inside, there were flowers everywhere and smiling staff faces, gleaming corridors and beautiful drawing rooms. In this haven of rest and comfort people waited for their end, watching television; or recovered and went back into the world to live, until some other kind of end overtook them.

Nirmala's room was surrounded by gardens on three sides. "Isn't it like Kishwar Apa's room in Nishat Mahal Hostel?" she said cheerfully to Talat. Gautam smiled sadly as she turned to him. "See, we had three hostels in Chand Bagh—Nishat Mahal, Naunihal Manzil and Maitri Bhawan—"

Gautam nodded. They were addicted to their past because it was safe and intact, more so for Kamal and Talat because there was no fear of Partition in it. "We were day students, as you know, but had so many friends in the hostels, didn't we, Talat? And also in Lady Kailash Hostel— I say, have you started work for the Majlis Mela?" she asked Talat eagerly.

"You'll be with us for next year's Mela, Insha Allah," replied Kamal.

"Insha Allah," she repeated with a cheery smile. After a while she said, "Bhaiya Saheb brought me to the hospital, he has been here several times."

"Cho chweet," Hari mimicked the girls. Everybody laughed.

Nirmala continued, "He told Roshan—she had come with him last time—what rakhi was all about, Pakistan notwithstanding. It's also Lucknow *wazedari*. Everyone has been here to see me except Champa Baji and Cyril. Well, I don't expect Cyril to come, I hardly knew him, but Champa Baji. . ."

There was silence. Then Hari mimicked some more people and made everybody laugh again. It was time to leave.

Suddenly Nirmala broke down. "You all will go away and I'll be left alone again—it's terrible when one's family and friends turn into Visitors."

A nurse came in and gave them all a broad smile.

52. The Boat-House

"Your Lucknow friends are over there, under the apple trees. Oh, they're leaving! Should we follow them to Lidhurst?" asked Cyril, looking out of the road-house window. "I came here with the intention of taking the road to Lidhurst but you didn't seem too keen," he added.

Cunningly, she tried to divert his attention. "Look, Shakespearean actors!" A touring company had just arrived at the inn, wearing Elizabethan costumes. They were also on their way to Lidhurst to enact a few scenes for the patients at the sanatorium.

Nirmala had already been taken to the hospital when Champa started working for Cyril Ashley in Cambridge. She could not tell him why she had such a bad conscience about Nirmala. In fact, she hadn't told him anything about herself or the way she used to confide in Gautam—she hadn't even told him about Gautam or Amir. Western men weren't interested in a girl's past, they weren't nosey. Thank god.

They boarded a launch and sailed downstream. The *Louisa Jane* passed through overhanging trees and creepers which formed dark watery tunnels. Cyril looked bored, like a husband. Everything seemed slightly worn out, including Cyril Ashley himself. The launch stopped in front of a boat-house and they went ashore.

A large Scandinavian woman stood on the wooden balcony overhead, and a number of people walked through the primroses carrying fishing rods.

Champa and Cyril spent several days in a riverside inn and went for long walks in the forest. "Champa," said Cyril one afternoon as he sat down on an up-turned canoe in the boat-house. "Tell me about your own milieu." He had discovered that this woman from a distant land had become strangely dependent on him. She was insecure, but he thought she might be comforted by memory.

He had become nosey too! "Are you also going to write a novel about me?" she asked unhappily.

"No. Who is?"

"Bill—William Craig."

"No, I don't wish to write a novel about you. You're not a freak, there are thousands of girls like you everywhere in the world, clever, sensitive, pretty."

So these three words describe me fully. She closed her eyes and tried to remember her own world. The drab locality in Banaras, cots scattered in the courtyard, Father reading depressing files of criminal cases. She cut out Banaras and went straight to Chand Bagh, Lucknow. She began telling Cyril about the Lantern Service, the Forest of Arden, the swimming pool, the American community songs sung around the bonfire. . .

Cyril interrupted her. "Look who's coming straight out of your Moon Garden!" he exclaimed.

She looked up. Kamal emerged from the crowd of holiday-makers. "Hello, Champa Baji, Cyril," he said. "We saw you the other day at a road-house, but were in a hurry to reach Lidhurst." He sat down on another up-turned canoe.

"I was just telling Cyril about Lucknow," she said, looking a bit crestfallen.

"How interesting!" Kamal smiled politely.

Champa heard the sadness in his voice and continued rapidly, with a certain bravado, "I was telling him about India—the smell of hay on a hot summer afternoon in the compound of our kothi in Banaras, the neighing of horses, the bullock-carts passing by. . . You know, when the wheels of a bullock-cart creaked in the distance at night our maid-servants used to say, 'This creaking of the wheels indicates that the goddess Bhavani is angry.' "

Kamal listened to her in grim silence.

"In the languid afternoons, the pankha coolie dozed outside—we have those long verandas with Georgian pillars in our country-home in Banaras district." She added hastily, "Now, of course, the house is fast crumbling. It may soon vanish. No, Cyril, you won't comprehend, your perceptions are different."

"I shall tell you. . ." said Kamal, leaning forward. He had suddenly entered a world which was far away and with which he was deeply in love. He wanted to escape from the tensions of the present, and set out on his own journey.

"Nirmala is not well at all—in Lucknow, her mother must have gone to the Hanuman temple in Aligunj and then proceeded to some Imambara and prayed to Imam Hussain for her speedy recovery. Gyanwati used to sing in the mode Yaman—

The House of the Prophet, the Children of Ali,
How I adore Hasan and Hussain, sons of Zahra. . .!

Can I translate this classical melody and the emotions they convey to me, into English? And during winter, at the time of weddings in our joint family, quilted curtains were dropped in the veranda of our ancestral mud-brick house in Kalyanpur and the mirasins crooned, *May the shadow of Ali fall on my Shyam Sunder Banra**. Can any western sociologist understand the beauty of this scene, this fusion of Muslim and Hindu

---

*Banna or Banra—bridegroom, derived from Ban Raj Forest Prince Krishna, Shyam Sunder; dark and handsome Krishna.

imagery in a song sung at Muslim marriages? And the peasants of my village sang the Ballad of Alha-Udal: *Alha sat by the Jamuna, Syed rushed forward crying, Ali—Ali—and ordered Udal: listen, sonny, King Prithvi has come with massive troops—drive him away.*

"Do you remember, Champa Baji, you and Gautam once came with us to Kalyanpur in the winter vacations, we sat under the tattered canopy of our village theatre and our nautanki orchestra played our favourite theatrical tunes! They were such good musicians. They staged *Laila Majnun* for us—Qadeer's nephew Master Chapati played Majnun—and he sang *Praise be to the Lord, Laila, I have come in thy Presence.*

"And he sang:

Laila, thy face is my Qibla. The ringlets of thy hair my faith,
To circumvent the Kaaba, I have come to thy Court.

"The mystic import of such ghazals was readily understood by our common people—the West doesn't have an equivalent in its culture."

Champa and Kamal were now transported to the mandap, sipping ginger tea out of clay cups. Master Chapati was singing:

Like Zuleikha when I fell in love with thee, Laila
I came to thy bazaar to be sold like Joseph—

They sat on cane stools watching Laila Majnun against the backdrop of a crudely painted fountain, a palace and the full moon. The nautanki percussionist played *kaharva* on his tabla. A motor launch went past noisily, they returned from Kalyanpur. "Our nautanki staged a first class *Nala Damayanti* and *Indersabha,*" said Kamal proudly and lighted Cyril's cigarette.

Champa asked him: "Do you remember Vasanti's song, *The jogan has gone forth in the search?*"

You won't get anything out of this search, my good woman, he wanted to tell her crossly. "It is an exercise in futility," he said aloud, "I mean, remembering the old songs—Pankaj Mallik for instance."

"Yes, *I was going to meet my man, fully made up and with braided plaits,*" she said. "How can you know, Cyril, who is Pankaj Mallik and Arzoo Lucknawi and Kallan Qawwal and Ustad Fayyaz Khan, what importance they have in our lives. . . And Jigar Moradabadi who says: '*A million suns went past and we continued to wait for the morn.*' And Kalidas: '*Passing over the Vindhyas and the Sindhu in the company of cranes, the cloud went forth carrying the message. . .*' "

Now Kamal wanted to come back to earth but Champa sat before him like the conscience of time. He felt she was flying about like a leaf in the maelstrom of eons. He frowned.

"Kamal, listen—" she was saying, "it is night-time, dogs bark, the bazaar is filled with silence. Birds are asleep, chowkidars are guarding the watermelon fields, gardeners are rattling the gondni's rattlers. In a short while the grindstones shall start moving—"

"Sarshar?"* Kamal asked her. She nodded and was lost in thought again.

"We used to assemble in Hari's tower room and solve the world's problems. Life was still very undefined. Sometimes we were picked up by strong beams of light; often we were surrounded by mists. We spent our youthful days in this light and shade of intellectual hide-and-seek. We aquired a kind of Gandhian humility, but it was not born of a sense of superiority. We felt as though the blood of mankind was on our hands and we had to wash it off. And, then, look what happened." He spread his hands in front of Cyril Ashley—"One morning we discovered that our own hands were drenched in blood, and we saw that all those fine people—intellectuals and authors and leaders—many of them had blood-stained hands too. Most of them were not willing to atone. They ran away, or took different avatars, but there were some genuine human beings, as well."

"Like Qadeer and Qamrun?" Champa asked humbly.

---

*Pandit Ratan Nath Sarshar, nineteenth century Urdu novelist of Lucknow.

Silently he took her permission to speak about them. They appeared like holy, shining beings.

"Yes, Qadeer and Qamrun, Ram Autar and Ram Daiya, our peasants and betel-leaf sellers, our chikan embroiderers who lose their eyesight doing intricate needlework for a pittance. They are our real backbone, Cyril."

Champa was still far away. She said, "Kamal, ask Gautam if he also remembers the wood-apples falling with a soft thud on the grass in Badshah Bagh. . ."

He pondered. How shall I tell her that Gautam has probably forgotten her? But, can he forget her? He must remember her, just as he remembers the river and the mossy houses and wood-apple trees. Kamal looked anxiously at his watch. "Er. . . Excuse me, Champa Baji, I've just come from Sir Ronald Grey's house—he's the surgeon, lives in a village close by—because I had to speak to him about Nirmal. May I take your leave? Bye, Cyril." He got up and strode away.

It was strange, he hadn't shown any surprise at finding her with Cyril in a boat-house. Everybody knew everything about her. She stood on a pinnacle, fully exposed. Why did I let this happen to myself, why? She looked at Cyril in abject terror. She had come back to the present like a wood-apple falling with a thud on English grass. She was living at the mercy of circumstances. Perhaps it was already much too late.

53. The Trumpeter

He used to play the trumpet regularly at the crack of dawn. He lived next door but she had never seen him. That summer morning it was ominously quiet. No trumpet sounded. Perhaps he was a student and had gone home. The morning seemed strangely empty. Champa had an uncanny feeling that it was the trumpeter of destiny who had given his last signal and vanished.

The project on Anglo-French relations was complete and Cyril had gone to meet his wife in Staffordshire. He was planning to visit the National Library in Calcutta for further work on Lord Cornwallis. Champa looked forward to her admission to the Middle Temple. This Indo-English relationship could not last. As Ghalib had said about human life, it contained the seeds of its own destruction.

The sun came up and she made her breakfast. Cyril's head appeared at the window.

"Hello Champa—damn good news!" he cried. "First give me a hot cup of tea."

She opened the door, and he blew in.

"What is it, Cyril? Found a lucrative job for me?"

He sat down at the kitchen table and grinned impishly. "Guess again!"

"You're going to become a don?" She poured his tea. He took a sip and said, "As our housekeeper Mrs Platt once told her wayward granddaughter, Jean—'Quit fooling around, luv, and get yourself the degree of M.R.S.!'"

"M.R.S.? Oh. . ." she blanched. This was most unexpected—they had never discussed marriage.

He lit a cigarette. "Rose and I are getting divorced. Now you and I can tie the knot—as they say in India."

"Divorce your wife in order to marry me? Have you gone off your head, Cyril?" she uttered, aghast.

He was surprised by her reaction.

"Have you really. . . because of me. . . I mean," she spoke in a crushed voice. "How on earth did you make such a tremendous decision?" She had never been able to understand the mysteries of decision-making. You resolve to get married, to separate, to change your career, change your country or religion. How did people do these things? She had made a decision once about Amir Reza—how had she done it?

"How could you. . . ?" she repeated.

Cyril frowned. Then he said coolly, "As a matter of fact, I suffer from fits of insanity from time to time and act strangely, you know—Give me one good reason why not?"

"Basically, because I am not a husband-snatcher—and secondly, I can't take you to my folks in India and say, 'Hello Pop, this is my Gora Saheb whom I have brought from Vilayat'."

"But you can have a roaring affair with a white man!"

"This is not Home, this is Abroad. You'll find many Hindus eating beef over here. . ."

"I remember your telling me once about an upper-class Muslim lady in Lucknow, Zakia something, who married an Englishman, Mr Stanley. An officer of the Indian Police—you said there was no uproar."

"Yes, but the Stanleys now live in Britain. I wouldn't leave my old parents in India and I can't take you to them in Banaras. . ."

"Why not? You always gave me to understand that you belonged to Anglicised landed aristocracy."

"Yes, indeed." She faltered. "But it won't do. My people are very modern but conservative in certain matters." She lapsed into silence. How could she take him to her dingy mohalla and shabby house after all the yarns she had spun about her "nawabi" family? And she didn't want her humble and innocent father to die of shock.

"Oh, Champa, why not? Can't you cite Mrs Stanley's example to them?" he persisted.

She paused and made another brave attempt— "After the recent Zamindari Abolition Act, my father has become very poor—you know all about Lord Cornwallis' Permanent Settlement—it's gone in a jiffy. So I must get back home, take up a job and help him."

Cyril was watching her intently. Champa began scrubbing the stove. He was silent for a while, then said ruefully, "I had always thought you were a bit of a waffler, Champa, that's what made you so interesting. Now don't let your fibs and fantasies catch up with you. I'm not concerned about your social status. Think it over. Every moment is unique, won't be repeated. Do not imagine, Champa, that these moments can be retrieved. Your life— myself—all this is unique. You cannot afford to laugh at the tragedy of passing time. Think it over, I'll ring you up tomorrow morning." He got up and left.

Champa spent the day in agony and lay awake all night.

Early in the morning Cyril telephoned. The little demon who had prompted her to be rude to Amir Reza all those years ago on the avenue in Badshah Bagh, whispered something in her ears. Cyril had called her a waffler, he had seen through her right away. She said coldly, "Cyril, it occurred to me, perhaps you want a wife-cum-research assistant for your Cornwallis project in India. You wish to legalise the arrangement, don't you? Maybe it's not blind love for an exotic, interesting native woman—am I right?"

"I beg your pardon. . .?" He sounded horrified. "What you're saying is perfectly outrageous!" his voice quivered with anger. "How can you be so. . . so crass!"

"Hold on, listen to me, your society will never accept me— a dark-skinned native. Your wife Rose may be Jewish and poor, but she's white and western. I wouldn't like to be looked down upon or have my children referred to as half-castes.

"At best, I would be tolerated and patronised. We have enough experience of Anglo-Saxon attitudes, Cyril, after all we were ruled by your nation for far too long.

"You opted out as a young rebel, but eventually you'll go back to the Establishment, revert to type. People do, you know, when they grow old. Or you may divorce me as soon as your fascination for the East is over. No, Cyril, I'm sorry. It won't do." She concluded archly, "Sorry if I have wounded your pride."

There was silence for a few moments. Then his frozen voice, "I misunderstood you, Champa. I am very sorry, too. Goodbye and all the best."

The day she was leaving Cambridge she went to his rooms and found him sitting at the window, busy working on *The New Statesman and Nation*'s Weekend Competition. The door was ajar. He remained absorbed even after Champa entered the room. When she sat down on a chair he raised his head and asked her about a possible clue. Champa pondered over it then gave him her opinion.

"Thank you."

She was taken aback. This young man actually was the Hon'ble Cyril Ashley who had gravely consulted her about an oblique reference to Christopher Marlowe, and thanked her formally.

"When are you coming down to London, Cyril?" she began conversationally.

"I have no idea at the moment. Anyhow, when I do, I may not be able to see you. All kinds of things to do, you know, when one is in London."

Rain pattered against the window-panes and the room was filled with fresh, vapoury air. They talked of common friends for a while. "It may start pouring. I must leave," she said looking at the wall clock.

He rose from the warm brown leather sofa.

Champa cast a glance about the room one last time as she stood up. At the door she extended her hand to Cyril. He bowed slightly and made way for her to leave. She kept her hand outstretched, and he held it in a light, limp handshake. "It was a pleasure and a privilege for me to have known you, Champa. Goodbye." He strode back into the room.

As she reached the end of the quadrangle, Champa paused and turned around. He was still busy with the crossword competition at the window. She knew she would never see him again.

54. *Queen Mary's Funeral*

Talat was about to step out of her office on an assignment when the telephone rang. It was Sajida Begum. "Champa is back to square one—rejoined Bill Craig's office. I want you to ask Bill Craig about my novel before this cantankerous old maid starts interfering—she hates younger women like us, you know. So ring up Bill now."

Talat smiled. "Sajida Apa, Bill Craig can wait, Queen Mary can't."

"Who—?"

"I'm off to Westminster Abbey to see Her Majesty—"

"So you're meeting Royalty these days?"

"Dead royalty, which makes them a little less royal I suppose. Bye."

Sajida was suitably impressed, and hung up.

Talat stood near the coffin of the late Queen Mary in Westminster Abbey and saw a 'close-up' of death for the first time. The serene, lifeless face of the dead queen was visible through a haze of lilies and candles. Talat had seen the queen's photograph in old magazines in Gulfishan—a young woman sitting ramrod straight in her hour-glass gown, imperious and haughty, the Queen Empress of India at the Delhi Durbar of 1911. If you are royalty you get married in Westminster Abbey, are crowned here, but even royalty is mortal so you lie in state here, too. . . Time was shuffling by outside the Abbey walls, like the old Eurasian who used to play haunting Scottish airs on his bagpipes in Lucknow. It was a fine summer's day and crowds undulated outside in the sun. It was a holiday for them—here was death in all its earthly glory, for commoners to gape at.

The story was to be filed immediately. Death may be eternal but its news got stale amazingly soon. One person's ceasing to exist triggered off a wave of activity among the living, for a day or two. Talat walked past rows of silent, grave-faced men and women, showed her press card to the guards at the door and made her way to the tower where the BBC Eastern Service was broadcasting a running commentary of the funeral. The tower was cold and grey and smelt of lived-in emptiness. Chacha was rounding off his commentary in Urdu. He grinned and told Talat, "I found Queen Mary's Indian cook outside. Go and interview him—just the thing for your Women's Page . . ."

Talat ran back to her office and informed her editor, "Miss Garnet. . . Queen Mary adored pulao—I mean pilaf—"

"Isn't that interesting."

"And King George V and Edward VIII loved shami kababs, and George VII. . . Miss Garnet, these are Indian dishes. Superfine Mughal delicacies. . ."

"Yes, yes?" She had removed her hearing aid.

"And the late Queen Mary often commanded her Muslim cook—"

"Muslim what?"

"Cook. The headline can be 'Queen Mary's Indian Chef in Tears'."

"Fine," Miss Garnet beamed. "Housewives will love the story. And do put in a bit about Queen Victoria's traditions as well, how she loved India and so on. Don't forget to add the recipes."

Talat returned to her room and started typing.

The telephone rang. Now it was Zarina who whispered, "There has been a minor crisis at your place. I came here to meet Saulat Rehman and found her reading Dante to Gautam in the original, which he was pretending to understand."

"That's no crisis. He loves such tomfoolery. . ."

"And Shanta is standing in your sitting room, looking like the goddess Durga in all her fury."

"Zarina, I have to send down copy in 20 minutes flat—on recipes I don't quite know. Tell me how much yakhni. . ."

"Shanta has walked out on Bill and told him it's either her or C—see?"

"How many almonds. . ."

"And she has come to tell G to tell C to leave B alone. Got it?"

"No. Can you quickly give me the recipe for *galawat-ke-kebab*?"

Zarina rang off.

55. End of an Exile

Shiv Prasad Bhatnagar 'Ranjoor' Barabankavi had come from Barabanki, U.P., before 1939, to study at Oxford. When the war broke out he stayed on in England and married a Latvian refugee whom he renamed Maya Devi. He was given to brooding and writing Urdu poetry, she ran a boarding house, their slender and only means of income. Any Indian or Pakistani who failed to find lodgings anywhere else headed straight for this shabby three-storeyed building in Camden Town. Ranjoor Saheb looked after his paying-guests as if they were his long-lost relatives. Often they disappeared without paying—he never complained.

BBC's Hamraz Fyzabadi was his tenant in the first floor flat. Ranjoor Barabankavi was a Hindu and an Indian, Mr Fyzabadi was a Muslim and a very staunch Pakistani. Still, both were Urdu poets from Oudh, and they shared the same Urdu culture. Ranjoor often took out the *Ramayana* in Urdu verse and after a few glasses of whiskey, said tearfully: "You unholy Muslims cut Mother India into two." Whereupon Hamraz, who did not drink, came out with some choice remarks about what the Kafirs had done to Muslims during the Partition riots.

Then Shiv Prasad would say, "All right, listen to this ghazal which I composed last night."

All his lodgers who belonged to Uttar Pradesh, attended the evening sessions in Ranjoor Saheb's front parlour, where a lot of Urdu poetry was recited. Once Kamal turned up and was amazed to find Hamraz Fyzabadi holding forth on U.P.'s glorious culture. "Your country is Pakistan, what on earth have you got to do with Uttar Pradesh now?" Kamal had said to him.

"One's heart is still in Fyzabad, even if one has taken up residence in Quetta or got a job in Peshawar. Every year when one goes to Fyzabad to meet one's old folk at home, one is shadowed by Indian C.I.D. Back in Pakistan it is said that refugees from U.P. have descended upon a young and struggling country only to exploit the new opportunities. For the rest they still look upon Bharat as their real country. In short, one is neither here nor there."

Hamraz Bhai offered some perfumed tobacco to Ranjoor Saheb who was busy preparing a paan with enormous gravity. Betel leaf was a holy object, specially flown from Karachi to

London, and Hamraz Fyzabadi gave Ranjoor Saheb two leaves, morning and evening, as a sacred offering. After finishing the paan-preparing ritual Hamraz Saheb turned towards Kamal. "The trouble is, Kamal Mian," he said mildly, "that you are a visionary. All young men are. Upright, honest. They don't like facing uncomfortable facts. The problem is that the world is run by politicians, not poets. Be realistic, for a change, Kamal Mian, and stop taunting me about Pakistan."

Maya was a homebody, quiet and complacent, and always cooking. She must have been beautiful when Ranjoor Saheb married her fifteen years ago. Ranjoor Saheb was too busy with his books to pay any attention to his wife. Then one day, a young Parsi student came to stay in Ranjoor Saheb's boarding-house. The London Majlis was going to stage a variety show in aid of the ailing Bengali poet, Qazi Nazrul Islam, who had been brought to London for medical treatment. Pakistan had also declared him a national poet. (The other national poet, Iqbal, had died in 1938.) Nazrul was a citizen of India and lived in Calcutta, and it was rumoured that he had been indulging in Tantric practices which adversely affected his reason. His mind had long been paralysed, and he was blissfully unaware of the partition of the subcontinent.

One Saturday afternoon, members of the London Majlis divided themselves in to several groups and went forth collecting funds. Talat and Feroze made for Camden Town. They met Hamraz Fyzabadi in the gallery of Ranjoor Saheb's house. "Hand over a fiver, Hamraz Bhai," Talat demanded sinisterly, Chicago-style.

At that very instant a catastrophe occurred in the life of Ranjoor Barabankavi, who was strolling in front of his house composing a melancholy ghazal.

At this time Maya Devi could usually be found arranging supper in the basement kitchen. However, today Ranjoor spotted something through the window which convinced him that his wife was conducting a passionate *affaire de l'amour* with their new lodger, Hoshang Matchiswalla. Right under his honourable nose! Mr Ranjoor darted towards the house.

Talat and Feroze were standing in the hall with Hamraz

Bhai when they heard a crashing thud in the basement. They rushed down and were appalled to find Maya lying prostrate on the ground, bleeding profusely. Her ten-year-old daughter Leela knelt beside her, howling with all her might. Ranjoor Saheb stood in the doorway, very quiet.

"What happened?" Talat gasped.

"Nothing," he replied serenely. "She slipped on the stairs. Don't you worry," and he went upstairs.

The next minute they heard another loud bang on the first floor, and by the time Talat telephoned 999 to get the ambulance, Ranjoor Barabankavi had finished beating the daylights out of Hoshang Matchiswalla. Hamraz Bhai and other lodgers hastened to the spot to intervene, and in the confusion, the aggrieved husband boxed all of them on the ears, one by one, and actually had a terrific fifty second free-style wrestling match with Hamraz Fyzabadi. The staircase landing was completely dark while this blood-and-thunder enactment took place.

It was discovered later that Hamraz Bhai and Ranjoor Barabankavi had both taken each other to be Hoshang Matchiswalla. Now Ranjoor Saheb was requested to get some brandy from the local pub for his poor wife.

He didn't return. A scout who was sent down to the pub, returned with the news that Ranjoor Saheb had settled himself at the bar and was drinking away happily. The ambulance arrived and Maya Devi was taken to the hospital for first aid. Hoshang Matchiswalla, meanwhile, packed up, hailed a cab and made himself scarce.

A few leading movie stars like Raj Kapoor and Nargis began arriving in London, but they failed to make a splash because the Indian population in the city was still quite small.

" 'The Beauty Queen of Indian Cinema' is in town these days," a London Majlis friend told Talat. "I have made an appointment with her to see you and Feroze. The lady has cartloads of jewels given to her by the four biggest maharajahs and nawabs of India. She's staying in a luxury flat in Knightsbridge, and is bound to give us a large amount for Nazrul's Aid."

Talat remembered her appointment with the Beauty Queen, and rushed to Knightsbridge along with Feroze.

The Beauty often came to England to visit her children who were studying in two very expensive schools. "This indicates the sociological changes which are taking place in our country." As usual, Talat started an academic discussion on the way to Knightsbridge. "When the British-educated son and daughter of the Beauty Queen go back home they will not be referred to as such and such Baiji's grandchildren."

"Yes," agreed Feroze, "but such classy Baijis were always accorded special status in our male-dominated feudal society. Chanda Bai of the Deccan was a child of her times, the troubled eighteenth century—so she even raised a little army of her own. She gave away millions in charity. The Beauty Queen is bound to donate at least twenty pounds—our demand is so modest."

They were welcomed by a smiling Beauty Queen. She introduced them to her very fat mother who was a beauty in her own time, and a famous singer. Once, during the First World War, Lawrence of Arabia had attended her mehfil in Delhi. The hostess spoke to the girls most charmingly and offered them pakoras which her mother had been frying. Both mother and daughter wore huge emeralds and diamonds.

"Remember the Princes' jewels and ask for thirty pounds," Talat whispered to her friend. Feroze made the request.

The legendary Beauty gave them an enchanting smile. "Unfortunately," she said in her silvery voice, "due to foreign exchange restrictions, I do not have a penny to spare. I offer my heart and soul to your good cause." She saw them off at the ornate door of the lift, made a little bow with her courtly salaams, and stood there till the lift went down. Talat and Feroze boarded a bus and settled down to another academic discussion.

"A few points are verified by today's episode," said Talat gravely. "(a) What the books say about these ladies being the last word in charm, culture, etiquette, etc. is absolutely correct; (b) this was the reason why besotted men crowned them queens or lost their kingdoms; (c) no man would thrash them for being unfaithful. Harrassed housewives like Maya Devi get bashed up."

Back in shabby old Camden Town they found all Ranjoor Saheb's lodgers assembled in Hamraz Fyzabadi's drawing room. Feroze told him about their unsuccessful mission and he said, "You should have asked me before going there. Mother and daughter are well-known for their meanness. The mother used to come to sing at the radio station when I was with AIR Delhi." He was about to lose himself in pre-Partition nostalgia when somebody resumed the discussion on the evening's fracas.

The curtain moved and Ranjoor appeared, framed in the doorway. "Do come in," his guests chorused, awkwardly.

The unhappy landlord glanced around. "No," he said, "I don't want to disturb your gossip session. Came up just like that—goodnight." He disappeared again.

Shiv Prasad Bhatnagar didn't return home. His wife resumed her household drudgery with bandaged head and poised demeanour: she was a woman of remarkable resilience and dignity. After a couple of days Shiv Prasad Bhatnagar, Ranjoor Barabankavi, was found lying frozen and dead on the Embankment.

56. Light on the Hilltop

The sanatorium glimmered at the top of the hill like a bonfire lighted by an unseen boy scout. Gautam drove uphill, passing through an immense silence. Mechanically he got out of his car and ascended the flight of stairs and, walking through soundless corridors, entered Nirmala's room.

Her eyes lit up when she saw him. She had been lying with her face to the wall. Away from the crazy, selfish world, what was she awaiting with such unnerving tranquility? He shuddered a little as she sat up.

Hurriedly she tidied her hair with her fingers, worrying unhappily if her nose was shining too much.

"Nirmal, how robust you are! Soon you'll start looking like Lala Rukh," he remarked with forced gaiety.

She smiled politely.

Nirmal, I never took any notice of you; and now you are a part of my being. Maybe it's too late. Champa was the tumultuous Ganga in flood in the monsoons. Nirmala had always been the gently flowing Gomti. Despite her schoolgirl prattle she had somehow remained detached, a silent devotee of Krishna. Or sublime like a goddess, hidden inside a white temple on a hilltop.

With great effort he had managed to banish Champa from his thoughts, and successfully avoided meeting her despite living in the same country and moving in the same social circle for some years. Grant me some peace, goddess. He placed his hand upon Nirmala's forehead.

"Gautam Mashter, tell me the latest."

"A new character has landed up from India, Mr Tughyan Bhagalpuri," Gautam began.

"Ha, ha, what a funny name. Is he a crack-pot too?"

"Absolutely."

"What is Surekha's new flat like? I believe it has a lovely garden room."

He described the said room in detail. "Get well soon and see it for yourself," he added.

"Yes, yes, I will," she replied with faked enthusiasm.

He told her the latest off-colour jokes about the Queen and Prince Philip. She laughed heartily and told him some jokes in exchange.

Before they knew it, the visiting hour was over.

"Oh, gosh, listen, I forgot to ask you. . . According to Champa-watchers, she has also hit town, back from Cambridge. Did you know that?"

"No."

"Oh," Nirmal said simply, "I thought Talat would have told you. You must meet her, poor old thing, drifting like an oarless boat."

Her new compassion for Champa upset Gautam. Those who have an inkling that they are about to go tend to forgive whoever has hurt them. Nirmala put her head back on the pillow, a little exhausted. With a woman's sixth sense she understood that Gautam had lied to her about Champa. She switched the light off after he had left and turned her face to the blank, white wall once again.

Gautam had telephoned Champa a day earlier. "This is Gautam," he said, a trifle nervously. "Is that Champa?"

"Ah, you Tarzan, me Jane," she replied flippantly. That put him at ease—she had certainly become hard-headed. She expressed neither surprise nor anger at his having materialised out of the blue after all these years. He arranged to meet her on Saturday evening.

She came to the door of her mews, and greeted him. "Ah, long time no see, no nothing," she said smoothly as though they were two Anglo-Indians meeting casually on a Saturday afternoon on the Mall in Hazrat Ganj. With great courtesy he gave her a bouquet of flowers and a musical box. She lifted the lid and it played 'Auld Lang Syne'. She felt like crying. He looked away. No. She had not become a Jezebel, she was the same old Champa of yesteryear.

"This is a cigarette box!" she said, wiping her eyes.

"I know you smoke."

"I remember you once said you didn't like women who smoked and drank. I do both."

"You do a good many things now that we don't quite approve of, but that is none of our business."

"And pray who is *we?*" she asked, raising an eyebrow.

"My friends—"

"The Lucknow Gang?"

"Yes. You always considered yourself to be too much of an individualist to identify with it."

He manoeuvered his American limousine out of the lane. "Charles Dickens once lived here," she told him.

"Oh, did he?" He was very quiet, thinking guiltily about Nirmala. It's pure hell for a man who is torn between two women. They headed for the countryside and had their tea in a road-house.

"I have bought a Mayflower," she told him, another conversation piece.

"Why a Mayflower? A Hillman is always better."

"Do you realise that we have met after so many years and you have started arguing with me all over again," she said ruefully.

"One doesn't change, the way you have."

She turned pale. He tried to soften the blow—"Both you and my Bhabi, Shanta, both of you have gone overboard, totally westernised."

"Ah! Please don't bring up that Bharatiya Nari Sati-Savitri business!" she answered curtly.

"No. But when I hear people calling you Nabob Cyril's Bibi I do feel unhappy. I've been away in the States all this time, so I didn't quite know what you had been up to over here. . ."

"You have become a gossipy old mohalla woman. And for your Information and Broadcasting, Cyril Ashley wanted to marry me. I refused."

"It seems to have become your pastime, refusing offers of marriage."

"He wanted to divorce his wife and marry me, but I am not a home-breaker so I said, no."

Gautam smiled fondly. Good old Champa. Living in Britain may have changed her as a person, but it had certainly not improved her English. "Home-wrecker, you mean," he said gently. "I'm sorry, I didn't know that. So once again you sacrificed your personal happiness for the sake of another woman. First Tehmina, now Mrs Ashley—that was very noble of you. Tell me, then, why are you trying to entice poor Bill?"

"Oh, that! You've done your homework about me all right."

"Shanta Nilambar is my relative," he reminded her.

"Well, I wanted to hurt her: a) because she was very uppity with me, b) I am intensely jealous of her. I know you still care for her a great deal, and I've always wondered why on earth you let her shack up with Bill. . ."

"I told you, I am a conservative person and she is still my bhabi. I can only admire her from a distance. She's a rare combination of beauty and brains, like Attiya. She is waiting for the Hindu Code Bill to become a law, then she will be able to divorce my cousin and marry Craig. So, please Champa, leave Mr William Craig alone—I hate talking to you like this."

"You think I've become a slut."

He winced. "Ladies don't use such language, Champa."

"Oh, forget it. Even in Chand Bagh/Badshah Bagh I had acquired a kind of reputation. And here, too, Indians love scandal-mongering. That's why I only meet foreigners."

He began to laugh. "Champa, we are the foreigners out here, Ashley and Craig, etc., are the natives."

She giggled, feeling hollow inside.

Slowly, it turned into a routine. On Saturday afternoons he took her out of town, drove around autumnal woods, had tea and dinner in country inns and dropped her back at her digs by nightfall. Sometimes she picked him up in her Mayflower and took him out. She dutifully asked him about Nirmal's health but never went to see her at the sanatorium on the hill.

57. La Paloma

The Nazrul Aid Variety Programme of the London Majlis of Indian Students was coming to an end. Finally, they began the Indian national anthem. Roshan slipped out through a back door of the Scala theatre, and found Amir waiting for her in the foyer.

"Despite my warnings you haven't stopped mixing with the wrong set."

"And I have told you so many times, Amir, that I am not interested in their politics. Some of them are very good friends of mine and it's great fun meeting them. Please don't shadow me like the CID or FBI."

"Let's go to the Istamboul for dinner," he said peaceably.

In the restaurant a Continental musician began playing La Paloma on the accordian. "I'm going to Spain next week, with my Bengali friends," Roshan informed Amir sweetly.

"Is this bunch of snooty Indian Bengalis and crazy East Pakistanis more important to you than me?"

"No."

"Then?"

"Perhaps you want to be more Catholic than the Pope. I have no such problem—I am native-born, a daughter of the soil. . ."

This unexpected remark rendered him speechless. They did not have the usual quarrel, instead, he told her he wanted to take her to his father's grave which he always visited when he went to the Continent. "I remember, when my father died, they had trouble finding a Muslim maulvi. Then, luckily, they got hold of two Albanian hojas who said the funeral prayers and buried him . . . One should always die in one's own country." He fell silent, for he suddenly remembered her caustic remark. Then he spotted a friend and called him over to their table, and told her he was soon shifting to a larger flat in Amala Roy's block.

"Attiya also lives there—so it will now be known as Lucknow colony," the friend chuckled.

Roshan wrote to him from Cordoba and quoted much Iqbal. Isherwood's Berlin had vanished. She motored through the Rhine valley and visualised all Germany as Vicky Baum's Germany, and all Austria as Dodie Smith's Austria. She would have liked to go to Switzerland and offer fateha at his father's grave, but he hadn't given her the cemetery's exact location.

She bought a lot of presents for all her friends and on her return, first went to Chelsea. She walked down the corridor to Amala's ground-floor flat, and found her and Nargis Cowasjee laughing their heads off over some incident the previous evening. "Oh, here comes Doña Spinoza!" Amala cried. "Let's go and say hello to Attiya."

This building in Chelsea seemed to be inhabited by eminently successful women: Nargis was a rich heiress and fashion designer, Amala was a career diplomat and dancer who invited celebrities like Dylan Thomas and Louis MacNiece to her parties. Attiya Hosain was an author, and her collection of short stories, *Phoenix Fled* was lying near the pineapple basket on Amala's window.

"A rare combination of beauty and intellect. You know, there used to be a saying that if you went to India and did not see the Taj in Agra and Attiya in Lucknow, you had seen nothing . . ." Amir had once told her when he was lecturing her on the superiority of U.P. culture.

He had recently shifted to this building, and because good girls did not visit bachelors in their dens, she handed the gift she had brought for Amir to the janitor as she was leaving. "Shall I keep it for him, Miss, or would you like to give it yourself? The Captain has gone to Karachi on home leave."

"Keep it for him," she said quietly, and gave Mr. Jenkins the little present she had brought for him. The kindly old janitor was overwhelmed—but he also understood the depth of disappointment and sorrow in her voice.

58. Autumn Journal

Auburn leaves float around like useless thoughts. Autumn has come to the forest of Hazelmere, young lovers walk across the wood, trampling dry twigs underfoot. They emerge on the other side and are confronted by decrepit pensioners sitting in a row on benches, waiting for nothing. The pensioners see the young couples through thick glasses and continue to wait for nothing.

She had obtained her Tripos. Before sailing for Pakistan she went through the woodlands and cast a last look at the glowing red oaks. She stopped her car in front of the old red-roofed church, attracted by the quaint engravings on the gravestones. She pushed the heavy door and went in. The chapel was hollow and empty. She touched the cold, grey stone of the font. Old Testament stained-glass faces scowled at her through faint multi-coloured rays. She read the brass plates which bore names of Gallant Englishmen Born in this Parish who fell at Cawnpore and Waziristan, defending the Empire. She yawned and dropped a few coins in the charity box.

"Hello, my child," the aged vicar said to her in a mild, quivering voice. He had quietly emerged from the cherry orchard and limped towards her.

"Good afternoon, sir." She smiled respectfully, dropped some more shillings in the box, and came out.

You move on and reach the Unreal City. You find your friends assembled in the Chicken Inn, discussing the morning's news. The most awful things are happening around the world—why should you bother when today's headlines are tomorrow's waste paper? Crowds are milling in Bond Street, enjoying the sunny weekend. Who are you to refuse to be a part of this ordinariness?

She drove on to King's Road and parked the Mayflower in the courtyard of Amala's block. Someone was playing the mridangam in Amala's studio flat, Talat Reza was singing.

Through the window the room looked like a cosy little stage-set seen from the back row of a club-theatre. The play was written by a favourite author, say Cocteau or Anouilh, or even Tennesee Williams, and the scene was absurdly peaceful. She would not disturb this peace. They are there, happy and safe and intact. I was merely an interloper. I shall send them picture postcards from Cairo, she decided, it's the simplest thing in the world, sending picture postcards from Cairo. She lit a cigarette and kept sitting in the car.

Feroze was addressing Talat. "O happy boatman of the Ravi, blah— blah—Prince Salim had said—do you remember when we played *Anarkali* in Kailash Hostel, autumn of 1946? We had a full moon painted on the backdrop for that scene. . ."

Talat remained silent and motionless.

"You look like a mouse that has drunk a pint of liquid lead," remarked Feroze, after a pause.

Talat spoke: "Do you know what happens when a mouse drinks up a bottle of liquid lead? It stands up on its tail and starts making a speech. Or it begins to sing, like yours truly in *Anarkali* singing as Dilaram—*At the edge of the carpet of moonlit water, Jamshyd's goblet in my beloved's hands* blah. . . blah. . ."

Ramanna Pillai sat crosslegged before his drum, deep in meditation. The two Dutch-Indonesian boys from Surekha's troupe dozed on the wooden floor.

Roshan rang the bell. Pillai opened the door and grinned. She came inside. "I heard you singing, Talat Apa," she said apologetically. "I hope I'm not disturbing your rehearsals."

Obviously they were getting ready for a show.

"Roshan Ara Kazmi, you are welcome," Talat replied solemnly and burst into another song like a character in a nautanki. *Because it was the time of flowers, we went into the glade singing, and lo! The caravan of spring had passed*— AIR Lucknow composition, sung by Talat Mahmud. When was it, Feroze?"

"1945," Feroze replied promptly, "which year has fled for evermore, like all previous years. . ."

"I've never heard this song again. Some day I'll compile a list of all the lovely songs I've heard only once, that keep haunting me. Whatever happens to them? Where do they go? Like those very old film songs whose records have vanished, their composers and singers dead and forgotten. Only snatches of tunes remain. What a terrible thing to happen—the death of a song. . ."

The telephone rang in the gallery.

"That was Gautam—wanted to know if he could bring an American ballerina as his guest this evening," Surekha announced.

"American ballerina?" Talat was astonished. "What about Princess Champa, Act II?"

"Curtains," Surekha answered in a tone of finality, and began practicing her famous leap in the air. Then she added, "He's back in circulation."

Talat turned towards Amala who had studied elocution at RADA—"Recite that bit from your friend MacNiece's *Autumn Journal—I loved my love with a platform ticket.*"

Amala dropped the Bharatanatyam costume she was taking out of the wardrobe, stepped forward, stood ramrod straight like a schoolgirl with her arms down, and began reciting mechanically:

I loved my love with a platform ticket.
A handbag, a pair of stockings of Paris Sand. I loved her
    long

I loved her between the lines and against the clock, Not
  until death
But life did us part. I loved her with peacock's eyes and the
  wares of Carthage.
With blasphemy, camaraderie, and bravado and lots of
  other stuff. And so to London and down the ever-
  moving stairs.

She sat down on the floor. "Why is this evening so depressing?
Do you remember once, at nightfall, we sat on the steps of my
house on Fyzabad Road and a group of mysterious sanyasins
wandered in? They demanded dakshina, muttered something
in some strange language and disappeared in the shadows of
the champa trees. We were so scared—-

"Have you noticed how mournful some evenings are? When
day and night touch each other, when we are laughing in
brightly lighted rooms, the black unlit hours sing underneath
in the hinterland of our separate private sorrows. Those
sanyasins meet us on lonely roads, they curse us and disappear
into the shadows. I have heard them weeping aloud on pitch
dark nights."

"My mother says," Talat replied in a small voice, like a child,
"my mother says, even if one dies at high noon one will be
surrounded by twilight. So, every evening, one's soul foresees
those last moments when day meets the final night, and that's
why we feel depressed."

"As a performing artist," Surekha addressed Roshan gravely,
"I would like to tell you the reality. It's all a question of props.
Stage scenery, backdrop, curtains, footlights. Only the empty
stage remains in the end."

"Corny," said Talat briefly.

Nargis Cowasjee entered the room, back from Lidhurst after visiting Nirmala. She had gone there with her English
fiancé, and on the way they had picked some heather leaves in
the Hazelmere woods. She gave a few to Roshan—"Congrats
on getting your Tripos, and best of luck, my dear."

"Time to leave for Comedy Theatre, Madam," Pillai announced respectfully.

"This is always my Zero Hour. Trring goes the third bell

and the curtain rises and we start all over again. What would happen if the curtains of the world's stages continue rising and there was no more me to dance?" Surekha uttered ruefully as she picked up her make-up kit.

The sound of the mridangam rose higher and higher *Na— dir-dam-ta-na-di-re-na*—chanted Talat with two South Indian ladies sitting with Pillai and Ranganathan at one end of the stage. Surekha arrived like a shaft of lightning and began her 'Tillana'.

Now I am dancing as usual, she said to herself, then Amala and Ram Gopal will dance. The show must go on. The question is, why the hell should it go on? *Kir-tik-tam-tit-tam; kir-tik-tai-tit-tai.* I've got to dance on TV tomorrow, on Monday I'm flying to Holland to dance before Queen Juliana. The river is flowing; *Dheem-ta-na-di-re-na, tana-di-re-na.*

The show must—-

The hall was empty. Surekha's English classmates from RADA lingered near the exit, talking. A number of press correspondents waited to interview the famous dancer.

"Dance. . . is my life. . ." she began soulfully.

"Good God, Surekha," Talat shuddered and longed for tea. She sat down on a sofa and dozed. *This little pig went to market, this little pig stayed ay home, this little pig had a bit of meat and this little pig had none. This little pig said, Wee, Wee, Wee, I can't find my way home. Dheem-ta-na-di-re-na—*

Gautam floated past, gallantly carrying the American ballerina's cloak on his arm.

59. A Bunch of Heather Leaves

"On Monday, 1st Zee Qaad, 1374 A.H. Syed Amir Reza Abidi was married, telephonically, to Miss Alema Khatoon," Kamal announced in a court-room voice. "The bridegroom had not seen the young lady before she reached Karachi from Allahabad."

The audience reacted appropriately. House-guest Chandra who had come from Washington D.C., rushed in from the garden. Talat and Surekha stopped making Swedish salad. The news was electrifying and unexpected. Hari spilled the tea he was drinking. He had come from New York, and was on his way to Cairo. Gulshan sat at the dining table, talking lazily to Hargobind Rai Tughyan Bhagalpuri, visiting Urdu novelist. He pointed towards Hari and said, "This fellow and Gautam are a pair of Ibn Batutas. . ."

"A pair of what?"

"Ibn Batutas."

"Gautam is also Huinsang—often comes from China," Kamal added from his corner in the garden room. It was a pleasant Sunday morning and everybody was feeling marvellous.

Champa turned up—as though it was the last act and the entire cast had assembled for the curtain call. She, too, looked radiant. Gautam had revived his friendship with her after all these years, and it was like old times again. However, her arrival dampened the high spirits of The Gang. Hari regarded her thoughtfully: how she had changed over the years! Now she reminded one of studio flats, the Latin Quarter, music festivals at Salzburg. Her golden brown complexion was glowing, she carried a bunch of heather leaves in her hand. She must have picked them up while strolling through the woods with Gautam in the morning, he thought, and with deep anguish remembered his sister who was lying in the hospital, only just alive. He had lost faith in God long ago—there was ample evidence to prove the non-existence of any sort of deity.

"What's happened to them? They've all become tongue-tied," Tughyan Saheb whispered to Gulshan.

"They are suffering from a surfeit of awareness, they are thought-addicts," Gulshan responded indifferently.

They greeted Champa formally. Hari Shankar brought her a cup of tea. "Hi, Champa Baji."

"Hi, Hari."

"Heather leaves! Sure sign of good luck according to the natives of this island."

She registered the taunt in his voice, and smiled politely.

He tried to make amends. Flopping down on the carpet he said earnestly, "I was meaning to contact you about something, glad to meet you here. See, there is a vacancy in the Indian quota at the U.N. Shall I try for you?"

It was very illogical, but all of sudden she felt that the end was near at hand. The room began whirling madly. Chandra, who wore a multicoloured sari, became a chinese lantern, Hari and Kamal produced strange noises like ventriloquists' puppets. Tughyan Saheb was a huge duck clucking away in low key. Her eyes brimmed over. I'll go bonkers, she thought.

Tughyan Saheb noticed her tears. (He was an ex-communist turned Sufi.) "My Pir Saheb says, Submit to the will of God and hope for the best."

"Kamal— what has Tim written?" Talat shouted in exasperation. "How?"

"Telephonically. Look, before he left he told me that as a member of the defence services of his country, he could not marry Roshan because she had foolishly become a high security risk. There were classified reports against her to the effect that she was a close ally of Red Indians. Communists were bad enough, *Indian* Communists—god forbid."

"Doña Spinoza a Commie? That's a joke!" said Talat incredulously.

"Anyway, so he asked me to write to Amma to find a nice, uncomplicated girl, preferably a graduate of Karamat Hussain Muslim Girls' College, Lucknow, or Muslim Girls' College, Aligarh or Lady Irwin College of Home Science, Delhi. As soon as possible, that is, before Moharrum."

Champa sat in the doorway, playing with Surekha's black Persian cat.

There was another round of tea. Kamal cupped his cigarette in his hand like a truck-driver, closed one eye, knocked off the ash with a jerk. More suspense. At last he began, "The situation at present is this: most of the eligible bachelors have gone over to Pakistan, the girls are in India. So the bachelors travel to India on leave and bring back wives from there, or they get married over the phone. My mother found the girl, she had graduated from I.T. College and her family lives in Allahabad.

Therefore my father sent the *paigham* to her father in customary florid Urdu: if your honour graciously accepts this lowly person's humble nephew in your sonship. . ., etc.

"Begam Ejaz said loftily: We are in no hurry. We have a lot of other excellent proposals, they are under consideration." Then he addressed Gulshan, Surekha and Chandra. "The tradition among us Moz-lems is that the proposal always goes from the boy's side and the girl's people act very high and mighty. There is a saying that till the boy's folk come pleading a minimum number of many times to the girl's house, that until the threshold is worn down, her parents won't say 'yes'. It's called *larkey walon ne dehleez ki mitti ley daali.*

"However, Tehmina writes that things being what they are today, Bhaiya Saheb was married to the Hon'ble Mr Justice Ejaz's eldest daughter within a month."

"But over the telephone, yaar, for goodness' sake!" exclaimed Hari Shankar.

"You know that Urdu saying, *Hum Dilli, tum Agre, to kaise baje gi bansuri.* * Now, a maulvi and two witnesses sit near the phone in Pakistan, likewise in India. The respective maulvis read out the marriage contract over the trunk-line and off goes the bride to Pakistan. Since Bhaiya Saheb is in the defence forces he couldn't get a no objection certificate to go to Bharat, therefore. . ."

"Wish we could have the *pheras* around the telephone, it would solve a lot of logistical problems for us settlers in America," Chandra mused aloud.

"He will return to London with his bride early next month." After this exit line, Kamal declared an Interval.

Champa came in from the garden, said a general goodbye, and left.

"Roshan told me before she sailed for Karachi that she was marrying a CSP officer chosen for her by her parents. On the one hand there was security, on the other the Security Act.† She was opting for the former, she said."

---

* I am in Delhi, you in Agra. How can we play a duet on the flute?

† A law in Pakistan under which a person could be arrested for political dissent.

"Now she will spend her life attending cocktail parties and cutting ribbons at flower shows," said Surekha. "I've been imagining how all of us will end up in the future— Champa as a retired, shattered school marm, me as a faded dancer, forgotten by the public, Talat as a . . . as a . . ."

"As an unsuccessful author?" Talat put in helpfully.

"Maybe. Then how different would we be from Roshan? Old age is a great leveller, especially for women celebrities."

"Girls are a tricky proposition, yaar," Hari said to Kamal. "It's so easy to break their hearts, they're so fragile. They ought to be treated like goddesses and handled like Dresden dolls. How could Bhaiya Saheb be so insensitive about Roshan? She's a great girl."

Hari was exaggerating as usual. Talat remembered him as a young bully who used to smash up her dolls. She turned towards him. "Mian Hari Shankar, economic independence is the real thing. Dolls and goddesses, indeed!" she fumed.

"Champa Baji is economically independent," Hari argued, "but look at the mess she's in. . ."

"Amir Reza, Gautam, Cyril Ashley, Bill Craig, Gautam again in the second round—why she's been merrily playing musical chairs," Talat replied. *"Kora Jamal Shahi, peechhe dekha, maar khai. . ."*

"Talat, you'll always remain Tatterwalla Girls' High School, Barrow Road, Lucknow," Kamal said sternly. "It's her life, let her be. However, would *you* like to play such musical chairs?"

"Good heavens, no," Talat replied primly.

"Being financially independent doesn't solve women's emotional problems," Hari repeated.

Talat was frowning. Hari Shankar pacified her. "Look, Bibi, I quite agree with you. You study some more, do your Ph.D. as well. Economic freedom is certainly the main thing."

Talat was in no mood to be pacified "A Ph.D. will give me ladoos to eat? Just a measly lectureship—Rs 300 a month!!! Only three hundred!" She waved three fingers in front of Hari's nose.

After Talat returned to the kitchen, Kamal said to Hari on the quiet, "I didn't tell these good ladies what Bhaiya Saheb told me before leaving, that he never wanted to feel *threatened* by his wife—which just goes to show."

"Yeah, which goes to show," Hari agreed. "To tell you the truth, I can see his point of view."

They shook hands.

60. The Garden Room

It had started snowing. The Anglo-Saxon lama looked out of Mrs Shunila Mukerji's drawing-room window, then turned round and fixed his gaze on his Anglo-Saxon audience. He was a clean-shaven middle-aged man with a shorn head which he covered with a ski cap. He wore the maroon robe of a Tibetan monk and held a prayer wheel in his right hand. He looked enormously picturesque. He was the same Englishman who had fled Lucknow fifteen years earlier, and Kamal and Hari Shankar had gone to Hardwar to look for him. He had returned to the mundane world as an ordained lama, author of a best-selling paperback titled *Himalayas of the Soul.*

Gautam arrived at Nell Gwen Court and found a heap of snow-boots outside the door of Mrs Mukerji's posh flat. He looked in through the half-open door and surveyed the crowd. He was about to go back when Nargis Cowasjee saw him and came forward, grinning. She carried a bundle of burning joss sticks, English fiancé in tow.

"Nargis, what's all the racket for?" he asked, peeved.

"Shsh—" she whispered. "All for the sake of Culture, Gautam, all for the sake of Culture. I am told he has been engaged by the Congress of Cultural Freedom to lecture on Buddhism in the West. Isn't he cute? It's such fun listening to him—his yak talks to him in English and so on. You only have to discover your own Inner Himalayas—I say, Gautam you look distraught. Is Nirmal all right?"

"Nirmal?" he gasped.

"Half her lung was removed last week. . . successfully. . ." she added as she saw Gautam blanch. "She's fine, I visited her yesterday. I'm thinking of taking the lama to her for her Enlightenment!"

"I. . . I was away in Moscow all this time. . . And now I am looking for Kamal—this envelope arrived addressed to him c/o India House. I found it this morning. He had applied for a post in the National Physical Laboratory and he has been called for the interview. At the earliest. I've phoned him everywhere but can't locate him. So I dropped by here—Mrs Mukerji may know."

"Oh." Nargis tiptoed out to the gallery, followed by the hostess who had recently taken to spiritualism. Gautam told her why he was looking for Kamal.

"Come in, come in. The lama is in touch with Hidden Masters and Unseen Yogis, he'll tell us Kamal's whereabouts in a jiffy. So, Kamal is also leaving? Cyril has gone away to East Pakistan, Michael is emigrating to Israel. . ."

"Sujata di, this is the way of the world. People come and go," Gautam said wearily.

"Yes, indeed. As Gurudev has said, Traveller, you must—"

"Excuse me, Sujata di, I'll see the reverend lama some other time," and he ran towards the lift.

"Try the BBC canteen and the Chicken Inn," Nargis shouted after him, anxiously.

The Chicken Inn was unusually quiet. A solitary girl in a powder-blue cardigan and black skirt sat at the counter, drinking coffee. It was Champa. "Hello," she said, "you done a Houdini again."

"Look, Champa, Kamal has been called for an interview. He is bound to be selected—he *must* airdash to Delhi."

"That's jolly good news. But why are you so glum?"

"Nirmal underwent major surgery last week. . . Didn't you know? I didn't, because I was away in Moscow."

He rang Surekha from the telephone on the counter. Gulshan answered: "Yes, yes. Nirmal is fine. Kamal has gone to Sir Roger's to get her reports. . . Surekha will come home late from RADA. . . Kamal said he would come straight to our

house from Harley Street, to collect some books for Nirmal.
You go there and wait for him. I have to rush to college, but
I'll leave the keys with Asha."

They came out of the restaurant. "Can I tag along with
you?" Champa asked. She seemed to be concerned, too.

"Yes, sure. Where have you parked your Mayflower?"

"Sold it to Roshan Kazmi. I needed the money and she
wanted to chase and impress Commander Amir Reza. Since I
had no one to chase, what was the bloody use of maintaining
a motor car?"

"So back to London and the ever-moving stairs!" He quoted
Louise MacNiece absently.

They reached the Aroras' house in St. John's Wood, took the
key from Asha and went directly into Surekha's garden room.
Champa opened the plate-glass door. He made for the phone and
dialled several numbers to locate Kamal. Then he sat down resignedly on a sofa, and began the wait for his elusive friend.

Outside, the hollyhocks were lit up by a dim winter sun.
Music rose from across the garden wall, the day was comfort-
giving and pleasant. Champa lit the fire. Surekha's unfriendly
black Persian who was fast asleep on the rug, woke up and
miaowed sullenly.

Gautam glanced around. Objets d'art. A huge Nataraj.
Hungarian and Spanish dolls. A Russian balalaika. Autographed
portraits of Margot Fonteyn and Robert Helpman. A sewing-
machine on the floor along with a basket of fresh vegetables.
"She is a world famous dancer, but basically a housewife. . .
And thank god for it. . . Actually, a dwelling reveals the character of its occupants." He began to elaborate on his Theory
of Rooms. In order to overcome his anxiety and tension about
Kamal and Nirmala, he obviously wanted to just go on talking.

"Now, Sujata Debi's place, where everything is so arty-crafty
. . ."

"How," Champa interrupted him, "can you detect the subtle
difference between pose and non-pose? I've always said that
you're a bit contrived, too!"

"Maybe I am. But, on the whole, we can hardly ever tear
ourselves away completely from our real background." He

paused for a moment and added, "Isn't it odd, that sitting on the stool in that Oxford Street restaurant you did not seem to have come from Banaras."

She nodded tiredly, "You told me all this the very first time you met me after six long years—when you came to my mews—that I had changed for the worse."

"Did I tell you that I wrote you a letter last year from the States? I was holidaying in New Jersey during the Fall, and one day I sat down under a purple tree and composed an epistle to you. I was unusually happy. I have never understood the reason for my elation from time to time. I did write to you but you probably never received my letter. I think I clean forgot to post it and went back to New York."

"I have received no letter, ever."

"Come, come, you're being dramatic again!"

Somebody had started singing a Bengali song in Asha's semi-detached next door.

"Gautam, stop being nasty to a poor exile." Tears welled up in her eyes.

"Poor exile, says you!" He looked at her expensive black net stockings and her chic dress bought at Liberty's. "What on earth hinders you from returning home, my dear?"

Ajit and Taruna were leading the chorus at Asha's.

"They're going to yell and sing far into the night—the entire London Majlis of Indian Students seems to have turned up there," she commented wryly. "They're leaving for Budapest tomorrow, for the Youth Festival."

He rushed out. "No, Kamal is not here," he was told. The next moment he had jumped over the wall and joined Asha's party.

He returned to Surekha's garden room after three quarters of an hour. "Did Kamal ring up?" he asked.

She was lying in front of the fire, reading. "No," she replied dryly.

Gautam didn't apologise for his disappearance. Indian men still take women for granted, she thought unhappily. Or perhaps he has lost all respect for me. He wouldn't dare behave like this with Talat.

Gautam found Surekha's empty Assamese bag lying on a chair and carefully stowed the envelope in it. Then he addressed Champa.

"You seem very angry with me, for some reason."

"You're a cheap mercenary, Gautam. You started seeing me all of a sudden after six years. You took me for a ride, in order to accomplish a mission on Shanta's behalf. You asked me to give up Bill. I did. Shanta went back to him, and then you dropped me again like a hot brick. Was that an honourable thing to do?"

"I always told you I was no good, Champa," he said stonily. "It's 2 o'clock. What with one thing and another, I have still not been able to contact Nawab Kamman."

"Such are the uncertainties of life," she remarked cynically.

"The notes are rising like a storm. They are eternal. . ." he said after some time, listening to the sound of music coming from Asha's house. "But they seem to stop before they reach total harmony." He got up and played an arpeggio on the piano. "One note is missing, in lower C. It must be the mice—they often take up abode inside and eat up the felt. Back home in Bahraich a fat old mouse used to play such difficult Wagner pieces, running up and down the chords! At the dead of night, too. My mother was convinced that some ghost had got inside it, till the servants discovered our furry pianist!"

"It sounds odd, playing Wagner in Bahraich," she remarked ironically.

"You see," he explained "like the Gulfishan folk, I belonged to the Anglicised upper middle class. Father was a high court judge in Allahabad and he engaged an Anglo-Indian pianist to teach me. He taught me upto the 6th grade. Then I went off to Santiniketan. . ." For the first time he was talking to her about his personal life. "Then Father settled down in our hometown, Bahraich, after he retired. I love Bahraich," he added stoutly. A few minutes earlier he had taunted her for not being faithful to Banaras, but as a diplomat with superior, international airs would he really feel at home in a drab and dusty small town?

"Would you like to settle down in Bahraich after retirement, like your Dad?" she asked archly. "Wouldn't you prefer London or New York?"

He looked at her in amazement. Her mind darted ahead of his with surprising speed.

Here we are, she and I. At last. At last. He grew nervous and went over to the window. We are living at each other's mercy, bound down, chained in time. Although this time was unreal, too. He looked at Champa who appeared so unnecessary, sitting there in front of the fire. Unnecessary and absurd, like himself.

We entered through one door, and now all exits are closed. I have lost the key.

"So what will you do now?" he asked sombrely.

"Oh, I'll eat a few dinners at the Middle Temple."

"It's futile, Champa, we'll never find the key, the password. Forget about it." He paced around and began examining the bronze statuettes. He rapped them on their heads. "Because," he said touching the nose of a South Indian goddess, "it is you and nobody else who will get caught every time. You think that you have arrived at a decision and now everything will be all right. But it isn't so easy, dear Champa. You shall have more trouble."

He returned to the window. The moment kept spinning, its whirlpool extending to the ends of the earth. Oceans of eternity drowned in it. Slowly it wound down, shining and dim by turns. Like a lantern on a windy night. Light entered the room, slipping over the garden snow. A perfect pattern. She remained motionless by the fireplace. Outside, cars passed by on Maida Vale, shoppers went in and out of the grocery store, the mossy old church round the corner cast a ghostly shadow on the street.

All of existence is a book which I have read and will go on reading till my last breath, Champa told herself resignedly.

Gautam said, "Two distinct worlds are present in me all the time. One of them includes these people," he pointed towards the room with its photographs and books, "in the other there are only you and me, by ourselves. Both worlds are connected to each other through a bridge. What'll happen when this flimsy bridge breaks down?"

"You will blow up the bridge yourself," she replied.

"No. . . These people have set up machine-guns everywhere, there are cannons hidden under the bushes. It's the crudest kind of jungle warfare you can imagine. And clouds are thundering in the sky above. I feel that one of these days this other world will slip into the yawning pit below and I'll be left outside, struggling to recover myself. It's a dreadful thought."

"You're hiding in the rafters with your spotlight, and you turn it in the direction of anyone who comes into view," she said. "And the poor fellow is exposed in that light. You have always done this." She recollected their conversation in Sita Dixit's cottage years ago.

"But I myself am in that light all the time," he protested.

"No, you have cleverly camouflaged yourself, lurking in the hollyhocks. What will happen when this searchlight hits you, too? I know what you will do. You'll jump down from your ambush and run! You'll knock around, peeping through lighted windows and see us inside, sitting around warm stoves, eating, talking, cooking dinner. You'll come prowling over the roof tiles, a tramp, nimblefooted tomcat. We'll see your face against the window-pane by the light of the moon. Bogeyman!"

"And at that time little will you suspect that I am right there, taking part in discussions near the stove, cooking, eating. No. You will see me peeping through the window. Bog woman!"

After a while, he said, " Looks like Kamal will never turn up."

Now, "afterwards" still remains. An afterwards which will extend till death, till eternity. Which shall remain for evermore, Champa said to herself. He and I have no destiny.

Gautam strode across and went to the bathroom. Champa stepped out into the garden. The telephone rang, she came back. Gautam was still in the bathroom. She picked up the receiver. It was a nurse from Lidhurst. "May I speak to Mrs Ahuja," she asked. Then the line disconnected. Surekha's black tomcat growled under the table, Gautam rushed in.

"Who was it?" he asked anxiously.

She was scared. "I dunno. It was from Lidhurst but the line got disconnected."

All of a sudden she saw Gautam transformed into an ashen-faced yogi. Terrible. Terrifying. Like Shiva, about to break into his Dance of Destruction. . .

"The whole day is gone, and I am still here. . . What am I doing here, talking bloody inanities." He made a dash for the gallery. Near the door he caught sight of a parcel of books lying on a corner table. It was marked "For Nirmala, with love and prayers for a speedy recovery, from Surekha."

He picked it up blindly and zoomed out of the room. He got into his car and drove in a frenzy towards Lidhurst.

Champa wiped cold perspiration off her face, and sat down weakly. After a few minutes she noticed the Assamese bag in which he had stuffed the envelope addressed to Kamal. He had forgotten to take it along in his tearing hurry.

The singing in Asha's flat stopped suddenly. An ominous silence. The black Persian who had got entangled in the telephone cords, freed himself and jumped out. Then he stared malevolently at Champa. She closed the glass door, picked up the Assamese bag and stepped out. She slipped the key in Asha's mail-box next door and began walkiing briskly towards the tube station.

On the platform Champa met June Carter. She was coming from Asha's party and looked grim. She asked, "Have you heard. . ."

"No. What?"

"She died. At 3.30 today. They telephoned Surekha, there was no response, they said. Then they rang up Asha. Champa, you need a good dose of Napoleon brandy. So do I. Let's go . . ."

Champa was struck dumb. Her legs trembled. The train arrived, and the two women got into it. Champa was feeling dizzy. She sat down and put the Assamese jhola on the seat next to her. After a few stations June nudged her, "Let's get off over here."

Champa stood up in a daze, leaving the bag behind on the compartment seat. She followed June blindly on the escalator, like a cocker spaniel. They emerged in the street and went into their favourite pub which they had nicknamed "The Duchess and the Bandits" in honour of the Duchess of Kent's recent visit to troublesome Malaya.

61. 'The Laurels'

'The Laurels' stood at the end of a quiet avenue, with a rock-garden and duck pond in front. The gallery was full of finished and unfinished canvases, including an incomplete sketch of Nirmala. It looked eerie.

There was still no central heating in many houses in England. During the winter Zarina Hussain could be seen,. clad in jeans, a scarf around her blonde head, going into the shed in the backyard to fetch wood for the fireplace. Once the drawing-room glowed with a log fire, the world suddenly seemed cosy and safe. Zarina and her younger brothers had come to England for higher studies immediately after Partition. Their father bought a house, named it 'The Laurels' (his English wife was called Laura) and returned to Allahabad. Every six months he visited his family in England.

The world was covered with a shroud of snow. Nirmala had been dead a week. One dark and dreary evening as Zarina sat in the kitchen reading, the door bell rang. Her brothers were away on the Continent with their school friends, Mrs Hussain was upstairs watching TV. The bell rang persistently. Zarina got up and peeped out of a bay window. Gautam Nilambar hovered on the porch steps, his face half hidden in the up-turned collar of his raincoat. His snow-boots were covered with slush; he'd obviously walked to the house. He looked a bit odd and mysterious. For some reason Zarina felt scared. Timidly, she opened the front door, and he stepped in.

"Hello, Gautam Mashter," she said, trying to sound casual. He put down his baggage and saluted her gravely.

"Take off your boots, Gautam," Zarina suggested politely.

"Shan't. I'm the Eternal Traveller. I am not going to enter

your drawing-room—houses have no meaning for me." He swayed a little, picked up his attache case and declaimed, "I am the Eternal Travelling Salesman, carrying samples of ruined lives. Would you care to have a dekko?"

"Please, Gautam, close the door. . ."

"I have a lot of people with me. They're standing outside in the snow," he said anxiously.

"Call them in."

"How can I? You wouldn't be able to see their faces in the glare of your spotlight."

"Who are they, Gautam?"

"Ghosts. Corpses. Their procession follows me faithfully wherever I go."

"Never mind, call them in. I won't be frightened."

"You ought to be. Because we ourselves are turning into corpses all the time."

"Gautam," she said gently. "You have returned, haven't you, from wherever you had gone. Your sudden disappearance was so baffling. We were all terribly worried about you."

"That was very kind of you. I'm grateful."

"I mean, welcome home, dear Gautam. Wherever home is . . . that is. . . the transit camp after every journey. . . etc."

"That's all right," he made a grandiose gesture of dispassion. "I accept your welcome." He looked around and added, "This is not the same house in which you used to live. . . Aunt Laura's house?"

"It is, Gautam Mashter."

"All right. . ." he said uncertainly, "it must be if you say so . . . Zarina. . . have I gone round the bend?"

"Of course not," she replied. "You're looking just a wee bit tired, that's all."

Mrs Hussain appeared on the staircase landing. She wore a pink housecoat and bedroom slippers. To him she looked like a tall and stately Roman goddess with flowing ginger hair. He saluted her.

"One does get tired after running continuously. Do you know how many *millions* of miles I have covered?"

"Where have you been, Gautam?"

"Why should I tell you?" he replied childishly. "I spent many nights in the forests, slept in desolate barns, hid myself in lonely boats and sat crouching in railway waiting-rooms."

"I'm sure you are exaggerating as usual, Gautam—you imagined all this in your stupor. . ."

"No. I was trying to dodge the police. . . Today I decided to come back and confess—"

"Police? Mummy!" Zarina called out in sudden panic.

"I have been roaming around seeking refuge. Knocked on all my friends' doors, peeped in through their windows and found them sitting around cozy stoves, talking, while I stood outside in the Bog with a fierce searchlight beating down upon me."

He was unconsciously repeating his conversation with Champa when he had spent that tragic, improbable day with her in Surekha's garden room.

Laura Hussain came downstairs.

"Gautam! He's roaring drunk. Throw a jug of water on his mug. . . Quick!"

Zarina obeyed her mother. He shook his head like a wet, shaggy dog and wiped his face. "Good evening, Ma'am," he said and did a quick pirouette.

"Come off it, sonny," Mrs Hussain said sternly. "We all like to take a holiday from our normal selves once in a while, but don't overdo it." She had grasped the situation immediately. Nirmala had died and he was drowning his sorrow in drink. She led him firmly to the kitchen.

"Now. Have a cuppa and tell me all about your metaphysical travels, but stop fancying yourself the hero of some Spanish tragedy."

"Why Spanish? Tragedy is universal, Aunt Laura, it has no frontiers," he declared, lifting his forefinger. He looked out of the window, turned round and declaimed:

"I hereby confess. . ." then he became incoherent again.

After piecing together his 'confession', Zarina rushed to the corridor and called her friends at St. John's Wood. Luckily Kamal, Talat and Hari were all at home, and Kamal answered at the other end. She spoke to him in an undertone. "Gautam has turned up, vastly disoriented. He is actually being very funny, but he's acquired an exaggerated sense of his own importance—a hero in some kind of melodrama. . ."

"All drunken people sometimes indulge in melodrama," Kamal replied sullenly. "You know, he just vanished from Lidhurst, leaving Hari and myself to cope with Nirmala's funeral arrangements—the cad."

"Now he's talking about ruined lives and stuff. Says he let Nirmal die and Champa turn into an alcoholic, and he lost the envelope with your interview call. Now the date has passed and he is entirely responsible for the possible loss of your career. So he ran away from Lidhurst—because when he was spouting high falutin' philosophy with Champa Baji in Surekha's garden room, there was a phone call from Lidhurst and when he reached he found four white screens around poor Nirmal's bed. . . He felt he had killed her, and ran back to town to get drunk. Then he realised that he had killed Champa Baji too, metaphorically speaking. Because while he was getting drunk at The Duchess and the Bandits he found Champa there and she was also smashed. That's like killing two birds with one stone, I said to myself. Ha-ha-" she laughed hollowly. "Black humour."

"He's talking bloody nonsense, trying to cover up his shameful disappearance from Lidhurst. Throw him in the duck pond."

"The duck pond is frozen."

"Oh well, we'll be there right away, and straighten him out. See you."

Kamal rang off. By the time Zarina went back to the kitchen Gautam had passed out blissfully.

62. The Fugitive

"Now Talat Reza and her Cats Club will float the rumour that I've hit the bottle."

"Have you?" asked Neil. He was busy making toast.

"No," Champa replied, painting her nails. It was an utterly depressing Monday morning. They were sitting in the dilapidated kitchen of June Carter's mews. "Although Talat Reza rang up just now, sounding very concerned. Even hinted darkly that I should not be drinking alone."

"Have you been drinking alone?" Neil asked her, like a physician.

"No. Yes. . . only after I heard that. . . that poor Nirmala had died. . . and when I realised that I had lost Kamal's interview letter. He missed the date because of that."

"Step out and face the world! Meet those very people you are trying to avoid, you have been 'underground' here for more than a week now. Go."

"Shunila Mukerji telephoned last evening to say that she had arranged a sort of requiem for poor Nirmala. Today at the Geeta Centre, eleven o'clock. They're bound to be there, all of them. Should I go, Neil?" she asked timidly.

"Go," he repeated. "Tell the whole world that you are Champa Ahmed, not a mole nor a cipher, that you are a good girl. And remember, no one is entirely alone. There must be many people who care for you and need you."

Neil's self-confidence reassured her slightly. She finished her tea and rose from the broken horsehair sofa, put on her favourite old rose silk sari and went downstairs.

"Nobody has turned up after all," Sujata Debi complained as she opened the front door. "Nirmala's brother and friends must be atheists. Loma Devikanand-ji had made all the arrangements, but these people do not wish to see the Path of Mukti. And do you know what they are doing at the moment? I'm told they get together and play rummy."

"Who do you wish to seek?" An American lady from California addressed her, leaning out of the window. "He is here . . . He is calling you, calling all of us unto Himself." She pointed to the large picture of Lord Krishna which adorned the hall of the Geeta Centre. "You need that Third Eye to see him which, alas, you Indians have lost. . ."

Champa rushed out and, reaching the kerb, slowly stroked

her forehead with her fingers. She felt as if all the passers-by had the Third Eye on their foreheads which stared at her, relentlessly. Panting, she boarded a passing bus and got off near the Indian Students' Centre in Exeter Street.

A new contingent of students sat in the little hall, chatting brightly.

"I am Champa Ahmed. . ." she announced in the doorway.

"Yes?" a young South Indian came upto her, looking askance.

Her heart sank. Her name was so unimportant. Neil was wrong—nobody knew her, nobody needed her.

"Nothing. . . nothing. . . It's all right," she muttered and was seized by sudden fright. "I just dropped in to see your social centre. . ."

The crowd eyed her suspiciously.

Back on the Strand she entered the elephant-flanked portals of India House.

"I am Champa Ahmed," she announced solemnly at the counter in the canteen. She wasn't one bit surprised by her persistent idiocy.

"Yes, dear?" the middle-aged Malayali woman at the adding machine asked her in a Lion's Corner House accent. "Lunch is over, but you can have a snack if you like."

"No, thanks. Thank you," she said, becoming more flustered. In the far corner, Surekha's cynical husband Gulshan sat drinking his coffee, absorbed in *The Economist*. She fled India House, too.

Now she made for Chicken Inn where she ran into Kamal who was telephoning the Thomas Cook office. He said a few casual, polite words to her, then left hurriedly. She remained standing near the glass door watching him vanish down Oxford Street. Next, she peeped into the BBC canteen down the road. Everyone was sitting around untidy tables, arguing fiercely as usual. "I am Champa Ahmed," she felt like saying to all of them, but backed out quickly.

She spent some time window-shopping mindlessly, then had some sandwiches at a drab Lion's Corner House. Exhausted by the sheer emptiness of it all, she walked to the Underground station and mechanically bought a ticket for Warwick Avenue.

She emerged in Maida Vale and rested against a leafless tree. Surekha and Asha lived in the neighbourhood, so did Talat and Kamal. Lights had come on inside tall, elegant houses. It was almost like a peaceful street scene painted on a Christmas card.

Surekha came out of a corner shop carrying her bag of groceries. "Hello, Champa. . ." she cried. "Why on earth are you standing there? Come along home. . ."

She followed the dancer meekly. Surekha entered her flat and went down to the garden room. A little bit of daylight still lingered outside the glass door. A handful of flaming leaves came sailing down and settled on the steps. The last rays of the setting sun formed a golden circle on the grass.

What is it one really wants in life?

"Make yourself comfortable, Champa," said Surekha amiably.

"The room would not be the same as it was that day, even if I sit on this sofa," Champa said half to herself, without realising that she was thinking aloud.

"That day. . .? Which day, Champa? What was the room like?" asked her hostess, going towards the fireplace.

"Don't know."

Dusk fell over clean, pure, almost holy snow; one's entire existence seemed light and sheer. Surekha wrapped a white-and-gold Kashmir shawl around herself and lit the fire.

"A lot of people are going home soon," she said.

"Who?" Champa asked, indifferently. Suddenly she felt she had nothing to do with anyone any more. Sanctified like this weather, she was spread all over. What need did she have of particular stations and personalities? She was not related to anything or anybody.

Surekha sat down on the carpet and began peeling potatoes. "Everyone," she answered. "Hari is leaving by Air India, taking poor Nirmal's ashes with him. Kamal is sailing, Gautam is leaving for New York. He has recovered from his massive hangover, or maybe it was a nervous breakdown."

Big Ben chimed over the BBC. Darkness settled rapidly on the garden, the darkness of winter nights which pounces upon the world all at once. Champa went into the kitchen to help Surekha. The effect of evening whiteness had gone, replaced by night. Champa returned to the room. It was empty. Everything was different. The shadows, the balalaika, the Hungarian dolls. The bronze Nataraja. Books. Time had fled for evermore.

Back in June Carter's lane she reached the stable door and stretched out her hand to switch on the light. Suddenly, darkness leapt forward and greeted her. Till now, she thought, night was against me, now perhaps it may be my ally. The wind came rushing, wave after wave, across sooty house tops. She heard the distant rustling of the grass, the snow on oak leaves. The waters of the night are gushing by over the earth and the currents have become separate. She laughed. Underneath, the earth is hard and real, and I must continue treading it till the hour of my death. Where else will my feet carry me? I shall reach daylight holding fast to the rope of darkness. Night, from this moment on, you are my friend. I have known you for ages. During the monsoons, in the time of flowers, under full moons, in the long hours studying for the exams, travelling by train through strange countries, I have known you in all your aspects and moods. You and I have spent our time together. One day you shall win.

Then she addressed someone else: 'I leave you now in the company of your dreams. I was reality, and you will never give up dreaming.' The night deepened and it became very cold. The waves of silence continued dashing against the walls of the mews. Time said: Recognise me. I'll never stop hounding you. You thought that the moments shall remain at their stations. You were mistaken. Look at me and know me. I am going, second by second, disappearing behind the folds of heavy curtains, sinking under layers of darkness. I am Darkness upon Darkness, I am the dividing line. You cannot go beyond me. Turn back—you have reached the frontier. The gate stands before you, a new country begins now. You will have to get new travel documents, fill new forms and write your signatures all over again. I have broken many a spell—yours was very insignificant. Recognise me, I'll keep walking along with you, you can't run away from me. People will leave you, I won't. See how quickly you reached the check-post? You were finding it so difficult to decide, I solve all problems. All decisions are made, all intentions become actions because of me, and through me.

You shall face more trouble but I'll teach you how to deal with it. Make peace with me. I am still here.

The window curtain fluttered in a strong gale. The stable was filled with frost and she realised that she was shivering with cold. She closed the window quickly and ran upstairs to her room.

63. *The Urn*

Talat was writing an article for *The Eastern World*, Surekha was reading a book on choreography, Zarina was sketching. The world went about its business as usual, peaceful and indifferent. As a matter of fact, ever since Nirmala's death, the world had gone about its business more peacefully than ever.

"Shouldn't we do something about Nirmala's Rites of Passage?" Hari Shankar asked Kamal, just as he used to earlier ask: "Shouldn't we do something about Nirmala's marriage?" They also had to do something about her belongings. Get up, put on your armour. Left, right, forward march. Pick up your tried and trusted weapons, go and bring back Nirmala's old armour and weapons which she no longer needs.

After this pantomime they drove up to Lidhurst, and on the way back stopped at the roadhouse marked 'Teas' where they always had their tea under the apple tree. Back in his flat in St. John's Wood Kamal put Nirmala's luggage in his room, which Hari Shankar was sharing, after which they both went out again. Talat entered Kamal's room and cast her eye around. The sideboard was cluttered with useless things. The landscape on the wall she had once bought for a few shillings in

Camden Town, old magazines and newspapers, bric-a-brac surrounded by Nirmala's suitcases and bags. Talat felt as though all of life was a junk shop, death its price-tag.

On the sideboard stood a little urn containing the ashes of Kumari Nirmala Raizada. Hari Shankar Raizada, next-of-kin, was going home to submerge the said ashes in the sacred Ganga at Kashi. Mr Raizada had gone out with Kamal Reza to finalise the arrangements. Death certificate. Religious service. Etcetera.

His Air India ticket for the flight back to Delhi lay on another table. Everything material and solid. That urn was as real as the chair or the sofa or the teacups bought in a department store's bargain basement.

What could be more trite than the event of dying?

One cries at other people's deaths, then dies oneself.

Nirmala had spent all her earthly days planning for the future, sitting up whole nights preparing for college examinations, praying fervently for a first division. All right. Please god, at least give us a good second division with perhaps a distinction or two. Okay, god, just see to it that I get through. Then she had this great anxiety about the Nation and the Country. Forever arguing, agitating, leading processions, discussing socio-economic problems. When she did get a first division she insisted that she be sent to no less a place than Cambridge. Well, she got a scholarship and was overjoyed.

For the first few days she hadn't quite believed that she was actually in Cambridge, but then she started making fresh plans. She would work and help Father pay off the family debts, she would find a lovely bride for her dear brother, Hari, later still, when she had saved a little money herself, she would embark on a world tour. First she would visit Outer Mongolia, then Mexico, Chile, Peru, etc. She was frightfully keen on Outer Mongolia—she simply had to go there. It sounded so remote, literally out of this world. She also vaguely hoped she'd have a house of her own with a lily pond. She would call it Neelpadam Kunj.

Then of course she wanted to buy all the saris in India. And she insisted on a pearl-and-turquoise jewellery set like her married sister, Laj. She would often make guest lists for her wedding. Tonight her friends had all assembled, but not for her wedding. Dinner was being made in the kitchen, Surekha's shadow moved to and fro on a window. Talat sat down on the floor and made an attempt to pack Nirmala's belongings. Saris, cardigans, shoes, slacks, bangles, books. She opened a handbag—it was full of bus tickets, half-used lipsticks, a one pound note and a few pennies, hairpins, bills. A half-torn envelope with the smudged post-mark of Behraich, 1943, slipped out of a book. Gautam's glossy picture peeped out. It had been mailed to Nirmala's parents after they had sent her marriage proposal to the 'boy's' father according to Hindu custom.

Talat looked blankly at the photograph. Then she picked up a red pencil and scribbled *"Dead Letter Post Office"* across the envelope, put it underneath some other papers in Nirmala's cabin trunk and returned to the living room.

64. *Windsong on the Heath*

" 'At Tehmina Appie's wedding,' Nirmala declared with much aplomb, 'I'm going to wear a gold-and-silver Ganga-Jamni lehnga.'

" 'I'll put on a Banarasi sari,' Malti said demurely, like a grown-up woman. Malti, Nirmala's cousin was sixteen, Nirmala was two years younger, and I was a year younger than Nirmala. I listened to them in awe, because I only wore frocks. . ."

After a pause, Talat said to Kamal, "Don't you see this is so futile. My past is important only to myself, others can find little meaning in it."

"My past is my own," Kamal repeated.

"And the world is only interested in the present," Hari Shankar's voice resounded.

"But the past is present and the present is the past, and also the future," Talat replied. "See, this is also the Qoranic concept of Time, an Egyptian scholar at the Islamic Centre once told me. He asked me to read Mohyeddin Ibn-el-Arabi, the Spanish metaphysician. But how much can one know? Time is a juggler, it goes on persecuting me. Why doesn't any one of you come to my rescue?"

"Even Einstein cannot help you, Talat Begum," said Hari Shankar heartlessly.

"What possible interest can the world have in my past, I ask you?" Kamal insisted. He buzzed around and stopped at the calendar. It was December 15, 1954. They were sitting by the fireside in a cosy pre-war flat in St. John's Wood. Their shadows made strange patterns upon the walls. A Mozart concert was being broadcast from Vienna, and the London Underground vibrated faintly underfoot, carrying multitudes to unknown destinations in the Black Hole.

In a similar darkness of time Talat had leaned against the veranda railing of Water Chestnut House in the month of July 1939, talking to Nirmala Raizada. She was no different from the girl in St. John's Wood, yet they were two different personalities. The Buddha has said that man changes every instant—he is different in childhood, in youth and in old age. You were not there before this moment, only a continuum remains. Glaciers floated on faraway oceans and blue winds roared across terrible mountains. Time was fluid. Time was frozen.

"We want to reassure ourselves by repeating our story," said Hari Shankar, "for we are scared as hell."

"Time shall devour us and darkness shall be our last refuge. It's sad to think that despite his high-falutin' philosophy Gautam Nilambar turned out to be a frightened little mouse," said Talat.

"Forget Gautam or we'll drift from the real issue. The point is, I was Hari Shankar fourteen years ago and shall be considered Hari Shankar fourteen years hence as well. And after all the experiments which we'll be subjected to, we, Time's little guinea pigs, will perish without a squeal."

Talat nodded. Though thousands of Talats existed on countless planes, scattered in myriads of pieces, the same face is reflected separately in the several bits of a broken mirror. One could only travel forward; to return was not possible.

Kamal looked at everybody through the eyes of a fly. Michael. Bill Craig. Zarina. Gulshan. Surekha. He buzzed around again and settled on the head of the Laughing Buddha. Then he flew up to the calendar and began crawling over December 15, 1954. Why should we flies be so upset by the death of one among us? Do we fly on to a heaven or to a hell after we stop buzzing?

Early next morning Hari Shankar was flying to India. After much discussion it had been decided that he would carry the urn with his sister's ashes in his handbag. Nirmala had turned into a piece of luggage with an Air India tag on it, it was as simple as that. He would carry the urn by train to Kashi and submerge it in the Ganges. And that would be that.

"A frightened little mouse, despite all his intellectual bravado," Talat repeated, shaking her head sorrowfully.

"What is Gautam? A mere illusion."

"Oh, Hari, don't start your pseud-giri at 11 o'clock in the morning," Talat said in tired voice.

For some moments no one spoke. To Talat they looked like dumb toys. A soldier with a little tin gun in his hand, Michael. Ancient, grey-haired, sad-faced, oriental philosopher, Hari Shankar. The almond-eyed dancer of Emperor Chandragupta Maurya's court, Surekha. The utterly sophisticated Nawab Kamman of King Ghaziuddin Hyder and Vajid Ali Shah's Durbar, Kamal. They sat there adorning the niches in the wall, clay dolls for Diwali, miniature figurines moulded by the expert potters of Old Lucknow. One of them, Nirmala, had recently fallen off and broken, so one niche was empty.

In accordance with Muslim folk beliefs, if somebody is missing in India, an Aamil or Muslim practitioner of white magic is summoned. He puts a little kajal—lamp-black mixed with ghee—on the right thumb-nail of an innocent child. Then he recites some Quranic verses and the child begins to glimpse the place and the person who is lost on his thumb-nail. Qadeer used to say, "First a sweeper appears and sweeps the ground, then the bhishti comes wearing his red apron, bent double with the weight of his water-skin. He sprinkles water. Then a throne is brought. The King of the Genii arrives and sits on it and the viewer gets to know what he wants to know."

Talat looked hard at her thumb and only saw Cutex nail polish on it. She felt very unhappy. "I wish we were back in Neelampur," she thought. "Qadeer would have told the village maulvi, 'We have lost Nirmal Bitiya. She has put on the Sulaiman topi* and can't be seen by anyone. Please find out where she is. Or maybe her enemies did black magic on her, that is why she died so young.' "

She saw Bill and Michael regarding her with concern as she stared vacantly at her right thumb-nail. She frowned. Shall I tell them about this occult practice of ours? Omigosh—they'll laugh their heads off. Do you really believe in voodoo? And then they'll think, well, after all, she is basically a backward, benighted, medieval Oriental, she really can't relate to us post-Reformation Occidentals.

Shall I tell them tales of black magic performed on moonless Diwali nights? And the *churails* whose feet are turned backward, who speak through their noses and live in bamboo clusters during the monsoons and in peepal trees on hot, summer afternoons. They eat handsome young men. . . . And there is this world of shining beings—devas and angels, and eternal happiness and light. Nirmal has crossed The Barrier. Has she seen the Unseen? She was one of us, now she is one of them, the light, airy, holy beings—or maybe there is absolutely no Afterlife.

When they brought Gautam back from Zarina's cottage in Osterly he remained ill and bedridden for a week. Sometimes in his delirium he came out with a lot of classical Urdu poetry. Once the doctor arrived while Gautam was quoting an eighteenth-century poet with much drama:

> *Chali simt-e-ghaib se ek hawa, ke chaman surroor ka*
>   *jal gaya.*

---

*Prophet Solomon's cap.

Magar ek shakh-e-nihal-i-gham, jise dil kahain,
so hari rahi.

He sat up and thundered—

Khabar-i-tahayyur-i-ishq sun,na junoon raha na
pari rahi.
Na to tu raha, na to main raha, jo rahi so
bekhabari rahi. *

He fell back against his pillows and closed his eyes like a stage Majnun.

The old physician was baffled. "What was your boyfriend saying, young lady?"

Talat was aghast. "He is my adopted brother," she replied stonily. Then she remembered, they did not have these adopted brothers, sisters, uncles, aunts, etc., out here in the West.

"Well, what was your adopted brother saying? Is he an actor?"

"No, sir, he is a part-time philosopher of sorts." She pointed towards the placard on the kitchen door which said, "Thinker's Den."

The doctor smiled, recalling his own student days.

"Sir, the poet my brother quoted, says:

From the direction of the Unknown arrived a gust of wind
and blighted the garden of joy

But a bough of the Tree of Sorrow, called 'heart', is green for
evermore.

Behold the wonderment of love, the madness and the fairy
both vanished

Neither the patchwork of sanity remained, nor the revelations
made by madness.

You did not remain you, nor I, I. Only non-awareness survived."

This must be the Wisdom of East, the good doctor decided. He wrote out a prescription in his state of awareness and left hastily. He wanted to get out of the room which contained the presence of death in the form of the sick man.

---

* Siraj Aurangabadi.

Kamal and Hari Shankar bullied Gautam into getting well within a week. He was well enough to return to his job in the United States, and after seeing him off at the airport his friends returned to Talat's flat for lunch. The rooms were full of packed luggage. Kamal was also leaving Britain.

"Let's get some fresh air," Gulshan suggested after lunch.

On the way to Hampstead Heath they passed little back gardens, crossed narrow, cobbled lanes and half-lit tea-rooms. Office girls were returning from work. It was an Eliotonian cityscape.

"Some peaceful scenes inspire pure terror in me," said Michael.

"Yes," Talat replied.

"We must never try to drag others into our own scenes."

"Or into our dreams," replied Talat. "My past, my time, my dreams are mine, they cannot belong to anybody else. Though you mustn't forget," she added hastily, "I am talking on a strictly personal level. The future is the same for all of us."

"For heaven's sake," Michael said irritably, "don't go on following the Party line. The bloody future lurks over there beyond the hill, with open jaws, ready to devour us separately . . . like Hari's ten-armed black goddess. I am going to Israel, Kamal to India which does not recognise Israel. Where the hell is a common destination for humanity? Only the process of extinction is common to us all."

"I was perfectly all right," said Talat and then, all of a sudden realised with a shock that people's minds are at different stages in the million year evolution of the human brain.

"There were other things, too, that scared me. The landscape after the rains; friends; comfortable houses. When I opened my bags all kinds of documents popped out—bank correspondence, stocks and shares, the biannual reports of joint stock companies. Strange names that were familiar in an impersonal sort of way. The world of the Boards of Directors— Lord Sinha, Sir Biren Mukerjee, Shri C Thapar, Dr. K. Hameed. There was another world hidden behind these names. Magnificent buildings, classy, modern offices. Money, money, money. Strikes, hunger, unemployment. Director's Meetings.

Trade Unions. Apex Diamond Mines of South Africa. Slums. The City of London. Clive Row, Calcutta. Bishop's Gate. Chowringhee. Tata-nagar. Andrew Yule, Calcutta. Martin Burns. Spencers, Madras. Indian Iron and Steel Ltd. Cipla Ltd., Bombay.

"I signed on their dotted lines. These shares belonged to me, given to me by my father. These papers perhaps symbolised my economic security and bore witness to my considerable status in society. What use is all this to me? Mere pieces of paper. Money, money. In 1947 I lost all sense of the value of money."

Kamal took his cue from her: "It was revealed that there was more confusion in the universe than we had imagined. The world had gone wonky."

A Salvation Army band marched past, playing *"Onward Christian Soldiers."*

Talat resumed speaking: "Before I knew it I had embarked upon the. . . shall I say. . . the dangerous journey of thought, sailing on a sea of words."

A dim sun was reflected in the lake. "What are words?" asked Talat. "What is reality? The books say: words are wrong, there is no meaning. Relationships are futile. Sometimes I felt that Brahaspati was imparting his knowledge to the demons. In medieval Europe they burned women at the stake. Often I saw myself as a little witch, blindly flying around astride the broom of my so-called learning.

"Many other brooms whizzed past, ridden by countless other young women. . . Tehmina, Nirmala, Surekha, Feroze, Nargis Cowasjee, Shanta, Champa, and many more. These brooms had flown so high that it was impossible now to bring them back to earth. In fact, the skies over the whole world were full of such brooms. Now, Champa Ahmed made the mistake of dozing. Look, I am a *daastan-go,* and for a *dastaan-go* all of life is an allegory.

"Now, if you are riding a broom and you fall asleep, you're bound to lose your way and crash-land in the middle of no-where.

"In her dream-condition she floated around singing like

the Vaishnava devotees of Bengal. Champa Baji also thought she was a seeker—while my own discovery is 'Seek. . . and Ye Shall Not Find'. She envied the Catholic nuns. When I was a teenager and very self-righteous, I disliked her immensely because I thought she was a happiness-grabber and tried to steal other people's happiness. She robbed Amir from Tehmina and Gautam from Nirmala. However, when she was coming down with her bag of loot somebody pulled the step-ladder from under her feet. Let's go for a walk, and I'll tell you more about Champa's Follies."

"I too have some idea of the symbolism of things," said Michael, spreading his hands in the dark air. "I have suffered a lot because of it." A plane flew overhead and disappeared into the clouds. They gazed after it.

"The City of Unknowing that we founded, we built its citadels with the bricks of philosophy," Talat said. "One day Death the Burglar broke in and tiptoed into our towers.

"Two years ago, we visited the Farnborough Air Show where poor John Derry died breaking the sound barrier—his aircraft exploded in mid-air, killing many. At the instant that its engine hurtled towards me from the sky, I knew my time had come. . . Instead of falling face downwards on the ground, I began scurrying around looking for Zarina and Chandra. I was worried only about them, it didn't occur to me that I should try to save myself. So, when Nirmala faced death she, too, wouldn't have been afraid."

"The Vedanta mentions four states of existence—the waking man; dream; dreamless sleep; and death," Hari Shankar intoned like a priest. "Death is the only human experience which cannot be shared. So we left Nirmal alone to conduct this experiment entirely on her own. She was carried away by the strong currents of the River, struggling hard to fight the waves in the dark.

"Maharaja Janak said: 'Mithila is burning, but I remain'. We are all burning." Hari Shankar turned to Michael, "Hasn't the heat of the flames reached you?"

Kamal had gone down the hill and begun to sing.

"When my grandma died the family pandit told us the soul

flees from the flames into the night," said Hari Shankar, "from the night into the waxing moon, from the moon into the world of gods and into the world of winds, passing through the atmosphere, smoke, clouds, rainfall and plants. The smoke of sacrifice changes from air to smoke, and then into frost and clouds and rain, and falls on the earth as snow. All souls evaporate in the atmosphere...Where did Nirmal go from the crematorium?"

"The winds shall carry away my breath, the sun shall draw a blind over my eyes, the moon shall put me to sleep. The hair of my body is being turned into shrubs and nettles, trees grow out of my head, blood is transformed into water," said Talat.

"Deep sleep, deep waters, deep dreams," intoned Hari Shankar. "The elements are meditation. The winds have gone to sleep, only death remains. The body thinks and feels; when it finishes, everything else finishes too. The burning fire, cool water, pleasant winds, have all come out of their own swabhav." He raised his right hand in a gesture unknown to himself. To Talat he looked at that moment like the red-robed priest of Kali she had once seen at Kali Ghat.

"Many have to die still, I am going before them. I am going with them. I look back—what happened to those who are dead already? I look ahead—what will happen to those who die after me...?" she said thoughtfully. "There is only one life and one death. There is no return."

"The little ant, it climbed the hill with elephants in its ear," Kamal was heard singing a Purbi folk song. "I saw a strange happening: the river was drowning in the boat."

"Light spread on the hills every morning. I repeat the seven voices with King David," said Michael who had turned into a rabbi.

Kamal went back to his singing.

"We have found the world wanting," said Hari Shankar. "Our innocence has been our doom. We are tied to each other with this bloody innocence. The day one of us cuts loose we shall be scattered. The rope of our culture has already snapped and we hang in mid-air on its separate ends."

"Forget your ghosts, forget your ghosts," said Gulshan the materialist.

"Whatever I do, I feel as if all my actions are directly connected with the cosmic cycle. I try to laugh in order to hide the importance of my actions which can adversely affect others. The voice of the Lord our God is above the waters, his terrifying, destructive, annihilating voice which breaks the cedars of Lebanon into pieces," Michael continued.

"Then the voice turns into Nataraj's Tandav Nritya," Surekha spoke through her own mystery.

"A thousand yogis sat in the forests, singing. I heard their chant," said Hari Shankar.

"I roamed the meadows of Babylon and Judea playing on my harp," said Michael.

"I heard your voice, too," said Talat, "but you picked up a machine-gun."

Kamal had come back. He began speaking abruptly. "Then the glass door opened. Champa was among those who came in. 'Hello,' she said, ambling towards me. 'Who are these people? What is this place?' This is The Rose of Sharon. And I am telephoning Cook's office. At the moment I am safe, surrounded by tall stone buildings. A solid, marble floor under my feet. Champa is in front of me, she has the same hair-style, same looks, same smartness and poise. She is in a silk sari, her favourite orange. She is glowing in the bonfire of time.

"And I also have the uncomfortable feeling that I am not particularly happy to see her. I haven't felt anything—sorrow, irritation, nothing at all. As a matter of fact I want to run away. Now what can I do if you are Champa Ahmed? How on earth can I help it? In fact, I won't mind in the least if I don't see you for another ten or twelve years.

"Today you look more beautiful than ever. More sensible, dignified, confident of yourself. 'I heard the other day that you were going to Rome, Champa Baji, to dub your voice for the Urdu version of "Bitter Rice" or something, someone told me at the BBC,' I said, to be casual.

"I felt that she wanted to tell me something very important, but checked herself.

"Outside it had started drizzling. 'What are they showing in Studio One, Champa Baji?' I tried to make small talk. People who were coming out of the cinema houses looked extraordinarily sad. The lights were dim, the street-musician on the kerb had never sounded gloomier. The double-deckers and cars in the traffic seemed to be lumbering painfully. Time went limping by on Oxford Street. She pressed her nose against the glass-and-chrome window and quietly observed the street scene. I said goodbye hurriedly and came out.

"Now I have left her far behind, and I am going home. She continues to stand in the noisy whirlpool of boundless silence, her little nose against the glass door. Why am I so tired? Let me sit down here quietly, let me be still," said Kamal and sat down on a rock.

"Like pious thieves we evoked special devas, but our gods betrayed us," said Talat. "Our Thieves' Kitchen has closed down."

"Now I remember nothing," said Kamal raising his face. "Passing years float around me like soap bubbles. Lights glisten on rain-filled streets, the moon rolls over sleeping chimneys, slipping away towards the sea. Sharp winds whistle tipsily across the southern moors, birds of the night are circling over the still, oily waters of heaving harbours.

"Crowds pass by on the bridge, canoes sail on shaded streams. I am on the shore.

"I have to search for a ship whose lights have gone out, a ship which will quietly enter the dark ocean, going towards a place where, I have this gut feeling, there is nobody to say, 'Welcome home, Kamal Reza'. . ." He stood up and started walking back towards the street. Then he repeated, "There is no one to say 'Welcome home'. . ."

65. Stateless

On a frosty morning, a few days later, Talat took the earliest tube to Chelsea. Warm gusts of air blew in the tunnelled gloom of the half-empty Underground station. She emerged on the road and started walking towards Amala's apartment.

Mr Jenkins was on morning duty. Poor old man, he had gone out to fight for his King and Country, lost an empire as well as an arm. The Big Boys had come back as generals and proceeded to write bulky memoirs, but many Tommies became crippled beggars and porters.

Sometimes Mr Jenkins looked like an Eliotonian character who saw women come and go, talking of Abbot & Costello. Did he have any children? Why didn't they look after him? One could not ask personal questions in the West.

"Lousy weather, Miss," he said, beaming. "But we'll hear the first cuckoo pretty soon."

Talat nodded. Optimism and fortitude had kept this nation alive.

Amala had been posted to Ottawa. She stood in the midst of her packed luggage and broke into a recital of lines from "Ash Wednesday". Then she said, "Do you remember how Hari used to copy Prof. Sidhanta: five long years with the length of five long winters—I spent seven years in this lovely country."

Nargis Cowasjee had come to say goodbye. She was soon going to marry her English fiancé.

"Rejoice, rejoice, the best is yet to be," she said happily.

Talat rushed back to St. John's Wood to finish packing for her brother, who was shortly leaving for India.

In her own foyer she was greeted by Mrs Harding, the caretaker. She had a flatlet on the ground floor and, like Mr Jenkins, was also the solitary, silent chorus of the drama.

Kamal was making breakfast. "Why are you sulking so early in the morning?" he frowned.

"I am all right, Jack!" she replied. "I was merely thinking that I'm also like Mrs Harding."

"You're not as fat. . . yet."

"I mean I'll always remain the reporter, the observer, the chronicler."

"You'll always remain the Super Idiot. You'll keep worrying about other people's problems and never give a thought to

yourself. Chances are you'll quite mindlessly miss your boat . .
. That reminds me. . . just find out the exact time of departure
of my boat-train, pack my jing-bang properly, and stop scowl-
ing. With a mug like that nobody will ever marry you."

The ship's orchestra played its farewell tune. Kamal leaned over
the railing and looked down at the quay. His eyes welled up.
He was as emotional as ever, despite having lived in cold Britain for so long. An old European gentleman who stood next
to him placed his hand supportively on his arm. He looked at
the stranger in gratitude; he introduced himself as Prof. Hans
Krammer from Vienna. Kamal went to his state-room. His
cabin-mate turned out to be an American, Thomas Samson,
an economist, going to India on a Fulbright scholarship.

All Kamal's friends had come to Euston Station—his Bengali
comrades had even burst into the Nazrul Islam chorus, "On,
on, on, drums are rolling in the sky. . . On. . ." He was a
soldier marching onwards to take part in battles whose purpose was not quite clear.

In Portsmouth he was all alone. The world had begun to
look strange from the moment he ascended the gangway. In
the afternoon he made a round of the boat. The voyagers included families of Pakistani and Indian diplomats, American
tourists, students returning home. He ran into Pandit Gaur, a
young Gandhian from western U.P. Kamal used to know him
in London. Together they befriended a group of European
Indologists who were going out to India. Some were planning to stay there for a few months to attend the 2500th birth
anniversary of the Buddha. The Government of India was going to celebrate the event with great fanfare as an international
festival. Dr Hans Krammar was an Austrian scholar of Pali,
and a British poet was en route on an assignment for the BBC.
All of them began to spend their time together.

A French bhikshu called the Rev. Premananda remained
aloof, engrossed in his meditation. A Pakistani Ahmediya missionary based in West Germany tried a couple of times to preach
Islam to the misguided White infidels, but they were too deeply
involved with Booda to pay him any attention. In England

Kamal had noticed two different kinds of Orientalists—the Islamicists were Pakistan-oriented while the scholars of Hinduism and Buddhism were indifferent or even subtly hostile to Islam. Well, everybody can't be omniscient like Arnold Toynbee, Kamal consoled himself. On board, they had all the time in the world to thrash out these matters. As they approached the Suez the world became sultry and Kiplingesque. Till only ten years ago it was still Pax Britannica.

While they were crossing the Canal the discussion drifted towards E.M. Forster. The British poet said, "Forster wrote his novel in 1924, at which time he created Dr Aziz as a representative Indian. Dr Aziz is no longer Indian—Muslims are now identified only with Pakistan." He glanced at Kamal and added, "Now, our Kamal Reza is not the typical Indian, only our Pandit Gaur is."

The remark hit Kamal between the eyes. He sat there motionless. Lightning seemed to have struck him. Perhaps he was now stateless. The friends continued to sip beer and talk of other things while they passed slowly through the date-palm lined muddy waters.

In another corner of the deck a Maharashtrian woman began singing a Mira song in which the naughty child Krishna told his mother he hadn't stolen the butter.

Maiyya mori, main nahin makhan khayo,
Bhor bhai gayyan ke pachche Madhuban mohe
*Pathayo, Maiyya mori. . .**

Kamal forgot the unexpected anguish caused by the Briton's realistic commment, and was instantly lost in the song. Pandit Gaur began to beat time with his hands and soon, both he and Kamal strolled towards the singer.

"Every culture has its secret language," said the British poet, "and Kamal and the Pandit share it. That is the whole point. If a westerner were to write a novel about India he probably

---

* I didn't steal the butter, Ma,
   At early dawn you sent me out with the cows to Honeywood. . . Ma,
   I did not . . .

wouldn't understand why they're both so carried away by that song."

Strains of a waltz floated out of the ballroom, outside an old Robert Taylor film was being shown. Kamal moved away and prowled around aimlessly, greeting some acquaintances with feeble 'hellos'. On the deck, Sikh businessmen from Glasgow were singing Heer* at the top of their voices. They also shared a secret language with the Muslims and Hindus of Punjab, and yet they had butchered one another in the riots of 1947. Politics has always been mightier than culture.

A full moon was rising sluggishly over the horizon. The boat moved forward with ease and dignity; the French Buddhist sat on a deck-chair in a corner. They entered the Arabian Sea.

Snow-white foam shone in the moon. Everywhere, on all the oceans of the globe, all manner of ships were sailing on this seemingly shoreless sphere of liquid moonlight. *The Constitution, The Queen Elizabeth, The United States*, yachts of the rich, cargo boats, destroyers, aircraft-carriers. All kinds of people voyaged on the high seas—diplomats, cardinals, American tourists. Gujarati and Sindhi businessmen. Indian dancers. Pandit Nehru and Maulana Abul Kalam Azad were in New Delhi and all was well with the world.

"I have probably become stateless, and this is not your sukhvati, your state of bliss, Brother Ananda," Kamal said politely to the French monk, and went back to his cabin. He banged the door shut and didn't go down for dinner.

Half the ship emptied at Karachi. The Indologists exchanged addresses and points of contact with Kamal as they approached Bombay harbour.

The Colaba lighthouse was sighted.

Kamal reached Lucknow, which by now had become a derelict and shabby city. Gulfishan looked deserted. The garden had

---

* Heer Ranjha, a seventeenth-century Sufi allegory by the mystic poet Waris Shah, a classic of Punjabi literature, popularly sung in rural Punjab.

withered, the garage and stable had been turned into godowns. ("All Pakistan-bound relatives dump their extra luggage in here," his mother told him placidly.) His eyes searched for Ganga Din, Qadeer and Qamrun. He called out, "Hussaini's wife, Ram Autar, Ram Daiya!" No one answered. They were not there. Ganga Din had died of old age, the driver had gone back to Mirzapur, Hussain to Karachi with Mrs Amir Reza. And Ram Autar had found a better-paid job as a gardener in Sikander Bagh.

Finally, Kamal went into his room, fell on his bed and began to cry. Was he really so disturbed by his father's destitution? He had spent his life railing against the feudal order. Now, after the abolition of zamindari, they were almost starving in Gulfishan. "Long live the Revolution! You ought to be pleased to see your old Mian Jan a pauper," Taqi Reza Bahadur told him bitterly. "They abolished zamindari first in U.P. because most of the landowners were Muslims."

"Oh, no, Mian Jan," he had protested.

His sister Tehmina had come to meet him from Jhansi. She told him, "The Raja of Nanpura is selling his crockery and Mummy has sold off half her jewellery. The money you and Talat have been remitting from Britain was all spent on Mummy's very expensive medical treatment. And, of course, they won't accept a penny from me, being a married daughter. However, I have sent this girl to cook for them."

Kamal went to Water Chestnut House and had a good cry, remembering Nirmala. Her aged parents were shattered because they had lost a daughter, his own parents didn't realise that they had unwittingly lost a country.

He asked his father, "What do you intend doing now? Migrate to Iraq like the Raja of Mahmudabad or go to Pakistan?"

"I will stay right here," the old man replied serenely. "Why should I run away?"

Kamal was puzzled, "But Mian Jan, you'd made such a show of joining the Muslim League."

"That's all right. Pakistan has come into being, well and good. In the circumstances, there was no alternative. Muslims had long been exploited economically. That does not mean that I run away from my own country," he said wearily and looked at the clock. He had to sell another government compensation bond at one-third its value for Kalyanpur lands today. That was their only means of income in Gulfishan.

"Do you think I would go and stay as a poor relation at Amir's place in Karachi? Certainly not!" said his mother. "At least we live in our own house over here."

Kamal began to look for a job.

"Get a letter of recommendation from some influential person," his father advised him.

"Why should I? Don't I have confidence in myself?"

"Yes. But you belong to the wrong community."

"Are Hindus given good jobs in Pakistan?" he retorted.

"No. But Pakistan does not claim to be a secular state."

Same arguments. Same answers.

Kamal wrote to Talat: "Continue working in London. Join the Indian diaspora, but don't go to Pakistan."

Talat replied: "Why are you so demoralized? This is precisely the time when your integrity and courage of conviction will be tested. Keep up the fight."

He heard from Gautam who was in New York, but didn't write back. Hari Shankar had returned from abroad and was posted in Bangalore. Kamal didn't contact him, either.

Amir Reza sent him letter after letter from Karachi: "Come over at once. We need highly qualified scientists like you. Stop being such an ass—a man's career should come before everything else. Don't waste any more time."

He stopped opening Amir's letters.

Amir Reza had opted for Pakistan in 1947. Somebody in the Department of the Custodian of Evacuee Property woke up to the fact after eight years. Since one member of the Reza family had become a Pakistani, Gulfishan was deemed evacuee property—Syed Taqi Reza and his son were declared 'intending evacuees'. They filed a suit challenging the Custodian's decision.

Now Kamal spent most of his time going round the law courts, briefing the lawyers, writing out petitions. He had become extremely bitter; he rarely laughed, and his natural gaiety had given way to sourness and irritability.

He went to Delhi in search of a job and, as usual, stayed at Laj's place on Bela Road. One morning as he walked up to the Maiden's Hotel post office, he ran into Thomas Samson who had travelled with him on board the ship from England.

"Hi, Kim! So glad to meet you again!"

"Ah! You did tell me you would be staying at the Maiden's. I was meaning to contact you. Have you 'done' Delhi, Tom?"

"Not yet."

"I'll show you 'round," Kamal said eagerly. In an instant he had became the Kamal of old, free from the worries of earning a livelihood, the zealous, proud son of free India. In the afternoon he took Tom to see the new National Physical Laboratory, in the evening he planned to go to Sapru House for a sarod recital by Ustad Ali Akbar Khan. He telephoned Gulshan to meet them at 'Alps'.

"What are you doing these days?" Tom asked him while they were sipping cold coffee in a restaurant in Connaught Circus. Gulshan had also joined them.

"Nothing in particular, looking for work," he replied, trying to sound casual.

"Unemployment is a major problem out here," observed Tom earnestly.

"It's a problem for everyone, not just for me. When prosperity comes to the land, it will also be for everybody, it won't go distinguishing between Hindus and Muslims. We shall sink and swim together. Now, with the Second Five Year Plan. . ."

"You are an aristocrat," Gulshan interrupted him with his usual frankness. "You can never declass yourself. . ."

"This is not true, Gulshan. Countless feudal families have been declassed in one stroke with the abolition of zamindari, reduced to abject poverty. And most of them happen to belong to my community," Kamal replied.

"Even you are talking like a communalist!" Gulshan remarked.

"Indian Muslims must pay the price in various ways for the division of India," said Tom.

"Yeah," Kamal shot back. "World Jewry must continue to be blamed for the crucifixion of Jesus Christ."

Tom kept quiet. He was Jewish.

"Why don't you go to Pakistan, yaar, they need scientists," Gulshan suggested gravely. "Droves of highly qualified non-Muslims come back to India, don't find suitable employment and return to settle down in the West. It's being called the brain-drain—join it. Your going away to Pakistan will not be such a world-shaking event. Personally, I woudn't have returned from London but Surekha wanted to build her dance career at home. And now she has found that the country is teeming with Bharatanatyam dancers. Anyway! Don't be such a damn fool idealist, yaar. Go."

Kamal was leaving for Lucknow by the night train, and met the Urdu poet Hamraz on the platform. Hamraz had gone to Karachi from London and was now on his way to Fyzabad to visit his ailing Indian mother.

"How is everything with you, Kamal Mian?" he asked with concern.

"Fine, Hamraz Bhai."

"Things don't look fine to me, Kamal Mian. What is the matter?"

"Nothing at all, Hamraz Bhai." Kamal quickly said goodbye to Hamraz Fyzabadi and hurried towards his compartment.

At long last Kamal obtained a visitor's visa from the Pakistan High Commission. He had spent many a sleepless night before arriving at this decision. For the last few days he had been trying to hide himself from the world. Shadows seemed to dance about in the empty rooms of Gulfishan. Kamal carried on a terrible dialogue with himself—You blasted coward. Rat. What happened to all your nationalism? Talat is right. One ought to become a grass-cutter and work for the Revolution. Damn you, mercenary weakling, no-good opportunist. Damn, damn, damn.

There were no vacancies at the moment, even in the Muslim University at Aligarh. He had decided, however, that he would just not forsake his country—he would be one of the eight crore Muslims who were citizens of India. Why had they been written off?

The Rezas lost their case. Both Khyaban in Dehra Dun and Gulfishan in Lucknow were finally declared evacuee property. Next morning when Kamal woke up he found himself a homeless unemployed refugee in Lucknow. On Monday morning police officers arrived to lock up the bungalow. Kamal requested them to wait so that they could pack their suitcases. On Wednesday Kamal boarded the train along with his aged parents, on Thursday the train reached Delhi. On the sixth day the train crossed the border, on the seventh day Kamal was in Karachi, Pakistan.

66. Letter from Karachi

Karachi, capital of the fifth largest state in the world. Beautiful houses in posh localities, witness to the fact that never before had the Muslim middle classes acquired such prosperity. But otherwise the situation is not very different from India. The nouveau riches ruled this land of the very poor, and how well the former natives of Uttar Pradesh have transplanted themselves on alien soil! The solid Muslim middle classes form the backbone of 'refugee' society. Once a year they go to India to visit members of their families still living in that country, and they still refer to India as 'home'. You will usually find a very ardent and patriotic Pakistani remarking casually that he or she is going home in December for two months. Therefore, home is Sandila or Moradabad, country is Pakistan— not unlike first generation Armenians or Poles or Greeks in America who refer to the place they come from as "the Old Country". This is a human problem. They even have a Bangalore Town in Karachi, but India would be a cipher for those Mohajirs' children who are born here.

Some intellectuals of my acquaintance often get together in a coffee house for lunch, and in the evenings they assemble in some rich friend's drawing-room to discuss politics. They are all very anti-Establishment.

Islam has become useful for politicians. It is being presented to the world as an aggressive, militant, even anti-culture religion. Its promoters are not concerned with Islamic humanism or the liberalism of medieval Arab scholars or Iranian and Indian poets and Sufis. But there are other encouraging signs. Purdah has more or less disappeared, girls are taking up careers and some have become high-ranking officers in the medical corps of the defence forces. Going abroad for higher education has become the norm for young women. What I find odd, though, is how upper-class women, the Begums, have taken to ballroom dancing en masse!

I don't think we realise what a terrible world our generation inherited from our parents. Look at the situation today, in 1956. When a young Muslim man graduates from an Indian university he comes over to Pakistan and becomes a pilot or a member of the civil service. He believes that even if he were to appear for the Competitive Examinations of the Indian Civil Service, he would not be selected. In other words, the demoralised Indian Muslims must continue paying the price for Pakistan, even though most of them had nothing to do with its creation.

In the demand for Pakistan, Urdu was most thoughtlessly declared to be the language of a "separate Muslim nation", so now it is also paying the price for the creation of the "homeland". In India it has almost become a non-language. The word 'Urdu' is now associated with Pakistan and creates an emotional and psychological block for most Hindus. Therefore it continues to be the language of films and film songs but is called Hindi. By abolishing Urdu in schools they have also impoverished their own culture.

It is Saturday night, and I have just returned from the posh house of a local intellectual. His friends include a few interesting foreigners, and I met two very well-read and pleasant Americans there tonight, Jacob Morrison and Mary Richards. Jacob knows a lot of Urdu too and is easily one of the most scholarly men I have met anywhere. (It is rumoured that both of them are

CIA.) *This club is a kind of Hyde Park Corner. Some of these young Pakistanis are real non-conformists. They remind me of my own old friends. They love to argue, and argue fiercely and brilliantly. A fine crowd. I mean to see more of them during my stay here.*

Tonight a very old American historian came to the Saturday Club, passing through Karachi on his way to Tokyo. He addressed me sadly: "The subcontinent would have been one of the Great Powers if you hadn't split. What would have happened to us if America had been divided after the Civil War? Don't repeat your famous theory that the real cause of Partition was economic. What else was it? That is what I want to find out. . ." He waved his hand and looked at me with his large, melancholy eyes.

"I merely wish to know the real cause of the Decline of the East. I asked Prof. Toynbee, too. Why did India fall in the 18th century?" Mary Richards wondered aloud.

"India had an inadequate irrigation system," replied Jacob Morrison gravely. "The problem is purely agricultural."

"Unlike the sea-faring medieval Arabs the Mughals were originally horsemen from landlocked steppes. They didn't build a navy to guard their vast coastline. Tipoo Sultan did. But it was too late."

"The Ottomman Turks were originally horsemen, too," I objected. "But till the 17th century, as a European naval power, they considered the Mediterranean to be a mere Turkish lake."

"O.K. But what was the basic cause of the decline of Islam?" Mary persisted.

"The Asharites," Tanveer, the host, replied shortly.

"Who?"

"The Asharites. Their philosophy of pre-destination replaced the doctrine of the Muattazalites— the rationalists who believed in Free Will. The Pre-destination School become all powerful, because after the Mongol Invasion and the Fall of Baghdad in 1256—" Tanveer paused and began again with some emotion, "Do you know that the Mongols threw all the books of all the libraries of Baghdad into the Tigris and used them as a bridge? The water of the Tigris turned black with ink."

"Who were the Asharites, for god's sake," Mary repeated her question.

"After the Fall of Baghdad people thought this must have been the Will of God that all the intellectual achievements of Islam be destroyed and the Caliphate knocked down by the barbarians. Pre-destination—this was the Asharite dogma— which is followed to this day by the majority of Muslims—-

"Another irony—Raja Rammohun had studied in an Arabic madrassa and was influenced by the Muattazalite philosophy. Thus those Rationalists indirectly figure among the founders of Hindu Reformation, while the Muslims discarded them eight hundred years earlier!"

"Ah, but the Sunni church could not very well adopt the Shia Muattazalites' doctrine—" Jacob commented knowledgeably.

Thus it went on and on. . . . till we dispersed at 1.30 in the morning and drove to the airport to have coffee. I have come home only an hour ago. I was too sleepless, so I started writing this letter to you.

Now, I must tell you the big news. Yesterday, I, Dr. Kamal Reza, revolutionary, ardent believer in the destiny and greatness of a United India and so on and so forth, ate my hat and was appointed on a post starting with a salary of twelve hundred rupees a month. I have to set up a laboratory in East Pakistan and may be sent to the United States soon to buy some apparatus. Next week I am leaving for the East Wing; shall write to you from Dacca.

Dawn is breaking. I have spent the entire night writing this disjointed letter. Just now I drew the curtains and looked out. Karachi has woken up. Karachi is going to work. Hundreds of thousands of people riding on bicycles and cycle rikshaws and buses are advancing towards factories and workshops. They are mostly Muhajirs. These are the people who were referred to as the 'lovable masses' in our Party jargon. It was not their fault, Talat. They deserved to live in peace, eat and sleep with at least a roof over their heads. I witness a sea of workers on their way to the P.I.D.C. Dockyards which are under construction at the moment. It is, honestly, a thrilling sight. They are the new proletariate and they will bring about the socialist revolution in Pakistan.

It is foolish to think that India Divided can be reunited again. The map of the world changes after every world war. It changed after 1945, too.

I once borrowed Lin Yu Tang's Leaves in the Storm from Hari Shankar and read it sitting inside my cosy room in Gulfishan.

So, shall I consider myself a mere trembling leaf, blown far away from my rose-garden—Gulfishan?

Think of the Palestinians. I have found a home, they haven't.

I have always dreamed of creation and not of destruction. Do you think I am going to allow myself to be lost in the vacuum of despair? Oh no, Talat, I shan't let this happen to me.

I will re-construct.

First I will construct a house for myself, ha, ha.

Amir Reza's mansion has been built by a famous firm of Italian architects. Mrs Amir Reza is an unmitigated bitch. Her lavish dinner parties are faithfully reported in the glossy society magazine called The Mirror. She is hell-bent on my rehabilitation (her younger sister is studying in Nainital, U.P.). This Abominable Sister-in-law of ours has just arranged for me to buy 1,000 square yards of land through one of her influential uncles and I'll get a house-building loan of sixty thousand from my department. Yesterday when the Signor came to see me with the blue-print, I wanted to tear my hair and howl.

Our parents will stay in Cousin Amir's annex till my house is built. Father spends the day reading newspapers and does not talk much. Mother keeps meeting her friends and relatives who have migrated from Lucknow. I understand my parents' plight. Asad Mamoo has died of old age and loneliness in Neelampur.

With love,

> *Yours,*
> *Kamal*

P.S. Met Roshan Kazmi at a party. She is married and looks O.K. Sajida Begum has become a political leader. She hasn't changed. "It's a sad tragedy," she told the press in her condolence message, when some worthy died the other day. Good old Sajida Apa. I wanted to ask her, what's a happy tragedy? Perhaps she would have replied, "Yours, dear Kamal."

67. The Road to Sylhet

India of the Middle Ages. Jaunpur, Gujarat, Bengal and Malwa of the Sultanate period. Mandu's Hindola Mahal, the Chaurasi Gumbad of Kalpi, pre-Mughal India. He placed his hands on cold grey stones which belonged to the past and the present at the same time. He contemplated the decorative motifs— arabesque, lotus flowers, Gandharvas, elephants. He touched the slim bricks of the minarets, paced up and down the labyrinths and peered into the dark underground halls of medieval forts. Often a village girl would pass through a broken arch, tending her flock of goats or an urchin would suddenly dive from a peepul tree into an ancient, murky well. Once a grasping, blind mendicant drifted into a deserted palace, sat down among fallen columns and smoked his coconut hookah. The glassy-blue sky hung low over glazed Persian domes and silent courtyards. Clouds rose from the mist-clad hills of the western ghats and broke over the Sufi hospices of Bijapur. The sorrowful, silent, deserted India of the Middle Ages was bathed in sea-like rain, the weeds and grass heaved in strong winds.

He returned to the local dak bungalow at sundown and had his glass of whiskey on the veranda. The khansama made him an excellent English dinner, followed by caramel pudding. How did the fellow manage to produce such a repast in god-forsaken places, and at such short notice? One of the wonders of Hindustan.

He felt a bit awkward for he was held in awe by the common people. Even educated Indians became self-conscious in his presence. The White Saheb's mystique was intact. Sometimes he too felt he was a very special person. Perhaps the solar hat and the tropics did it. Now he understood what Champa had told him that last day over the phone about the inherent superiority complex of Englishmen.

In the former princely states he found that commoners still held their erstwhile feudal masters in affection and esteem. That may be the reason why, down the centuries, Indians had continued to be ruled by a variety of rajahs, sultans and British viceroys—they loved pomp and splendour, and kow-towed to authority.

The dak bungalow's khansama came in and said deferentially, "Huzoor, the gharry is ready to take you to the railway station." So he went back to Calcutta, took a Dakota plane to Dacca, and travelled to Sylhet on an over-crowded train.

Sylhet, at last, was his destination.

The train stopped with a jerk at a small wayside station. All manner of voices reached his ears swimming through his drowsiness.

"Boiled eggs. . . Hot tea. . . Hot tea. . . Boiled eggs. . . Bananas. . . Bananas. . ."

He pushed up the window shutter and looked out. A cool wind brought in the earthy fragrance of freshly ploughed land. An old and bent Hindu carrying numerous little bundles walked briskly down the platform. Hindu women with glittering red sindhur on their foreheads and in the parting of their hair, little girls in multi-coloured cotton saris, Hindu gentlemen in white dhotis, Muslims in chequered sarongs. Half-naked children, Anglo-Indian guards, palanquin-bearers. The train moved. The babel of Bengali voices dissolved in the running dark as the train puffed along past little lakes covered with water-lilies.

Sometimes a woman could be seen standing in the doorway of her thatched hut among wild orchids. In an instant her purple sari mingled in the dark. Women carrying lanterns— what would be the stories of their lives? Their world-view? Their philosophy? The distance of time covered by them between birth and death? Suffering. Destitution. Famines.

He closed his eyes again.

'Allah give us rain, give us rice. . . give us clothes.' The words of the Bengali ballad song in his ears. He had heard it the other day at a cultural function in Dacca. 'Allah, give us rice. . .' And how he had always romanticised Bengal!

The train came to a halt at another little station. The starched turban of a dignified bearer loomed before his sleepy eyes.

"Dinner, Saheb?" the bearer whispered reverentially.

He nodded and pulled up his blanket.

Labourers from eastern U.P. worked on his tea estate in Sylhet. Ram Daiya, and Ram Autar; Lachman and Sita, Trilochan and Chambelia. . . Two names seemed to be very popular among the purbis. . .Ram and Sita! Ram and Sita!!! The Golden Era of India, the classical period. The Heroic Age—Ayodhya, Lakshnavati, Shravasti. Ram Chandra and Oudh and Janak Kumari Sita of Mithila. Ram and Sita. . . The undernourished labourers of his tea-garden. . .

"Dinner, Saheb. Coffee or tea?" The bearer placed the tray in front of him. Cyril sat up and remembered that he had to reach Srimangal on time. He was to tour Rangamati and Chandraghona and Bandarban; he had to make more money.

The train arrived at Sylhet in the morning, and the Eurasian, Peter Jackson, as usual, awaited him at the station.

It was late in the evening and they drove straight towards the Surma river. Old men and women carrying smoky lanterns boarded the country-craft. Others were coming ashore in hordes—the outboard motor-boat had returned from the other bank. A blind beggar recited Quranic verses, his loud monotone, awe-inspiring. Two blind men had climbed into a canoe, one blind woman sat under a tree, motionless. Planks were attached to the motor-boat and the Mercedes was driven on to the deck.

Peter hired a *nauka*. The river bank was left behind. Suddenly a strong wind rose and the canoe began to rock.

Cyril Ashley picked up the lantern and looked around anxiously. "Peter, have we run into a storm?" Then he called out to the boatman. "I say, look here, er, what do they call you, boatman?" he asked in broken Bengali.

"Abul Monshur, Saheb. . ."

"Abul Monshur, let me help you with the oars."

"It's all right, Saheb, Allah is my Captain," he replied placidly. Cyril peeped under the roof. The little boat contained all the earthly belongings of old Abul Mansur Kamaluddin. Lantern, the prayer mat, pots and pans, a coconut hookah. This was the white-haired boatman's entire world, rocking on the angry waves of the Padma.

Cyril felt strange. He rubbed his tired eyes and tried to convince himself that it was real, that a meaningless sequence of events had scooped him out of the lanes of Cambridge and deposited him in this boat, in this fantastic, beautiful land called East Bengal, Pakistan. He looked around again. A streak of bright yellow extended over the dark waters. A big sampan sailed past majestically, the moon rose slowly behind the willows.

68. *The Circuit House*

Happier times they had spent together continued to swill in their tumblers. Cyril Ashley gazed at the distant blue mountains across which lay the mysterious country of Burma.

"Can we get there by candle-light?" he wondered.

"How many miles to Babylon?" responded Kamal, in the same vein.

A starving pye-dog climbed up onto the veranda through the wooden rails. Cyril gave the hungry visitor a meat pie.

"He may have fled Red China," Kamal said, looking soberly at the dog. "He is an anti-communist doggie. He's come here in search of Freedom."

"You still talk like you used to in Cambridge!"

"I dare say, you are frightfully observant," Kamal replied, and gave the dog a chicken sandwich. "No Cyril, I can prove my bona fides." He took out a brand new, shining green passport from his pocket and showed it to his friend.

"Have you come here to plan the Karanaphully Paper Mills? Most people do."

"I have come here to eat my hat. Is it any of your bloody business? Haven't you turned up to suck the blood of poor miserable Bengali labourers. . . like your famous ancestor did? Bah. . . Well. I admit I'm a lousy renegade. So?"

He is about to go in for another bout of self-pity, thought Cyril gloomily and picked up his cup of tea.

The Hon'ble Cyril Howard Ashley had reached the Chittagong Hill Tracts the day before after crossing many a river, hill and thicket on the tortuous way. He had journeyed from Srimangal to Chittagong, from where his tea was exported to the great markets of the world.

On hearing the news that he had divorced Rose, his brother, Lord Ashley, heaved a sigh of relief—the prodigal had returned from Bohemia. Lord Ashley still owned tea gardens in Sylhet. One evening he called Cyril to his club near Green Park and said, "Would you like to become a tea-planter for a change? You'll have plenty of time to do your Lord Cornwallis."

Cyril nodded in agreement. There was no further scope in life for argument.

He was visiting the Hill Tracts on business. Last evening he had returned to Rangamati Circuit House and caught sight of a young man leaning on the veranda railing overlooking the Karanaphully River. On hearing his footfall the young man turned and saw him. It was Kamal Reza. "Dr. Livingstone, I presume?" he grinned, and told Cyril how he had had to migrate from India to Pakistan. He was touring the East Wing before setting up a laboratory in Dacca. They talked of old friends. "I've been here more than three years," said Cyril, "lost touch—"

"Champa has become a barrister. She has come back to India. Talat keeps me informed. Soon after the Hindu Code Bill was passed Shanta obtained a divorce from her husband. She has married Bill Craig. And Nargis Cowasjee was murdered."

"*Murdered?*"

"On her honeymoon. Cruising aboard her own yacht. Allegedly by her British husband. Presumably for money."

The bamboo cinema-hall was located at the bend in the river. The Urdu dialogue of "Baiju Bawra", the latest musical hit from India, became audible in the intense stillness of the night. Lata Mangeshkar's crooning wafted across the Karanaphully, and Kamal listened thoughtfully. Lata's voice is a bridge which unites the two enemy countries, he thought.

"Are you aware of the existence of Lata Mangeshkar?" he asked Cyril, pointlessly.

"Lata. . . Mang. . . who. . .?" repeated Cyril, startled.

The Head Cook brought fresh tea.

The Governor-General of Pakistan, General Iskander Mirza, a former member of the British Indian Political Service, had returned to Karachi from Bandarban after an elephant-trapping expedition. The bamboo Circuit House had been specially redecorated for his visit, and the pomp and circumstance of the Governor-General's visit had reminded the Head Cook of the good old days of Sir Fredric Bourne.

"There must have been quite a do here last week," said Kamal.

"Yes, Huzoor, the Laat Saheb is as magnificent as the real white Laat Sahebs from before. Huzoor," the cook glanced around and whispered, "the place is full of trouble-makers. They are over here, too. They are everywhere. . ."

"Over here. . ."? Kamal felt as though desperate terrorists lurked in the surrounding forests—any moment they could attack the Circuit House and kill him. Then maybe he would be called a martyr. The thought consoled him.

Kamal and Cyril stayed in Rangamati for a week.

The local rajah, who was the chief of one of the hill tribes of East Pakistan, had been educated at Oxford. He invited Cyril and Kamal to dinner. In the Raj Bari across the river, Kamal saw the touching spectacle of a dying Princely India. A little cannon adorned the garden, nearby stood a white stone temple. The modest royal mansion was lighted by dim electric bulbs. The hall was lined with oil portraits of royal ancestors in Mughal dress. "Some of these fellows included the Mughal governors of Bengal and Assam," Cyril promptly enlightened Kamal in an undertone, referring to a tattered volume of the *Imperial Gazetteers* of this region which lay on a shelf in the Circuit House drawing-room. "Therefore, racially, this chap is partly Mughal. His religion is Hindu-Buddhist, and ethnically he may even be Mongol or Tibeto-Burman. The labyrinths of Indian history can drive one up the wall."

"Have you come from Pakistan?" the Rajmata graciously asked Kamal.

He was a bit confused. Isn't this Pakistan as well? Or is it? He pondered the question. What exactly is meant by country?

This Raj Bari and the special world contained within it belong to which country—India or Pakistan?

"You must visit Sitakund," the Rajmata suggested. "There are sulphur deposits on top of the hill and a fire burns all year round in the temple. It's a beautiful place."

When they took their leave Kamal made a formal bow, unconsciously reverting to the feudal etiquette of Lucknow. "Goodbye, Rani Saheba, Raja Saheb," he said with a flourish. The next morning they motored down to Chittagong and boarded a train for Sitakund. A ticket-checker entered the compartment, saw their tickets and leaned against the wall.

"Do sit down. Do you smoke?" Kamal offered him a cigarette. He stared at Kamal in disbelief. Then he sat down at the edge of the seat with some hesitation.

"Do you belong to this part of the province?" Kamal asked, to put him at ease.

"Yes, sir. My village is right there, across the betelnut grove," he replied pointing out of the window.

During the journey, Kamal learned many other things about him. The ticket-checker was suffering from T.B., he was low-paid and had to support five marriageable sisters. He was not at all satisfied with the present ministry at Dacca.

His political insight was amazing. He argued like a university student and spoke fluent English. A mere tubercular babu whose life was spent checking tickets on a branch line of East Bengal Railways.

"Before the creation of Pakistan one hardly ever came across a Muslim travelling first or second class, the Bengali Muslims were so depressed economically," he continued earnestly. "Now I feel thrilled when I see my own brethren-in-Islam lounging in air-conditioned coaches."

The train approached the next halt.

"Shall I tell you something," the ticket-checker rose from the seat and addressed Kamal, "I have been travelling on this line since 1947. You are the first high-ranking official from West Pakistan who has spoken to me courteously, and asked me to sit down. I will always remember you." He got out of the compartment and vanished into the crowd.

"We would like to visit Sitaji's Temple," Kamal said to a passing coolie when they got off at a wayside station.

"Do not go there at this time, Saheb. The hilltop is very high, there are leopards and pythons and it will get quite late by the time you come back," the Station Master said respectfully, coming forward.

"No, we have got to go," Cyril insisted.

Immediately the news of their arrival spread in the hamlet. A palanquin was brought on to the platform, and the young girl sitting inside peeped through its red curtains.

"Our Maulvi Saheb's daughter. She is going back to her in-laws' house," a coolie informed them.

Now the railway constable approached the visitors. "Come with me, Saheb, if you insist, I'll take you to the village." They came out on the mud track. The cool air was full of the sweet smell of wild roses. The police constable immediately started discussing politics—high prices, artificial famine, the Awami League, A.K. Fazlul Haque. Kamal's head reeled. Every single individual in this province seemed to have a distressingly acute political consciousness. There was no doubt that he was in Bengal.

Soom Kamal noticed that a little boy had started following them along the way and he was saying something to the constable in Chittagongian dialect.

"Prafulla here says he will take you to the temple," the constable told Kamal.

"Hello, Prafulla." Cyril and Kamal solemnly shook hands with the boy.

The mud street of the bazaar had been freshly sprinkled with water. People gathered in front of little shops, chatting and reading newspapers. Cyril entered the tiny bazaar like a white giant. They stopped in front of a little bamboo restaurant. Inside, a few men squatted on wooden benches reading Bengali newspapers. A gramophone blared a Tagore song sung by Laila Arjumand Bano, East Pakistan's famous crooner. The bamboo walls displayed advertisements for the latest Bengali films from Calcutta. This was another world, entirely different from West Pakistan. "We want very hot tea on our return," Kamal said to the restaurant owner "we are off to the Hill." The villagers had already brought fruit and sweets for them from their homes.

"You are our guests, it is our duty to serve you, sir," a bearded Muslim said to Kamal, urging him to eat the bananas.

"Were these the very people who butchered one another in 1947?" Kamal wondered, bewildered.

"Every individual mind," Cyril remarked, "is the net result of a million years of evolution. Sometimes the animal part of the brain takes over."

They made for the hill accompanied by a very serious-faced Prafulla. Local Hindus had started preparations for Saraswati Puja although it was many months away. A number of beautiful and fragile clay statues of the goddess lay about on the grass, painted a shining white. The village potters had placed them outside in the sun to dry. After a short distance they came upon a red-stone tank surrounded by red-stone temples. A curtain of banyan branches hung over the tank steps. They came into another harbour where young girls sat chatting at the edge of a pool.

Through dense foliage, winding stairs led to the hill-top. Ancient, bell-shaped Hindu monasteries stood hidden among the trees all the way up to the peak. Nameless yogis were buried in their sitting postures in these tombs. The fire burned in the sulphur deposits on the peak.

"Queen Sita was left here for a few days by Ravana before he kidnapped her and took her to Ceylon," Prafulla informed them in a matter of-fact kind of running commentary. Sadhus were going downhill. Cyril and Kamal began climbing the stairs again. Now the top was not very far. A waterfall sang under a broken arch. The whistles of homing magpies, the rustling of leaves, the ripples of the cascade, the slow hissing of sulphur flames and the chanting of mantras mingled together and rose slowly like heavy incense. Prafulla climbed up like a contented monkey. "Saheb, be careful," he warned, "the place is full of scorpions and snakes."

Sunlight faded in the leaping dark. "Let's go back. We have to catch the eleven o'clock train," Kamal reminded Cyril after a few minutes.

At the village tea-house their return was being anxiously awaited. They went in like old inhabitants and sat down on a wooden bench. Cups of sweet steaming tea, cheap biscuits and local sweetmeats were placed in front of them reverently. The hosts stood at a respectful distance, shy and eager to please. They did not accept any payment from the "pilgrims". Many villagers accompanied them to the station. Prafulla was walking beside them, silent like an old friend.

Urchins did not pester them for bakshish, and Prafulla refused to accept a tip. He looked very hurt when Kamal offered him a five-rupee note.

"Ban Bibi* will look after you in your journey," the constable said as their train arrived.

69. The Tea Planter

Having crossed streams, forests and the picturesque regions of Maulvi Bazaar, Kamal and Cyril finally arrived at Cyril Ashley's headquarters at Srimangal, Sylhet district. His bungalow stood on a hillock, its lights visible from a distance.

All of a sudden Kamal felt that the old familiar Cyril Ashley had, through some mystic transformation, turned into a Burra Saheb, the traditional White tea-planter. His car entered the imposing porch. Head held high, holding his handkerchief to his nose and looking straight ahead, Cyril ascended the veranda steps. His household staff rushed forward to take his solar hat and binoculars from him. Some labourers who were standing outside, kow-towed meekly. Cyril called out in a peremptory voice: "Abdul Rahman, *pani lagao*—" Then he walked majestically towards the guest-room. "Take your bath first. Dinner at nine," he said to Kamal.

---

* Fatima, daughter of the Prophet, is revered as the patroness of the woods by the forest-dwelling Muslims of East Bengal.

The bungalow was full of expensive teak furniture, its walls decorated with tiger-skin, and stag and bison heads. Kamal felt as though he had stepped back into the India of 1938. He remembered a similar atmosphere from Gulfishan in Lucknow and Khyaban in Dehra Dun. Abdur Rahman brought back memories of Amir Khan, and when Cyril called out to the chauffeur, Kamal thought for a moment that Qadeer would come running.

Exile, exile. . . Oh my god, why did you let me become an exile. . .? He lay himself down on an armchair in his room and covered his eyes with his hands.

Servants were passing through the jute-carpeted gallery. The Bengali accountant hovered in the veranda, a representative of the labourers sat on the porch steps. They were all waiting for Cyril. The hush of obeisance pervaded the bungalow. The bearer, the khidmatgar, the cook, the 'boy' and the Anglo-Indian clerk, Joseph Lawrence, the peons, all stood about deferentially. Cyril Saheb had returned after several weeks and a number of affairs needed his immediate attention. There was only one Cyril Ashley but his personal staff seemed to include any number of men. The gardener, the 'grass-cut', the syce, the water-carrier, the chowkidar. His personal motor-launch was tied to a jetty nearby.

He was the same Cyril Howard Ashley who, just a short while back, had ambled in the quiet lanes of Cambridge with books by Baudelaire and Mallarme in his hand, and eaten fish and chips in a restaurant in the demoralising company of Michael and Denis.

In the morning they had their breakfast in the 'morning room', after which Cyril put on his sola topi and they climbed into his Mercedes. The accountants and clerks led by Joseph Lawrence and Peter Jackson, climbed into a number of jeeps and the whole procession advanced towards the tea-gardens. Cyril showed Kamal his factory, after which they went on to the Planters' Club where Cyril continued enlightening Kamal on the various aspects of high finance. Then he discussed the day's Narayan Gunj Share Market with his fellow-planters and glanced through the financial pages of Calcutta's *Statesman* and *Amrita Bazar Patrika*, and Dacca's *Morning News*. They were sipping beer before lunch, when Kamal disappeared.

"Have you seen Mr. Reza?" Cyril asked Peter Jackson after a while.

"Er. . . I think I saw him going towards the tea-gardens with Nurul Islam Chowdhry, sir," came his reply, heavy with meaning.

"Nurul Islam Chowdhry. . ?" Cyril repeated. Chowdhry was the labourers' spokesman and had come to meet him the night before. He had been told to come to the office in the morning. Cyril drove out to his estate in search of his friend, and parked his car under a flame-of-the-forest. He walked down to the shrubs. The trees were full of birdsong, and the sun, streaming through delicate branches, made lovely patterns of light and shade on the undulating surface of the tea-garden.

He heard the tinkling of glass bangles. A Purbi girl was dextrously plucking tea-leaves, but as soon as she saw him she pulled the anchal of her sari over her dusky face. The Burra Saheb stood right in front, and smiled. Drifting on a slow current of thought he came ashore and asked her in kitchen Bengali, "What is your name?"

"My name? Champa. . ."

"Champa," he repeated, as though he had heard the name for the first time. "Champa," he mumbled again. "Nice name . . . Champa. . .," and made off rapidly towards the car. The girl gazed after him, somewhat amazed, as he vanished in the light-and-shade of the slender trees. Champa, and a whole generation of workers, had come across all sorts of Britons on these estates—eccentric, arrogant, good-hearted, drunk—this particular Burra Saheb was mad.

Cyril returned to the Club and threw himself into a deep armchair. Elizabeth II smiled down at him from the mantelpiece. In another photograph, an English lady, in a sola hat and pre-1914 high-necked dress sat perched uncomfortably in an elephant-howdah. The Maharaja of Cooch Behar sat near her. The English lady's condescending expression reminded Cyril of his own grandmother, Lady Penelope Ashley of Barnfield Hall, who came to India for an occasional tiger-shoot.

"Good morning Granny," he whispered hoarsely and wondered again at Kamal's whereabouts.

Kamal returned to the bungalow late at night. Cyril waited for him in the drawing-room.

"Where have you been?" he demanded crossly, when Kamal entered.

"Oh, nowhere in particular," came the nonchalant reply.

"Did you go to the labourers' village?"

"Yes."

"Look. You belong to this set-up as much as I do, so don't be self-righteous."

"The workers get one rupee four annas a day as their wages?"

"They do."

"Are the communists trying to organise them?"

"I don't know."

"Of course you do. You know everything damn well, because you're sabotaging their attempt to form a trade union."

"Kamal," Cyril lit a cigarette. "You know I once carried the world's cross on my puny shoulders. It was futile, so I threw it off. You have rid yourself of this cross too, remember. Early tomorrow morning we're leaving for Raj Shahi to have a dekko at a Paharpur Gupta sculpture. Now have your dinner and go to bed. Goodnight."

In Raj Shahi district the villas of Hindu zamindars stood very silent in the orchards. Their owners had migrated to India.

"This area is an anthropologists' paradise," a documentary film-maker from the West told them at the Raj Shahi Circuit House. Kamal and Cyril accompanied the film unit to the beautiful interior of the district.

"The Santhals are so poor they eat roots, yet they are so dignified," the foreign camera-man exclaimed.

"We'll keep them hungry and dignified," the young Bengali escort said in a bitter aside to Kamal. "Excellent subject for *National Geographic.*"

"Cyril, East Pakistan is poised for a socialist revolution," said Kamal happily.

The day Cyril and Kamal were returning from Santhal country, the entire population of the last village on the way back gathered in front of the jeep. A jet black, astonishingly beautiful young girl stepped forward, garlanded the visitors with marigolds and bowed gracefully, hands folded. The village headman had tied a stick to the stump of his broken leg, and worn his only ragged shirt in their honour. He came limping to the end of the village to see them off. A lithe Santhal boy dived into a pond, plucked a red lotus with a long stalk and presented it to the departing guests.

The Ganges flowed by the Circuit House in the Civil Lines of Raj Shahi town, and on the other bank lay Murshidabad, in India.

The two friends spent the day in the museum looking at the exquisite Gupta sculpture, and after dinner they strolled by the starlit river.

"The East humbles a person," Cyril told Kamal reflectively. "When I first came to this amazing subcontinent and stayed in out-of-the-way dak bungalows, I marvelled at John Company's efficiency. Then I learned that the Ommaya Caliphs had introduced a postal service throughout the Arab empire way back in the eighth century, and that there were dak chowkies every few miles in the Sultanate in India, complete with rest-houses and wells for couriers and travellers. The I.C.S. is still governing India and Pakistan, but we merely superimposed our system over Akbar's administration. . .

"In our library in Barnfield Hall, we have a rare manuscript of Prince Dara Shikoh's translation of the Upanishads. The fly-leaf carries the name of Babu Radhey Charan who presented it to my forefather, Nabob Cyril. This country gentleman had worked as an accountant in Siraj-ud-Daulah's government over there—" he pointed towards the river, "in Murshidabad."

A boat was coming towards the bank and for an instant, Kamal thought that Babu Radhey Charan, in court regalia, would step ashore. Instead, they heard a gunshot. The patrol boat went past with army jawans—the Ganges formed a natural frontier between India and East Pakistan. Kamal and Cyril turned back towards the circuit house and Cyril continued to talk about Dara Shikoh.

"Do you realise," he said accusingly, "how very Eurocentric even you people have become? The Upanishads were introduced in Europe though Dara Shikoh's book, but only the Orientalist who translated the Persian book is remembered, not that unfortunate and amazing Mughal prince."

A second shot was fired in the distance.

"Another smuggler shot. Or perhaps another border incident," remarked Cyril pensively.

On the way back to Dacca the train stopped at a busy pier of the Ganges and passengers boarded the waiting steamer. Ant-like swarms of coolies transferred luggage from the train to the boat carrying tons of heavy crates, ascending the treacherous gangplank, to the accompaniment of rhythmic noises. Third-class passengers came aboard and flopped down on the floor of the steamer across a grill. The place was teeming with old Hindus. Then the first-class passengers arrived. They went into the cabins, or loitered on the glistening deck. Binoculars and cameras were taken out, newspapers unfolded. Two smart West Pakistani Punjabi begums began knitting, two Bengali maulanas heatedly discussed Awami League politics. A high-ranking West Pakistani official relaxed inside a cabin, drinking beer. He was a former member of the Indian Civil Service now called Central Superior Services in Pakistan, and the Indian Administrative Service in India. Kamal and Cyril surveyed the scene as they stood in a far corner of the deck. What rigmarole was this? What kind of world had come into existence? How many millions of human lives had been lost in the process of the creation of this particular world, how many homes destroyed, how many millions became refugees and exiles? How many millions who used to starve then, continued to starve now?

The high-ranking Punjabi official emerged from his cabin and offered Kamal a cigarette. The river had become molten gold, shining brilliantly in the rays of the setting sun. A huge black jute cargo boat sailed past. Kamal watched it spellbound, experiencing a thrill.

"Magnificent," he muttered.

"Ah," the Punjabi official remarked. "As a matter of fact, these vistas look pretty only from a distance. If you have to actually live out here you begin to realise what is what when you deal with the locals. Lazy. Past masters of intrigue. Parochial. It's a feat of endurance to govern them and keep them out of mischief.

"I assure you, the Bengalis are a self-contained lot, what with their Tagore, there jute and all that. Believe me," the official continued with spirit, "the day this region secedes from Pakistan I shall celebrate that happy event by remaining drunk for a whole week."

They were approaching Narayan Gunj. The sun shimmered in the purple clouds like a burning red caste-mark. Countless boats glided about sailing right up to the sharp outline where river and sky seemed to meet in infinity. A shrivelled old woman shot past, rowing her little canoe with amazing speed. A mighty overpowering distinct world existed over the mighty river. Soon little lamps lit up in the sampans, as though the river was celebrating the Festival of Lights. Muslim boatmen began chanting their prayers in their sailing craft. The wind rose and the masts swelled and fluttered like the gleaming white wings of a thousand cranes.

Back in Dacca the two young men were soon reabsorbed in their respective work. They met at the Dacca Club in the evenings and returned to the rest house together. On a Sunday they went nosing around the medieval lanes of the city and came across old-fashioned horse-carriages rambling slowly through crooked, seventeenth-century streets. The Armenian churchyard was hidden behind the walls and arches of a meandering and mysterious Armani Tola, and they read Armenian names on old tombstones. Hatoon. Aram. Aratoon. Who were these people? How did they live, how did they die? Mrs. Hesipsima Harlary. Aratoon Gregory Sameon. Cathick Avietick Aram Thomas. Hatoon Aram Aratoon of "The Pagoda Tree", Calcutta. . .

Clouds flooded the night sky. The two friends sat in the rest house drawing-room. Cyril was reading a book of medieval Bengali folk songs, in translation.

Champa flowers blossom around the pond. Dark clouds thunder in the sky. Emotions rise in my heart like a flooded stream in August. Stream! Why do you flow so fast, for you know not where you go—Pitcher! Drown yourself in the water like a drop of rain. I, too, am drowned like you.

The pale blue light of the table-lamp looked weary. Lightning blazed across the black sky, typhoons raged in the distance.

"I am leaving for Karachi via India tomorrow," Kamal was saying. Cyril looked up.

"Yes, I suppose you are," he replied.

"I'll be seeing you off and on."

"I hope so."

Asoka leaves under the veranda heaved.

The crow is dark, Cyril read, *the koel is darker, and dark is the water of the Sanjakhali River... but her hair was the darkest...*

Outside, the rain played jal-tarang on a lily pond. Trees and *aparjita* flowers lit up for an instant when lightning flashed again. Cyril read aloud, *"Old Ganga weeps uselessly beyond the champak trees."* He uttered in a strange voice, *"Tell her that I have closed my ears against their call. I have tied my boat to the shore. Tell her."*

"I will," Kamal replied sombrely.

The following morning Kamal left for Tejgaon airport and emplaned for India. From Dum Dum he went straight to Howrah Station. At the platform he noticed a police officer coming towards him briskly. Unnerved, he felt for his passport and travel documents in his coat packet in order to assure himself that he had not entered India illegally. The police officer went his way without looking at him. Kamal continued to feel acutely miserable.

The train began its westbound journey. Burdwan. . . Asansol. . . Patna. . . Mughalsarai. . . Banaras. . . Allahabad. . . hurtling through a strange, unknown land. A year ago this was his own country, the land of his forefathers. Today he was a foreigner here. He felt as though people were looking at him suspiciously. "You are a Pakistani," they seemed to be saying, "Come to the police station. You ought to be in the lock-up. You are a Pakistani—Muslim spy—Muslim spy." The wheels of the train also seemed to be repeating the same clangorous, harrowing, blood-curdling refrain—spy—traitor—spy—traitor—traitor—traitor—-

He opened his eyes, trembling. The train, as usual, glided into Charbagh Junction.

Charbagh, Lucknow.

Lucknow?

He stayed in Golagunj with some relatives for a couple of days. Now he had to proceed to Dehra Dun to have their house deed verified for filing urban property compensation claims in Karachi. He left on the third day. He had nothing to do with Lucknow any more—why should he stay any longer? He was different now, and changed. Lucknow had changed too. Historical monuments were falling to pieces. Hazrat Ganj looked like a slum, the Mall was full of stray cattle. Lucknow had gone to seed.

70. The Pomegranate Tree

Talat had informed him from London that Champa was also back in India and, according to June Carter, staying with her uncle in Moradabad. Kamal had managed to have Moradabad added to his visa for India before leaving for Dacca, and had taken Champa's Moradabad address from Sita Dixit who was still living in the same cottage in Chand Bagh.

"Like Champa, I have also become a wallflower," she said to Kamal with some unconscious inner satisfaction.

The train from Lucknow reached Moradabad at midnight. The first-class waiting room, its regulation railway furniture redolent of British times, was empty. Kamal recalled how the family used to pass through Moradabad on their way to Dehra Dun: Qadeer and Hussaini would jump out of the servants' coupe to appear like grinning genii at the compartment window. Kamal, Tehmina and Talat would stay awake waiting for the midnight wonders of Moradabad platform—tiny brass kitchenware for dolls, blunt Rampuri daggers for Kamal, velvet caps for the servants. . . Every railway station of his childhood had its own special gifts—the petha and miniature soapstone Taj Mahals of Agra, laddoos of Sandila, mangoes of Malihabad, oranges of Nagpur, brass toys of Banaras. Oh, India, India, why did you forsake me? A lump rose in his throat. He shook his head. No, this drooling sentimentality won't do. He stretched himself out on an armchair and dozed. When he awoke, he had his breakfast in the first-class refreshment room, too, and recalled the spick and span Spencers of pre-Independence days. Wait a minute, have I started missing the splendours of colonial India? He came out of the railway station and hired a tonga.

"Police station," he said briefly. The tonga-wallah was a Muslim. He understood and took him to the thana where visiting Pakistanis' arrivals and departures were recorded. The S.H.O. was a Muslim too. The Hindu constable wrote down the necessary details in Urdu calligraphy, taking Kamal by surprise. One year in Pakistan had already disoriented him about India. The police officers offered him steaming tea in a glass and discussed the latest Indo-Pak cricket match.

He gave Champa's address to the tonga-wallah and they made their way through the bazaar. The town seemed to be teeming with Muslims. In the streets people were shouting cheerfully to one another in colourful, colloquial Urdu. How had Partition solved the Muslim problem? Those who had migrated were only a fraction of Muslims in India. The bazaar walls displayed posters in Urdu announcing mushairas, qawwalis and saints' festivals even though there was a preponderence of Hindi signboards on shops.

The tonga reached a seedy locality. Broken terraces gaped in front of arched gates, A drowsy eagle sat on the white-washed wall of a little Shia mosque. Was this where Champa Baji actually belonged? She had always obliquely referred to a stately home in Moradabad.

She needn't have—why spend half her life fantasising about

herself?

A little window opened in a crudely carved wooden gate. He pushed it gently and peered into a damp, hay-filled, airless hall. A few cots lay in the semi-darkness. He lingered for a while uncertainly, then clambered in through the opening and immediately came upon a staircase. It was dark and narrow and crooked and seemed to belong to an earlier century. He called out several times but there was no response. After a few minutes he mustered up his courage and ascended the worn-out steps.

Striking a match in the tunnel-like gloom he soon emerged onto a first floor courtyard, and a room. Its only furniture was a dusty armchair and a four-poster. The trellised balcony over-looked the mosque down below where a solitary maulvi was reciting the Holy Book. He sat near the ablution tank. A plate-ful of something was placed near his prayer-rug. Straining his eyes Kamal saw that it contained fried liver.

Soon the heads of a few street urchins appeared above the mosque wall. The boys began chanting in a monotone: "Goat-liver, goat-liver, Mulla-ji's legs shiver!" This was obviously some kind of local prank! He probably detested the sight of goat's liver and the plate had been placed near his prayer-mat as the result of a wager. So, life was passing peacefully in this obscure little neighbourhood, too!

Kamal went downstairs again and came out into the lane, puzzled by the silence. He espied the local cemetery on a grassy slope adjoining the mosque. Living souls, dead souls. Where are you, Champa Baji? A goat bleated, tied under a shed. A girl peeped through a high window in an ancient wall and moved away the moment she noticed Kamal staring blankly at her. He trudged round the mosque and came upon another gate which seemed to be a replica of the gate-house he had already visited. He reached a sagging terrace and rattled the chain.

"Who is it?" somebody called hoarsely from within. Kamal's own voice drowned in his parched throat. He had never felt more dismayed.

"Who is it, I say?" An old woman in tight black pyjamas

looked out of the gate-window.

"It's me. . ." he faltered.

"What's that? Tell us your name, beta."

"Kamal Reza. From Pakistan."

The crone went in and after a few minutes came shuffling back to open the window.

"Come in, come in, beta," she said absently, chewing paan in her toothless mouth.

He went in, ducking his head through the window. A solitary pomegranate tree stood in the middle of the courtyard. How was it that from Andalusia to Bihar they had always planted a pomegranate tree inside their homes? What was its significance? Most Muslim houses, humble or grand, had a pomegranate tree—they had one, too, in their garhi in Kalyanpur. Kamal was lost in thought. Then he saw Champa— she was sitting on a wooden divan inside the dalaan.

"Champa Baji!"

"Kamal!! Good god!!!" She rose slowly and began to smoothen the faded counterpane.

"I trespassed into the house in front," he said. "Sorry I've turned up like this, but there was no time to inform you."

"Everybody has gone to Barey Abba's place. Let's go there, we must have a long, long chat," she said calmly and took down a light, quilted wrap from the washing line. She covered herself with it, ready to leave. They came out into the lane. "We do not wear the new-fangled burqas out here, *chaddars* and *dulais* are still the proper thing," she explained. Then she led Kamal into a by-lane which branched off from the mosque and continued along the grave-yard slope. Weeds and little peepul tendrils stuck out of the ancient walls on either side.

He followed her timidly into the courtyard where a few chairs and cots were placed in a semi-circle. The sharp smell of fried spices wafted out of the kitchen.

"Barey Abba, this is Kamal Reza," he heard Champa's voice call out in the darkness.

"Aha! Welcome, welcome, son," the old man who had been lying on one of the cots said warmly, sitting up. "Sit down, here on this chair. No, no, not on this—this one is more comfortable. You have honoured us indeed with your kind visit."

A young girl went into the kitchen, another sat in the veranda, studying. A pile of books lay in front of her on the
table. "My cousins," Champa said to Kamal, "the one in the
kitchen is Zebun, she has just done her M.A. in sociology
from Aligarh Muslim University. The one over there is Mariam
Zamani, doing her M.Sc. in agriculture. They were babies when
I went to Lucknow for my B.A. Why are you so quiet, Kamal?
What's the matter?"

"Nothing, Champa Baji."

Her uncle talked to him at some length in a slow, dolorous
tone, going over the same old topics—the impending war between India and Pakistan, the distressing economic problems.
"We U.P. Muslims have been ruined because of the creation of
Pakistan," he concluded.

"Why is this place so quiet? Where has everybody gone?"
Kamal's voice trailed off.

"Over there— where you gave gone," replied the old man.
"Most of our family members packed up and left with just a
few old fogeys like myself here. The place will be haunted by
ghosts after we die."

"But I saw the city chockfull of Muslims," Kamal argued.

"Only the hoi-poloi," Barey Abba replied dismissively. "The
gentry has more or less emigrated."

"Moradabad is one of the towns of U.P. where Muslims are
a majority but they're mostly artisans," Champa explained in
an aside to the perplexed visitor. "You are here for too short a
time to get the hang of the socio-political situation. Have
some tea," she added as Zebun appeared with the tea-tray.

"As long as Jawaharlal is alive everything will be all right.
But what will happen after he goes? Only Allah knows. In the
long run, our succeeding generations will face the same fate as
Spain's Muslims."

Kamal shuddered. Does Spain still haunt the Muslim mind—
especially in times of crisis? He looked at the pomegranate
tree swaying in the gentle evening breeze.

The old man puffed at his hookah and continued, "Now
tell me about Pakistan. I hear all manner of riff-raff from India

have prospered. Weavers and butchers from U.P. call themselves Syeds over there, and Punjabis are hobnobbing with the
refugees."

Kamal had seen Champa today perched on another rung of
her ladder, against another backdrop, another set of props. At
least this was her real milieu. He closed his eyes. The Champa
of Lucknow, Paris, Cambridge and London, and now the
Champa of this joyless, half-lit house in Moradabad. The sadder and wiser, the serene Champa of new India!

Rain-laden winds blowing across the river Ram Ganga ruffled
his hair. The painfully alluring rainy season of his country. But
this was not his country any more. His visa was about to expire,
soon he would set off in the direction of his homeland.

Moradabad. This murky staircase, Champa Ahmed, Zebun-
nisa, Mariam, Barey Abba—all this will remain behind. Ought
he to shed a tear over this unalterable fact? He felt he was a
lone traveller like Abu Rehan Al-Beruni who had trekked down
the dusty, craggy road of centuries and seen it all, and now the
Spanish mystic Ibn-ul Arabi seemed to have stopped travelling with him. He felt bewildered and alone.

"Where is Hari Shankar?" asked Champa in her former voice.

"Champa Baji," he said indignantly, "Hari Shankar is not
my alter ego any more. Why should I know his whereabouts?"

"Why not? Don't you write to him?"

"What on earth should I write to him about, and why?" he
replied, sitting down on the cot.

"You are still very emotional!"

"Most certainly not," he answered impatiently, "I am just
sick of this Indo-Pakistan melodrama."

"You still haven't become strong," Champa replied peaceably. "Why did you come here? To see me? Was this a senti-
mental journey?"

"Well, one does like to look up one's old friends once in a
while," Kamal faltered. "And besides, Moradabad was on the
way to Dehra Dun," he added with a long face.

Rain pattered on the balcony. The fragrance of wet earth
reached Kamal's sensitive nostrils. A woman in scarlet churidar
pajamas passed by in the lane, hawking Amroha mangoes.

Champa continued to sit on the doorstep.

"What are you going to do now?" he asked.

"I," she replied, "am going to set up law practice in Banaras and help my father. Do you happen to know the real name of my mother's hometown?"

"Shivpuri."

"Yes, the City of Bliss. It is going to be the city of bliss sooner or later, like all the other towns in this subcontinent. It's up to me to do my own job conscientiously, others can think and act as they choose."

The call for afternoon prayers rose from the little mosque. Unconsciously she covered her head with the anchal of her sari.

Downstairs the girls were busy frying monsoon delicacies. They had put on traditional rainbow-coloured cotton dupattas and saris in honour of the rains. "Send up something for us, too," Champa called out to them through the window.

"Okay, Bajia, wait a bit," one of them shouted back merrily and resumed singing, "Who, oh who, has hung the swing on the mango trees?" This popular song had been composed by Bahadur Shah Zafar, the last Mughal king of India. He, too, had been a musician king.

Kamal became restive. A gharara-clad Zebun appeared on the stairs and came up and placed a plateful of hot and spicy pakwan on the floor. Then she went back, humming the rain-song.

Champa was still sitting on the threshold. "You must be wondering," she said slowly, "who will come to my doorstep *now!* But Kamal, I think that as far as personal success goes, I have been luckier than you. I have found the magic key. Gautam told me once, in London, in his pseudo-philosophic manner, that we had all lost the key. When I received your sister Tehmina's letter in the rainy season of 1941 in Banaras, welcoming me to Chand Bagh College, I thought that letter was the password to fairyland!"

Rain fell tunefully in the pool downstairs. The trees appeared lush green, little streams rippled in the lanes, a tank of lustrous water sparkled in the courtyard. The saplings in the cracked china vases swayed in the breeze, and little waterfalls spilled down from rain spouts. "This," Champa said, *"is mine own Water Place. Herein flows the stream of my tears."*

A shower of rose-apples fell from the over-hanging tree. Champa removed a wet green leaf from her hair.

"Kamal," she said thoughtfully, "do you remember that Pakistani artist in London? She painted yard after yard of canvas as the years rolled by. She wandered from studio to studio all over the western world, she held one-woman shows in London and Paris and Rome. Diplomats' wives and society ladies came to attend the inaugurations, cameras flashed and reporters mobbed her. Meanwhile, she would stand in a corner, talking and smiling politely. At the end of the evening when they left, the hall became empty and she was alone in the company of her celebrated paintings. She took the last bus home, all by herself—Kamal, eat these pakoras while they are hot, they get cold in no time."

The following morning he left for Dehra Dun. Champa came to the small window in the creaking old gate and said a surprisingly cheerful, "Khuda hafiz" signalling that she had made her truce with life. He should, too.

Once again Champa was left behind, a shadowy figure in the distance, just as he had left her once standing behind a glass door on Oxford Street. And just as she had stood on the lonely road in front of Gulfishan when Amir Reza went away to Pakistan. But perhaps today she was not alone, she was part of the crowd. She had at last, and unconditionally, accepted the comradeship of her fellow-beings.

Kamal used to think that while he was forging ahead, Champa had stayed behind. He would march on to new worlds, new visions, newer horizons. Today, he realised that perhaps he was receding and Champa, who was not lonely any more, was moving forward. She had the sorrowful little priest of her mosque for company, Zebun and Mariam, the veiled women and ragged urchins of her lane, the under-nourished coolies with their push-carts. Champa Baji had become their fellow-wayfarer. At this point the invisible cobwebs of Kamal's new philosophy of despair snapped with a jerk.

The tonga was passing through Qazi Bazaar. The muezzins' call went up from the mosque's loudspeakers and Muslim shopkeepers were closing their shops for evening prayers. One or two solitary kites fluttered across the horizon. Kamal saw a red kite which had been cut and was adrift in the deep blue sky. Gautam should have been here to appreciate the symbolism of this scene! He smiled sadly. "What can I do, yaar," he said to himself, "my end has been pretty inglorious."

71. The Elusive Bird of the Doon Valley

The Shivalik hills came into view. The familiar panorama unfolded—mountain streams, waterfalls, temples, sadhus. Rocks, baboons, woods, clusters of lilac and hawthorn.

The Doon Valley.

Dehra Dun railway station. Ragged Garhwali coolies surrounded him at the tonga and taxi stands. Saab want go Mussoorie? Want go Rajpur? First-class hotel run by English Memsaab. . .

On the way to town in a tonga he was suddenly confronted with the newly dug up, denuded mountainside facing Dehra Dun. "They are cutting down forests for timber and dynamiting rocks to do some kind of mining," the tonga-wallah told him.

What are they doing to my beautiful country, Kamal thought with rage and horror. Does Panditji know what is going on over here? I must inform him at once. The next moment the irony of the situation hit him—he had nothing to do with Pandit Nehru any more, this was not his country. In fact he had come here to perform a kind of requiem—to wind up his property matters and sever the last remaining bonds with the land of his ancestors.

He spent a couple of hours in the district magistrate's office poring over real estate documents, and discussed Movable and Immovable Property, Agreed and Non-agreed Areas. Afterwards he repaired to a hotel, and in the evening, loitered on the tranquil avenues of Dalanwalla and read the name-plates on the gates.

The Rispana flowed by.

"Hari Shankar," he mused aloud after a while.

"Hum."

"Come to think of it, the Prof. is dead right. We are in a mess."

That evening they pondered over the philosophy of renunciation, mouthing profundities.

"Let's read the names on the bungalows, the choice of names reveals the psychology of the owners," said Hari Shankar stopping in front of a garden gate.

"We shall never build a house, for the falcon doth not make a nest," observed Kamal, quoting Iqbal.

"To think that people have built houses, lovely houses of all kinds. The world is full of houses."

"Yes, isn't it strange."

They sat down on a little Chinese bridge which connected a villa with the avenue. "There must be some meaning to this," observed Hari Shankar gravely.

"There must be," Kamal agreed.

They read more name-plates in the deepening twilight. 'Jasmine', 'Shamrock', 'Doon Haven', 'Rose Mount', 'Ashiana', 'Fairy Cottage', 'Khyaban'.

Dolefully they strolled down Rajpur Road and observed the rippling waters of the Eastern Canal. A broken shoe sailed past, bobbing up and down in the gushing current.

A gleaming Chevrolet pulled up near him. Kamal rubbed his eyes and looked around. Hari Shankar had vanished. This was not 1942, but the Dehra Dun of 1956. He rubbed his eyes again. He was sitting on the foot-bridge of his own house, Khyaban. A well-dressed, genial-looking Sikh climbed out of the car and eyed him suspiciously, taking him for some fashionable thug who would make off with his new music system.

"Yes?" he asked.

"I. . .I. . .," Kamal stammered, confused, his heart beating faster. He looked again at the marble slab on the gate-post:

Khan Bahadur Syed Taqi Reza Bahadur of Kalyanpur. This was doubtless his house. He rose to his feet, his throat dry. Nervously he took out the documents from his pocket as proof of his bona fides.

"Oh, I see! You have come in connection with movable property," the Sikh said cordially. "Do come in, Bhai Saheb, your store room is safely locked. Have you brought the keys?"

"Yes," Kamal replied, looking down at the blue pebbles under his shoes.

The Sardarji led him to the front veranda and offered him tea. The new owner of Khayaban belonged to Lahore and had come to Dehra Dun as a penniless refugee during the Partition riots. Now he was a wealthy contractor, busy cutting down alpine forests. He almost wept as he talked of Lahore with deep nostalgia.

"May I come tomorrow morning to open the box-room?" Kamal asked hastily.

"Certainly, please treat this as your own home, *Apna hi ghar samjhen.*" The Sardar repeated the customary Indian phrase of hospitality.

Kamal returned to his hotel.

In the morning he went to Khyaban and made his way down to the store-room. Sitting there on the red brick staircase he realised that he was a member of India's Lost Generation. The world his gracious family had inhabited was one of autumn woodlands, hillside cottages and the gleaming silver of afternoon tea. The path through the oaks in front of him had been trodden by elegant ladies of his family, looking like the heroines of some old French or Turkish novel, as they languidly carried Burmese parasols or tiny Italian bags made of beads in their delicate hands.

Whenever they had come here during the winter to see the snows of Mussoorie, logs were burnt in the grates and satin quilts piled up on the carpets where they sat and drank green tea. Talat would make a little igloo of her quilts, and sit inside with her "John & Mary" colouring books.

There had been a sprawling bread-fruit tree near the kitchen, and Hussaini's wife diligently counted its fruit every morning to see that they were not stolen by the neighbour's cook. A painting in the front veranda depicted a shikar scene, in which a pack of greyhounds chased a stag among the reeds of the Terai. The drawing-room cornice, covered with gold-embroidered black fabric, displayed a row of family photographs in silver frames. Chinese palms stood in brass planters on tall tripods in all four corners of the room. The wash-basin in the dining room was filled with fresh neem leaves every morning, the table was laid in English style on formal occasions, complete with rose petals floating in finger bowls. The silent khidmatgar, Amir Khan, was dressed in a spotless white 'chapkan' and scarlet sash and pinned the silver monogram of Father's name on the red band across his white, crisply starched turban.

On warm summer afternoons when everybody was fast asleep in the cool rooms inside, Kamal would sneak out to sit under the shade of the lichi trees. A deep cosmic silence descended over the world, suffusing one with cosmic languor and extremely tranquil thoughts. A lone bird cried ceaselessly among the distant deodars. Its cry resembled the words—*Main sota tha, main sota tha*. 'Alas I was asleep. . . I was asleep. . .' This elusive and invisible bird was found nowhere but in the Doon Valley. It remained hidden among the leaves and poured out its lamentation on long summer afternoons. According to a mountain legend, god distributed various boons to his creatures when he created the world. The peacock got his feathers, the koel her voice and so on. At the time this stupid bird was fast asleep somewhere in the woods of the Doon Valley, and consequently it got nothing. This had been its complaint ever after.

The Sardarni went from one room to another and closed the pantry door with a bang. Kamal returned from the Dehra Dun of 1936.

He unlocked the store-room, went in and aimlessly opened and closed the dusty almirahs. He peered into chests and caskets, and wondered about the usefulness of possessions. He looked at the pile of junk which one is pleased to call 'property'—there was more junk of a similar kind locked up in the

store-rooms of Gulfishan and in the country house at
Kalyanpur. . . He stood on a little island amidst the litter and
reflected. . . people are desperately keen to possess *things*.

Now he knew why they renounced the world and took to
the woods. He sat down on a stool and tried to be methodi-
cal. First he opened the little steel boxes containing family
documents, but closed them again weakly. His eyes wandered
to a mountain of old and rare Urdu magazines. Not knowing
what to do next, he picked up a battered attache case marked
"Correspondence", and opened it with tired curiosity. The
letters carried strange post marks: Aurangabad, 6th July, 1933.
Indore, 24th October, 1928. Mysore, 3rd March, 1937. Who
had sent these letters and what had they written in them? Where
were they now and what were they doing? Or, in which grave-
yards were they buried?

For instance, this letter from Dr. Ras Bihari Lal dated Pilibhit,
29th July, 1931. Who was Dr. Ras Bihari Lal? Or Vishwanandan
Pandey from Ranikhet, and Mohammad Ahmad Abbasi, Sub-
Judge, Gonda. . .? He sat on the floor and wondered and wondered. He shoved the attache case back onto the shelf and turned
to a number of files under the carpets. Kalyanpur litigations,
papers connected with the legal separation of Aunt Chunni
Begum and her no-good husband, Mir Banney (both of them
long dead). One copy of the *History of Oudh* in Urdu written
by Syed Kamaluddin Hyder and published by the celebrated
Navalkishore Press, Lucknow, ages ago. Its yellowed pages
crumbled to pieces when he picked up the book. He opened it
tenderly. The frontispiece had a preposterous pen-and-ink
drawing of 'His Highness the Hon'ble Maharaja Sir Digbijay
Singh Bahadur, of Balrampur and Tulsipur, the Province of
Oudh, on whose gracious command the present history was
compiled.' It also carried a preface written by H.H. the Maharajah in exotically florid Urdu. He began reading at random.
*'In short the Nawab of Bengal was disheartened because of these
things and after a great deal of meditation, put on the ochre
robes of a mendicant and sat down on a piece of mat. The Court
also wore the same lowly garb and was the object of much adverse
comment by the ignoble world. . .'*

Kamal turned another page.

'— *Thus the great and glorious English Sahebs realised that they had conquered the land of Ind that very day. The reality was revealed from east to west. Therefore they sought to strengthen their position as Ministers to the Emperor. After which they knew that it would be easy to annex the entire Mughal Empire. And that one should not enter somebody's house all of a sudden and should take one's time. It was obvious that there was disunity in the Indian nation, as if all the lamps of Hindustan were put out one by one. . .*

'*The Pathetic Demise of Mirza Ali Khan, June, 1816.*

'— *He was buried in Calcutta's Kasi Bagh wherein the son of Tipu Sultan is also enjoying his eternal repose. Some humble folk of the town accompanied his bier considering him to be, after all, Vizier-i-Hind, Prime Minister of India. The Sahebs ordered that the Tommies should guard the bier. That was the reign during which John Lamsden Saheb was the Resident at Lucknow and John Cherry Saheb was the Resident at Benares who was later murdered by Naib Taffazul Hussain Khan. . .*

'— *Mirza Muzzafer Bakht, son of Delhi's Prince Mirza Sulaiman Shikoh, tried to venture out of Lucknow wherein he lived as a pensioner of the Court of Oudh. Some down-and-out loafers of the town also accompanied the Prince. When he returned to Lucknow disappointed and dejected, he married Sally Begum, one of the English widows of General Claud Martin, and lived on his White wife's pension.* After her death he continued living in her house. . .*

'*The Departure of Col. Dubois and Ferrell Saheb and Maulvi Mohammed Ismail to London with the Embassy and Priceless Presents for George IV, King of Kings. . .*'

Kamal threw the book back in the basket, and for some moments looked sadly at the dust which clung to his hands. He did not wipe them for some time. These things shall not go anywhere. Let them be taken over by the Government of India and sold to a kabariwallah, he said to himself.

---

* Sally Begum was also known as Gori Bibi.

He was about to leave the room when he caught sight of an old group photograph in a corner. He picked it up and shook off the dust—it was his uncle, heavily garlanded and seated in a row of serious-faced worthies. The picture had been taken when this deputy-collector uncle was being transferred from one district to another. District officials sat next to him in the row, stood at the back, and leaned sideways on their elbows on the carpet in front. Under a high-arched veranda in the background stood a number of liveried peons, very erect and solemn. He read the names printed on the grey mount. Mr. L. Saxena, Mr S.A. Rizvi, Thakur Ram Narain, Masudul Hasan Naqvi.

He remembered some of them. What strange men they must have been—innocent, gentlemanly, civilized, completely unaware of fraud and racketeering. Silly people. They had their own peculiar, old-fashioned illusions, humour and interests. Poetry symposia, litigation, shikar, classical music. What peaceful, uncomplicated lives they led, what a peaceful uncomplicated society theirs had been! He looked at this group for a long time. How did we prove ourselves to be better than them? You poor old things! But I'm ashamed of myself in front of you. That is why I am running away, to hide myself in distant places. Goodbye. He dropped the photograph gently on the floor and emerged from the store-room.

The bird continued to cry in the trees, *Main sota tha*. Stupid bird, you didn't lose anything, he muttered, locking the door after him.

72. Sudarshan Yakshini of the National Museum

"Hello Laj—I am at the police station," Kamal airily informed his childhood friend, trying to sound jovial.

"Police station? Whatever for?" Laj was shocked. She had never had a Pakistani visitor before.

"To report my arrival, stupid. I had checked in at the Maiden's. Let me collect my luggage from there. See, I was not very sure if I'd find you all at home."

"Where would we go from here, Kim? You remember the address or shall I come over to fetch you?"

"Of course, I know the address!" He had rung off. When he returned to the hotel lobby, he ran into Laj's cousins who also lived in the vicinity. It was again a cheerful long-time-no-see kind of encounter. They had come in with a group of Texan advisors wearing white shorts and chappals. This country like Pakistan seemed to be overflowing with American advisors. An expansive Sardarji drove him across to the old civil lines. The locality, like the hotel, was still very British although the Koi Hai's had left a decade earlier. Kamal thought, well the Mughals faded out a century ago but their impact still lingers. Civilizations do not vanish overnight. At the Civil Lines police station the thanedar entered the details of his arrival in rapid Urdu scrawl. This surprised Kamal because everywhere else he had seen a preponderance of the official Hindi script.

The Civil Lines seemed tranquil as ever. A koel sang somewhere in the distance.

Some of the bungalows were inhabited by the sophisticated descendents of Munshi Jeevan Lal, a friend of Ghalib. After 1857 Munshi Jeevan Lal had taught Urdu to the Tommies stationed in Shah Jahan's fallen citadel, the Red Fort.

Kamal noticed the old name-plates on the bungalows' gates. He was coming from a country full of displaced people and he was one of them. Here were families living in their houses where they had always lived. He remembered how, as a school-boy prank, he and Hari had jumbled up name-plates on the gates of Dalanwall, Dehra Dun. Now he had exchanged his complete address and identity for a totally different one.

The cab drove up to the potted palms of a pleasant kothi on Bela Road. He found Laj standing on the veranda steps waiting for him. The moment she saw Kamal she rushed towards him and broke down. "Don't go away, Kamman," she said tearfully. "Nirmal is dead, Hari is always abroad. And now you have run off to Pakistan."

They went in and sat down on a sofa. "Why are you crying?" he said slowly. "Don't cry, please."

His train was leaving for Amritsar in the evening. Laj had a mental block about Gautam—she didn't have his phone number. He picked up the directory and went through the Jungle Book of Central Government numbers. He came across two familiar names, Zarina Hussain, AIR, External Broadcasts and Saulat Rehman, Ministry of Education, Then he located Gautam in the Ministry of Information & Broadacasting.

Kamal dialled the number. "Hello! So you are here, you so-and-so. . ." he said, trying desperately to assume his old manner. "Yes? Yes. This morning from Dehra Dun. . . Came from Dacca. Stopped over at Lucknow. Tehmina sends you her love. She is fine, happily married to a kinsman who is in the IAS, a deputy commissioner somewhere in U.P., queening it over the district. Quite forgotten her revolutionary zeal.

"Everybody is fine except yours truly. . . Qadeer and Qamrun. . . My god! You remember them! You remember everything! Everything, you said? Well, you do have an excellent memory! Qadeer went back to Mirzapur after the car was sold. Why was the car sold? Yaar, entire lives have been sold, mortgaged, auctioned off, thrown away, and you're worried about an old motor car!

"You have not sold yourself, you say. No. No. I was talking about myself. . . I got a good price and market conditions were favourable.

"No, I am afraid I can't meet you, no time. Very tight schedule. No. What is the bloody use of waiting for me in Alps? Right now I'm going to meet the Custodian. . . P Block. Okay, I'll try to come, but don't wait for more than fifteen minutes. I may not turn up at all, may be held up in that bloke's office. Bye."

He replaced the receiver. "Okay, Laj, I'm scooting."

"What should I cook for the train journey, Kim?"

"The same that you always cook," he replied curtly. Go on, try to trap me in this mushy "Rakhi sister" business of yours, it won't soften my heart. My steps shan't falter. I am strong.

I'm a world-weary old man, I have attained Restraint and Balance and Peace. . .

In Connaught Circus he mistook a passing woman for Surekha and went up to her, quickly apologised and resumed loitering in the veranda. Standing in the midst of prosperous, happy, self-satisfied human beings, he felt apprehensive. He also remembered that before going to the railway station he had to report at the Civil Lines police station again and inform them that he was leaving India. Clearing out.

The scorching sun of the month of Bhadon beat down on him mercilessly. He wanted to rush back to Karachi and decided that he would never come to India again, even though his sister Talat and a lot of relatives lived here.

"What a pleasant surprise!" he exclaimed with forced bonhomie as Dr. Hans Krammer came out of a bookshop. A young, efficient-looking girl, apparently from the Information Division, accompanied him.

"I am taking the Professor to the National Museum, do come along," the young woman (who was introduced to him as Kumari Aruna Bajpai by a gushing Dr. Krammer) said to Kamal. He closed his eyes for an instant. Nirmala would have been working somewhere like this if she were alive today.

"We travelled together on the voyage out to India from England," the good Professor told Miss Bajpai.

They picked up two French intellectuals from the Imperial Hotel and were taken to Rashtrapati Bhawan by Kumari Bajpai in a station-wagon. Dr. Hans Krammer and his colleagues lived in that rarefied little world to which Kamal had belonged not so long ago. They, too, had a larger-than-life outlook and possessed perception in addition to cognition. They had all come to India to attend the Buddha Jayanti, and for the last few months Dr. Krammer had been living in a houseboat in Srinagar, writing a book on Gupta sculpture.

The former Viceregal Lodge had been renamed Rashtrapati Bhawan after Independence, and a portion of the presidential palace had been converted into a museum. "This is only a temporary arrangement, you know," Kumari Aruna Bajpai said to

Kamal-apologetically. "A proper museum, under construction, will do justice to our glorious heritage."

Kamal winced at the cliche. "Yes, of course," he replied politely. Twelve months ago he had been talking to Tom in exactly the same strain, minus the platitudes, bursting with national pride.

Kamal did not think it necessary to tell her that he had belonged to this country, too.

The marble halls of the presidential palace were cool and immensely rest-giving after the blazing sunshine of the outside world. The statues of antiquity stared at Kamal at blankly. The foreign visitors stopped at each glass case and exchanged their erudite views in undertones. In the Durbar Hall where the viceroys of India used to hold court with all the glory and splendour of the Mughals, the viceregal throne had been replaced with a colossal statue of the Buddha. A velvet cascade of maroon curtains fell in the background.

Kamal sat down on the steps of the throne. He bent his head and recalled another tranquil Buddha Hall he had visited as a youngster, when he and Hari had accompanied their sisters to Banaras. . . years ago. . . in 1941. The world was young then, because they were young and full of hope and joy. They were all sitting on the marble floor of the Buddha temple when Talat suddenly stood up and started dancing before the bronze image of the Enlightened One.

So what was enlightenment all about, anyway, Kamal reflected with amazement. Once again his thoughts were disturbed by Kumari Bajpai. "Come along, please," she said, briskly shepherding her flock into another room. "Here is the Dancing Girl of Mohen-Jo-Daro, India's earliest civilization . . . five thousand years old."

It's Pakistan's earliest civilization, he wanted to correct her officially, but the situation was too funny for words.

They gazed spellbound at the tiny figurine. She looked like any Negroid woman of the Makran coast. In modern Karachi they worked as labourers, so at this moment I have solved the mystery of the world-famous Dancing Girl of Mohen-Jo-Daro. She was merely a Makrani labourer. He chuckled to himself.

They proceeded to the sections marked Chan-ho Daro, Swat Valley, Harappa, Taxila, Ruper.

They moved on to another section till they came upon a lighted glass case. It contained an archaic bas relief of a plump woman with arched eyebrows. "Excavated recently from the ruins of Shravasti," the caption read, "circa 4th century B.C."

The lady stood cross-legged. She had a puffy face, arched eyebrows and pointed chin. With one arm she had bent the bough of a kadamba tree over her elaborately coiffed head. She looked strong and earthy. She was bare-breasted and wore heavy ornaments.

"The ancients liked rotund women, and they didn't wear saris," Mons. Raoul commented with glee. Miss Bajpai blushed. Dr. Krammer began gravely: "Future theories of India, roop and aroop, form and formlessness, bhav and abhav, took root at this time. This piece," he addressed the gathering, "is probably earlier than Bharhut and Mathura."

"The problem facing the sculptors of that age must have been one of communicating pure thought through known symbols. This and the Bactrian-Greece Buddha-heads of Gandhara gave rise to idol worship." Dr. Moreland spoke in a lecture-room voice.

With whom am I going to talk about my concepts of form and formlessness, roop and aroop, bhav and abhav? thought Kamal. All those theories have proved pointless. This statue has no message for me.

"In the Vedanta, pure aesthetic experience is indivisible like lightning. The beholder becomes one with the creator. What is your opinion?" Dr. Moreland asked Kamal.

"I have no opinion, sir," he replied glancing at his wrist-watch.

"This murti reveals the strength of the earth. It is life instead of beyond-life. A complete fusion of the sense of peace, balance, movement. A Terrible Beauty Is Born," said Dr. Moreland.

"Wish we knew the name of the sculptor who created this girl under the kadamba tree. But in India history has no meaning. Events are not important. Reality, myth and tradition all get mixed up. Historical time does not exist. The moment is eternal, man remains nameless. His creations get lost in this ocean of eternity. No crisis affects the Indian mind because crisis is also part of time and time has no meaning," Dr. Krammer intoned. "That is why the artists of the East hardly ever bothered to inscribe their names. You know the artists of Iran left one tiny leaf unfinished because for them only Allah was the Perfect Artist." Kamal slipped out and entered the gallery.

". . . the realisation that we are Time itself," Mons. Roul was saying.

"You can feel the space, you only think about time," Dr. Krammer's voice chased Kamal as he hurried out of the gallery.

After seeing the Custodian in P block he didn't go to Alps to meet Gautam Nilambar. He went directly to Laj's house and said to her: "In case anybody rings up, please say I am not at home." After which he bolted his room from the inside and went to sleep till it was time to go to the railway station.

Gautam waited for Kamal for nearly an hour in the restaurant and telephoned him at several places. When he gave up all hope of meeting his friend he returned to his office.

After a while he called his deputy, Kumari Aruna Bajpai, in connection with an important file. He was told that Dr. Bajpai had gone to the National Museum with Dr. Krammer.

"Damn. . ." he muttered crossly. He was vastly depressed since he had missed meeting Kamal.

Gautam was furious. . .

He was furious at this country, at himself, at Kamal, at every thing in the world. He would have eaten Dr. Krammer and Miss Bajpai and the rest alive, if it were possible.

This file was Top Secret and Most Immediate. He got into his car and drove to Rashtrapati Bhawan. Miss Bajpai and her party had already left. He wandered thoughtlessly in the hollow rooms of the museum.

A few pamphlets of the Information Division lay at the base of the statue of Sudarshan Yakshini, which his colleague had probably forgotten there. He picked them up. Then he looked at the statue vacantly. The girl from Shravasti gazed back stonily.

A fine example of archaic sculpture, he reflected. There should be an article about it by Dr. Mulk Raj Anand in *Marg* and one by Karl Khandalawala in *The March of India*, he thought as a publicity expert. After which he came out of the museum.

Kamal emerged from Laj's house at sundown. "You have been roaming in the hot sun all day, a bit of fresh air will do you good," Jeejaji said to him. They got into the car and drove all the way to the Ridge. New, flourishing localities of post-Partition Delhi glimmered on the horizon. The friends came downhill and proceeded to New Delhi where they drove around aimlessly. A concert by Ustad Bare Ghulam Ali Khan was in progress in Sapru House.

"Our Surekha is playing Heer in the Sheila Bhatia opera tonight," Laj informed him enthusiastically.

"How nice," said Kamal.

"And she is also going to play Vasantsena in *The Clay Cart* from next week. Begum Qudsia Zaidi's production, directed by Habib Tanvir. But you are not staying even for a couple of days."

"Must get back to my work in the lab, you know." Kamal replied tonelessly.

The car slowed down in front of a new temple. Devotees lay prostrate all over the marble floors of the mandir. Kirtan was being sung on the harmonium. Throngs of complacent middle-class men and women squatted in the prayer hall. The idols represented the new Indian kitsch.

It was time to go.

He said goodbye to his host and hostess and got into the compartment. The train slowly came out of Old Delhi railway station. Jamuna Bridge. Citadel walls of the Red Fort. Bazaars, streets, level-crossings. Flat-roofed houses. Flowering trees. He kept looking out of the window. He was going away.

Jamia Nagar, Nizamuddin Aulia. Lodhi tombs. Everything will be left behind. Life shall continue. The falling off of one man does not make any difference. These were different people now, they had been travelling on a separate road. Kamal had nothing in common with them any more. He would have nothing to do with them. They, too, wouldn't miss him.

The reporters of the world's press must be drinking hard, as usual, in the Press Club. Surekha Devi must be dancing on the stage of Begum Qudsia Zaidi's Hindustani Theatre. Pandit Nehru was meeting a delegation of French Quakers at his residence.

Soft winds blew across Roshan Ara Bagh and Bela Road. Roses bloomed in the bungalows of the old Civil Lines and New Delhi.

The train came out into the country. Every journey is symbolic, Gautam had observed once when he used to (according to Talat) converse in the manner of Al-Mustafa of Kahlil Gibran. "The entire symbol of India is the journey. The habit of always travelling, always searching. . ." Spengler had said. Listlessly Kamal picked up S. Radhakrishnan's paperback that Kumari Bajpai had bought from the railway bookstall and presented to him as a parting gift.

"In Indian philosophy, nobody decrees that you must not do this, or that you ought to do that. . . Here everyone is free to do what he likes."

Oh, yeah . . .?

He closed the book after turning a few pages and lay down on the berth.

East Punjab stations passed by. Their walls displayed garish Urdu posters advertising the latest films. The once colourful silk salwars of Sikh women were reflected on the newly washed platform of Jullundur. Hawkers sold hot tea and pakoras.

Morning. The train was approaching Amritsar. Groups of Sikh women were passing by on village paths. Sikh peasants had already reached their fields with their ploughs. Crowds of veiled Muslim women and old bearded Muslim men sat across the bars on the Amritsar platform, waiting patiently for their visas to be checked and cleared. A fat Sikh police officer was asking an old woman, "What is your name, ma-ji?"

"Amina," she replied plaintively. "This is my daughter, Sakina. She is a Pakistani. I have come from Delhi to receive her. Her father is on his death-bed."

Pakistani Sakina stood on the other side where Pakistani passengers had to wait. She was looking at the police officer with frightened eyes, separated from her Indian mother by the iron bars. "Her papers are all right, beta?" Her mother asked the police officer hopefully. . .

A Pakistani officer of the Border Police climbed into Kamal's bogey.

The Express moved. The soldiers of both countries boarded the rear compartment. This was the usual Indo-Pak armed guard which travelled back and forth with the trains.

Kamal had been mustering his courage all these days to remain intact. He broke down finally when the train crossed the border and he saw, for the last time, the grinning, jovial face of a Sikh soldier who stood alert with his gun under a telegraph pole.

Suddenly, the other country began. The gun-toting Sikh soldiers were left behind.

I am in Pakistan. I have come from India. Refugee. Muhajir. Displaced Muslim from Uttar Pradesh. . . how terrifying. . . . Refugee . . . displaced. . . homeless. . .

Abdul Mansur Kamaluddin wept.

After a few moments he realised that his fellow passenger, the Pakistan Border Police officer who was returning to Lahore from Amritsar, was looking at him intently.

Kamal was crestfallen. He felt as though the police officer was saying : "You still stand at the cross-roads of conflicting loyalties, don't you?"

The eyes of the whole world were glued on him. You are an Indian Muslim. . . Indian spy . . .

The train's wheels seemed to be repeating the same refrain— traitor. . . spy. . . traitor. . . spy. . . traitor. . . spy. . .

He opened his eyes, trembling. The train was slowly entering the barred portion of Lahore railway station. His heart beat faster.

In the evening he boarded the P.I.A. plane from Lahore's
Walton Airport and began flying towards Karachi.

Now his new life lay before him. He took out his morocco-
bound notebook. What a lot of things he had to do when he
got back to the Federal Capital. First thing, Uncle Nazir had
to be asked to dine with him at the Gymkhana Club. This
influential relative could help him purchase cement, etc. in
the black market. He was going to build his house in a posh
locality of Karachi. Cousin Munne has married the daughter
of the Minister of Industries, must remember to invite them,
too. Tell me, where can I go from here? he asked himself.
How can I avoid becoming a part of the System?

A beautiful Pathan air hostess brought him coffee. She was
impeccable in a green uniform designed by Pierre Cardin. He
gave her an appreciative once-over. For a moment he felt good
and self-assured. For a brand new people we are not doing
badly at all, thank you. He tried to shun his very negative
thoughts and picked up *The Dawn*. Soon he was engrossed in
the political news of his country. . . Crisis in the Cabinet. The
Prime Minister resigns. The new Prime Minister addresses the
nation in Jehangir Park. . .

After a while he looked out of the window. The sky was
overcast. Soon it would start raining. The clouds need no passport. He drew the window's green curtain, stretched his legs
and leaned back in his seat.

73. *The Highway to Shravasti*

They had crossed the Gulwa Ghat bridge over the Sarju and
entered Behraich. The government jeep shot forward, emit-
ting a black cloud of exhaust fumes. A sturdy lad was driving
his bullock-cart on the main road and shouted at the chauffeur of the station-wagon which overtook the jeep. "Hey, Mister! Can't you be more careful? You have upset my bullocks."

The American journalist photographed the gesticulating boy who did not seem to be at all in awe of the big saheb-log.

"India's new democracy!" the American said to Lady Nilima Banerjee, the Supreme Culture Vulture who had accompanied the VIPs on the Buddha's trail. Why does she still stick to her British title, he wondered.

Lady Banerjee was talking to a Japanese professor of Indology. The lorry behind them carried ordinary pilgrims— Buddhist men and women from the Chittagong Hill Tracts and Cox's Bazaar, East Pakistan. They were going straight to Sahat Mahat, the present-day name for the ruins of Shravasti. The dusty yellow bus was followed by limousines carrying more Buddha Jayanti delegates.

"I would like to get off here and walk home," Gautam said to Miss Bajpai. "There is a short-cut through the fields." During the three-hour drive from Lucknow and the crossing of the Ghagra by steamer, he had been listening to Dr Krammer's discourse on Zen. He wanted a little respite. "See you early tomorrow morning, sir, at the Circuit House. And then we leave for Shravasti. Excuse me, Mons. Raoul."

The Sikh driver stopped the car, Gautam got out and stretched his legs. The vehicles disappeared behind a clump of blazing gulmohurs. He looked around and inhaled the fresh country air. Flame-of-the-forest was in flower, wild frangipani was laden with red blossoms. The entire woodland seemed to be on fire. Dark clouds rumbled in the sky and a drop of rain fell on his nose. He turned towards a forest path and walked on. As a youngster he often used to paint these wild flowers. He remembered how he had once made a water-colour of the young Prince Siddhartha standing under a mango tree looking mournfully at a dead bird shot down by a hunter's arrow. Gautam had insisted that he be sent to Santiniketan. How long ago it all seemed today. How did that young dreamer turn into a hard-headed diplomat? He walked on. It started raining and he took shelter under a huge banyan. The moist easterly breeze hit his face. The trees had turned into an orchestra of wind instruments. They are playing ragas Malhar, Des and Gaur Sarang, he mused.

As suddenly as it had started, the downpour stopped. He heard the faint roar of a tiger. Oh, my god! He looked back at the mud track and realised that he had lost his way and wandered into a dense forest. His fine Italian shoes were covered with slush. Kadamba flowers glittered like little red lamps, a lone peacock danced under a laburnum. Cranes stood about gloomily by a lake, soaked in rain. Beyond the woodland, Gautam recalled, lay the vast complex of the shrine of Salar Masud Ghazi, the culture hero of the region. That must be many miles away, too. Leaping across puddles and rippling brooks he found his way back to the main road. His expensive trousers were splashed with mud.

He sat down on a milestone, waiting for a passing lorry. I could be eaten alive by a tiger and that, he thought sorrowfully, would be a grotesque end to a distinguished career. He tried to think of something pleasant and recollected his boyhood days when his father would take him to the hunting lodges of the rajas of Nanpara and Pyagpur, the biggest feudal lords of this district.

The tiger roared again. Just then a tractor appeared at the far end of the road. It was heading for the city—he ran up and shouted for a lift.

The tractor was overloaded with a wedding party which welcomed him heartily and made him sit next to the bridegroom. Gautam chatted with them in dialect, feeling gloriously at home and happy. The baratis dropped him right at the gate of Nilambar Bhavan, Civil Lines, Behraich.

His father was away in Lucknow. Lady Nilambar stood on the front lawn, talking to the gardener. She was not in the least surprised to see her son and heir arriving in a tractor full of singing peasants—he had always done such crazy things.

"Look at you! Have you been wallowing in mud?" she chided him. "Did you wade through the rivers on the way?"

He grinned sheepishly and touched her feet.

"Oh, Mummy, my suitcase has gone in the car to the Circuit House." He rushed upstairs to his room and fished out some old clothes from his wardrobe. "How is Aunt Damyanti?" he shouted through the half-closed door of the bathroom.

"Fine," his mother replied from the veranda. "Are you all right, beta? Happy?"

"Yes, Mummy." The soap got into his nostrils. "When is Pushpa getting married?" he yelled again.

"Next Sahalak*. . ." came the answer.

"Has Uncle Prakash built his house?"

"No. Do you remember Khan Bahadur Mohammad Hussain, the retired judge? He went away to Pakistan. His bungalow was being auctioned, so Prakash bought it. For a song."

The word Pakistan reminded him, he would have to explain the Kashmir case next morning to the western visitors.

"I'll have a little snooze," he said to his mother after lunch and went back to his room. She had lovingly preserved his boyhood things in his dressing-room—roller skates, paint brushes and sketchbooks. Sheets of graded music, stacks of *Boy's Own* and *Film Fun* were lying heaped in a corner. Whenever he came home he looked at these things with nostalgia.

He lay down on his bed but remained wide awake. After a few minutes he got up again and went into the treasure trove of his dressing-room. He picked up an old copy of *Film Fun*, sat down near the window and looked at a cartoon captioned: Doing the Lambeth Walk—

The wind had dropped and the room was stuffy. There was no electricity. Gautam felt suffocated. The magazine fell from his hand. All of a sudden he was seized with the fear of Being. He stood up and went across to his mother's room.

"Mummy, I'm going out for a drive," he said, slightly shaken.

She regarded him with concern. Something was troubling him. What was it?

"You've just come all the way from Lucknow by car, shouldn't you take a little rest?"

"I'll go up to the highway to Shravasti and see if it is motorable. All these VIPs, you see—I'll be right back."

He took the Plymouth he had brought from America for his father from the garage. He drove fast on the road to Gonda,

---

* Season of weddings.

and remembered the tiger's roar as he passed the heavily wooded regions and caught a glimpse of the river Sarju sparkling through the mahua trees. He was twenty-five miles out of Behraich town. Little stupas erupted on the landscape. An intensely hot sun emerged from behind the clouds, and the air was warm and humid. He spotted the yellow lorry of the East Pakistani pilgrims in the shadow of a brown stupa. Little men and women were busy picking up dry wood-apples as holy objects. The Enlightened One had walked on this ground.

He drove on and came to the bend of the road. Shravasti was not far now. He parked his car under a tree and strode down towards the river which encircled Behraich district. He reached the grassy bank and looked around for some place to sit, then noticed a mound of stones on a riverside knoll. It looked like a shrine. A deer darted out of the shrubs. No leopards, hopefully, he thought and approached the grotto. It was probably dedicated to some totem or goddess of the adivasi Bher tribes who had given this district their name. Out of curiosity Gautam climbed up the stair-like stones and peered in. The walls were covered with the soot of oil lamps that had burned through the centuries. He could not see the face of the goddess, perhaps it was an uncut stone pasted with red sindhur. In the Beginning there was no image, just the idea. Perhaps aboriginal shrines like this inspired the idol worship of the early Aryan settlers. He leaned against the stone wall. All was very quiet. He wanted to be perfectly devoid of all thinking. For the first time in his life, it occurred to him—if only Nirvana were possible. Fear, the sense of being alone, grief, defeat, despair, hatred, anger, the wish to escape, the concept of space and relativity—Nirvana, which is beyond life, death, sleep and wakefulness, love, compassion, dispassion, and yet is the ultimate reality. . .

He heard a footfall.

"Who are you up there. . .?" a voice from below asked.

"I. . ." for an instant he was unsure of his identity: who the hell am I?

The other young man climbed into the rough stone enclosure.

"Hi—" Hari Shankar shook his hand as though it was the most natural thing in the world for them to meet in a rain-forest in the middle of nowhere on a humid evening.

"How. . . ?" Gautam asked briefly.

"Laj trunk-called. I rushed to Delhi, but Kamal had already left. Phoned your office, they said you were out on this junket. Came to Lucknow to see my parents. Thought I may as well look you up, too."

"That was nice of you." Perhaps Hari had forgiven him for Nirmala. This was the first time they were meeting, and in the unlikeliest of places, after that dismal morning in December 1954 when he had been seen off at Heathrow airport.

Hari Shankar sat down on a brick and regained his breath. "It has been a helluva wild goose chase. First went to Behraich Circuit House where one Miss Bajpai said, go to Nilambar Bhavan. Lady Nilambar said he has gone towards Shravasti to inspect the road. He has joined the PWD.

"So I took this route, saw your automobile on the roadside. This is dangerous tiger country, yaar, let's get the hell out of here. Quick." But he kept sitting.

The wood burst into birdsong. "They're coming home to roost," Hari observed rather pointlessly.

"Yeah."

They looked down at the flowing stream. "I am told the Sarju is a crystal clear river. You throw a coin in it and see it shining at the bottom."

"Yeah."

Hari took out his wallet. A coin slipped into his hand. He grinned. It was a silver dollar. He threw it in the water. It lay gleaming on the grey sand of the river-bed.

"Amazing!" he exclaimed.

Both fell silent again, too depressed and world-weary to speak. The sun was going down, the river turned amber in the twilight. After a while Hari said, "Yaar, Gautam. . ."

"*Bolo.*"

"Kamal has deserted us. Betrayed his friends, gone away for good and let us down. Together, we could have challenged the galaxies."

"We have all betrayed one another," Gautam replied quietly. Can these western visitors to Shravasti understand the pain in our souls? In India's, in Kamal's, in mine?

They watched the river ripple past. Words were temporary and transitory. Languages fade away or are forced into oblivion by new tongues. Men also come and go, even the river and the jungle are not eternal. After fifty years a jungle of concrete may spring up here. The river may dry up or shrink or change course, just as human beings disappear or change the direction of their journeys.

> *Ghazalen, tum to waqif ho, kaho Majnun ke marney ki,*
> *Diwana mar gaya, aakhir ko, veeranay pe kya guzri**

Hari recited softly. The dirge mingled with the rustling of kadamba leaves.

"You are being over-sentimental. Kamal is no Siraj-ud-Daulah, he's very much alive and at this very moment must be dancing with some lovely begum in the Karachi Gymkhana," Gautam remarked cynically.

"You don't understand him, really. I have known him since my childhood," Hari retorted, exactly in the manner of his sister Nirmala, who had rebuffed Gautam all those years ago in the Koh-i-Noor restaurant in Cambridge—"You don't know Champa Baji, really, we have known her since our childhood—" He was felled by a sudden wave of agony. He grasped the crag near him, assailed by the feeling that he was alone in the cosmos, alone against the galaxies. In the enveloping black void he heard Hari Shankar's melancholy voice: "Kamal was over-sensitive, an incorrigible, fanatical idealist. He was let down by a relentless world. Something within him has died, otherwise he would not have avoided meeting you and me so scrupulously. It is his new incarnation in the other country, dancing in the Karachi Gymkhana. At this moment."

"You make it all sound quite eerie," Gautam came back and answered, trying hard to sound casual. A peacock fluttered its

---

*Gazelles of the desert! You know how Majnun died. Tell me, what happened to the wilderness after the Crazy Lover was gone?

wings and flew up to the sprawling jack-fruit tree in order to settle down for the night. Hari looked at his watch. "Let's go. By the way, Kumari Aruna is hosting a dinner tonight at the Behraich District Club, and has especially invited us eminently eligible, though slightly jaded, bachelors."

"Caste no bar?" Gautam asked lightly.

"We have been abroad far too long, yaar. Indian society has changed," Hari Shankar replied and clambered down. "This cave is so spooky, even the adivasis have deserted it."

Gautam followed him out. They began to walk towards the highway where they had parked their cars.

A petite female figure in white appeared at a short distance. Hari stopped dead in his tracks. He had turned quite pale. He rushed forward but returned at once. "That. . . that woman over there. . ." he stammered, "didn't she resemble Nirmala. . .? Same face. Same gait and height. For one wild moment I thought my kid sister had come back. How foolish of me."

The woman walked briskly ahead on her clodhoppers.

Moments later Hari said, "I attended an Indo-Pak Conference in Lahore last year, after which they took us to Taxila."

"Oh, you have been to Taxila!" Gautam exclaimed. "I want to see Taxila very much."

"Over there, in the museum, I came across this Gandhara frieze depicting the Miracle at Shravasti," Hari continued. "You know, Lord Buddha performed a miracle to convince the haughty Brahmins of his Buddhahood. . .

"Well!" he laughed bitterly, "there are no blessed miracles in Shravasti today. For a second I thought my sister had come back, but how can she? Poor Nirmal is dead and gone forever."

Gautam kept quiet, stoically. He could hear his heart beat. His legs trembled—just a little.

More women in white materialised carrying bamboo sticks and lanterns. It was like a procession of will-o'-the-wisps. They were on their way to the stupas. A band of ochre-robed bhikshus from Cox's Bazaar followed the women.

"Pilgrims from East Bengal," Gautam commented in a toneless voice, "on their way to the site of Jetvan Vihara."

The yatris' wooden sandals produced an awesome, rhythmic sound on the cobbled path. Slowly the clip-clop, clip-clop receded in the depth of the primeval jungle.

The silence became absolute.